Kenneth

MW00413459

By Keith A Pearson

For more information about the author and to receive updates on hi new releases, visit…

www.keithapearson.co.uk

"You were a stranger to sorrow: therefore Fate has cursed you." – *Euripides*

1.

Questions posed in song titles. What is love? Is this love? Where is the love? The Pet Shop Boys even suggested love is a bourgeois construct but I never really understood what they meant by that. Perhaps I'm not supposed to.

The fact so many musicians continue to wrestle with the complexities of love suggests we're no closer to understanding it.

Five months ago a brown envelope dropped onto my doormat. It contained a letter from the County Court, or more specifically, a decree nisi. At that point, I began to pose my own questions about love. How much does a marriage need? Can two people love each other in different ways? Can any marriage survive without love?

I must have thought I loved Nathan at some point but eleven years after we exchanged vows, I couldn't recall. I certainly appreciated him and, at the time, I definitely felt gratitude, but love? I don't know.

Two months after that first brown envelope arrived, the County Court sent another. It contained our decree absolute and it stung more than I expected. The media, when talking about the breakup of a celebrity couple, always say the marriage failed. Marriages don't fail — people fail. When a marriage just ends because neither party has the motivation to keep it alive, that's proper failure. And with failure comes regret. I should have tried harder, compromised more.

It all comes back to love, though. Maybe we did love one another but it was the wrong flavour of love — more vanilla than passion fruit.

This introspection is doing me no good. I should really get up.

Sunday mornings are for long, lazy lie-ins but it's already too warm in my airless bedroom, and it's not even nine o'clock. I peel the sheet from my sticky skin and stare up at the ceiling. Even with the window open I've just spent another night broiling in my own sweat.

Still half-asleep, I get up and plod to the bathroom where I'm jolted into full consciousness at the sight of a jaded woman looking back at me from the mirror. The clumps of hair plastered to her clammy forehead aren't a great look, and her expression says as much.

I brush my teeth while sitting on the loo. After thirty-nine years of existence, I'm beginning to appreciate the simple joy of taking the weight off my feet for a few minutes. Another simple joy is expelling a buttock-shuddering trump without having to worry about anyone hearing it. It's not ladylike but like a tree falling in a forest, if there's no one around to hear it …

Still pondering quantum theory, I hop in the shower and turn the thermostat down to the coolest setting. Ten blissful minutes pass and I emerge invigorated and non-sticky.

Coffee beckons.

The kitchen is almost as stifling as the bedroom so, after putting the kettle on, I open a window and the back door. A visitor is waiting for me.

"Good morning, Frank."

Frank looks up and meows before rubbing himself against my shins. I don't know who owns the ginger tom, and I'm almost certain his name isn't Frank, but he first showed up at my door the day after I moved in. It took several hours to establish Frank wasn't going anywhere without a bribe: half-a-tin of tuna. I've checked with the dozen other homeowners in the street and none of them know who Frank belongs to.

He invites himself into the kitchen and sits at my feet as I search for a can of tuna in the cupboard.

"Did you have a good night?"

He doesn't reply.

Frank's owners didn't see fit to have him castrated which leads me to believe he spends his nights whoring himself far and wide. He's certainly handsome enough and has that look of mischief in his eye.

"Have you been out breaking hearts?"

His yawn is almost an answer.

Once I've forked his breakfast into a bowl, Frank does what Frank always does and jumps up onto the kitchen table in anticipation. We're both creatures of habit and perhaps that's why we've bonded.

"Enjoy."

I make a coffee as my guest tucks into his breakfast. He makes light work of it and then follows me out to the garden.

One of the many reasons I fell in love with this house is the walled garden. It's not particularly big but there's no grass to mow and the six-foot high wall provides an oasis of privacy. I sit down at the bistro table and sip coffee. Frank leaps up onto the other chair and commences his post-breakfast ablutions.

The coffee is good and the slight breeze divine but I'm not as content as I should be. Perhaps it's the sudden rush of caffeine, but I already feel restless, fidgety.

"What am I going to do with the day, eh, Frank?"

My feline friend responds by curling up on the chair and closing his eyes.

"I appreciate the input."

There is an inherent problem with being a thirty-nine-year-old divorcee. All my friends are married or in long-term relationships; their free time consumed with partners, kids, or family. I have no partner, no kids, and no close family. Those of a chirpy disposition will always argue the benefits of a blank canvas. To them, it's an opportunity to create the new without the hindrance of the old. It's one perspective. I'd guess there are plenty of artists who find a blank canvas fairly depressing; particularly if filling that canvas is a necessity to pay the bills. I'm in that camp, albeit my blank canvas has left a gaping hole in my social life rather than my finances.

My phone rings.

I scoot into the kitchen and grab it from the table, only to groan when I spot the caller's name.

"Hi Hannah," I chirp through gritted teeth.

Hannah and her brood moved into my former marital home in Kensall Gardens. I rue the day I gave her my number and suggested she call if there were any problems.

"Oh, Kelly. Thank God you're up. I'm so sorry to trouble you on a Sunday morning."

"It's okay. What's the problem?"

"It's the lagging in the loft."

"The lagging?"

"Yes, I've been up half the night worrying about it."

"Err, why?"

"I can't recall seeing the paperwork. Do you know when it was installed, and if it met fire regulations?"

"I … no Hannah. I don't."

"Good God," she gasps. "We could be living in a tinderbox."

"Hannah, the house is barely fifteen years old and I'm fairly sure fire regulations haven't changed much in those fifteen years. You're probably worrying about nothing."

"That's easy for you to say, Kelly. You don't have children to worry about."

"Thank you for reminding me."

"What am I going to do?" she whines, ignorant of her offence.

"I don't know. Call the fire brigade?"

"Oh, yes. I hadn't thought of that. Do you think they'll come out on a Sunday?"

I was kidding but if it gets her off the phone.

"Considering the severity of the situation, I'm sure they will."

"I'll call them now."

"Great. Good luck."

"Thank you."

"And Hannah. Just so you know, I'll be indisposed all day, so I won't be able to answer my phone."

With barely a goodbye she ends the call. I never liked Hannah, or her pretentious children and arrogant arsehole of a husband for that matter, but I particularly don't like her this morning for reminding me about that bloody house and unfulfilled maternal aspirations.

Nathan and I moved to Kensall Gardens a few weeks after we married. My new husband had a good job in investment

7

management with an income to match — our new home testament to his success with bedrooms aplenty, a kitchen the size of a squash court, and a large plot accessed via a gated driveway. It was to be the safe, secure home in which we'd raise our children. There were no children, and that's why I'm now living in an end-terrace house, chatting to a cat.

Our lack of offspring certainly wasn't through lack of trying. Initially, we had sex twice a day, every day, but after three months I felt like an unpaid prostitute and Nathan like a badly maintained sex robot. I concluded that married sex was a bit like chocolate cake — the occasional slice is lovely but imagine eating a slice the minute you wake up in the morning, or when you'd rather be slumped on the sofa drinking wine and bingeing on a box set.

We agreed to limit our efforts to three times a week in the hope we'd maintain some semblance of romance but the damage had already been done — we were sick of chocolate cake. And to make matters worse, our unenthusiastic humping had only resulted in a dozen negative pregnancy tests. Something wasn't right.

We booked an appointment at a fertility clinic and I can still remember every detail of the journey there. Nathan kept offering reassurance he would love me no matter what any test might reveal; the implication clear. In his defence, I felt like I was the problem too. I'd endured so much trauma; I felt broken in some way.

A week later, a sympathetic doctor confirmed my husband's infertility. Nathan demanded a second opinion but another test only confirmed the diagnosis. Over the following weeks we discussed our options, which were limited to sperm donation or adoption. For six long months Nathan did all he could to avoid a decision and eventually admitted he'd already come to terms with our childless existence. It didn't come as much of a surprise as I knew there was no way my perfectionist husband would accept a child that wasn't the genuine fruit of his loins.

I should have left him at that point, but Nathan was all I had. I've never been career orientated but left with a gaping void

8

in my life to fill, I threw myself into work. Until that point I'd been employed as an admin assistant for a personal finance company. I started at Marston Finance shortly after leaving college, and a decade later I remained rooted in the same position. I didn't care about promotion, or the tedious nature of the work, because I knew it'd be over once I met Mr Right and settled down to start a family. A flawed plan, as it transpired.

Over the ensuing months I put everything I had into my job. I turned up early, stayed late, and applied for every position the company advertised to demonstrate how much I wanted to progress. My persistence eventually paid off, and they promoted me. Another promotion soon followed, and then another, to department head. The long hours and extra responsibility took my mind away from the house which would never be a home. I couldn't stand being there — the empty bedrooms and manicured garden a constant reminder neither would see the happy chaos of children.

Nathan and I continued on the same trajectory for nine long years; both embracing our respective careers while neglecting our marriage. We saw less and less of one another and even decided separate bedrooms made sense so we could both get a decent night's sleep when one of us worked late. We reserved cake for birthdays and anniversaries but, in the end, we both lost our appetites.

No couple could survive such an existence, and two brown envelopes later we became another divorce statistic.

I haven't completely given up on having children but I'm a realist. Yes, women are leaving it later in life but even if Cupid comes calling in the next twelve months, it's unlikely he'll bring a man in his forties who wants to start a family. Realistically, I'm playing the lottery on a timer.

I wander back out to the garden where Frank is now fast asleep.

"Oi, sleepyhead. Don't be so anti-social."

He doesn't stir. Shit, I can't even talk to a cat now.

With nothing else better to do I rescue a dog-eared paperback from beside my bed and read for a couple of hours, stopping only to grab a couple of bagels for breakfast. Frank eventually wakes up, stretches, and promptly pisses off.

I'm about to consider walking into town when my phone rings again. Expecting it to be Hannah, I'm in two minds whether or not to answer but I'm so bored I'd rather listen to her whining than the voices in my head.

It's not Hannah. I prod the screen.

"Hey, Martha."

"Just put it in the sink," she yells.

"Pardon?"

"Bugger. Sorry, chick. I'm multi-tasking."

With twin eight-year-old girls, my best friend spends an inordinate amount of time multi-tasking.

"What are you up to?" she asks; her focus back on our conversation.

"Nothing really."

"Great, I'll be over in an hour. I need cold wine and adult conversation."

"On a Sunday?"

"The girls are driving me insane. I need to get out of the house before I kill one or both of them."

To validate her point, one of the girls shrieks in the background.

"I'll put some therapy juice in the fridge. I take it you're not driving?"

"Stuart is taking the girls to the cinema so I'll get him to drop me off on the way."

"You didn't fancy it?"

"They want to see the latest Spiderman movie. Honestly, giving birth to a ten-pound porcupine would be less painful."

"You have sex with a lot of porcupines?"

"They're so cute," she chuckles. "What's a girl to do?"

"Weirdo. I'll see you soon."

"Shortly, shorty."

I hang up but my grin lingers.

Martha and I met during our first week at Shaw House Girls School. I was tiny for my age and an obvious target for bullies.

One lunch break, a girl from the year above decided I should be relieved of my lunch money. At that point, a tall girl with permed blonde hair came to my rescue, and threatened to stab the girl in the tit with the sharp end of a plastic set square. The bully fled and Martha then admitted she almost pissed her knickers in fear but couldn't stand by and do nothing. I knew in that moment we'd be friends for life, and so it has proven.

It appears she is coming to the rescue again; to save me from abject boredom.

2.

Seventy minutes after my phone call, the doorbell chimes. I dash down the hallway and open the door to the explosion of colour and wild blonde hair that is Martha Miller.

I'm greeted with an enthusiastic hug.

"Lovely to see you, chick," she purrs. "Now, where's the wine?"

Martha follows me through to the kitchen where I extract a bottle from the fridge. I fill two pre-prepared glasses and hand one to my friend.

"Christ, I need this. What a morning."

Martha then relieves the glass of half its contents.

"That bad, eh?"

"From the moment they woke up this morning, the girls have been a nightmare. I've put the adoption agency on speed dial."

"You don't mean that."

"Oh, I do. At half-eight this morning, they asked if they could cook pretend breakfast in the kitchen, with Play-Doh. Ten minutes later the smoke alarm goes off and I rush in to find them frying Play-Doh sausages on the hob."

I try hard to stifle a laugh.

"It took me half an hour to clean my best pan. And the smell … you have no idea."

"But you still love them, eh?"

"Most of the time. Anyway, I came over so I could forget I'm a mother for a few hours."

"And I thought it was my company that enticed you here."

"Not gonna lie. It was mainly the prospect of wine in a child-free zone."

"I guessed as much. Shall we go sit in the garden?"

We head outside and sit at the table. Martha puffs a long, satisfied sigh as she stretches out in the chair.

"I envy you, Kelly."

"Do you?"

"On second thoughts, no," she sniggers. "But I do love your

home."

"Thank you."

"It's so quiet ... and tidy. If I could keep my home tidy for just one hour, I'd be happy. If it isn't the girls creating carnage, it's my husband."

"The reason my home is so tidy is there's no one here most of the time."

"Yeah, about that."

"Oh dear."

"Do you know what you need, chick?"

"A time machine?"

"If only. No, what you need is a decent man. It's time to get back in the saddle."

"Hmm, you think? I'm still trying to work out where I went wrong with the last relationship."

"Don't let one bad experience put you off. Not every man is as awful as Nathan."

"He wasn't that bad."

"But he didn't ... you know ... push the right buttons."

"Err, if you're referring to what I think you're referring to, our sex life was like those new tills they have in Sainsbury's."

"Eh?"

"Self-service."

Martha almost spits a mouthful of wine in my direction.

"My God. And how often did you find an unexpected item in your bagging area?"

"Haha ... most Sunday mornings while Nathan played golf."

If you took away the wine and the cellulite, you could be forgiven for thinking we're giggly fifteen-year-old girls again. If only.

"Seriously, though. You might have wasted eleven years with Nathan but it'd be a travesty to waste another eleven years on your own. You're too good a catch to fester on the shelf."

"Aww, thank you, hun."

"And besides, you'll be fifty by then. No man will want to go near your dusty old snatch."

My turn to choke.

"My God," I splutter. "You're incorrigible."

"That's why you love me."

Martha then grabs her mobile phone and starts tapping the screen.

"Checking up on the offspring?" I ask.

"Sod them. I'm setting up a Tinder profile for you."

"You are bloody not. The last thing I need in my life is a constant stream of dick pics."

"If there's an overflow issue, just send them my way."

"Martha!"

She fixes me with her blue eyes and I know what's coming.

"You might have given up on the prospect of meeting Mr Right but as an old romantic I'm not so easily defeated. I know he's out there and you just need to lay the right bait."

"Bait?"

"Say cheese."

Before I can argue, she takes a photo and inspects the screen.

"Nothing a few filters won't fix."

"Please, Martha. I'm not giving up — I just don't trust Internet dating. I've heard some horror stories from the girls at work."

"Really? Do tell."

"Tanya in accounts met a guy online and he invited her to some swanky restaurant for their first date. Apparently, he worked in the City and drove a Mercedes."

"Sounds promising."

"After they'd eaten, and consumed two bottles of Cristal Champagne, he told her to go powder her nose while he settled the bill. Tanya thought he was just being chivalrous but when she returned to the table, he'd done a runner, leaving her to pay the four-hundred quid bill. Still, she found out later he hadn't lied about everything. He did work in the City, delivering parcels, and he did drive a Mercedes, albeit a panel van."

"That's awful. Poor cow."

"And that's the reason I don't want to get involved in Internet dating. Too many chancers and bullshitters."

"You could try speed dating."

"No, thanks."

"I could ask Stuart if he knows any single guys."

"Again, no thanks."

"Or, you could …"

"Will you give it a rest, please?"

My words are delivered with a little more force than I intended.

"All right, stroppy arse. I'm only trying to help."

"Sorry, hun," I sigh. "I know you are."

We both take a time-out with a large glug of wine.

"Listen, Martha. I hear what you say about wasting another eleven years but I don't want to force the issue. If I meet someone then great, but I don't have the stomach for the whole online dating malarkey. It feels … I don't know, a little desperate."

"I'm sorry, too. You're right, but I just want you to have what I've got."

"A washing machine full of skid-marked underwear?"

"Precisely," she giggles.

"Well, one day I might, but I think I'll let fate decide when I'm worthy of such a treat."

"Fair enough. I won't say another word."

"Thank you."

"And in the meantime," she adds, raising her glass. "Here's to self-service checkouts."

The subject put to bed, Martha moves the conversation on.

"So, what are your plans for this place?"

"Err, plans?"

"To restyle it, freshen it up. No disrespect to the previous owners but it's a bit bland, don't you think?"

"I like it."

"But don't you want to put your own stamp on the place?"

Besides the garden, the neutral decor was one of the main attractions when I first viewed the house. It isn't far from what I'd have chosen myself.

"Honestly, Martha, I'm happy the way it is."

"But look at the kitchen. Imagine how much brighter it would be if you painted the walls. I saw some ideal colours in the DIY store last week."

One reason Martha and I have remained friends for so long is because we're very different people, and they say opposites attract. At school, Martha cultivated her bright, vivacious nature whilst I had a tendency to shrink into the background. Those same traits have flowed into adulthood and extend to our tastes in fashion, and interior design.

"Let me guess. One of those colours was a shade of yellow, and the other orange?"

"How did you know that?"

"Lucky guess," I chuckle.

"Why don't we order some sample pots to see how it looks?"

"No thanks."

"If you're worried about the cost, there's no need. The paint will only cost forty quid and I'm sure Stuart will be happy to apply it if you keep him fed and watered. It'll keep him out from under my feet for the day."

"No, the cost isn't an issue."

Unlike so many couples, Nathan and I avoided a financial shitstorm during our divorce. Nathan, ever the pragmatist, suggested we sell the house in Kensall Gardens and after recouping his original investment, we split the remaining equity fifty-fifty. Anything we had before we married would remain ours. That suited me as I already had a sizeable chunk of cash in the bank before I met Nathan, and all I really wanted was enough money to set up on my own. With no children or even a pet to squabble over, there seemed no point inviting lawyers to take a third of our assets in fees.

Noting my reluctance, Martha accepts defeat.

"I'm not likely to change your mind, am I?"

"Sorry, hun, but no. I like my decor just the way it is."

"Spoilsport. I'm deeply hurt." She adopts a pouty expression like a sulking child.

"Aww, will more wine make it all better?"

"Probably," she huffs.

Sniggering, I return to the kitchen and top up our glasses. It's a journey we take turns completing over the next three hours until five bottles stand empty on the kitchen side.

"I'm feeling a bit squiffy," Martha admits, collapsing in the chair after another visit to the toilet. "You're a bad influence, Mrs Thaw."

"Excuse me. You're the bad influence … and it's Miss Coburn now. Mrs Thaw is … she's gone, forever."

"I'm glad," she slurs. "I much prefer Kelly Coburn."

"So do I, hun. So do I."

The doorbell rings.

"That'll be my hubby."

"I'll see you out."

We stagger back through the house — bouncing off the hallway walls — and open the door to Martha's husband, Stuart. He takes one look at us and bursts out laughing.

"Christ. How much have you two had?"

"Just … hic, a glass or two," Martha replies. "Where are the girls?"

"My parents. Mum asked if they wanted tea in the garden."

"Okay, cool. How was Spiderman?"

"Bloody brilliant."

"You're such a child … but I love you."

My best friend stumbles into her husband's arms. He looks over her shoulder to me and smiles.

"Probably best I get this one home," he says.

"I think so."

"Did she mention …?"

"She did, yes," I interject. "And thanks for the offer, but I'm happy enough leading the single life for now."

"You're probably right, and I suspect I'll feel a pang of envy as my wife throws up on the way home."

"Good luck."

"Cheers. See you, Kelly."

Martha tries to give me a goodbye hug but her legs don't cooperate and Stuart has to hold her upright. She just about manages to blow a kiss in my direction before being guided to the car.

I close the door.

As the hallway spins, I'm forced to concede I may have also drunk too much. I stumble into the lounge and collapse on the sofa; intent on resting my eyes for an hour until the wooziness passes.

And there ends my Sunday.

3.

I wake up with a start; soaked with sweat and my heart pounding. The only clue to the time is the shard of sunlight leaking beyond the partially closed curtains. Sitting upright, I take a dozen deep breaths to calm myself.

There was a time I'd wake up like this with alarming regularity. The only consolation on this occasion is I didn't wake up screaming, or with my tear-stained cheeks stinging red. It's been at least a year since that recurring nightmare played out in my dreams and I thought I'd got past it. Perhaps the alcohol is to blame. It's certainly to blame for the thick head and dry mouth.

I check my watch: just gone six in the morning. Too early to be awake but too late to go back to sleep. With the harrowing imagery still fresh in my mind's eye, sleep isn't where I want to be anyway.

I crawl off the sofa and make my way to the kitchen. Employing the now-rusty coping mechanism, I switch on the radio to fill the silence and allow my thoughts to drift towards yesterday, and Martha's visit. I need to occupy a happy head space.

Kettle on, painkillers consumed, I open the back door.

"Morning, Frank. You've no idea how pleased I am to see you."

Without waiting for an invitation, he gets to his feet and saunters in through the open door; stopping only to rub his head against my shins. I squat down and run my hand through his thick fur. He responds with a purr so deep it thrums my fingertips.

"Pleased to see me too, eh?"

I've grown fond of Frank but his daily visits have created a dilemma. I've always wanted a pet but Nathan didn't, and although I'd love a dog, it's not fair with the hours I work so I decided to home a refuge cat at some stage. However, I'm not sure how that cat would feel about a casual interloper popping by every morning. It's akin to postponing the commitment of marriage because you don't want to lose a fuck-buddy.

"You do realise, Frank, we can't go on like this."

He stares up at me through eyes wide and green. I know what he's thinking, and it probably doesn't involve a conversation about our relationship status.

"Typical male. You only want me for one thing."

He responds with a meow.

"At least you're honest about it."

I serve Frank his breakfast and head upstairs to the bathroom.

The simple act of taking a long shower and putting on freshly laundered underwear proves a boon. I consult my wardrobe for an outfit comfortable enough to get me through the day's promised heat. I settle on a sleeveless mauve dress short enough to air my legs but modest enough not to attract unwanted attention from pervy Leonard in the finance department. As the painkillers nudge the dull ache from my head, I return to the kitchen feeling considerably better than I did when I left.

Frank is sitting on the table, doing what cats do best: very little. His eyes follow me as I make another coffee and prepare some breakfast. A favourite tune from my teenage years plays on the radio and I turn the volume up a notch.

"Frank, I'm guessing your favourite Spice Girl is Ginger Spice, right?"

I might be mistaken but I'm sure his pupils widen a fraction.

"Oh, more of a Baby Spice fan are we?"

He yawns and, after listening to me slaughter one verse and the chorus of *Wannabee*, he jumps down off the table and shoots out the door.

"Everyone's a critic."

Despite the one-way conversation, it's nice to enjoy breakfast without the frantic clock-watching I endure most workday mornings. By half-seven I'm mildly bored though and decide to get the earlier bus.

I grab my bag, lock up, and don a pair of sunglasses to hide the dark circles under my eyes. I might have had a sufficient quantity of sleep but it lacked any quality. Today will be a challenge.

Turning left out of the front gate, I make my way down Juniper Lane.

As lovely as my home is, it'd been on the market for nine months before I put in an offer. The reason, and the issue with Juniper Lane itself, is a lack of parking. The lane is a single track with a ten-foot-high hedge opposite the houses; planted decades ago to dull the noise from the railway track thirty yards beyond. When the dozen terraced houses were built during Queen Victoria's reign, parking probably wasn't much of an issue but these days it is, and I've since learnt that houses in Juniper Lane are a tough sell.

As I don't drive, it's not a problem for me. As long as the pizza delivery guy can abandon his car in the road for a minute, I'm happy.

The bus stop is only a few streets away and, at this earlier hour, I arrive to find the usual half-dozen regular faces are all absent. The only other passenger is a youngish guy in overalls, plugged into a pair of oversized headphones. I smile but it seems he doesn't want to risk conversation as he just nods and stares at his phone screen again.

As I wait for the bus, I think back to my conversation with Martha yesterday, and my love life. I was a late starter with the opposite sex and didn't lose my virginity until the ripe old age of eighteen. Simon and I dated for three months before I felt ready to do the deed — from memory, a wholly underwhelming experience — and a week later Manchester University confirmed they'd accepted his application for a place. Despite promises we'd survive a long-distance relationship, we didn't.

Over the ensuing ten years before I met Nathan, I dated three more guys but I can't say I came close to falling for any of them. I'm a sucker for a rom-com movie and maybe all those dreamy, heart-warming happy endings raised my expectations to unrealistic levels. I wanted Hugh Grant but fate delivered Steve the mortgage broker, James the ophthalmic optician, and Kelvin the unemployed actor. All three were nice enough but butterflies never danced and love resolutely failed to blossom. Richard Curtis had lied to me.

I started to think maybe I was the problem but Martha insisted I just hadn't met the right guy. Buoyed by my friend's words, I remained optimistic … until that day. Even now, I try not to think about it and on the whole, I succeed — or at least my conscious mind does. It's a different matter when I'm asleep; as last night proved.

The bus arrives and the man in the overalls waves me on first. Perhaps chivalry isn't dead.

My journey, as usual, takes about fifteen minutes. After a quick detour to Starbucks, I make my way towards the imposing office block which houses the four hundred employees of Marston Finance.

When I started eighteen years ago, there were just fifty of us. Now, Marston Finance is a publicly listed company; having completed the two-decade transition from a small, family-owned firm to a soulless corporate entity.

If I were the type to embrace change, I might consider seeking employment elsewhere, but I'm not. I like routine and familiarity.

After the usual fight with the revolving front door, I make my way across the brightly lit foyer to the lifts. On my way, I pass the security guard who mans the reception desk until half-eight; when he'll be replaced by a blonde, twenty-something girl with a saccharin smile and excellent telephone manner.

For once, one of the two lifts is waiting with the doors open. I step inside and press the button for the tenth floor.

It doesn't come as much of a shock when I enter my department and all the desks are empty. There's no contractual obligation for any of my colleagues to be here at eight in the morning and it wouldn't surprise me if at least half of them are still in bed.

I wander through to my poky office; a space I seem to spend more time in than my actual home — a point Martha made yesterday after the conversation moved on from my love life. She asked a question which I couldn't answer, and still can't: what's my end game? I'm not sure it's a question anyone can answer.

At work, I strategise and plot the course of my department with some degree of confidence; but life isn't so predictable. Some folks claim they know exactly where they're heading but how often does fate throw them an unforeseen curveball? It's like planning a road trip without a reliable car or map. I see no point in trying to predict my destination when I can't see any further than the end of Singleton Street.

Taking a seat behind my desk, I wake the computer and open my email program. I like to begin every day by emptying the inbox, and the earlier start means I can hit the ground running when my colleagues arrive. One by one, the emails cascade. I scan the first few and they're mainly trivial issues I can address with a canned response. One email, however, leaps off the screen because the subject line is in upper-case letters: REMEMBER ME? My eyes scan left, to the sender's name.

"What the hell does he want?" I mumble under my breath.

I open the email from my ex-husband.

4.

The unexpected email is brief and to the point; a request I call him as soon as possible. It's time-stamped an hour ago.

I can't imagine there's anything left to be said but Nathan isn't one for small talk so there must be a genuine need to speak with me. I grab my phone and call his number. He answers on the second ring.

"Hi, Kelly. Thanks for calling so promptly."

"It's okay. What can I do for you?"

A silent pause punctuated by the sound of a pen tapping a desk — one of Nathan's annoying habits.

"I was wondering if we could have dinner tomorrow evening."

"Err, don't take this the wrong way, but why?"

"Because … well, why not?"

I don't really know how to answer. It's not that I harbour any ill-will towards my ex-husband — I just don't feel anything. Our divorce may have been amicable, but it ended in the same clinical manner you might terminate a business contract, with neither of us suggesting we remain friends or stay in touch.

"I don't know if it's a good idea."

"It's just dinner."

"Yes, I get that. What I don't understand is why."

Another pause and more pen tapping before he answers.

"There's something I want to discuss with you."

"Right, and you can't discuss it over the phone?"

"No."

My turn to pause for thought. I'm curious enough to consider his invitation but I detest dining in the fancy restaurants Nathan prefers.

"We can meet, but I'd rather not have dinner."

"But, I've booked a table at Jerome's."

His choice of restaurant, and presumption I'd agree, nicely sum up why we're now divorced. He considers a meal at Jerome's a treat while I loathe everything about the place from the overpriced, pretentious food to the condescending staff.

"Let's meet at The Three Horseshoes."

"Very well," he agrees; probably through gritted teeth. "Shall we say eight o'clock?"

"Fine. I'll see you tomorrow."

After a perfunctory goodbye, I hang up.

I turn my attention back to the screen but my mind wanders off in a different direction. I can only guess why Nathan wants to talk, and that guesswork sits between two possibilities. The first would relate to a loose end from our divorce; a forgotten insurance policy or warranty which requires my signature. Nathan is a stickler for admin.

The other reason could be his mother.

Beatrice and I had a strained relationship. On the outside, it would be easy to mistake Nathan's mother as a sweet-natured octogenarian; her pearl-white hair neatly tied into a bun and her lined face always painted with a warm smile. Behind that facade lurked an uber-bitch. For the first year or two after we married, Beatrice made a veiled effort to be civil but that veil eventually slipped and she made it abundantly clear I wasn't good enough for her precious son.

Then, four years ago, my already-fractured relationship with Beatrice imploded after she suffered a stroke. It would have been impossible for her to continue living alone so I agreed she could move in with us.

Big mistake.

The stroke affected her mobility, but it didn't blunt the sharp edge of her tongue. She became unbearable and after six weeks I gave Nathan an ultimatum — he either moved Beatrice into a care home where she could receive professional help, or I would move out. By that point, even Nathan had to concede his mother required full-time care. With some reluctance, he moved her into the best nursing home money could buy. Of course, Beatrice blamed me for ousting her.

To her credit, though, she won the war because her refusal to be in the same room as me marked the beginning of the end for Nathan and I.

I understand more than most how precious our parents are, so I never let on to Nathan how his mother treated me. Maybe Beatrice has finally shuffled off, and he wants to break the solemn news under the misconception I give a shit. It'll be an effort, but I might muster a few crocodile tears for the old cow.

Theories exhausted, I return my attention to the long list of emails and with no further distractions I make good progress. I've all but dealt with my inbox when the hordes arrive on the dot of nine o'clock.

My department's primary role is to process the hundreds of personal loan applications which ping through the company website each day. It's a never-ending struggle to meet targets set by the board while ensuring we adhere to the regulatory guidelines. When you also throw unreasonable customer expectations into the mix, the department is never too far from a meltdown.

Natalie, who works on the new applications desk, pokes her head around the door and asks if she can book some holiday.

"Sure, but I'd like to discuss some issues regarding fraudulent applications first. You processed four cases last week alone."

"Do you mind if I grab a coffee first? I'm gasping."

I glance at my watch.

"It's five past nine, Natalie. If you want to have a coffee before starting work, might I suggest you get here earlier?"

I know I'm being harsh but I have to be. When I took on this role, our productivity levels were an embarrassment, and it's not been easy re-tuning the attitude of some individuals in my team. At twenty-eight, Natalie is a bright, intelligent, young woman but her work ethic is distinctly lacking. If there's a corner to cut or an opportunity to skive, she'll grasp it with both hands.

She looks at me, incredulous. Even with a frown there are barely any lines creasing her perfect skin.

"You're saying I can't have a coffee?"

"I'm saying it's Monday morning and we've got a lot of work to get through today. Remember … the work you're being paid to do?"

Rolling her eyes, she trudges over and slumps in the chair opposite. If this were my business, I'd hand Natalie her P45, or at least deliver a severe bollocking about her attitude. Neither option washes in the corporate world, and she knows it. Any disciplinary issues must go through the human resources department and they'll then instigate a process of arbitration and resolution before anything approaching action occurs.

For those of us who care about our work, it's infuriating.

My sulky subordinate sits and half-listens to my recommendations before departing with a frown. No doubt she'll be in the staffroom later slagging me off to anyone who cares to listen. Trouble is there are plenty who will as I don't think I'm the most popular person in our department. I find it odd that when my male counterparts demand high standards from their team, they're considered assertive. Yet, when a woman makes those same demands, she's labelled a hormonal bitch. Ironically, it's usually my female colleagues who are the worst offenders for staffroom slander. So much for the sisterhood.

I get on with my work and the morning progresses without incident or corporate catastrophe. At half-twelve, my stomach reminds me it hasn't seen food for five hours. Some days I don't get the chance to leave the office at lunchtime but today isn't one of them. A packet of crisps and a chocolate bar from the vending machine won't sate my hunger.

I grab my bag and make a dash for it while I can.

Out on the street I'm hit with a blast of super-heated air; akin to stepping from a fridge to a furnace. I quickly cross the road to the shade and follow the path towards my favourite sandwich shop. It's a bit of a stroll but their smoked salmon and cream cheese baguettes are to die for.

Halfway there I'm accosted by a young woman distributing leaflets outside a hair salon which I don't remember seeing last time I passed.

"Do you have a moment, madam?" she asks.

"Err, not really."

She thrusts a leaflet at me.

"Today is our first day so we've got a special offer — fifty percent discount on cuts and colours."

I've been going to the same salon for years. Consequently, I've had the same hairstyle forever; as Martha likes to remind me on a near-daily basis.

"Our head stylist, Ruby could do something amazing with your hair," she adds.

I look beyond the young woman towards the salon itself. It's the height of modernity compared to the dated salon I frequent — all smoked glass, polished chrome, and black leather seating.

Another woman appears in the doorway.

"This is Ruby," the young woman confirms before telling her colleague I'm interested in their offer, which I don't recall claiming.

Before I can object Ruby is at my side, fingering the tips of my hair.

"Your face would suit a much shorter style," she states. "Have you ever considered a pixie cut, maybe with a darker colour?"

"I, um …"

"You'll lose ten years, easily."

I'd love to lose ten years and divorce Nathan before my thirtieth birthday but I suspect Ruby is referring to my aesthetics.

"I would?"

"Definitely. You've got just the right cheekbones to pull it off."

"Thanks. Let me have a think …"

"Come on in and I'll show you some photos."

Between them, the two women then abduct me from the street. Inside the salon, I'm escorted to a leather sofa where Ruby begins cooing over a photo album. Admittedly, the short hairstyle looks great on the young models but I'm not sure it's really me. I raise every objection I can think of but she bats every one of them away. One last go.

"Unfortunately, I work full time."

"What time do you finish today?"

"Oh, err, sixish."

"Perfect! I'll book a slot at six-fifteen for you."

Shit. I assumed they close at five-thirty.

"Trust me, your other half won't recognise you, and I guarantee he won't be able to keep his hands to himself."

I'm about to use my lack of another half as a final objection when a thought occurs. Although I'm not one to embrace change, Nathan used to object if I hinted at having my long locks cut even a fraction shorter. It would be worth having my hair cut short just to see his reaction, and perhaps proof I've finally stepped from the shadow of his controlling ways.

It's also half-price — my favourite two words, after 'free' and 'wine'.

Ruby and her colleague smile at me, expectantly. Would it hurt to be impulsive just this once? It's only a haircut; it's not like I'm having a tattoo.

"Okay. I'll see you at six-fifteen."

Decision made, I escape the salon and continue on my way to the sandwich shop while also texting Martha the news she's waited years to hear. She replies instantly with just three words — AT FUCKING LAST — followed by a celebrating emoji and a kiss. She then sends me a second text to say she feels like utter crap and will never drink again. I know Martha is kidding herself.

Rather than return to my poky office, I eat my baguette at one of the small tables outside the sandwich shop. I devour every morsel and sit back in my chair. With the midday heat and a full belly, all I want to do is take a nap. I glance at my watch. Five more hours of petty problems, difficult staff, and testy customers. I'm consumed by an air of laziness and it takes a real effort to get up off my arse.

With minimal enthusiasm, I wander back to the office.

There's a tiny consolation upon my return; the chilled air which embraces me in the reception area. There is a conspiracy theory doing the rounds that the company keeps the building cool because the ideal temperature for maximum staff productivity is nineteen degrees. It's certainly the ideal temperature for maximum nipple protrusion; even amongst the male staff. I've taken to wearing a bra with extra padding at work.

The afternoon passes like a kidney stone — slow and painful. At one point, one of my more militant team members asked if staff were still permitted to visit the loo on company time. Natalie had clearly been in her ear, stirring up trouble. I told her the company didn't mind loo visits, but they were considering a cap on toilet paper usage: a maximum of two for liquids, and eight for solids.

No doubt a humourless handful will complain to human resources tomorrow but it was worth it to see their outraged little faces.

At six o'clock, I pack up and get ready to leave for the hair salon. Not for the first time, I try to talk myself out of it but a nagging voice in the back of my head keeps telling me to stop being a fanny. That voice sounds a lot like Martha's.

To silence the self-doubt, I switch to autopilot and don't disengage it until my head is resting on a basin and a seventeen-year-old apprentice is washing my hair.

Next stop, the chair.

I'm gowned up, and the point of no return arrives as Ruby gets to work with her scissors. I try to avoid the mirror; instead focusing on the mound of clumped hair forming on the floor. In my limited experience of hair stylists, you can tell those who've spent a long time honing their craft. They have a sixth-sense with conversation and seem to know precisely how much chat each client wants to hear. In my case, I don't mind the odd question about holidays and the weather, but I'd much rather Ruby concentrates on her job. She obliges.

After a good hour of scissoring, I'm ushered back to the sink. Ruby herself then begins a chemistry lesson which I pay little attention to as my now-short hair receives the first part of the colouring treatment. Then, piss-weak coffee, waiting, more chemistry, followed by more waiting. I decline a second cup of coffee.

As my will to live slips away, Ruby finally unleashes the hairdryer. I don't have to avoid the mirror as my heavy eyelids droop shut. They remain that way until the styling part of the process is complete.

Suddenly, the hairdryer falls silent.

"Well, what do you think?"

I cautiously open my eyes to see a stranger looking back at me from the mirror.

"Oh ... um. Wow."

"Is that a good wow?"

The change is dramatic and I can't decide. My long flowing locks are no more; swapped for an abbreviated head of hair swept to the right with the tips skirting my forehead in short bangs — my face now the focal point of everything above my shoulders. The colour change, mercifully, isn't too dramatic with the auburn softened to a darker shade of bronze.

"I love the colour."

"It really accentuates the green in your eyes."

"You think so?"

"Definitely. What about the style?"

I turn my head left and right while keeping my eyes fixed on the stranger.

"It'll take a bit of getting used to but ... yes, I like it. I really do."

"You wait until tomorrow morning when you're getting ready for work. Trust me, you'll never want long hair again."

Barely able to pull my gaze from the mirror, I'm then de-robed and escorted to the reception desk. Even at half-price, the cost of rebranding my head is still three times what I usually pay for a cut.

Ruby books me in for a trim in six weeks' time and I leave the salon with a final glance in the mirror.

I smile at the stranger. Nathan will shit a brick when he sees me tomorrow, and for that reason alone it's money well spent.

5.

My evening comprised of a microwave meal, an hour of television, and the taking of several selfies which I sent to Martha. Her glowing feedback crushed any lingering doubts about my new look. I then dragged my exhausted but happy carcass upstairs at ten o'clock and flopped onto the bed. I just had enough time to enjoy the exquisite sensation of a draught circling my newly exposed neck before sleep took hold.

I wake to an alarm rather than a nightmare. Not a bad start to the day.

That start remains positive when I shave five minutes off my usual preparation time. The problem with long hair is you experience more bad hair days than good, particularly if you're in a hurry — that is why God gave us hair bobbles. I require no bobble this morning; just a wash, a quick blow dry, and a light misting of hairspray.

I skip down to the kitchen and open the back door.

Frank looks up at me.

"What do you think of the new hairstyle, then?"

Can a cat shrug its shoulders? It kinda looked like he did — not a single shit given.

To make amends, he rubs himself against my legs and purrs loudly.

"You can't just flirt your way back into my good books, Mister. I'm not that desperate."

Not yet, anyway.

Like an old married couple we go through the same routine we do every morning until Frank saunters outside and curls up on the bistro table. Nathan had many failings but at least he never ended a conversation by falling asleep on the patio furniture.

I check my hair in the mirror for the twentieth time and leave for work.

As I walk to the bus stop, my mind turns to tonight and the meeting with my ex-husband that I'm now looking forward to;

albeit for reasons of vanity and pride. Whatever he needs to see me about, I intend to stroll in, wait for his jaw to hit the floor, listen, then sashay my arse out of there within an hour.

The final act of closure.

I reach the bus stop and swap thin smiles with the commuters who make the same journey as me every morning. We know nothing about one another besides our mutual whereabouts this time every weekday. I don't even know their names. To me, they're just bus stop seven; or six some days.

Our chariot arrives and we file on. There's an unwritten rule we embark in order of who's been waiting the longest which means I'm the last to climb on board. I swipe my travel card and turn to face the aisle in search of an empty seat. Today, they're in short supply at the front and I can't quite tell if there are any free towards the rear. As the bus pulls away, I stagger down the aisle.

There's just one empty seat — next to a chubby, middle-aged guy with bad teeth.

He looks up at me and smiles; too close to creepy for my liking. However, I've painted myself into a corner now. With no other empty seats it would be even more awkward to turn around and retrace my steps to the front of the bus.

Skin prickling, I sit down next to Mr Bad Teeth, with one buttock hanging over the edge of the seat so there's no chance of bodily contact.

Please don't talk to me. Please don't talk to me.

In lieu of forgotten headphones, I make it clear I'm not up for conversation by staring intently at my phone whilst randomly stabbing the screen with my index finger. I'm tempted to report my discomfort to Martha via text but it would be too easy for Mr Bad Teeth to glance to his right and see what I'm typing. I check the news app instead.

I'm partway through a depressing article about another mass shooting in America when I'm interrupted by the sound of a throat being cleared.

"Excuse me, darlin'."

I turn to Mr Bad Teeth.

"Can I squeeze past?" he asks.

His voice is exactly as I imagined; like a raspy sex offender poring over Facebook photos of teenage girls. Sometimes, my imagination gets the better of me.

"Oh, yes ... sorry."

I get to my feet and take a few paces back; clutching a vertical pole for balance as the bus turns a corner. Mr Bad Teeth gets up, steps across, and smiles again.

"Cheers, darlin'."

I'm not sure if he expects a response, but he doesn't get one. He then waddles off down the aisle towards the exit. The encounter is a reminder why I don't like the idea of Internet dating — too great a risk of awkward situations with creepy men.

I sit back down and return to my phone.

The rest of my journey passes without incident although the temporary roadworks on the outskirts of the town centre add another five minutes. The delay means I don't have time to visit Starbucks so my first port of call is the staffroom. It's no great shock to find I'm the first to arrive.

I fill our antiquated kettle and switch it on. As I wait for it to boil, I search the cupboard for a clean mug.

"Morning."

I recognise the voice but as it's only eight-thirty, I must be hallucinating. I turn around and to my surprise, Natalie stands in the doorway. As our eyes meet, we swap the same look of mild surprise, but for different reasons.

"Morning, Natalie. You're ... early."

"Oh, my God," she gasps. "I'm loving the new look."

Due to a lack of practice I always struggle to find a suitable response to compliments. I settle on a smile that I hope appears sincere.

"Thank you."

"You look amazing, so much younger."

"That's lovely of you to say."

"You'd easily pass for forty now."

"Bless you ... wait, what? Forty?"

"Yes, easily."

Judging by the look of innocence on her face, I can only assume Natalie is unaware of the insult she's just thrown my way. Either that or she's a bloody good actress. I'm about to correct her but stop myself. What's the point?

"I'll pass your feedback on to my stylist," I reply with a withering smile. "Anyway, it's good to see you heeded my advice."

"Your advice?"

"Coming in early."

"Oh, right. No problem."

I make myself a coffee and leave Natalie to make her own as a punishment for bursting my bubble.

For reasons we've never been able to ascertain, Tuesday is the slowest day of the week for loan applications. Consequently, it's a good day for clearing the backlog of overdue reports and forecasts. One major gripe I have with working in a corporate environment is there are too many in senior management who justify their existence through the medium of other people's work. I'm forever being asked to collate data so the Operations Director can demonstrate his value via a weekly PowerPoint presentation to the board. Justin isn't a bad boss but over the years he's become gradually indoctrinated into the corporate cult. For all the perks, such as a six-figure salary and private medical cover, I don't think I'll ever become a convert.

I barely leave my office most of the day but when I venture out to grab a sandwich, a handful of my colleagues offer positive feedback on the new look, with that feedback ranging from pleasantly surprised to outright gushing. It goes some way to rebuilding my confidence after Natalie's comments. Perhaps one day, when one of us has tendered our resignation, I might ask her how old she thinks I am. In the meantime, I'd rather not know.

The day ends with an empty desk and all my reports up-to-date. I'm not at Nathan's obsessive level but I take some satisfaction in having all my admin in order.

As I shut down my computer it confirms I need to install an update. Wearily, I click the button and sit back in my chair. My attention then drifts to the framed photo next to my monitor, and the two smiling faces looking back at me. Of course, they're not looking at me but a camera which captured the moment fifteen years ago. Both in their early fifties at the time, Dad had skippered their cabin cruiser, Kellybelle, from Southampton to Cowes for the weekend; the bright blue sky and their sun-kissed skin a clue to the time of year.

My parents adored that boat and took her out at every opportunity; sometimes just across The Solent to the Isle of Wight and sometimes, work-permitting, as far as Southern Portugal. Whenever Dad met someone, he'd jokingly tell them he owned a yacht, but Kellybelle was a tatty old bird requiring constant maintenance. I remember when he proudly confirmed the name he'd bestowed upon her — we even had a naming ceremony where he attempted to smash a bottle of cheap supermarket wine against the hull. It took four attempts before the bottle eventually won, and Dad had to spend an entire Saturday patching up a bottle-sized hole.

The only fly in their happiness proved to be their daughter's lack of sea legs. I took a dozen trips and threw up every time. No matter how quiet the sea, or how many anti-sickness pills I took, we always ended up returning to port within an hour. Fortunately, Martha's parents suggested I might like to holiday with them and that became a regular occurrence throughout my teenage years. My parents were then free to explore the seas alone for two whole weeks, and the occasional weekend when I stayed with my grandparents. That arrangement continued until I turned nineteen and they were comfortable leaving me at home on my own while they gallivanted around the ports and harbours of Europe. They were so happy living their dream I didn't mind, plus I had my own life to forge by that point.

Their dream only lasted another four years.

Just as my thoughts drift in a direction I'd rather they didn't, the update ends. I take a final glance at the photo and offer the same silent prayer I offer every day before leaving the office.

I manage to secure an empty seat on the bus home and, in an attempt to shed the lingering sadness I brought with me, spend the journey contemplating which outfit to wear tonight.

There's a delicate balance to be struck.

On the one hand, I don't want to look like I've made too much of an effort but on the other, I want Nathan to see I'm revelling in my independence. I need a Goldilocks outfit — not too plain, not too sassy; just right.

Once I've had a bite to eat in the garden, I head upstairs to my stifling bedroom and scour the wardrobes. At least half-a-dozen outfits are considered and then discarded on the bed. By outfit eight I'm a hot, sweaty mess, and I find myself trapped in a tight-fitting number which clings to my skin like a rubber wetsuit. Frustration mounting, I'm about to text Nathan and cancel when I spot one final contender lurking at the end of the rail.

I purchased the ivory-coloured dress for a friend's fortieth birthday party last month but a bout of mild food poisoning derailed my plans to attend; not least because explosive diarrhoea and ivory-coloured dresses aren't a great combo.

Hoping it fits as well as I remember, I pull it from the rail. I'm about to try it on but decide a shower might be in order first. Not only is my skin stickier than a cinema carpet, my deodorant is struggling to live up to its promise of day-long protection.

The twenty-minute blast in lukewarm water does the trick and I emerge from the shower feeling human again. After dousing myself in talcum powder and double deodorant, I return to the bedroom.

The dress slides on without incident and I turn to face the mirror. It's erring towards the sassy end on the Goldilocks scale, with the hem several inches north of my knees and the low neckline offering third-date levels of cleavage but, as Martha would say, fuck it.

"Not bad at all," I coo, as I check out various angles in the mirror. "You'd almost pass for forty, love."

Outfit sorted, I blow dry my hair and apply enough makeup to look like I've made an effort — just not much of an effort. There's just one final finishing touch; a deliciously sweet perfume Nathan detested because he said I smelt like a chocolate cheesecake. Most men would consider that a good thing, but not Nathan.

A few squirts of perfume and the transformation from sweaty office worker to self-confident, slightly sassy, divorcee is complete.

Showtime.

6.

The Three Horseshoes is my local and only a ten-minute walk from Juniper Lane. Barely one minute into that walk my right foot catches the edge of a protruding paving slab. My next step is decidedly lopsided.

I stop and inspect the cause. The three-inch heel is hanging to the sole by just a few strands of leather; probably beyond repair.

"Bollocks!"

My sass takes a knock as I'm forced to limp back home and source an alternative pair of shoes.

New footwear acquired, I'm sixty quid out-of-pocket by the time I reach the same protruding paving slab, and late. I quickly snap a photo so I can complain to the council; not that they're likely to cover the cost of replacing my shoes but at least I can vent my annoyance. The paving slab itself appears unconcerned.

As I turn into Kiln Road, I check my watch — four minutes past. Knowing Nathan, he'll give it until ten past before calling to check my whereabouts. With The Three Horseshoes only a hundred yards up the road, I should arrive before he gets too agitated. He's a stickler for time-keeping.

I push through the door at five minutes past.

My local is rarely busy but being a Tuesday evening it's particularly quiet. Besides two grey-haired men nattering away at the bar, there's only one customer; a middle-aged man alone at a table near the window. He spots me and turns away, only for his head to snap back in my direction a second later in a double-take. He gets to his feet and ambles over.

"Evening, Nathan."

"It's lovely to see you, Kelly."

As he comes to a stop, he appears unsure of the correct protocol for greeting an ex-wife. Nathan is the least tactile man you could meet, therefore, a hug is unlikely, but even he might consider a handshake too formal. I remove the decision by turning to the bar and asking the landlord for a large glass of white wine. Nathan then edges up beside me and slaps a tenner down.

"Please, let me get that."

"Thanks."

The glass has barely touched the bar before I grab it and down a thirsty gulp; a slight and unexpected nervousness threatening to breach my confidence.

"You've had your hair done."

"Yep. Fancied a change."

"It's ... different. Very trendy."

His use of the word 'trendy' makes me inwardly cringe. And from a man who considers beige cords the height of fashion, it's not much of a compliment. He, on the other hand, hasn't changed one iota. The same tawny hair neatly parted at the side. The same clean-shaven face. The same achingly dull, conservative attire. Although Nathan is only eight years my senior, he's always possessed the sensibilities of a much older man.

"Shall we sit?" I ask, changing the subject.

"Of course."

He follows me to the table by the window and we sit opposite one another. Nathan takes a sip of Coke before posing a question.

"How have you been?"

"Good, actually. You?"

"Oh, not so bad. Busy with work as usual."

"And how's your mother?"

"She's ... well. Her mobility has deteriorated a little which she finds frustrating, but on the whole she's in good spirit."

My first theory shot down. The Munchkins will have to put off their celebrations for another day — it seems the witch is hanging on.

"Give her my regards."

"I will."

Topic exhausted, he gazes out of the window for a few seconds. I didn't expect our meeting to be a festival of hugs and high-fives but even so, the awkwardness is palpable.

"Where are you living now?" I ask, just to break the silence.

"I'm renting an apartment in that new development down by the river."

"Nice."

"It suits my needs, although it feels too much like I'm living in a hotel."

"You couldn't find a place to buy?"

"The timing isn't right. I've got a strong inkling the property market is about to nosedive."

"Well, I guess you'd know."

"What about you?"

"I'm not so sensible. I bought a little house on Juniper Lane, with no parking."

Now we're on to his favoured topic of conversation, his body language becomes increasingly animated.

"You really should have sought my advice, Kelly. But, if you hurry there's still time to sell while the prices remain inflated. I know a few people in the property game so I could make some calls tomorrow if you like?"

"No thanks, I don't want to sell. It's my home, Nathan, not an investment."

"Yes, but ..."

"I'm not selling."

"Your loss," he huffs. "Don't say I didn't warn you."

Irked, I move on from the small talk.

"I'm guessing we're not here to discuss my property affairs, so can we get to the point of this ... whatever it is? You said you needed to discuss something with me."

"I'm sorry; I didn't mean to lecture you."

"Old habits die hard, eh?"

He frowns at my barb.

"I've changed," he suggests in a low voice. "I'm not the same man you divorced."

I've only been with him for five minutes but time enough to determine little has changed.

"Really?"

"Yes, and that's what I wanted to discuss with you. I've had a lot of time to myself since the divorce; time to reflect, and to think about the future."

I don't like the direction of this conversation any more than I like Nathan's attempt at sincerity.

"And what have you concluded?"

His left hand disappears beneath the table and emerges a second later. He places a small box in the centre of the table.

"Please open it," he requests.

The box is too small, too fancy to contain anything other than … no, that's ridiculous. I stare at it for a moment and then look up at my ex-husband.

"What is it, Nathan?"

"Open it and you'll see."

"I don't want to open it."

"Please. I'll explain all once you've seen what's in the box."

"If it's what I think it is …"

"Just open it."

More agitated than curious, I snatch the box from the table and flip the lid open. The content of the box is, in one way at least, a surprise.

"A ring?"

"Not just any ring," he says proudly. "That's an eighteen-carat gold ring with a one-carat diamond."

There's no denying it's a stunning piece of jewellery which probably cost as much as a new car. It's a far cry from the modest ring Nathan offered when he proposed. He argued large diamonds were vulgar, and prone to being dislodged when worn every day. I should have realised then he didn't have a romantic bone in his body.

"It's lovely," I concede. "But I don't understand why you're showing it to me."

He sits forward and fixes me with an intense gaze.

"Kelly, will you marry me?"

"I beg your pardon."

"I said will you marry me?"

Saying you're speechless is rarely literal but on this occasion I physically can't find the words. There are lots of questions, though — the most pertinent relating to Nathan's sanity.

"Listen," he continues. "I've thought long and hard about this, and where our marriage went wrong. I accept I wasn't the most spontaneous or romantic husband in the world but, as I say, I've changed."

"I ... err ..."

Undaunted by the lack of an answer, he presses on enthusiastically.

"I've booked a slot at the registry office for eleven o'clock Monday morning. Two hours later, we'll be heading out on a flight to Paris for five nights at the Park Hyatt — it's that swanky hotel we passed on the way back from the Eiffel Tower, remember? You said you'd love to stay there one day."

There must be a punchline but from the look on his face, it appears Nathan is completely serious. Still dumbstruck, I empty my glass in the hope alcohol will help. Doubtful, but it sure as fuck won't make the situation any crazier.

"Another?"

I can only nod.

Taking my silence as a positive sign, he skips off to the bar.

Left on my own with the ring, I attempt to order the list of questions I haven't been able to ask. It strikes me I might be in shock, and that's the reason I can't think straight. If Nathan had told me he'd set up home with a Dutch mime artist called Ruben, and they were madly in love, it would have been less of a shock. On some level, at least that would have made sense. His proposal — his second proposal — doesn't.

"Here you go."

Another glass of wine appears and Nathan retakes his seat.

"I suspect you've got questions," he says. "I do appreciate my proposal might have been a little unexpected."

Another gulp of wine oils my mouth sufficiently so I can finally stammer a few words.

"This is ... why, Nathan?"

"You always said I lacked spontaneity. This is me being spontaneous."

"No, I mean ... why on earth do you think we should get

married again?"

"Because I still love you. Because I realise what an absolute fool I was, letting you go. But mostly because I want a second chance to prove I can be the husband you deserve."

"And what kind of husband is that?"

"I think you know."

"I do, but I want you to tell me. You say you've changed, so prove it."

"Do you want me to spell it out?"

Now I've got past the ridiculous reason we're here, it's an opportunity to vent some angst I never shared in the divorce settlement.

"Let's just step back for a moment. We're divorced, and that didn't just happen by mistake, did it?"

"I know, but I now accept I was to blame. I became so obsessed with work, and ensuring mother was being properly cared for, I neglected you."

"We both worked hard, and I don't blame you for looking out for your mother. We divorced because we'd grown too far apart."

"And why did we grow apart? That's the key question."

"Is it?"

"Absolutely, it is. If we'd just spent more time together, I doubt we'd be here now."

"You think it's that simple?"

"I do, and you have my word it'll be different next time. We'll take holidays together at least twice a year, and have weekends away; go out in the evenings to the theatre and for dinner."

"Okay, where would we go on holiday?"

"Anywhere."

"So, you'd be happy on a two-week beach holiday in Spain?"

A loaded question. Nathan detests beach holidays almost as much as he detests Spain, but I've got a point to prove.

"Um, well, we could talk about it, but I'm willing to compromise."

"Come off it, Nathan. I might be happy lying on a beach for

two weeks but you'd hate every minute, and that's the problem — we're such different people we'll never be able to find a workable compromise."

"Other couples do."

"Yes, but those couples typically have something we lost a long time ago."

"Namely?"

"Love."

The corner of his mouth twitches; a tell-tale sign I've struck a nerve. However, Nathan being Nathan, there's no immediate comeback. Instead, he sits back in his chair and presses the tips of his fingers together; calculating his next move like a chess grandmaster.

"You realise," he says calmly. "Love is rarely enough on its own. Many marriages fail despite both parties loving one another."

"I understand that, but if there isn't love, what's the point in being married?"

"Support, companionship, friendship … plenty of good reasons. In some cultures, the bride and groom are strangers on their wedding day, and they build their entire marriage on friendship. Love develops later."

"Maybe so, but I don't want a friend, or a companion. I want what I always wanted: romance, affection, passion. In short: love."

"And that's what I've realised. I can give you all of that."

"No, you can't. I'm sorry, Nathan, but there's nothing there anymore."

"So, you won't give me a chance to make amends?"

He looks at me almost pitifully. An unfamiliar expression on a familiar face.

"I can't. We both need to move on."

The expression quickly changes to one I have seen before. Many times before.

"So much for gratitude," he snorts. "This is the first time I've ever asked you for anything, and you deny me without a thought."

"What? This isn't a favour you're asking of me, Nathan. Were you seriously expecting me to remarry you because of some misguided sense of debt?"

"Why not? It wasn't as if our marriage was that bad, was it? Granted, I could have made more of an effort but we learn from our mistakes."

"Dear God. You're actually serious?"

"Completely serious."

"But, really …"

"Look, all I ask is for you to think about it. Just give yourself a day or two to digest it and I think you might find it's not such a terrible idea once you weigh up all the pros and cons."

His statement nicely sums up why I could never marry a man like Nathan again.

"It's not about pros and cons — it's about how I feel. You must admit, in those final few years we lived like housemates. We never had dinner together, never went out, rarely talked, and don't even get me started on our non-existent sex-life."

"We both agreed separate bedrooms made sense."

"Yes, but we still lived in the same house so why didn't we ever have sex?"

"You never seemed that bothered about it."

"And neither did you. Couples in love want to have sex with each other — we didn't."

"It'll be different next time. We'll share a bedroom and I'll happily commit to having sex at least once a week … more, if that's what it takes. Maybe, we could sit down on a Sunday evening with our diaries and commit to the exact days and times? That way, we can monitor our love-making and ensure we don't fall back into the same rut as before."

I'm tempted to bash my head against the table but a time-out trip to the toilet might involve less pain.

"This is ridiculous," I huff. "I'm going to the loo."

I storm to the toilets and seek refuge in a cubicle to gather my thoughts. On reflection, if I'd gathered them at the table, I'd now have my handbag and phone with me. Seeing as I'm unable to text Martha and seek her input, it looks like I'll have to work out a suitable response on my own. It takes several minutes to decide what I'm going to say.

Returning to the table, I sit down and calmly confirm my position.

"In your succinct, pragmatic way, Nathan, you've demonstrated just how little you've changed. What kind of couple pre-book sex on a schedule?"

"Okay, maybe that wasn't the most sensible of suggestions, but I have changed. If you're just brave enough to accept my proposal, you'll see just how much."

This is pointless. Pointless and exasperating — much like our marriage.

"Look, I'm not willing to marry someone I'm not in love with, and there's nothing you can say to change my mind. I'm sorry if it hurts, but I don't love you, Nathan."

The twitch returns.

"You loved me once, when it suited you."

"Eh?"

"You were a broken mess when we first met, and I put you back together. You loved me then, didn't you?"

"Hold on a minute …"

"No, you hold on," he snaps. "How many sleepless nights did I sit and comfort you? Who was there to wipe away the tears whenever and wherever you broke down? Who paid for all those therapy sessions, and who supported you through your darkest days? From the very first moment we met, I looked after you, didn't I?"

My mind serves up a montage of memories; most of which I'd hoped never to recount.

"I'm not denying you were a rock and I'll always be grateful, but that was twelve years ago. I'm not the same woman."

"Just answer one question: did you love me?"

"I … yes, I suppose."

"Well, then. If you fell in love with me once, you can fall in love with me again."

There's a hint of insistence to his tone. Not a question but almost an instruction. Nothing I say seems to be sinking in so there's only the nuclear option remaining.

"I want children."

"Fine. We'll use a sperm donor, or adopt. Whatever you're happy with."

"Sorry?"

"If I'd listened to you at the time, we might now be living happily in Kensall Gardens as a family — you, me, and our children. I regret that decision; denying you the opportunity of motherhood."

A complete one-eighty turnaround in attitude but I don't believe him.

"But you don't want children, do you?"

"I want whatever makes you happy."

"Don't ignore my question. Do you want children?"

"I can see myself as a father, yes."

"For crying out loud, just answer the question. Do you want children? Yes or no?"

"Yes."

"I'm sorry, but I don't believe you."

"Then let me prove it to you. I swear I'll make you happy, and I think deep down you know I deserve the opportunity to at least try."

As I take another glug of wine, he picks up the small box from the table and takes out the ring.

"Marry me, Kelly. Please."

Calmly, I put my glass down.

"No."

"Will you at least think …?"

"Stop, Nathan. Just stop."

I grab my bag and stand up. I don't wish to be cruel but I need to close the door on this madness and nail it shut once and for all.

"Let me make my position clear, Nathan. I don't love you and I don't want to marry you because we're not right for one another and we never will be. It's time for us both to move on so please don't contact me again."

"Please, sit down."

"I'm going."

"If you leave, that's it. I know you, Kelly, and if you change your mind, it'll be too late. It's now or never."

"I'll take never."

"You're making a mistake," he says flatly.

"Goodbye, Nathan. Look after yourself."

I turn and stride away.

As I reach the door, he calls after me. "You'll regret shunning me, Kelly. Mark my words."

I don't look back. The only regret I have is not shunning him twelve years ago.

7.

Strange, but within a few minutes of leaving The Three Horseshoes my thoughts turn to Father Christmas. My parents did such a good job convincing me of his existence, I was eleven years of age before I learnt the truth.

Although I didn't realise it at the time, it was a watershed moment in my childhood — the moment I discovered my parents were competent liars. I think it's also the moment I began questioning their judgement on other aspects of my life. If they lied about the jolly man in a red suit, what other lies had they spun? I hated carrots yet my eyesight seemed perfect and, despite my mother telling me I'd definitely catch a cold without one, I rarely ever wore my scarf in winter. Granted, parental lies are usually of the white variety and for the good of the child, but they're still lies. And once you know parents lie, you begin to question everything, and develop your own opinions. Over time, you push the boundaries and learn to think independently.

When I first met Nathan, my mental state was as fragile as any child's. Looking back, perhaps I needed someone to protect me from the truth and make decisions for me, but I didn't realise my marriage vows gifted control of my thoughts and decisions forever more. It took me eleven years but I now realise, unlike my parents, Nathan never wanted me to think independently — our brief meeting proved as much. Perhaps he does genuinely think he's changed but beneath all the promises and the gestures, he's as unyielding as he ever was. The only person who has changed is me, and for the better.

As I turn into Juniper Lane, I sway between the pride of putting Nathan in his place, and the painful memories our conversation stirred up.

The solution is another glass of wine, and a friendly ear to bend.

I arrive home and change into a pair of shorts and a vest top. Once I've poured a large Pinot, I grab my phone and sit in the garden.

Hoping the girls are in bed, I call Martha.

"Hey, chick. How's it going?"

"Great. Have I caught you at a good time?"

"I've got a glass of wine in hand and the girls are asleep, so yes."

"I thought you were never drinking again after Sunday."

"I lied."

"What a surprise. You okay to chat?"

"Of course. What's up?"

I relay the evening's events, or at least I attempt to but Martha interjects when I get to the proposal part.

"He did what?" she shrieks. "No fucking way."

"Yes way, and the ring must have cost a small fortune."

"I wouldn't accept that man's proposal if he turned up with the Crown Jewels. Wait … you said no, right?"

"Obviously I said no. Repeatedly, as it goes."

"God, I bet he threw a hissy fit. That man hates not getting his own way."

"Ah, but he's changed, apparently."

I'm treated to the sound of raucous laughter for a full ten seconds.

"That's priceless," she snorts, still chuckling away. "There's more chance of the girls changing their own beds than Nathan changing his ways."

"Quite. Anyway, he had it all planned out, to the point he'd actually booked the registry office for next week, followed by a trip to some posh hotel in Paris for the honeymoon."

"He didn't? The bloody cheek!"

"I suppose, in his head, it seemed like a romantic gesture but it only demonstrated how little he's actually changed. He then suggested we share a bedroom and set up some kind of sex schedule."

"What the fuck?"

"I didn't ask how he thought that might work, but can you imagine it?"

"Oh, God," she giggles. "You could give each day a name so you don't forget what's on the schedule. How do you fancy

51

Missionary Monday?"

"Or Fingering Friday?"

"Sodomy Sunday?"

"Yeah, too much."

We spend five minutes taking the piss out of Nathan and laughing hysterically before I touch on the other reason I called. The tone crashes.

"He said I owed him for all he did for me … you know … back then."

"I still hate myself for not being there when you needed me."

"Don't be silly. You did what you could, considering you were on the opposite side of the world when it happened."

"I don't know. I regret going back to Perth so soon after the service. I wish I'd stayed."

"And jeopardise the opportunity of a lifetime? I'd have felt even more awful knowing you'd given that up just so I had a shoulder to cry on."

"Stuart understood. He'd have been okay on his own for another month or so."

"That's not the point. And besides, there's something I never told you."

"Oh, what?"

"I was planning to come out to Australia once I'd dealt with the house and all the legal crap. Part of me hoped the change of scenery might have helped."

"Shit, really? You never mentioned it."

"I know, but … well, I met Nathan before I had the chance. And the rest, as they say, is history."

"Christ, I bet you wish you'd turned right instead of left that day."

"If only."

I can still recall the exact moment I met Nathan as if it were yesterday. I'd just been to the solicitor's office for the reading of my parents' will. I'd kept the grief bottled up throughout the meeting but once I stepped out onto the street afterwards, the finality of it all hit me like a train. I remember the tears streaming and scrambled thoughts clouding my mind to the point

I lost my bearings. I should have turned right and headed back to the bus station but I turned left.

Sobbing uncontrollably, I staggered along the pavement as the grief took hold until I could barely breathe. I collapsed against a shop window, and that's when a stranger came to my rescue. Somehow, he calmed me down and established why I was in such a state.

At that moment, I'd have sought sanctuary from anyone. As it was, my saviour turned out to be Nathan Thaw.

He took me for a coffee and listened as I poured my heart out for over an hour. He then drove me home and promised to pop by in the evening to check up on me. It seems crazy now but at the time I felt so alone I couldn't think straight. I needed kindness and support, and it pains me to say it but Nathan offered exactly that. I was a willing victim.

Over the ensuing days and weeks, I saw more and more of Nathan as he gradually worked his way into my trust. We talked, we walked, we went out for dinner. With a steady, reassuring hand on the tiller, he guided me through the worst of the storm; helping, advising, and even pushing me to seek the help of a therapist when I reached my lowest ebb. With Martha getting on with her life in Perth, I couldn't have wished for a better substitute friend. If only we'd remained just friends.

Eight months later, and still not in the right frame of mind to be making such a life-changing decision, I became Mrs Kelly Thaw.

It's so easy to look back on it now and wonder what the hell I was thinking, but there was one driving force behind my decision to accept Nathan's proposal; a chance to have a family. With no siblings and both parents gone, the urge to create a new family proved overwhelming; to the point it consumed my thinking. I knew Nathan wasn't entirely right for me, but I thought marrying him and having children would go some way to filling the yawning hole in my heart.

That hole is smaller now, but it's still there. Nathan never came close to filling it.

"Look on the bright side, chick."

"There's a bright side?"

"Now you've finally purged that dickhead from your life, you can start looking forward. You might be older, but you're a hell of a lot wiser now."

"You're right on the older part. I'm not so sure about wiser."

"Don't do yourself down. You've got a lot going for you: a lovely home, a great job, and a stunningly attractive best friend."

"Jennie isn't my best friend, hun, you are."

"Bitch."

"Aww, you know I'm only kidding."

"Course I do."

"Good."

There's a brief pause before Martha continues.

"And you do know, don't you?"

"Know what?"

"Your mum and dad — they'd both be so proud of you."

"Thank you," I gulp.

"I miss them too. Every day."

"Stop it. You'll have me blubbing."

"All right. Just as long as you know."

"I do."

I just wish I didn't have to theorise how proud they might be. Meeting Nathan might have been an unfortunate twist of fate but the Devil himself must have had a hand in what happened to my parents; to lose them so tragically.

Martha might be right in that I've got plenty of good reasons to look forward, but I'll never stop looking back and wondering what might have been.

8.

After an hour-long chat with Martha, the first spots of rain dappled the patio. As I retreated to the kitchen, thunder rumbled overhead, and the heavens opened. I've never seen a storm like it and watched the accompanying light-show from my bedroom window.

The cloudless blue skies are back this morning but there's a crisp breeze rather than the suffocating, muggy air which has more than outstayed its welcome.

I open the back door and scan the patio. There's no sign of Frank but that's not unusual — he turns up when it suits and no doubt he'll be purring at my ankles when he's hungry.

Focusing on my own rumbling stomach, I put the kettle on and slide two thick slices of white bread in the toaster. I know it's not good for me but I spent eleven years eating muesli and natural yogurt for breakfast because Nathan suffered from a mild gluten intolerance and wouldn't allow bread of any kind in the house. I don't know why I put up with his demands for so long, but I guess all newlyweds have to compromise in the early days as they adapt to married life. Before you know it, those compromises become habits and you stop thinking about how those habits formed in the first place.

Now though, living alone has rekindled my inner-child. Free from the constraints of an oppressive husband, I eat my own bodyweight in gluten-rich foods, watch every episode of the soap operas Nathan detested, and I never put the toilet seat up. I eat biscuits in bed, drink wine on school nights, and I spend many an evening vegging out in just a pair of tatty old knickers and t-shirt.

Perhaps I'll never have a child but at least I can live like one. I've become pretty adept at seeking silver linings.

I get ready for work and leave the house a few minutes earlier than usual. Frank's loss is my gain. Those extra few minutes secure a bronze medal in the bus queue.

The journey is now so routine I barely pay attention to the

passing scenery. I get on, sit down, and stare at my phone screen for fifteen minutes. It's now so ingrained I instinctively know when my stop is approaching. The only difference this morning is the brief period of introspection while we wait in traffic. I make a promise to myself: never to think about Nathan again. Yesterday's meeting provided definitive evidence I made the right decision cutting him from my life.

I arrive at my stop and head to Starbucks.

I'm old enough to remember a time before coffee shops. I vowed I'd never fall into the trap of buying an overpriced coffee in the mornings but a colleague dragged me in last year and before I knew it, I'd formed an addiction to Latte Macchiato. As addictions go, I suppose there are worse.

I skip through the door and make for the counter. A particularly chipper barista takes my order and processes it with the usual efficiency.

"One Latte Macchiato," he confirms, handing it over. "Have a great day."

"Thanks. You too."

I take a sip, turn around, and bump straight into the man queueing behind me. Startled, the cup slips from my hand and three quid's worth of coffee splats across the tiled floor.

"Cripes," I splutter. "I'm so sorry."

"No apology required," the man replies. "Accidents happen."

His unflustered tone is almost a parody of the old-fashioned radio announcers on the BBC; crisp and assertive, but with a warm, reassuring undercurrent. It's not the kind of voice you're likely to hear while wandering the aisles of Primark, that's for sure.

I take a step back and assess whether I need to offer payment for dry cleaning. Fortunately, his suit is the same shade of brown as the coffee and I can't see any obvious stains. My inspection stops on the white lily fixed to his jacket lapel. Unusual, unless he's off to a wedding shortly.

"Lilium Candidum."

"Sorry," I reply.

"I noticed you admiring the flower. The Latin name is Lilium

56

Candidum, although it's more commonly known as the Madonna lily."

"Oh, right."

He continues to smile at me expectantly. His face is unremarkable in every way, from his mousy brown hair to his chestnut-coloured eyes.

I'm not comfortable making small talk with random strangers but I'm even more uncomfortable with the awkward silence.

"Did they name the lily after the singer?" I ask, tongue-in-cheek.

"Which singer?"

"Err, Madonna."

"I suspect not."

I nod, and a staff member arrives with a bucket and mop.

"Please, allow me to buy you a replacement coffee," the man suggests.

"Oh, there's really no need. It was my mistake."

"I insist."

Before I can argue, he approaches the counter and requests a replacement for my order, and a bottle of water. He pays for it with the exact change, plucks the bottle from the counter, and turns to face me.

"Your coffee will be ready in two ticks," he confirms.

"Thank you."

"You're most welcome. Have a splendid day, Miss."

If he were wearing a hat, I'm sure he'd have doffed it in my direction. As it is, he nods once and walks away.

Not a great start to the day but no real damage done. A minute later than I envisaged, I grab my coffee and set off for work.

It's exactly eight-thirty on the dot when I step out of the lift and make my way past the rows of empty desks to my office. I poke my head around the staffroom door to find it deserted. She's not due at her desk for another half-hour but I suspect Natalie's early arrival yesterday was a one-off.

On autopilot, I enter my office and begin the same old routine which begins with switching the lights on and hanging my handbag on the back of the door. I then boot up the computer and click the inbox icon.

One of the last emails to arrive is from my boss, Justin. I sent over the report he requested yesterday afternoon and it appears he isn't happy with the content. Predictably, my projections for the next month don't convey enough optimism. Reading between the lines, I'm guessing he wants me to base the forecast on wildly optimistic guesswork rather than hard data — he's probably in line for a bonus and doesn't want to jeopardise it by giving the board bad news. I'm sure he'll get his bonus once he presents my embellished report, and I'll get a bollocking next month when we fail to reach the wildly optimistic targets. This is the circle of corporate life.

I open up Excel and choose a random percentile between ten and twenty — sixteen, as it goes. I then add that random percentile to every projection and email the forecast back to Justin.

Two minutes later, his succinct reply arrives: Much better. I'm sure you'll smash those targets.

Knob.

I'm about to close the report when I notice an issue. I inadvertently added sixteen percent to my forecast for staff sick days. I've always argued there's no point trying to forecast how many of my team will call in sick each month, and Justin's failure to even notice the random increase validates that argument.

I should have been a vet.

Just as I return to my inbox, I hear two voices from the main office. Gradually, as more of my team arrive, those voices develop into a steady hum of white noise as phone calls are made and answered, and keyboards are tapped. Like the dawn chorus, it's the same waking sound you'll hear in a thousand offices across the land. Marston Finance is open for business.

I get up and poke my head around the door to check everyone is at their desk. My team leader, Ben, always conducts a morning brief and reports any absentees but it never hurts to check myself. I spot an empty desk at the far side of the room —

Natalie's.

"Everything okay, boss?"

Ben appears from the staffroom doorway opposite my office.

"Where's Natalie?"

He scratches his overgrown hipster beard for a second.

"She's not well."

"What's wrong with her?"

"Stomach ache, apparently."

"How original. Why is it stomach aches and migraines account for seventy percent of staff sick days?"

"Err, I don't know."

"No, neither do I, but my guess is they're a great cover for a hangover. You wake up feeling sick, with a banging headache, so it's technically not a lie to say you've got a stomach ache or migraine."

He shuffles awkwardly on the spot, avoiding eye contact.

"You had a migraine last Friday, didn't you, Ben?"

"I get them from time to time and usually a few pills do the trick, but last Friday's was a killer."

"Hmm ... that must have been awful. I hope it didn't ruin your friend's birthday celebrations the day before."

"My, um. Sorry?"

"Yes, you went out on the town Thursday evening didn't you?"

"I, err ..."

"You do remember you added me as a friend on Facebook, don't you? Judging by the photos you posted, you had a great time. I particularly liked the photo of you knocking back Sambuca shots in a nightclub at half-one in the morning."

"Oh, I ... err, only had the one. I think that's when the migraine started."

"Convenient."

"I wasn't hungover, boss. Honestly."

"I'll take your word for it. However, I'd like you to warn the team I'll be taking a keen interest in any reported sick days from now on. Make sure you inform Natalie by email."

"I will."

"Oh, and one other thing. Justin is expecting a sixteen percent increase in gross lending next month. I'll compile an action plan and email it to you later. Be sure to include it in tomorrow's briefing."

"Will do. Was there anything else?"

"Nope."

"I'll get back to work then."

He scuttles away and I return to my office.

The only reason I decided not to punish Ben's blatant skiving is because he's usually good at his job. It's a role I fulfilled myself for a year so I know how tricky it is to cultivate a good working relationship with the team while maintaining discipline. Being honest, I might have skived once or twice myself back then.

The day progresses with no great dramas but Natalie's absence grates by early afternoon. I'm not a vindictive person but she is the one member of my team I'd love to sack if I can find concrete proof she's broken her employment contract. I turn to Facebook and search her profile in the hope she might, like Ben, have posted damning evidence to undermine her claim of a stomach ache.

Unfortunately, she hasn't posted anything in over a year. I then try searching Instagram and although I find Natalie's profile, it's protected and so only her followers can view it.

Natalie is clearly more web savvy than Ben, and if I'm to find good reason to sack her, it won't be via social media.

Annoyed with myself for wasting time, I'm about to get on with more pressing tasks when my mobile rings. I don't recognise the number.

"Hello? Hello?" a confused voice barks when I accept the call.

"Err, hello."

"Is that you, Kelly?"

"Yes. Who's this?"

"It's Donald."

Donald has me at an advantage. I'm struggling to place his name.

"You still there?" he asks. "Hello?"

"Forgive me, Donald, but do I know you?"

"I'd bloody hope so. I pay you three hundred quid a month to rent your yard."

"Oh, I'm so sorry, Donald. Of course."

The reason I couldn't place his name is I've only ever met Donald once and spoken to him a handful of times. What he calls a yard is nothing more than an acre and a half of scrubby land Dad bought years ago to store Kellybelle during the winter months. Technically greenbelt land, it was dirt cheap as the farmer who owned it needed the cash and the local council wouldn't allow any kind of development. However, it already housed a dilapidated wooden barn which proved perfect for storing Dad's old boat while she underwent her never ending list of repairs.

If memory serves, Donald called me after hearing about the barn from my parents' solicitor. He wanted to rent it for his hobby of restoring classic cars and once we'd signed a lease and set up a standing order for the rent, there wasn't any reason to stay in regular contact.

"I'm calling about that man you sent over," Donald continues.

"What man?"

"The surveyor bloke."

"Sorry, I'm not with you."

"My lad drove past earlier and saw some bloke in a suit taking measurements of the access lane. He called me and I got myself down there sharpish. This bloke said he was surveying the land for a valuation."

"Eh? A valuation?"

"Yeah, and I'm not too pleased no one told me. If you're thinking of selling the yard, I hope you're gonna give me first refusal."

"Wait. Who said anything about selling it?"

"The bloke in the suit … well, not in so many words but he suggested the owner might have requested the valuation cos' they're thinking of selling."

"Did he now?"

"Yeah, which is why I'm calling."

"Look, Donald. I've no intention of selling the yard and I certainly didn't hire a surveyor."

"Someone did."

"Obviously, but it wasn't me. Did he give you a business card?"

"No, but he had one of those posh double-barrelled names."

"Can you remember it?"

"Now, let me think. What was it?"

I'm left hanging while Donald vocalises his thoughts.

"I think it was something like Foster … Foster … Stowe."

"Foster-Stowe?"

"Yeah, I'm sure that's what he said."

"Did you get his first name?"

"Afraid not."

"Right. Leave it with me and I'll look into it. Rest assured I've no plans to sell the yard."

"Thank you, but if you change your mind you will let me know, right? I've got thousands of old car parts stored in that barn and it'd take me an eternity to shift them elsewhere."

"You have my word."

He ends the call.

My work-related tasks are temporarily shelved while I sit and unpick the strands of my conversation with Donald. There are two questions I can't make sense of, let alone answer: why would anyone pay a surveyor to value land they don't own, and in particular, a plot with no real value to anyone other than Donald? I'm far from an expert on land values but I do know it isn't worth much unless you can obtain planning permission to build houses, or adapt it for commercial use; neither an option for the yard because of its greenbelt location. It can't be worth more than thirty grand; forty at a push.

I could spend all afternoon pondering possibilities but there's only one person who knows the answer — the surveyor himself.

A quick google confirms there are three firms of surveyors based in the town. I check all three websites but there's no mention of a Mr Foster-Stowe. I widen the search to neighbouring towns but five more website checks prove fruitless.

As a final roll of the dice, I call one of the local surveying firms.

"Good afternoon," a male voice promptly trills. "Ramsey Rowe & Associates."

"Hi, I'm hoping you can help me with an odd request."

"I'll try my best. I'm Richard, by the way."

"Thanks, Richard, I'm Kelly. I'm searching for a surveyor by the name of Foster-Stowe. Unfortunately, I don't know his first name."

"Well, there's only one surveyor I know with that surname — Nigel Foster-Stowe."

"And does he work for a firm in town?"

"He does, or at least he did. He left one of our competitors last year and set up on his own. I haven't seen or heard of him lately, though."

"Right, so you don't know where I might find his office?"

"I don't think he operates from an office as such. Last I heard he was working from home. He's sort of semi-retired."

"Locally?"

"Yes, but I couldn't tell you where."

"Not to worry. You've been incredibly helpful, Richard, and if I ever need a surveyor, you'll be the first I call."

I hang up and google Nigel Foster-Stowe. The results don't suggest he has a company website, but Google does kindly list a residential address for Mr Foster-Stowe's practice, together with a phone number. With my questions at the ready, I call the number. It rings three times and then nothing — no voicemail or recorded message to say there's a fault — just a faint, crackling sound. I try again but reach the same telephonic dead end. Three more attempts over the next half hour fare no better.

As I ponder my next move, an email from Justin arrives — he's spotted the discrepancy with the number of sick days I projected, and wants an explanation.

Mr Foster-Stowe will have to wait.

9.

I can't recall the last time I left the office at the same time as my colleagues, but I do so today. After my attempts to contact Mr Foster-Stowe, my mind-set began a slow journey from curious to annoyed as the afternoon progressed — not helped by a testy conversation with Justin and a host of other irritations.

I've decided I need to vent some of my annoyance and, as I can't yell at my boss, Mr Foster-Stowe will be bearing the brunt. He had no right trespassing on my land and even less right hinting to my tenant I might be looking to sell it. I doubt he'll appreciate me turning up outside of office hours but seeing as his phone line doesn't work, and he turned up on my land without permission, I hold the moral high ground.

I step through my front door just after six o'clock.

The address I'm heading to is only a twenty-minute walk away so I've time to grab a bite to eat. I head straight for the kitchen and open the back door.

"Ah, there you are."

I do wonder how much time Frank spends waiting at my door. His patience is an admirable quality.

"Come on then. Let's get you some dinner."

I throw a linguine in the microwave for myself and serve Frank his usual bowl of tuna. He makes light work of it and leaps down from the table before the microwave pings.

"Hungry, were we?"

Without so much as a glance in my direction, he casually saunters out the door. Frank might well be a beautiful creature but he really does need to work on his manners. If he were human, he'd be the type to turn up for sex at one in the morning and then expect you to sleep in the wet patch. He'd probably demand breakfast in bed too.

I shovel down the linguine and lock up.

Half way up Juniper Lane I turn around and head back home to grab a jacket; there's a slight chill in the air. I set off again and browse through my various playlists on Spotify as I walk, settling on a collection of upbeat nineties tunes. I've got a fairly eclectic taste in music but, like most people, I usually gravitate to the music of my youth. Every track provokes an associated memory: some make me smile while others are bittersweet. They're all precious, though, and nearly all feature my parents.

By the time I turn into Grenville Way — the road in which Nigel Foster-Stowe lives — the fond memories have quelled my irritation a little. Probably just as well.

I've no idea what surveyors earn but if his home is anything to go by, I'd guess Mr Foster-Stowe has done well for himself. The detached house isn't as large as my former marital home in Kensall Gardens but it's still the kind of house you'd price in fractions of millions.

I make my way to the front door and ring the bell.

Seconds pass before a squat man with thinning grey hair opens the door.

"Yes?"

"Are you Nigel Foster-Stowe?"

"That depends."

"On?"

"Who you are?"

"My name is Kelly Coburn, and assuming you are Nigel Foster-Stowe, I want to discuss a valuation you conducted earlier today."

"You do know what time it is?"

Instinctively, I glance at my watch.

"Yes, and if your phone line worked, I wouldn't be calling around at this hour."

"If this is in relation to business, you need to make an appointment. The office is closed and I'm rather busy."

"So am I, and I'd rather avoid a civil case against you for trespassing."

"I beg your pardon?"

"You trespassed on my land earlier today. And for reasons I can't comprehend, you suggested to my tenant I might be selling up."

"I … what land? I don't know what you're talking about."

"Springlake Lane ring any bells."

He looks at me with a puzzled frown.

"Yes, I valued a plot of land on Springlake Lane earlier today but my instructions came from the owner."

"Well, I am the owner and I certainly didn't instruct you. You can check with the Land Registry Office if you don't believe me."

"I'm not suggesting you don't own the land. I'm simply stating I received instructions from an individual who claimed they owned the site and wanted it valued as they intended to sell. I visited on the basis I had the landowner's permission to be there."

"Can I just check we're talking about the same plot of land here? It's about an acre and a half, bordered by Springlake Lane and Bulmer Lane?"

"Yes."

"With a large wooden barn and a forty yard access road?"

"Correct."

"Okay, so who instructed you?"

"I'm afraid I can't tell you."

"Why not?"

"Client confidentiality."

"I won't tell anyone if you don't."

"That's hardly the point, Mrs Coburn …"

"It's Miss, actually. And I'm afraid if you don't tell me, I'll have no option other than to pursue my trespass claim. If it goes to court, you'll need to reveal your client's name."

His frown returns.

"Fine," he sighs. "But it'll have to wait until tomorrow as I'm heading out to dinner and I don't have time to check the file. If you give me your mobile number, I'll call with my client's name on the proviso you don't tell a soul where you got the information."

"Fair enough."

He waddles away and returns with a pad and pen.

"You'll definitely call me tomorrow?" I confirm, after quoting my number.

"Yes, yes."

With my number jotted down, he's about to shut the door when another question comes to mind.

"Sorry, Mr Foster-Stowe. Can I ask what you think the land is worth, just out of curiosity?"

"You threaten legal action," he says indignantly. "And then expect me to give you a free valuation?"

"Err, pretty please."

"If you want a professional valuation, you can either hire your own surveyor or I'll provide a copy of my valuation for three hundred pounds."

"How much?" I splutter.

"The cost is three hundred pounds. Do you want a copy, or not?"

"I think I'll pass."

"In which case I'll bid you a good evening, Miss Coburn."

He slams the door shut.

I retrace my steps back up the path; unsure if I've sated my curiosity or stoked it. Despite my initial annoyance, I did question if Mr Foster-Stowe's visit was an admin error as the yard is surrounded by paddocks and farmland; owned by different people. However, he confirmed the unique details of Dad's yard and they don't match any other piece of land around Springlake Lane. Whoever hired him definitely wanted to know the value of the yard.

But why?

I wrestle with that question all the way back to Juniper Lane but, without knowing the identity of whoever paid Foster-Stowe's invoice, there's no way to answer it; until tomorrow.

Arriving home, I change into a pair of joggers and a sweatshirt; intent on spending the rest of the evening slouched on the sofa catching up with the soaps. I make it halfway through an episode of Hollyoaks, and a large bar of Dairy Milk, when my mind drifts back to the yard. Irrespective of Foster-Stowe and his mystery client, maybe it might be time to let it go.

Somewhere up in the loft are a dozen boxes of detritus from my parents' house. Prior to their arrival here, those boxes spent over a decade in the loft at Kensall Gardens. They don't contain any family heirlooms, nor pieces of jewellery or ornaments with sentimental value — just random household objects I couldn't bring myself to throw away. In amongst the bric-a-brac, I think there's an old toaster, a kitchen clock, a pair of bedside lamps, and a ceramic fruit bowl my parents used for storing everything except fruit.

I used to take comfort having the boxes close by but when I moved all my possessions from Kensall Gardens to Juniper Lane, the removal men questioned the logic of transferring a dozen boxes of junk from one loft to another. To me it's not junk, but they had a point; one which has played on my mind ever since.

Now my divorce is out of the way, perhaps it's the ideal time to start the final cycle of life laundry. Twelve years is a long time and I'm sure it can't be doing me any good clinging to the remnants of my parents' lives.

I grab my phone and return a call from earlier today.

"Hello."

"Hi, Donald. It's Kelly Coburn. We spoke earlier about the yard."

"Right, yes."

"Sorry for calling so late but I wanted to chat to you while I'm in the right frame of mind. Hypothetically, if I were to sell the yard, what would you be willing to pay for it?"

"Can't say I've given it a lot of thought but I could probably muster fifty grand, at a push."

"Oh, okay."

Much more than I reckon the yard is worth but I'm not going to argue.

"When you say hypothetically, what do you mean?"

"It means I'm just thinking about selling the yard, and I'm nowhere near making a definitive decision yet. However, I promised I'd give you first refusal, and I wanted to see how much you're willing to pay."

"Fair enough. If you can give me a couple of days, I'll crunch the numbers properly and come back to you with a formal offer."

"That would be great."

"So, what's changed your mind? You said earlier you had no intention of selling."

"As I say, I still haven't decided but knowing how much I could sell it for might have a bearing; hence the call. I'm yet to discover who sent that surveyor down but they might have done me a favour. I've put off dealing with this, and a host of other issues far too long."

"Understood. I appreciate you calling, and I'll be in touch when I've got a firm offer."

He says goodbye with a promise to contact me before the weekend.

I lay back on the sofa and for the first time since the yard came into my possession, give some serious thought to selling it. Although fifty grand is a lot of money, it's not money I need. I don't have a mortgage to pay off or any major bills to settle. And with no dependents, I can't use it to help anyone else. If I decide to sell, I guess the money will just sit in the bank gathering meagre levels of interest until the day I find a use for it.

Financially, it'd make more sense keeping the yard and the modest income it brings in every month. This isn't about money, though. In the same way the boxes in the loft provide a tangible link to my parents, they, and the yard, also keep me tethered to the past. I should focus instead on all the happy memories; many captured and stored in photo albums. Why do I need a scrubby patch of land and a dozen boxes of bric-a-brac to remind me of my parents?

After twelve years, perhaps it's time to let that past go, and maybe those embers of grief will finally fizzle out once and for all.

10.

Martha's shrieking is so loud I have to hold the phone away from my ear.

"Oh, my God," she continues. "I'm so excited."

"Alright, stop screaming. I am at work, you know."

"Sorry, chick."

She takes a breath and with it, some level of composure returns.

"You're absolutely sure you're up for it?"

"Yes. One hundred percent."

Ever since I split with Nathan, Martha has been nagging me to go away on a girl's weekend with her and our friends, Jennie and Rachel. Her nagging intensified after she spotted an online advert for a nineties-themed weekender at Butlin's, featuring some popular, and not-so-popular, chart acts from our teenage years.

"Do you want me to book it?" she asks.

"Nope. I'll book it and pay for it."

"I can't ask you to pay for all of us."

"I'm due an unexpected cash windfall soon so I absolutely insist — this is my treat."

"That's so kind. Just book the cheapest chalets, though."

"Not a chance. If we're going to do this, we're going to do it in style. I'll book the best rooms in the hotel."

"This is brilliant!" she shrieks. "Roll on September. I can barely wait."

"Me neither."

"But for now, I'd better go change my pants. In all the excitement, I might have just done a small wee."

"You're gross. See you later."

"Shortly, shorty. Love you."

I hang up and chuckle to myself.

I've had a constructive morning so far, although not necessarily on the work front. Having slept on the decision about the yard, I woke up with a new-found sense of clarity — my

70

parents would hate it if they knew I'd spent twelve long years in mourning. If I'm to respect their memory, I should embrace life with the same zest they did. I won't be navigating a cabin cruiser around Europe but I will attempt to do more, see more, and enjoy more. With that in mind, I've decided to sell the yard and invest every penny creating new memories; starting with a weekend away in September.

The decision alone has put a spring in my step. Now, there's just the practical details to contend with.

Having never sold land before, I decided it might be wise to seek professional advice. As he was so helpful yesterday, I made a call to Richard of Ramsey Rowe & Associates and he's agreed to see me at lunchtime so we can discuss the process, and I can confirm if Donald's offer is more or less the right price. Not that I've heard from him but Nigel Foster-Stowe can piss off, as can whoever instructed him. Neither will be my concern once I've struck a deal with Donald.

I turn my attention back to the work I'm being paid to do, which includes an email to all my team members about the increase in sick days. Natalie has blessed us with her presence today; right as rain after her supposed bug. Now she's on my radar I'm determined to catch her out. It's just a matter of time before she pushes her luck too far. I shall be waiting.

My final task of the morning is to book our weekend break. It only takes ten minutes to go through the online reservation process but it sets me back the best part of a grand. I don't expect to pay for a single drink the entire weekend.

That sorted, I grab my bag and head off for the meeting with Richard at his office; a short walk away.

I reach Union Road within five minutes and wander up and down looking for Ramsey Rowe & Associates. It isn't where I thought it would be. A quick call confirms my stupidity — their office is on the first floor of the building I walked past several times. I backtrack and locate the ground floor entrance between a dry cleaners and a firm of accountants.

I'm met at the reception by a tall, distinguished looking chap with silver hair.

"Miss Coburn, I presume?"

"Yes, but please call me Kelly. And you're Richard?"

"Correct. You found us in the end."

"I walked past the door three times."

"You're not the first," he chuckles. "Come this way."

He leads me through to an office which, unlike mine, has actual windows and enough space to swing a dozen of Frank's friends.

"Please, take a seat."

We sit down on opposite sides of his vast desk.

"So," he begins. "I understand you've got a parcel of land you're hoping to sell?"

"That's right. I've received a tentative offer from the tenant but I want to make sure that offer is fair, and how the sale process works."

"Well, you've come to the right place. We've got years of experience dealing with all manner of commercial property transactions, including land."

I nod, although I'm tempted to question why they haven't used that experience to relocate to an office their clients can find.

"Where is your plot situated?" he asks.

"Oh, it's on Springlake Lane. Do you know it?"

"I do."

He opens a drawer and pulls out an Ordnance Survey map which he then unfolds on the desk.

"Can you show me your land on the map?"

To save me from scanning the entire map, he points to Springlake Lane. I lean over and run my finger along the two-dimensional road until it meets the junction of Bulmer Lane.

"It's that entire section. I think it's about an acre and a half."

"You own it all?"

"I do."

"Interesting."

He sits back in his chair.

"And can I ask: how much is the offer you've received?"

"Fifty thousand."

"Right."

He extracts a calculator from his desk drawer and begins tapping the keys. After a good half-minute of silent tapping, he returns the calculator to the drawer.

"Your land is worth a shade more than fifty thousand pounds," he declares.

"Oh, okay. How much more?"

"It's just a ballpark figure but about twenty-five times more."

I stare back at Richard, open-mouthed.

"You what?"

"I said it's worth about twenty-five times more."

I heard what he said, but my brain is too busy dealing with his revelation to work out the maths.

"Are you okay, Kelly?" he asks. "You look a little pale."

"Err, yes. Twenty-five times? You're sure?"

"Give or take a little, but yes."

"But that would make it worth … um …"

"At least a million, but more likely one and a quarter million."

Either he's got a warped sense of humour or his claimed experience is in spouting outlandish bullshit.

"I don't wish to question your judgement, Richard, but I'm struggling to see how it could be worth anywhere near that amount. My dad paid ten grand for it."

"When?"

"I'm not exactly sure, but maybe twenty years ago. I think the farmer who owned it had financial problems and needed a quick sale; probably involving an envelope stuffed with cash, knowing my dad."

"Even then, a plot that size would have been worth twenty thousand plus. Your father struck a good deal."

"Right, so how on earth does it increase in value from twenty grand to over a million in just two decades?"

He leans over the map again.

"See this boundary line?"

I can just make out a thin horizontal line pencilled on the map.

"Yes."

73

"Everything north of that line was once within the designated greenbelt, including your plot. Greenbelt land has limited value because of the strict planning restrictions. However, back in January the local authority — under pressure to build more homes — proposed moving the boundary half-a-mile south to encompass large swathes of former farmland. You don't recall hearing or reading about the public consultation?"

"Nope."

"There were several objections but ultimately, the boundary move was approved and, as far as I'm aware, the local authority are currently in negotiations with several major housebuilders to develop the land. In a few years' time that farmland will form a development of roughly nine-hundred new homes."

"So, you're saying my plot of land is now suitable for development?"

"Exactly. I'd need to conduct a proper site survey but based on current demand, an acre and a half would fetch well over a million pounds in the open market … subject to planning, of course."

"But my plot doesn't have planning."

"No, but considering the local authority are about to grant permission on the neighbouring land, it's almost a given they'd have to grant permission for any development on your land. Once a precedent has been set, it becomes planning policy."

"Holy shit."

"Quite."

"Sorry. I thought I said that in my head."

"You're excused, considering the circumstances. You can now officially call yourself a millionaire, Miss Coburn — congratulations."

"I'm … wow! I'm genuinely stunned."

"If you don't mind me saying, I'm surprised by, well, your surprise."

"Sorry?"

"Considering this change of policy has been on the cards for a while, I'm surprised you haven't been inundated with offers from developers. They're usually proactive in such

circumstances and would typically canvas local landowners to
see if they can strike a deal."

"As you can probably tell, I had no idea until a few minutes
ago. How would they have contacted me?"

"They usually write. Every landowner's address is on the
Land Registry database."

"Ah, that would explain it. I moved home earlier this year
and you know what it's like — there are a million different
people to inform but the Land Registry office wasn't top of my
list."

"You might want to get on to that."

"Yes, I will."

"That sorted, there is some bad news."

"Oh."

"It's not bad news, as such, but I would warn you not to rush
back to work and resign. It can take months if not years to
conclude a land transaction; particularly if it's subject to
planning approval. In all likelihood, it'll be well into next year
before a deal might be completed."

"Right. I wish I'd known that before blowing a grand this
morning."

"On what?"

"Just a weekend break for my friends."

"If you're keen to sell sooner, there are other options.
Because the chance of obtaining planning approval is relatively
high, there are a number of speculative land buyers out there
who'd be willing to take a punt. At best, you'll only receive fifty
to sixty percent of the full market value but the sale won't be
conditional on planning."

"So, if I sell before the land has planning consent, it'll
potentially cost me half-a-million?"

"That's the deal. Patience, or a much smaller payday."

"I think I'd rather wait."

"In your shoes, so would I."

"Okay. That settled what should I do next?"

"If you like, I can put a proposal together? If we're instructed
to act on your behalf, we can conduct a full site survey and put

the land out to tender on your behalf. We'll handle all the negotiations, and once we've secured a suitable buyer, we'll manage the transaction itself."

"Great and how much will it cost me?"

"We charge two percent commission on the final sale price, and as a goodwill gesture I'll conduct the site survey for free."

"That sounds okay but I need to have a chat with the current tenant first. I think we can safely assume he won't be offering the kind of money a developer will pay so I need to give him notice."

"Not a problem. I'll get the proposal drawn up, and we can meet again early next week, if that suits?"

"Perfect."

He turns to his computer screen and clicks the mouse a few times.

"Monday lunchtime work for you?"

"Same time?"

"Excellent."

With another meeting booked, Richard hands me a business card and shows me out.

Still somewhat dazed, I amble back in the general direction of the office but I'm not ready to return to my desk just yet. There's so much to process, and scores of questions I'm only now considering. It's true to say in this day and age the word 'millionaire' doesn't have the same kudos it once did but even so, it's a life-changing sum of money.

More than ever, I wish Dad was here to witness how his investment panned out. My parents weren't rich by anyone's standards. They bought our council house in the late eighties and sold it eight years later; making just enough profit they could afford a semi-detached house across town. Despite moving to suburbia, Dad never lost that council estate, wheeler-dealer mentality necessary to survive when you're always one pay cheque away from the breadline.

Over the years, Dad's company promoted him several times and the extra income nudged my parents a few rungs up the social ladder from their working-class roots, but never in their wildest dreams could they have imagined being millionaires.

Wherever they are now, I'm sure the champagne corks are popping for me.

My stomach rumbles but I've no appetite. If I'd won a million quid on the lottery I'd be running through the streets screaming in celebration but this isn't so black and white. As Richard warned, there are a lot of hoops to jump through before I'll see any money, which is probably why I feel more nervous than excited. The carrot dangled, it'll be a long time before I can take a bite.

By the time I reach the office I've made one decision. Apart from Martha, I'll keep my potential windfall to myself until the deal is signed, sealed, and the cash delivered to my bank account. There is, however, one person I definitely have to tell: Donald.

Rather than attack my to-do list, I consider when might be the right time to tell my tenant he'll need to move his thousands of car parts.

I need to get it over with. It's only fair I give him as much warning as possible. Reluctantly, I call his number.

"Hello."

"Hi, Donald. It's Kelly again. We spoke last night about the yard."

"Oh, yes. You're keen, I thought you were gonna give me a few days."

"Yes, I was, but there's been a change in my circumstances. I'll get straight to the point — I'm afraid I need to serve notice on your tenancy."

"You what?"

"I'm giving you notice on the yard. Three months."

"But why?"

"I'm selling it."

"Now you hold on a moment," he blasts. "Only yesterday, you promised I'd have first refusal if you decided to sell."

"And up until this morning, you had first refusal. However, I've just had a chat with a surveyor, and your offer is significantly short of his valuation."

"I did say I might be able to up it a bit."

"By a million pounds?"

Silent seconds pass as I wait for a response.

"Are you taking the piss?" he eventually coughs.

"No. That's what the land is worth now. I'm sorry, but what else can I do?"

"You could stick to our deal."

"Firstly, we never had a deal. Secondly, who in their right mind would sell anything for a fraction of its true value?"

"I've already made an appointment at the bank."

"Then cancel it."

"This is a bloody outrage. You can't do this."

"I can, and I'm trying to be civilised …"

"Civilised?" he barks. "You don't know the meaning of the word. I've been a bloody good tenant all these years, and this is how you treat me?"

He then goes on a lengthy rant about how folks used to respect verbal agreements back in his day, whilst also questioning if my decision will change when I'm less hormonal. I can't get a word in edgeways until my phone buzzes to signify an incoming call. With my patience and sympathy exhausted, I grab the excuse to cut Donald short.

"I've got another call coming in. I'll write to you confirming what we've discussed, minus the casual sexism."

"Don't you dare …?"

"Goodbye."

I jab the screen to terminate Donald's call and accept the incoming one.

"Kelly Coburn."

"This is Nigel Foster-Stowe."

"Oh, good afternoon."

"I'm calling regards our meeting yesterday."

"Great, you've got a name for me?"

"No."

"Sorry?"

"I've had time to think about it and if you wish to sue me for trespass, Miss Coburn, go ahead."

That's my bluff called; not that it matters now. Still, I'm not going to let the smug old git have the last word.

"Nah, I don't think I'll bother suing you," I reply nonchalantly. "And I won't be paying you three hundred quid for a valuation report either. I've had a chat with another surveyor so I know what the land is worth."

"You do?"

"Yep, so I think we're done, Mr Foster-Stowe. Have a good day."

I hang up.

Tossing my phone on the desk, I puff a long sigh; the double serving of churlish old men taking the gloss off an otherwise remarkable day on the good news front. I do feel a sliver of sympathy for Donald, and a tiny part of me is still curious who hired Foster-Stowe, but I won't let either man get under my skin.

To celebrate, I call the work experience girl into my office.

"Can you do me a favour and nip to the bakers up the road? I need something sweet and calorific."

"No problem," she squeaks. "What would you like?"

"Hmm … I fancy a large slice of millionaire's shortbread."

11.

Everyone does it — you buy a lottery ticket and despite the astronomical odds of winning the jackpot, the daydreaming begins. It's part of the appeal, I guess. Right up until the machine spits out the wrong balls, you can picture living in luxurious mansion, holidaying in five-star resorts, and perusing a wardrobe bursting with high-end designer clothes.

My aspirations aren't as grandiose and my potential windfall is several million quid short of a lottery jackpot, but that didn't stop me researching ways I might spend it. After several hours browsing the web from the comfort of my sofa, I went to bed more confused than excited. The fifty grand I thought I might be due wasn't enough to change my life and therefore didn't invite any taxing questions. A million quid is, and the questions kept coming.

I considered investing in property, where I might earn enough rental income to give up work and still maintain a modest lifestyle, but what would I do with myself? I've no desire to spend my days learning how to weave baskets or play the oboe.

Dismissing the idea of buying properties to let, I switched my research to buying a house to live in, and wasted an hour trawling through Rightmove. The problem with million-pound houses, outside of London, is they all inevitably come with more bedrooms than I need and a huge garden I don't want. It would be like living back in Kensall Gardens, and I hated that house. I eventually dismissed the idea of buying somewhere bigger; not least because I'm perfectly content in my current home.

I then thought of other ways I could invest the money. I've zero interest in stocks or shares, but I then pondered the possibility of starting a business. With such a lump of money behind me, I'd have a better chance of success than most, and it'd keep me busy while also providing a return on my investment. The problem, I conceded, is I don't know much about anything beyond the corporate world. I have management skills which I'm sure would come in handy if I had some other skill or passion to base a business upon.

Reaching a dead end I fell asleep.

I woke up just after six and my brain, like an excited toddler, decided we'd had enough sleep — it wanted to play. It began with an analysis of how I got here, and more importantly, where I go next. I've spent the entirety of my adult life working for the same company but do I want to spend the next eighteen years working for that same company?

I'll be fifty-seven.

Fifty-seven.

Even at thirty-nine my colleagues already think I'm a wizened old spinster so God only knows what they'll think of me as I near the end of my sixth decade. I've heard what they say about the older staff members in other departments and it's not nice; 'cottontops' being one of the more polite terms they use. The only older members of staff they respect are senior management but the chances of me ever reaching that level are slim on account I never went to university and I don't have a penis.

Thinking about it, I don't really want to join their club, anyway.

It's too early to call it a decision, but I can't see myself spending another eighteen years at Marston Finance. That concluded, what the hell do I do with myself?

I sit up and stare into space; forcing my brain to stop playing and start focusing.

"Think, Kelly."

The same thoughts and questions I pondered last night return. They circle around and around, going nowhere but distracting enough I can't see past them. Maybe they're still circling for a reason — have I missed something?

And then it hits me so hard my heart skips a beat. I can't believe I didn't see it but now, with eight hours of sleep behind me, I'm functioning on full charge.

I can give up work, but what would I do with myself?

It's so obvious, but almost too perfect an answer. A swarm of doubts descend — too good to be true, surely?

I feel a little sick.

In my head, I used to picture a perfect little family: me, my husband, and a couple of children. It was all I wanted, all I dreamt about. That mental image became so ingrained I never considered replacing it with a new image — one without the husband.

There is a good reason I never considered it: practicality.

Being a modern woman is all well and good but how do you work full time and raise a child? I can continue to enjoy the financial security of a full-time career, or have a child — not both. I know some mothers do, and they have my utmost respect, but it was never a choice I wanted to make. The thought of hiring a nanny and then watching every precious moment in my child's life relayed to me as second-hand news, holds no appeal. Who wants to watch their child's first steps via a live video on Facebook?

The realisation dawns. My parents have potentially gifted me the ultimate inheritance. The land in Springlake Lane is the key to my financial independence and with that, the chance to become a mum.

I grab my phone and open the web browser. With shaky hands I type two words into Google's search box: sperm donation.

The excitement mounts as the initial results add credence to my idea. After scanning just half-a-dozen websites, it appears perfectly possible for me to become pregnant at a clinic, without the underwhelming foreplay or three minutes of sweaty grunting.

I'm about to get up and dance around the bedroom when the sensible side of my brain joins the party. I can't get too carried away with the idea just yet. There are still numerous obstacles I need to traverse before I hear the pitter-patter of tiny feet.

But there is hope now. Real hope.

I hop in the shower, get dressed, and wander down to the kitchen where I open the back door.

"Morning, Frank," I chirp. "Beautiful day, eh?"

I serve his breakfast and skip around the kitchen while

preparing my own. Eating while you're fizzing with nervous excitement is never easy but I force down a bagel.

The routine helps to bring me down from the ceiling and, fifteen minutes later, I leave for work having calmed down a fraction.

I arrive at the bus stop to find I've just missed out on a medal position; three of the regulars already queueing. With my fellow passengers all sporting headphones, we swap nods and smiles but there's no conversation. There rarely is.

I've often wondered why these people take the bus every day. We live in a society where the car is king yet the bus stop regulars are all, like me, reliant on public transport for their daily commute. Perhaps it's the cost of running a car, or maybe they don't have a licence because it's been taken away, or they've never passed the test.

When I turned seventeen Dad took me out for a handful of lessons. He then changed his mind, citing medical grounds; symptoms included the urge to evacuate his bowels every time I got behind the wheel. In his defence, he did set me up with a professional driving instructor and I took scores of lessons but couldn't cope with the gears. I moved to an automatic car but fared no better. After four failed driving tests I gave up, but it's never bothered me. For all the complaints people make about public transport, I quite enjoy travelling on buses and trains.

I'm duly delivered to my destination on schedule and after a quick detour to Starbucks, make my way to the office.

The usual routine ensues. I sit at my desk and switch on the computer. I'm about to open the email inbox when a message pings on my phone. The only person who ever texts me is Martha so I open the message without checking who sent it.

The second I read it, I wish I hadn't. It's from Nathan: We need to talk — call me.

I message him straight back: No, we don't. I'm blocking your number.

The beauty of a smartphone is it only takes two taps of the screen to fulfil my promise. The reward is a sense of deep satisfaction — I only wish I'd done it months ago.

The irritation dealt with, I get on with my day.

For the rest of the morning I struggle to maintain focus. Partly because of Nathan's text but mainly because I'm too weak to resist the temptation of googling information about artificial insemination; a search term which excluded some less savoury results I received when searching sperm donation.

Whilst researching the various options for insemination, I stumble across an online forum for women in a similar position and waste almost an hour reading the various threads. One of them — simply entitled 'Joy' — contains photos of newborn babies. Every photo represents a success story and stokes my own hopes.

I'm halfway through reading a thread on the pitfalls of one-night-stands as a method of insemination, when I notice the time.

"Shit."

I still have bills to pay and if I don't do my job, I'll find myself unemployed long before I see any money from the land. That would be a problem on so many levels; I've no choice but to refocus on the tasks I'm contracted to perform.

By lunchtime, I've caught up with my work but the excitement continues to bubble beneath the surface. I need to vent it, and I need to vent it in Martha's direction. I ping off a text to see if she fancies a drink later. She replies with an apology she can't make it but suggests tomorrow evening instead. I send a confirmation text back, hoping I don't explode in the meantime.

I'm about to pop out for a sandwich when I remember another personal task I promised myself I'd deal with. I call a charity shop.

"Hi, I've got a dozen boxes of household items I'd like to donate, if they're of interest?"

"Oh, definitely," the woman confirms. "Feel free to drop them off at our shop whenever it's convenient."

"Slight problem with that. I don't drive and I'd rather avoid a dozen round trips on the bus."

"Not a problem. We can collect but there's a bit of a wait as one of our drivers is on holiday."

"There's no rush."

She checks the schedule and offers a date two weeks tomorrow.

"That's fine. What time will they arrive?"

"We don't arrange their route until the day, although the driver will call you an hour in advance of his arrival."

"Perfect."

The woman jots down some details and confirms the collection.

That sorted, I put the phone down and look towards the photo of my parents.

"Sorry," I whisper. "I hope you understand."

Knowing my parents, I think Mum would understand my need to de-clutter more than Dad. He was a hoarder while Mum was meticulously tidy, on an almost OCD level. I lost count how many times Dad would bring home a battered piece of furniture or an old television which no longer functioned — his hope to fix them up and sell them on for a tidy profit. Our spare bedroom became a storeroom for his junk but he'd often use the kitchen as a makeshift workshop, much to Mum's annoyance. I think it was probably why she was so supportive when the opportunity to buy Kellybelle came up — at least Dad couldn't drag a boat up the stairs.

Having made peace with my parents, I sit back in my chair. It's been a constructive morning, although not necessarily for Marston Finance.

With no great urgency, I take a stroll to the sandwich shop and enjoy a leisurely lunch. I know it's a risky attitude but if my future doesn't involve this job; I don't see why I should continue to work more hours than my contract states. Everyone else in the office works to rule so why shouldn't I? Besides, if I am to fulfil my dream, I need to look after myself which means less stress. It also means less wine, but I think I'll wait until next week before implementing that regime.

I arrive back at my desk exactly one hour after leaving it.

Midway through the afternoon, a stress test arrives in the

form of Natalie. She saunters into my office and asks to change the holiday dates she only booked a few days ago. To her, it's a simple enough request, but for me it involves additional paperwork and changes to the staff rota I've already updated once. It's these little annoyances which, over the years, begin to grate; particularly where Natalie is concerned.

As difficult as it is, I keep a lid on my stress pot and agree to the change without complaint. I even find a half-smile.

The rest of the afternoon proves less taxing, and at five-fifteen I wind down with the intention of leaving at the same contractual time as my colleagues. The phone on my desk rings. Instinctively, I stretch across to grab the handset but stop myself at the last second. Penny to a pound it'll be Justin wanting some last-minute data which will require an hour of my time to collate.

I don't want to pick the phone up but old habits die hard. I answer it.

"Kelly Coburn."

"Hi, Kelly," a female voice replies.

The voice belongs to Amanda on the main switchboard. A relief.

"I've got a caller on hold for you," she continues. "Want me to put him through?"

"Who is it?"

"A Mr Graham. He says it's urgent."

I dredge my mind in search of anyone I know with that surname but nothing comes.

"Okay. Put him through."

I'm treated to a few seconds of classical music before Mr Graham's call directs to my phone.

I state my name again and wait for a reply.

"Kelly, please don't hang up. It's important."

I didn't recognise the fake name but I sure as hell recognise the caller's voice — Nathan. The devious arsehole has bypassed my block.

"Go away," I hiss. "I don't want to talk to you."

"All I ask is two minutes of your time. If you don't talk to me now, I'll just keep calling."

"What do you want, Nathan?"

"As I said in my text, I want to talk."

"The last time we talked, you threatened me."

"I was angry. I'm sorry."

"I don't much care. There's nothing left to say."

"Oh, but there is."

"What?"

The line falls silent but I can hear background chatter like he's in a coffee shop.

"Come and meet me."

"What? No."

"Please. I'm in The Three Horseshoes."

"Still, no."

"Don't be like that, Kelly."

"Goodbye, Nathan."

"Wait," he huffs. "I'll tell you."

"Hurry up then. I want to get home."

"It's about your father's old yard on Springlake Lane."

"What about it?"

"Let's just say it would be in your best interests to meet me."

"I doubt it."

"This isn't a game, Kelly. Meet me or you'll regret it."

"Are you threatening me again?"

"No, I'm stating a fact. We need to discuss your father's yard."

"We don't. It's none of your business."

"Yes, it is, and if you meet me, I'll explain why. If you don't … let's just say that for you it would be a costly error of judgement."

My annoyance ratchets towards anger. I'm about to release a volley of expletives down the phone but bite my tongue at the last second.

"I'm not meeting you," I growl. "Leave me alone."

"Fine. I'll just start legal proceedings so expect a large solicitor's bill."

"What the hell are you talking about?"

"Last chance, Kelly. Hop in a cab and come to The Three

Horseshoes now … or face the consequences."
    He hangs up.

12.

I slam the phone down with such force the sound of cracking plastic echoes around the office.

"Wanker," I spit under my breath.

Despite passing the Natalie test earlier, my stress levels are now off the scale. I draw a long, deep breath to ease the spiking adrenalin levels.

It takes a minute to ease the rage but then concern jostles into the unoccupied space. Nathan knew about Dad's yard but he's never shown any interest in it before. What's changed, and why mention legal proceedings? We're divorced, so he has no rights over my property. Why should I give a shit what he's playing at?

But I do, because I know my ex-husband.

Throughout our marriage he proved calculating and manipulative, and when he wanted something, he'd use every psychological tool in the box to get it. Sometimes, it was a trivial matter like a restaurant bill or a tradesman's invoice. He'd seek a discount due to some spurious claim; making threats he'd leave a bad review online, or make a formal complaint if he didn't get his own way.

Other times it would be for more serious issues, like when selecting a nursing home for his mother. He played one home off against the other to get the best care for the lowest price, and when one of those homes decided they'd had enough of the haggling, he showed them a list of spurious health and safety issues he'd identified. They were all minor but collectively enough to warrant a visit from the local authority inspectors. In the end, they admitted Beatrice to one of their best rooms at a heavily discounted rate just to keep Nathan onside.

The very last person I want to see this evening is my ex-husband but avoiding him won't make him go away. And if it's a choice of worrying why he's developed an interest in Dad's yard or finding out, I'd sooner know.

I call a cab company.

It takes a few minutes to get myself together before I take the lift down to the reception foyer. The cab is already waiting.

Fortunately, the driver isn't the chatty type so I can sit and stew in silence. Fifteen minutes, and a resentful twelve quid fare later, I barge through the door of The Three Horseshoes.

Nathan is already at the bar and hands me a glass of wine by way of a greeting.

"First round is on me," he quips.

"First, and only round," I reply flatly, taking the glass. "You've got twenty minutes and then I'm leaving."

"Fair enough. Shall we take a seat?"

Without waiting for my reply, he strides over to the same table we occupied the other evening. I follow and flop down in the chair opposite; my body language confirming how little I want to be in Nathan's company.

"How are you?" he asks.

"Forget the small talk. Why am I here?"

"I told you on the phone."

"No, you told me the best part of nothing. If I recall correctly, the main gist of your conversation was a threat."

"That wasn't a threat."

"No? What was it then?"

To demonstrate who's in control, he sits back and takes a long, slow sip of his Coke.

"It's flat," he complains. "And not chilled enough."

To double check, he empties half the glass before getting to his feet.

"I'm not paying good money for a sub-standard drink. I'll be back in a sec."

I take a long gulp of wine; not giving one jot about the temperature or effervescence as long as it's wet and contains alcohol.

Nathan returns with a fresh glass he won't have paid for.

"Sorry about that. Where were we?"

"You were getting to the point."

"Oh, yes. Your late father's plot of land on Springlake Lane."

"The plot of land which is none of your business?"

"It wasn't ... but it is now."

I'm still none the wiser but I won't play his game. I don't respond and we sit in silence. Realising I'm not about to take the bait, he sits forward.

"I've had some bad luck," he sighs. "A few of my recent investments have turned sour."

I shrug my shoulders.

"I just about steadied the ship after the first one, but the second one ... well, it's cleared me out."

Another shrug.

"I've got just enough in the bank to cover rent and the fees for mother's nursing home for two months. After that, I'm in serious trouble."

"So?"

I can see in his face how much my indifference irks. He sits back and changes tack.

"Can I tell you a little story?"

"No."

"I'll keep it brief."

"Whatever."

"After we moved out of Kensall Gardens, I paid to have the mail forwarded for six-months. As you know, I'm fastidious when it comes to paperwork, and I didn't want to miss a potentially important letter."

"Good for you."

"I must have included the option to cover all recipients with the surname Thaw, so the Royal Mail forwarded a handful of letters addressed to you. I intended to forward them on, but quite a few looked like junk mail so I took the liberty of checking first."

"What?"

"I opened them. Sorry, but I thought I was doing you a favour."

"How dare you," I blast. "That's illegal."

"So?" he shrugs. "Report me to the police if it makes you feel better."

"I might just do that."

I empty my glass and grab my bag; intent on getting up and leaving.

"Wait. I haven't finished my story yet."

"I don't care."

"You should, because four of those letters mentioned the land at Springlake Lane. Interesting reading."

"And for the third time, none of your business."

"It is, because of this."

He reaches into the inside pocket of his jacket and pulls out a letter.

"This letter is for you," he says, placing it on the table in front of me. "From my solicitor."

"I don't want it."

"Shall I tell you what it says?"

"You'll tell me no matter what I say."

"True, but I'll keep it brief. That letter confirms we never signed a financial agreement as part of our divorce settlement, and therefore what's mine is still yours, and what's yours is still mine."

"I … what?"

"Sadly, I no longer have much in the way of assets but having accidentally opened those letters, you clearly do. I want my share, Kelly."

"No, this is bullshit. We both agreed to walk away with what we had before we married … you kept your original investment in Kensall Gardens and I kept my parents' inheritance. That was the deal."

"Things change. I didn't need the money then, but I do now. I'm afraid to say the profit I made from the sale of our home has all gone."

I want to scream at him. No, I want to reach across and slap the smug expression from his face.

A few deep breaths and I decide both options would show weakness. Fortunately for me, Nathan has already shown his. He's skint.

"Fine. We'll go to court but I promise you one thing — I'll drag it out for months, maybe years. Both you and your mother will be on the streets long before you see a penny of my money."

"You've changed. When did you become so heartless?"

"The day I married you."

"Sticks and stones. Anyway, whilst you're right that it could take months to go through the legal channels, I have a proposition for you."

"Not interested."

"Don't be too hasty — it's a good offer."

"I said I'm not interested."

"I'll tell you anyway. I've brokered a deal with an old acquaintance and he's willing to pay six hundred thousand for the land and complete a deal within a month. It's a good price and you won't have to wait for planning permission. We'll split that fifty-fifty and you'll never hear from me again."

If someone had offered me three hundred grand for Dad's yard last week, I'd have bitten their hand off. Today, it's insignificant compared to the hope on the horizon if I'm patient.

"I've already spoken to a valuer, Nathan, so I know how much that land is worth with planning."

"So do I, but time is not on my side."

"I don't … wait. It was you, wasn't it?"

"What?"

"You hired Nigel Foster-Stowe to conduct a survey."

Now everything makes sense. As Richard suggested, developers had written to me and those letters doubtless hinted at the potential value of Dad's yard. They weren't to know I'd never see them as Nathan had set up the mail redirection and duly opened them himself. Then, he hired a surveyor to determine the exact market value and set up a deal with an old contact. A devious, underhanded plot to save his sorry arse from financial ruin.

He probably didn't reckon on my finding out about the true value of the yard — Foster-Stowe must have relayed that information.

"I had to move quickly, so yes, I organised a formal valuation."

"Whatever you paid him, and your solicitor, it's money

wasted. Even if there was the tiniest chance you could make a claim on Dad's yard, there's no way I'll agree to sell it at that price when it'll be worth double when the council grant planning permission."

"If they grant planning permission. My offer guarantees you three hundred thousand in a month's time."

"I'd rather wait."

"If you agree to sell now, I'll take that three hundred thousand and leave you alone. If you don't, I'll still take half of the money whenever you sell, plus I'll claim fifty percent of your home on top. Don't you also have quite a healthy pension and shares in that company of yours, too? Take my offer or I'll fight for half of everything you own."

"You're forgetting one thing, Nathan."

"Am I?"

"Yes, you're running out of time and don't have the money to pay a solicitor."

"Make me an offer then. This won't go away, Kelly."

"Okay. How about I give you fifty percent of …"

I drum my fingertips on the table while contemplating a fair offer.

"Nothing. How does fifty percent of nothing sound?"

His cheeks adopt a ruddy hue as he draws breath through flared nostrils.

"I'm being reasonable here," he spits. "After all I've done for you; it's the least I deserve."

"Yes, you've repeatedly mentioned everything you've done for me … particularly during our conversation on Tuesday when you proposed to me."

"I mention it repeatedly because it's a fact."

Another realisation strikes home.

"My God … how did I not see it? You only proposed so you'd have some legal right over the land as my husband. That's why you wanted us married so quickly."

"No, you're wrong," he protests. "I proposed because I still love you."

"Ha! You love what I'm worth more like. I should have

94

known you had an ulterior motive when I saw that ring. It represented everything you hate."

"I offered it to you in good faith."

"Yeah, right. I bet it was a fake, and how were you going to pay for our five-star honeymoon if you're as skint as you say?"

"I'd have found the money … for you."

I sit back and fold my arms.

"I'm going now, but let me tell you one thing before I do. Once I sell that land, I'll invest the money so I can finally have what you denied me — a child. Now, if you have any respect, any feelings, anything at all left for me, you'll forget this nonsense and let me have what I deserve."

"A child? You never said you were seeing someone."

"I'm not. As long as I have money, I don't need a man."

It takes a moment, but my words eventually sink in.

"You want to waste all that money funding a bastard child … spawned from a test tube?"

"No, I'm intending to spend that money raising a child, or children, who will be loved and cherished — without a manipulative, controlling arsehole like you in their lives."

"We'll see about that."

I get to my feet and flash a smile so insincere it would shame a politician.

"Nathan."

"What?"

"I hope you and your mother will be very happy together wherever you both end up. And, finally … fuck you for wasting another twenty minutes of my life."

I walk away.

13.

They say you should never go to bed angry. I was apoplectic.

Once I arrived home, I tried every possible way to drag my thoughts from the meeting with Nathan but the rage simmered all evening, and into the night.

How dare he? How fucking dare he?

I wasted a good two hours googling legal advice but little of it made sense, and I slammed the laptop shut none the wiser. I may have won the battle but knowing my ex-husband, I feared it was a mere skirmish ahead of a long drawn-out war. He's a proud man, so for him to have admitted his financial meltdown, suggests desperation. And desperate people are prone to desperate actions, although proposing marriage to an ex-wife is a new one — talk about brass-necked cheek.

At one point I considered calling him and making an offer — a gesture of goodwill just to get rid of him — but my principles wouldn't allow it even if I thought he'd accept a lesser amount. By two in the morning I half-convinced myself he's in too weak a financial position to fight. It allowed me to snatch a few hours' restless sleep but now, in the cold light of day, I'm no longer sure of anything.

As I chew on a piece of cold toast, my jaw remains taut with tension. Every part of me is still tense. Notwithstanding his claim, Nathan has also stolen the joy I unearthed yesterday. In just a few days, my feelings for that man have swung from total indifference to hatred, and I don't like it. Hatred is a draining emotion and I'm doubly annoyed it's ruining my Saturday morning.

To find balance, I call Martha.

"Hey, chick. How's you?"

"Don't ask, unless you've got a couple of hours spare."

"I wish I had, but I'm about to take the girls to dance class."

"I just wanted to check if you're still up for a few drinks later? I really need to talk to you, and I mean really."

"Oh, dear. What's up?"

"Imagine going to Weight Watchers next week and being told you've put on four stone."

"Ohh ... that bad?"

"Kind of, but don't worry ... it's just that ex-husband of mine. We'll chat later."

"I'll pop over about five if that works for you? I can only stay for an hour or two, though."

"No worries. Have fun at dance club."

"Fat chance. Seeya later."

I end the call and glance up at the kitchen clock. It's not even ten yet and I'll drive myself to distraction if I don't find something to fill the seven hours before Martha arrives. A quick check of the weather and I formulate a plan: a bit of retail therapy and then maybe a late lunch in the park; seeing as the forecasters promise a nice day.

Decision made, I get myself sorted and leave just after ten-thirty. With my headphones on, I select a cheery playlist which helps ease the tension and I arrive at the shopping centre less of a coiled spring.

With no real plan, I meander from shop to shop. There's nothing I really need and nothing catches my eye to qualify as a must-have.

I continue wandering aimlessly until I pass a shop I've subconsciously avoided for a long time. On this occasion, it draws me in. It's busy with expectant parents; most meticulously inspecting the wide range of prams and car seats, or cooing over rails of babywear. I head towards a table of neatly stacked clothes for newborns and browse the tiny garments; some of which aren't much larger than the clothes I used to dress my dolls in.

There was a time, before Nathan's diagnosis, I used to visit this shop every week. Not wanting to tempt fate I resisted buying even a bib, but the urge to nest grew stronger every week — until that fateful conversation with the doctor. This is the first time I've stepped foot in the shop since that day.

I pick up a babygrow, patterned with pictures of a cute bear cub. The feel of the soft fabric piques my resolve — I will come back here soon, and I will leave with as much merchandise as I can physically carry. Nathan took away my dream once; he won't do it again.

"When are you due?" a voice asks.

I turn to my right. A woman a few years younger than me is perusing clothes on a nearby shelf.

"Oh, err. Spring next year," I lie.

"Early days, then?"

"Very, but I couldn't resist a quick nose. I shouldn't, really."

"Yes, you should. Savour every moment."

I can't help but glance at her small bump.

"When are you due?"

"Bloody Christmas," she laughs. "He wasn't planned."

"Aww, a Christmas baby. That's so lovely."

"Yeah, it is."

We swap smiles and the woman wishes me luck before wandering off to another aisle. I then realise I'm still clutching the tiny babygrow. The last time I browsed the shelves in this shop, I didn't want to tempt fate by making a purchase — it made no odds. Perhaps this time I should tempt fate.

I head to the till and pay for the babygrow.

Outside the shop, I neatly fold it into a parcel and tuck it into my handbag. It'll stay there as a constant reminder of my goal. Who knows, maybe the tiny piece of patterned fabric will prove a good luck charm.

With no appetite for clothes shopping, I decide a good book might help me while away a few hours this afternoon. There's now only one bookshop in town and it's situated on the third floor where the rents are probably cheaper. I wind my way through the bustling crowds to the lifts.

As luck would have it, one of the two lifts is waiting empty with the doors open. I step inside and press the button for the third floor. A few seconds pass before the doors slide shut, and the ascent begins. That ascent is cut short when I reach the first floor and an impassive female voice announces the doors are opening. I use the delay to check my phone messages, and I'm relieved to see the inbox is empty. I then remember I blocked Nathan's number so he can't message me even if he wanted to.

The female voice announces the doors are closing just as I look up from my phone screen.

Stood just inside the door is the same man I bumped into at Starbucks. The same brown suit, the same lily in his buttonhole.

Coincidences happen all the time; I get that. However, if you bump into the same stranger twice in four days, typically there would be a jokey acknowledgement of that coincidence. The man doesn't seem in the least bit surprised to find himself in the same lift as the woman he purchased a coffee for a few days ago.

"Err, hello again," I gush.

"Hello, Kelly."

It almost slips by unnoticed. Only when I attempt a reply and realise I never told him my name does the situation lurch from coincidence to concerning.

"How … how do you know my name?"

He doesn't reply.

The lift begins its vertical journey at the same moment I decide I want to get out. I make a step towards the panel of buttons but then, without warning, the lift comes to a sudden halt somewhere between floors one and two.

"Oh, dear," Mr Brown Suit sighs. "It seems the lift has developed a fault."

"Just hit the alarm button," I demand. "I don't like confined spaces and I don't like strangers stalking me."

"I can help you with both those issues," he replies calmly. "Though not necessarily in that order."

He thrusts out a hand.

"I am Kenneth," he confirms. "And now you know my name, we are no longer strangers."

In any other situation, I'm sure most people would find his polite manner and geniality endearing. I don't and keep my right hand firmly away from his.

"Are you following me?"

"I'm not following you. I'm monitoring you."

"You're … what? Monitoring me?"

"Yes."

"Why?"

"I'm afraid I can't say. However, I mean you no harm; that I can assure you."

His inability to answer another straightforward question is irritatingly familiar. I hold my phone up and capture his photo.

"You've got ten seconds to explain how you know my name and why you're following me, or I'll tweet this photo to the local police force, and tell them I'm being held against my will."

"Tweet?" he muses, seemingly unconcerned by my threat. "A form of social media communication, is it not?"

"Are you kidding me?"

"Alas, not," he replies, apologetically. "I'm afraid I've always found humour a difficult skill to master."

"My question wasn't literal."

"Oh, apologies."

The situation now feels more like a farce than a stalking.

"I want to get out. Will you please hit the alarm button?"

"Certainly."

Calmly, he reaches across towards the panel of buttons. Before he presses any of them, a series of mechanical clunks sound from above and the lift continues its ascent. We reach the second floor and it stops again.

"My floor," Kenneth announces, as the doors slide open.

He steps out of the lift and turns around to face me.

"A word of warning, Kelly: fate has sent you on a path you must not follow. Change direction, please."

The doors slide shut.

"What the fuck?"

That is one of many questions I can't answer but it's not the most concerning. How did he know my name?

I dart across to the panel and repeatedly jab the button to open the doors. The lift ignores my instruction and continues on. After a painstaking delay I reach the third floor but I've no interest in buying a book now. I jab the button for the second floor and with the same lazy response, the doors eventually close.

"Come on. Come on."

Every second feels like an hour but I finally escape onto the second floor.

If you want to lose yourself in a crowd, there are few better places than Saturday lunchtime in a shopping centre. I scan left and right but, with a continually changing sea of faces to appraise, the futility soon dawns.

With no better plan, I walk up and down the concourse; continually scouring the crowd for a man in a brown suit while hoping he isn't in one of the shops. Even if he isn't, he's had sufficient time to reach the exit, and once outside there are any number of different ways he could have gone.

It doesn't take long to realise I'm wasting my time. I pass an empty bench and reluctantly accept it might be sensible to sit down and gather my thoughts.

I open the image gallery on my phone and tap the tiny thumbnail of my potential stalker. The full-size image offers little in the way of clues. Besides the flower planted in his lapel, Kenneth couldn't be more ordinary; to the point it would be hard describing him without the photo. Even with the photo, there's nothing even remotely striking about the man. His neatly combed hair is almost the same shade of brown as his suit and hints at a conservative career — maybe an accountant or a solicitor. His choice of black pullover rather than a shirt and tie removes another level of identification. Even a coloured shirt or patterned tie might make him identifiable. Perhaps it's a deliberate ploy.

I zoom in on his face but hit the same problem. He could be in his early thirties, or his late forties, or anywhere in between. Even his bloody eyes are brown. If Kenneth were a colour, he'd be beige. You could paint a room beige and most people wouldn't remember the colour of the walls after they'd left. The guy is, to all intents and purposes, invisible.

Frustrated, I put my phone away and attempt to recall our brief conversation. My initial shock at his appearance has fogged the first seconds but one word is hard to forget: monitoring. Is that really the kind of word a stalker would use, let alone admit to? It's a verb closely associated to a government organisation like the police or social services.

But who would want to monitor me, and to what end?

I let that question sit for a while but an answer stubbornly refuses to join us. I'm a nobody, with a mundane, ordinary life; there is no good reason for anyone to monitor me.

What I do know is I don't need this complication in my life right now. It's stressful enough dealing with Nathan's threats without some weirdo bumping into me and making cryptic statements.

And then I make the connection.

"You idiot," I mutter under my breath.

It's too much of a coincidence. In the same week Nathan hatched and deployed his plan to rid me of three hundred grand, this Kenneth character suddenly starts showing up.

The more I consider it, the more it makes sense. It's just the tactic Nathan would deploy: unorthodox, unsettling, and psychologically effective. Even the timing works. I expected some fallout from our meeting yesterday but I haven't heard a peep. Instead, he sent his advocate to threaten me. What was the last thing Kenneth said? Something about a path I shouldn't follow?

It also explains how he knew my name.

The dots join up. This has to be some bizarre ruse Nathan concocted to get inside my head. My guess is Kenneth will keep appearing and his warnings will become increasingly dire until I break.

That will not happen.

Now I know his motive, Kenneth is in for a frosty reception if he shows up again. As for Nathan, I'm actually relieved. He must be desperate to employ such a ludicrous strategy.

He's shown his pathetic hand, and it's a losing one.

14.

"So sorry I'm late," Martha pants, as I open the front door. "I had to park in a neighbouring county."

"Really?"

"No, but it felt like it. Why did you buy a house on a street where it's impossible to park?"

"Quit moaning. The exercise is good for you."

"I get enough exercise chasing around after my husband and kids, thank you very much."

I beckon her through to the kitchen where I've already got a bottle of wine at the ready.

"Drink?"

"Just a small one, ta. Unlike you, I couldn't cope without a driving licence."

"You might be surprised."

"I'll let you take the girls to school one morning, on the bus, and we'll see if you still feel the same way. Are bus drivers willing to turn around halfway to fetch forgotten homework or PE kit?"

"Point taken."

I pour two small glasses of wine and we sit at the kitchen table.

"Come on then, chick, let's have it. What's the problem?"

"I don't even know where to begin. The last couple of days have been … ridiculous."

I begin by recounting how I discovered the potential value of Dad's old yard.

"Holy shit," Martha gasps. "You're minted."

"Not quite. I won't see a penny until next year."

"Yeah, but … that's amazing! Have you thought about what you're going to do with it?"

"I have."

"Let me guess — a cosmetic surgery makeover? You could start with a proper pair of zeppelins, and then arse implants."

"What? Why would I want a bigger arse?"

"It's all the rage. Apparently everyone wants a fat arse these days."

"Err, not everyone, and if I had bigger tits I'd topple over all the time."

"Good point. Okay, so not cosmetic surgery."

"No."

"What then?"

I pause for effect.

"A baby."

"You're gonna buy a baby?"

"Not buy one, dummy. I'm planning on artificial insemination, and then I'll invest the money to provide an income so I can give up work."

"Wait … just roll back a second. Artificial insemination?"

"Yes."

"Sounds expensive."

"Not as expensive as you might imagine, and I can be sure the baby's biological father doesn't have any defective genes or hereditary conditions."

"That makes sense. It's a shame they can't do anything about the mother being a ginger."

"My hair is auburn, you cheeky cow."

"If you say so, but still, why pay all that money when you could go to Cheeks on Saturday night and get yourself knocked up in the back alley for free?"

"Hmm … tempting, but I'm not sure I fancy being impregnated by the kind of man willing to have sex up against a dumpster in a piss-ridden alley at two in the morning."

"Don't knock it. Stuart even treated me to a kebab afterwards."

"Aww, how romantic. No wonder you two are still so much in love."

With her usual brand of humour administered, Martha reaches across the table and grips my hand.

"Seriously, I think it's a brilliant idea and I'm chuffed for you. If anyone deserves a shot at motherhood, it's you."

"Thank you, but I've already encountered a slight hitch, I

think."

"Oh?"

Another lengthy explanation ensues as I recount the meeting with Nathan yesterday evening, and events at the shopping centre.

"What the fuck is going on with your life lately?" she gasps. "It's a soap opera."

"Tell me about it."

"I don't even know where to start."

She scratches her head for a few seconds.

"I'm no lawyer but Nathan's claim sounds sketchy," she says dismissively. "More importantly though, what kind of sick bastard employs a random nutjob to stalk his ex-wife in the hope of intimidating her?"

"A sick bastard like Nathan. He must be desperate."

"You should call him, and ... no, wait. You should let me call him."

"Why?"

"To say you've sussed his plan. Oh, and to tell him what a twenty-four carat wankspangle he is."

I almost spit a mouthful of wine across the table.

"You've no idea how tempting that is, but one thing I've learnt about Nathan is to act dumb. If he thinks I know what he's up to, he'll change strategy and I'll be none the wiser. At least this way I can play along until he runs out of money. He's already invested quite a lot in this charade so the longer it goes on, the weaker he'll be."

"Is his situation that bad?"

"Apparently so. He can't afford to keep Beatrice in that plush nursing home much longer."

"What a shame. Still, a spell in a state-run nursing home will probably do the snooty old bitch some good."

"After the way they've both treated me, I hope they rot in hell together."

"I'll drink to that."

Martha raises her glass and chinks it against mine.

"Now, let's get back to a more pleasant topic of conversation.

Have you thought about names yet?"

"God, no. It's a bit early."

"It's never too early, and at least you won't have to debate it with anyone else."

"True."

"If it's a boy, you should call him something unusual."

"Like?"

"Gary, or Malcolm … or Duncan."

"What? Are you serious?"

"Absolutely. Think about it: every classroom is full of kids called Jack, or George, or Ethan. No one calls their kid Gary these days."

"For good reason."

"And if it's a girl, I'd go for Tracy, or Wendy. Maybe Pamela."

"Are you taking the piss?"

"Yes."

I deliver a playful slap to her arm.

"I'm not calling my child Gary or Pamela."

"Spoilsport."

"But I like the idea of Douglas or Fay; either as a first or middle name."

"That's a lovely idea — naming him or her after your parents. You have my blessing."

"Thanks," I chuckle. "And it goes without saying he or she will need a godmother."

"Indeed."

"But, I don't know any responsible, upstanding candidates so you'll have to do."

"I'm honoured … and mildly offended."

We continue chatting nonsense for another half-hour before my friend has to leave. It's date night apparently, and Stuart has booked a table for eight o'clock. Probably at a kebab shop, Martha surmised.

We hug goodbye at the door, and I watch her wander up the street as she begins her epic journey back to the car park three hundred yards away.

I close the door and sigh. It's been a long time since I had dinner with a man I'd want to have dinner with. On the upside, at least I can now go watch whatever crap I want on TV without a heated discussion beforehand. The pros and cons of marriage — I had too many of the latter, unfortunately.

The chat with Martha has helped ease my concern so, feeling a little more relaxed, I order a pizza and change into my slobs. I'm twenty minutes into the first episode of a box set when the doorbell rings. A thin crust Hawaiian duly delivered, I settle back on the sofa. I watch another two episodes while browsing baby products on my phone. That pursuit ends when I tell myself off for thinking too far ahead.

Needing a break, I switch from Netflix to regular television just as the news is about to start. The stony-faced newsreader begins by reporting on yet another mass shooting in America. Some crazed lunatic has apparently wandered through a shopping mall with an automatic assault rifle, firing indiscriminately as he went. Twenty innocent people left home this morning and won't be returning — it's so awful.

The newsreader quotes the mind-boggling number of gun-related deaths in the US so far this year. If those deaths were attributable to any other cause, the Government would ban it in a heartbeat but, for reasons I'll never understand, they consider guns sacred. If I lived in America, I'd honestly think long and hard before bringing a child into such a scary world. How American parents sleep at night is beyond me.

A sudden shiver prompts me to reach for the remote control. Unsurprisingly, it isn't where I thought I left it. It never is.

I'm about to get up and search the sofa crevices when the newsreader moves on to another story. I didn't catch the introduction, but the camera switches from the newsroom to a windswept reporter who could be anywhere as the backdrop is just an inky blue sky. Fortunately, a graphic on the screen confirms the location as Crawley in West Sussex.

The reporter adopts a solemn expression as he picks up where the newsreader left off. I turn away from the television and continue searching for the remote control while half listening to the reporter.

"… eye-witnesses state two bodies were recovered from the vehicle …"

My head snaps back towards the screen; the reporter's face replaced with the smoking remains of a saloon car. Fire has destroyed every combustible element, leaving behind just the blackened skeleton and no clues to the car's make or model.

"… it is feared both victims were trapped …"

Bile rises in the back of my throat. Frantically, I turn my attention back to the sofa in a desperate attempt to find the remote control. I can still hear the reporter but I try to block out his words. Using my left hand I toss cushions to the floor while I dig my right hand into every crevice.

"Where the fuck is it?"

I can't bear to look at the television but I need to switch it off or change the channel — anything to silence the reporter and take away the imagery. I realise I've only ever switched the television off using the remote control. I've no idea where the power button is.

As desperation mounts, I run my hand around the outer edge of the set while keeping my eyes locked on the wall above. Even then, there's no ignoring the strobing blue lights of emergency vehicles reflecting off my white t-shirt and tinting the wall.

My fingertips catch a raised surface which could be a button. With no idea if it controls the power, the channel, or the volume, I press it repeatedly. The blue lights stop strobing and the reporter's voice is replaced by canned laughter.

Too late — the damage is done.

Somewhere in the deepest recesses of my mind, I've kept a jar, brimming with dark, but safely contained memories. The news report has removed the lid from that jar and the memories are now sloshing around in my head.

As I crawl back onto the sofa, the sloshing becomes a torrent and I'm swept back to the day I've tried so damn hard to forget — a day in late May, twelve years ago.

The first five months of the year had not been great for me. I'd split up with my boyfriend in February, and in April, Martha broke the news that she and Stuart were heading to Australia for a year. They had married two years previously, and I presumed they were planning to start a family. Instead, they had planned a year-long adventure together; a kind of gap year before being tied down to parenthood and all the other associated commitments.

Once they'd both given notice to quit their jobs, booked flights, organised visas, accommodation, and planned the budget down to the nearest penny, they were all set.

Two weeks later, I blubbered a goodbye to my best friend.

Without a partner or Martha to occupy my free time, Dad came to the rescue. Every Saturday, and one or two evenings during the week, he'd drag me down to Springlake Lane and I'd help him ready Kellybelle for her first outing that year. My assistance stretched to passing tools and keeping a plastic cup topped with tea from a flask, but it kept me occupied. Looking back, that was obviously Dad's plan as he knew how much I missed Martha.

Some weeks later, Kellybelle was hoisted onto a trailer ready for her overland journey down to the harbour near Southampton, where she'd stay until late autumn. Mum and Dad had already planned their first trip of the season — a shortish hop across the English Channel to Le Havre in Northern France. The journey across the sea would take the best part of nine hours and they planned to stay for three days before returning on the following Tuesday.

On a Friday evening in late May, I kissed them both goodbye at the doorstep of our family home as they began the first leg of their overnight journey to France. In truth, I was looking forward to having a little space to wallow in. Being an only child, my parents had a tendency to fuss whenever they suspected I wasn't myself, so I planned to enjoy five days of not being continually asked if I was okay.

They would never get to check on my wellbeing again.

The next day, I awoke to doorbell chimes at eight in the morning. Half asleep, I was minded to ignore it but my unwelcome visitor proved persistent and I reluctantly crawled out of bed on the fourth chime.

I stomped down the stairs and opened the front door. The irritation caught in my throat at the sight of two men in police uniform. They confirmed my name and asked if they could come in. I don't remember agreeing but the next thing I recall, I'm sitting in Dad's armchair with both policemen perched on the sofa opposite. One of them, with thinning hair and greasy skin, took the lead and asked if anyone other than my parents had been aboard Kellybelle when she left Southampton. I must have said I doubted it, or words to that effect, as the police officer then cleared his throat and adopted a solemn expression.

Only fragments of what he said next sank in.

A light aircraft reported seeing flames in the sea halfway between the Isle of Wight and the French coastline. The coastguard deployed a helicopter but, by the time it reached the coordinates given by the aircraft pilot, all they found were a few fragments of smouldering driftwood — no sign of Kellybelle or my parents.

The police officers weren't there to tell me my parents had perished; their job was to relay the limited facts. Kellybelle had disappeared from radar within minutes of the aircraft pilot reporting a fire. There were no flares deployed, no mayday signal issued, and no communication from the boat. One minute it was bobbing along merrily over the sea, the next it was ablaze. Finally, it disappeared beneath the waves.

The police officers left and I spent the next three days clinging to the hope my parents had set off on a life raft, and any moment a passing vessel would pick them up. I spent every waking hour by the phone, willing it to ring with good news. It never rung, with good news or bad.

Days became a week, and then two. By that point, any lingering hope had gone. As impossible as it seemed, my parents would not be coming home.

My Uncle Terence — Mum's older brother — flew down from Edinburgh where he'd lived for years. I'd only met him a handful of times and he was no more a comfort than the police officers. Lots of kind words and sympathy but all hollow when offered by a stranger.

As horrendous as I felt, worse was to come.

Despite an extensive search, the Coastguard were unable to recover my parents' bodies. At some point, they must have confirmed it was unlikely they ever would as Uncle Terence decided we should hold a memorial service; essentially a funeral without a cremation or burial. He sat me down and explained it would give the family closure, and he'd arrange everything. I was in no fit state to argue.

So, three weeks later I stood in a church and watched on as the service unfolded around me. Many of my parents' friends and colleagues attended, and several stood at the pulpit and said the nicest things. Hymns were sung and Uncle Terence had arranged for the first song from my parents' wedding to be played: *Lovin' You*, by Minnie Riperton.

Even now, if that song comes on the radio I'll change the station. It still breaks my heart every time I hear it.

If it hadn't been for Martha returning, there's no way I could have got through the day. As soon as she heard about the service, she spent a large chunk of their budget on a plane ticket and flew home. She held my hand, hugged me when I needed a hug, and wiped the never-ending stream of tears from my cheeks. I, in turn, felt guilty for dragging her halfway around the world when she should have been having the time of her life with the love of her life.

A week after the service, I virtually frogmarched Martha back to the airport.

After another tearful goodbye I returned to the house which was no longer a home. Uncle Terence had already left for Edinburgh a few days earlier, and he must have taken the promised closure with him as there wasn't any to be found anywhere in the empty rooms. I couldn't imagine any human feeling more alone than I did at that moment.

And yet, the nightmare lingered on.

The coroner's office eventually wrote to me, confirming the date for an inquest in to my parents' accident, as they labelled it. Without an inquest, my parents were technically missing rather than dead, and I remained in a heinous limbo where I couldn't obtain a death certificate. Every day, I had to deal with unsympathetic bureaucrats who often refused to talk to me without my parents' permission. Most of those calls ended with me slamming the phone down or completely losing it. Either way, without a death certificate they weren't interested in finding a solution.

The day of the inquest came, and I was in two minds whether to attend or not. Still searching for Uncle Terence's elusive closure, I decided I had to be there.

The proceedings didn't take long because of an absence of evidence. Kellybelle, they concluded, had been consumed by a catastrophic fire but no one could say why my parents didn't react. They offered theories; the most likely being my parents had somehow lost consciousness before the fire started, but no one could say how, or what caused the fire in the first place. In essence, it was like attending a court hearing with no witnesses, no evidence, and no charges.

The only conclusion the coroner could reach was accidental death. Months of waiting to be told what I already knew — nothing. However, the verdict meant I could at last secure death certificates. They had warned me I might have to wait seven bloody years, but mercifully the coroner saw sense.

With the deaths official, I then had to deal with my parents' estate and that involved a meeting with their solicitor for the reading of the will. It was the final punch to my already beaten soul, and I left their office in tears.

Twelve years on, I'm left with a jar of dark memories, eleven wasted years in a loveless marriage, and a pathological fear of fire.

I switch the television off and vow never to watch the news again.

15.

I'm in that space between asleep and awake. I can hear faint birdsong and I'm about to roll over when I feel it — a weight on my chest. In a fraction of a second, I take several steps closer to being awake as my brain boots up and works through the possibilities. My first thought is it's a medical issue like a stroke or heart attack, but surely there would be other symptoms, and pain? A more troubling thought comes next. Is it a large hand pressing down?

I'd rather not open my eyes for fear of finding an intruder stood at my bed, holding me down with one hand while brandishing a knife in the other.

Suddenly, the weight shifts a fraction. Could it be the intruder making a slight adjustment to ensure I'm properly pinned to the bed?

I have to open my eyes, not least because I'll likely soil the sheets if I don't get out of bed in the next few seconds. As the fear builds, I slowly let my eyelids ease open.

"Jesus!"

A fat, ginger, furry face with large green eyes is only inches from mine.

"Frank," I rasp. "You scared the shit out of me. How did you get in here?"

Reluctantly, I cast my mind back to the blur which preceded my coming to bed.

I go through the same routine every night where I switch off all the electrical devices, test the smoke detectors in the hall and on the landing, and check the doors and windows are all locked. Last night I came up to bed in a daze and must have forgotten to close a window.

Frank stretches out his front legs and two meaty paws massage the exposed skin below my neck, accompanied by a deep purr which reverberates through my ribcage. I might have enjoyed my wake-up massage if I'd known I had a guest in the first place, and that guest kept his bloody claws retracted.

"Ouch! Easy, Mister."

I lift his bulk from my chest and place him on the floor.

"Stay there. I'll be back in a minute and then we'll get breakfast."

He ignores my command and trots at my heels all the way to the bathroom. As I sit on the loo, he rubs his head against my legs.

"Can't a girl even have a piss in peace?"

I find a smile. Maybe one day it'll be a toddler demanding attention, rather than a fat ginger cat. It's only the hope of becoming a mother which kept the dark thoughts at bay last night.

The therapist Nathan insisted I visit all those years ago didn't fix me, but she imparted one piece of advice I've continued to heed. She said whenever it felt like I was being consumed by the darkness of negative thoughts, all I had to do was find a light; a beacon of hope to guide me forward. That beacon, she suggested, could be anything from the promise of a favoured takeaway meal at the weekend, to a day out or a short break. My beacon at the time proved to be the creation of a new family. It gave me the strength to push through the darker days. When a doctor snuffed out that beacon, my career provided an alternative light source.

Now, I have a new one, albeit a repurposed one.

I finish up in the bathroom and Frank follows me down the stairs to the kitchen. The window is open. Fortunately, of all the windows I could have left open, the kitchen one is less of a security risk because of the high brick wall surrounding the garden. It's also bordered by my neighbours' gardens on both sides. Nevertheless, I vow not to be so careless in the future, particularly as I don't know when or where Nathan's creepy stooge might pop up next.

I serve Frank his tuna and put the kettle on. While I wait for it to boil, my mind drifts back to the days when my ex-husband last exercised control over me. In the months after we married, I wanted a family so badly I'd have danced to any tune he cared to play.

Once I knew there was no chance of a family, the child grew up and sought independence. And, because Nathan was so consumed with his own career, it never crossed his mind I might be forging my own. By the time he realised, it was too late — his fragile girl had grown into an independent woman and he no longer served a purpose. He struggled to accept the new dynamic in our marriage and the cracks became a chasm. Even now, I think he continues to underestimate what I'm capable of, and that is his weakness.

Fuck Nathan, and fuck Kenneth.

With little else to do on a wet Sunday, I intend to use a large part of the day planning my own moves. I know it's premature but there are two good reasons to be bold: firstly, I'll be forty later this year and time is not on my side. Secondly, I'm determined my beacon will shine with the light of a thousand suns by the time I crawl into bed tonight.

The kettle boils just as Frank trots off — to seek his next conquest probably. I make a coffee and toast some bread. Once I've eaten, I grab a shower and set the laptop up on the kitchen table along with a notebook and pen.

After my earlier research I've a reasonable understanding of what I'm looking for, so I start by googling donor insemination clinics. An hour of browsing the results and one clinic stands out from the rest as they offer both the sperm and the insemination treatment. They also state a third of their clients are single women; a reassuring statistic.

I read every word on the website while making copious notes. I then google the clinic to check their online reputation. Virtually all the reviews I find are positive.

Satisfied I've found the right clinic, I scroll down to a form which, once submitted, will set the wheels in motion. I fill it in and let the cursor hover over the button at the bottom for a second.

"This is it, girl," I whisper to myself.

It's just a collection of coloured pixels on a screen and, if I click the mouse, it'll simply transfer my information across the web to a server somewhere. It is, though, so much more than that. It's the first step in realising a lifelong dream. I gulp hard and click the mouse. The screen changes and I'm offered a new page confirming the clinic will deal with my enquiry as soon as possible. That won't be until tomorrow but I don't care. I've done it.

I'm about to get up and celebrate with another coffee when my phone rings. With Nathan safely blocked, I answer.

"Hi. You got a sec?"

It's Martha, but even though she's only said a few words, I can tell it's not the bubbly, carefree version.

"Sure. What's up?"

"We need to talk, Kelly."

She rarely uses my actual name and her tone is odd; not angry but not friendly.

"About what? You sound pissed off."

"I'm not pissed off, just … I'm not sure how I feel but it isn't nice."

"Right."

"Were you drunk last night?" she asks, although it sounds more like an accusation.

"No. I had a couple of glasses with you, and that was it. Why?"

"So, you were stone cold sober when you sent that email?"

"What email?"

"Come off it," she huffs. "Don't make this worse than it already is."

"I've no idea what you're talking about."

"If you're embarrassed, that's fine, but please don't lie to me. I thought we were friends."

"Seriously, Martha," I snap back. "You're starting to piss me off. What email?"

"The bloody email I'm looking at now."

I pause for a second to settle my growing agitation.

"Right, so you're looking at an email I apparently sent?"

"Yes, to my husband."

"Okay, can you forward it to my Gmail address so I know what the hell you're wittering on about?"

I hear the tapping of keys at the end of the line and open up Gmail on my laptop.

"Sent, and I've left the subject title exactly how it was when Stuart received it."

A quick refresh of the page and Martha's email arrives. The subject is to the point: Please Don't Share.

I open it, and stare at the screen.

"You still there?" Martha asks.

"What ... what the fuck?"

The email contains a single line of text and a photo.

"I ... I didn't send this," I plead. "I swear on my life: this is nothing to do with me."

"It came from your email address."

I scan the page to the original sender's email address, kelly@marstonfinance.com, and right above it is Stuart's email address.

"Yes, but I sure as hell didn't send it. Why would I send Stuart ... this?"

The line of text contains two sentences: *I've wanted you so long but never been able to find the words. I hope this picture demonstrates how much.*

The picture below is of a woman lying on her back, naked on a double bed with her head turned to the side so you can't quite see her face.

"Do you understand why I'm so angry?" Martha asks.

"Yes, of course, but ... I've never seen this photo before."

"But it's you, isn't it?"

I lean in and look for tell-tale signs I fear will confirm Martha's claim. It isn't the naked body which confirms those fears but the bed linen and headboard I recognise.

"I ... this is my bedroom at Kensall Gardens."

"So, it is you?"

I look closer and even though the resolution isn't great, I can just make out the distinctive watch on her wrist. It looks remarkably similar to the one on my wrist.

"Yes, it's me but I don't know who took this photo."

"Come off it," she snaps. "Are you telling me you didn't spot someone at the end of your bed, pointing a camera?"

"Just hold on a sec. If I were in your shoes, I'd be livid, too, but at this precise moment I've got greater concerns."

"Such as?"

"For starters, I'm absolutely mortified Stuart has seen a photo of me naked."

"So am I."

"Yes, hun, but you're not the one being secretly photographed, and ... Jesus, look at my lady garden. If I was trying to lure your husband, which I'm not, I'd have at least booked a wax before bearing my wares."

"Hmm, you make a convincing point."

"Exactly," I state. "Come on, Martha — I love Stuart but not in that way. Even if I did, there's no way I'd do anything to jeopardise our friendship. I hope you know that?"

The line falls silent again.

"Sorry, chick," she eventually sighs. "You know me — act first, think later."

"I know you better than anyone, Mrs Miller, and you know me better than anyone. And right at this moment, you can probably appreciate how freaked out I am. Not only did someone take a photo of me in bed without my knowledge, but they also sent it to my best friend's husband ... from my work's email address."

"There's an obvious suspect."

"Yep, there is."

I study the photo again. Nathan and I decided on separate bedrooms a few years prior to our split. I can't even recall who suggested it, but it made sense as we both worked long hours, with Nathan often getting up at the crack of dawn to catch a flight and sometimes not arriving home until the early hours of the morning. He also snored, and I had occasional nightmares which resulted in me waking up screaming in the middle of the night. In the end, it seemed crazy not to make use of the empty bedrooms.

The photo was definitely captured in my bedroom and only one person could have taken it.

"You must have been asleep when he took it," Martha suggests.

"Clearly. What I don't understand is why."

"I can think of one reason."

"Go on."

"You two weren't getting it on back then, were you?"

"Err, no."

"So, perhaps he needed inspiration."

"For?"

"Do I really need to spell it out?"

The sordid penny drops.

"Eww! You think he took a photo of me in the buff to wank over?"

"Why not? Men are more visual when it comes to that kind of thing. No imagination."

"Yes, but … that's gross, not to mention creepy as hell."

"We're talking about Nathan here. It's the kind of thing a man like him would do, don't you think?"

Suddenly, I have an overwhelming urge to take another shower.

"Whatever his motives, I agree he must have taken the photo, but my greater concern is how he used my work email address and why he sent that photo to Stuart."

"I can't say how he sent it, but it's obvious why he sent it."

"To punish me because I didn't cave in to his demands."

"Yep."

"Well, despite our initial … misunderstanding, his plan has backfired. Apart from putting poor Stuart off his breakfast, he's only proven how utterly sad and desperate he is."

"I like your thinking."

"Thank you."

"Your vaginal topiary, less so."

"Sod off," I giggle.

Our heated exchange is officially forgotten but beneath the laughter, I still have one worry. Having already dragged Martha and Stuart into my domestic mess, it's a worry I need to address by myself.

I let my friend get on with her day, but not before asking her to pass my apologies on to Stuart. He's an easy-going guy but I'm already dreading the next time I have to face him.

For the next half-hour I remain rooted in the chair while I decide what to do. I don't know how Nathan used my work email address, but he's crossed the line. I conclude there's only one way to deal with him.

16.

The rain clouds have moved on but the forecast suggests more will arrive later this afternoon. I packed a foldaway umbrella in my handbag, just in case they turn up early. It's still warm, verging on humid.

I arrive at The Three Horseshoes one minute earlier than the hour I demanded. As I push open the door, I'm not even sure if Nathan will be on the other side — he doesn't like being told what to do.

The bar is busy with folks in need of a Sunday roast without the washing up. I scan the room and spot Nathan at a table in the corner, nursing a glass of Coke. He spots me but doesn't get up. At least he's here. One-nil to me.

Wanting to keep a clear head, I order a glass of orange juice and then casually saunter over to Nathan's table.

There's no greeting as I take a seat opposite.

"I loathe this place," he mutters, without making eye contact.

"I know."

"So, what's the emergency? I'm hoping you've seen sense about my proposal?"

I ignore his question and ask my own.

"Why did you do it, Nathan? And more importantly, how?"

"Do what?"

"Don't play the innocent. You know damn well what I'm talking about."

"No, I do not, and if you've dragged me here just to play guessing games, I'm leaving."

"The email."

He rolls his eyes.

"What email?"

"The one I apparently sent to Martha's husband. The one which contained a compromising photo of me taken in my bedroom at Kensall Gardens."

"Still none the wiser," he shrugs.

I pull my phone out and open the email; covering the photo

with my thumb.

"This email."

Nathan leans forward and squints at the screen.

"The photo is of me," I confirm. "Taken while I was lying in bed."

"Can I see it?"

"No, you can't."

"Why not?"

"Because I'm naked."

"Don't be so ridiculous," he scoffs. "It's not as though I haven't seen you naked before."

"Yes, when we were married. Now we're not, I get to choose who sees my body."

He leans back and looks to the ceiling. Seconds pass before he puffs a tired sigh.

"Well? Are you going to explain?"

He returns his focus to my face and looks me straight in the eye.

"I didn't send that email."

"You took the photo?"

"No."

"Bullshit. Who else could have taken it?"

"Nobody, because I don't think it's a photo. That's why I wanted a proper look at it."

"Is there vodka in that Coke? Of course it's a photo."

"It's not. From what little I saw, the resolution suggests it's a still image taken from a video."

"Oh, great," I hiss. "So, you were videoing me while I slept? What sort of sick bastard …"

"Just wait a second," he interrupts. "I didn't video you, and if you keep your temper in check for one second, I'll explain."

I fold my arms and frown.

"Make it quick."

"Do you remember the second time we viewed the house? I think it was a month or so before we moved in when we were listing all the improvements we had in mind."

I nod.

"You said you wouldn't feel comfortable moving in until we had smoke detectors and carbon monoxide monitors fitted in every room. Remember?"

I nod again.

"I called in a home security company and they recommended their top-of-the-range detectors. Their units provided smoke and carbon monoxide detection with the added benefit of an integrated security camera. It made sense to have that extra level of protection."

"Are you saying those smoke detectors had a video camera built in? In every room?"

"Not quite every room and I did tell you."

"No, you never."

"Yes, I definitely did. Whether you believe me or not, it's immaterial now."

I'm about to launch into a tirade about my privacy rights but decide there's no point — it is immaterial. I can't change the past and I'm more concerned with the present.

"Ignoring the fact I was being filmed without my consent, explain to me how that photo ended up in Stuart Miller's inbox?"

His head bows forward a fraction and his eyes fix on the table.

"Nathan? I want an answer."

"Fine," he huffs. "But promise me you'll stay calm."

"I'm not promising anything."

"You can shout and scream all you like, but it won't solve the problem."

"What problem?"

"Let me start with an apology. I haven't been entirely honest with you."

"In what way?"

"The money I asked for. It's not because I made some bad investments. I'm being blackmailed, or at least I thought it was just me, but it appears you're now a target too."

"You ... what? Blackmailed?"

"I know. On reflection, I shouldn't have lied to you but they warned me there would be repercussions if I told another living

123

soul. So, I told a few white lies in the hope you'd give me the money to pay them off. It's not as though you can't afford it."

"A few white lies? You threatened me!"

"I only did that because I'm desperate. I may have lied about the investments but business is tough at the moment. I have little in the way of free cash so I could only partially meet their demands. I've already paid the best part of two hundred thousand."

"And you thought I'd stump up the rest?"

"That was my hope, yes. I'm sorry, but I was … I am, desperate."

"Who's blackmailing you, and what have they got over you?"

"Remember the computer we had in the study?"

"What about it?"

"Two weeks ago I set it up in my flat. I booted it up for the first time in nearly a year, and I was prompted to download an update — I thought nothing of it at the time. The next thing I know, I receive an email claiming I'd downloaded some kind of script which gave the blackmailer access to the hard drive. They copied everything, including dozens of confidential client files."

"So what?"

"Some of those files have the potential to ruin me if they fall into the wrong hands."

"I don't see how your files have anything to do with my email."

"If I recall, didn't you use that computer for sending work-related emails?"

"A few times, yes."

"I received a text from my bank to say they'd blocked an attempt to access my account from an unknown device. They had somehow extracted my username and password from our computer but fortunately the bank software blocked access. I'm guessing your email passwords wouldn't have had the same level of protection."

"You're saying some dodgy scammer has access to my work email address?"

"It looks that way. It would explain how Stuart received an email you didn't send."

"And the photo?"

"I paid a monthly subscription to the security company and the system automatically uploaded all the camera footage to a secure website just in case we ever needed to review it. I must have logged on to that website a few times, and the browser obviously stored my username and password. If the blackmailer found the login credentials, it would be easy enough to download all the security footage."

His calmness stokes my indignation.

"How could you have been so stupid?" I blast. "Have you considered what those bastards now have?"

"I didn't know. I thought they were only interested in my files."

"And now they have access to every moment we lived in that bloody house and … wait, was there a camera in our bedroom?"

He nods, grimly.

"And how long did the security company store the footage?"

"They guaranteed five years, as long as I maintained the monthly subscription."

"For crying out loud. They've got five years' worth of footage covering every one of our private moments, including what we did in bed together."

"They'll need to search long and hard to find that footage."

"Don't be flippant," I snap. "Have you considered how humiliating it'll be if a video of us having sex ends up on some dodgy porn website?"

"I appreciate you're not happy at that prospect but it's the least of my concerns. If I don't stump up the rest of their money within seven days, I'm finished."

I take a moment to gather my thoughts and contemplate where I go with this.

"I called you stupid."

"Yes, you did."

"I was wrong. You're an absolute moron, Nathan."

"I beg your pardon."

"You shouldn't have given them a single penny. Any sensible individual would have gone straight to the police."

"And what would they have done?"

"Their job. They'd have investigated these scumbags and put a stop to their plans."

"Ah, there she is," he sneers. "That naïve girl I used to know."

"What did you just say?"

"Do you think these people are amateurs? I discussed the situation with a tech expert and he said there's no way of tracing the blackmailer's location. Realistically, what can the police do if they don't even know where in the world to look?"

"They could trace the money through the banking system."

"They insisted I pay in bitcoins — it's a digital currency and untraceable."

"This just gets better and better. What happened to you, Nathan? You accuse me of being naïve but there's only one naïve idiot at this table, and you'd need a mirror to say hello."

"As I say, the contents of those files could ruin me … permanently. I had no choice. None."

"Call their bluff. If they know you don't have the money, what can they do?"

"That's the thing. They know I've got the money, or at least I had money. I used to compile an annual analysis of our finances, just in case anything happened to either of us. Those spreadsheets contained a list of our assets including properties, savings, investments … everything."

"So, they think you're still wealthy?"

"Yes, and married. You see my problem?"

I down the remaining orange juice.

"I do, Nathan. And it is your problem — not mine."

"It is your problem if they send more emails from your work account."

"I'll get the guys in IT to change the password tomorrow. As for the video footage, I'll just have to suck it up if they do anything with it. I've had much worse in my life and I won't be blackmailed … particularly as this is all your fault."

126

He grabs my wrist.

"I need that money, Kelly. I don't wish to sound dramatic but I'm genuinely concerned for my safety."

"No. Call the police or call their bluff. Either way, I'm sure they'll soon move on to the next sucker."

I snatch my hand away.

"Oh, and while we're on the subject of the police, if your creepy friend, Kenneth, or whatever his name is, comes within a mile of me, I won't hesitate to call them and report him for stalking. I'll be sure to let them know you're behind it."

He looks up at me with a puzzled frown.

"I don't know what you're on about, but will you please sit down so we can talk about the money?"

"And listen to more lies? No thanks."

"Do you want me to beg? If that's what it takes, I will."

"Beg all you like but I'm not selling Dad's yard for half its value just to save your arse."

"Don't then. There are other ways."

"What?"

"I checked, and your shares in Marston Finance are now worth over a hundred thousand. And, you could easily raise another two hundred thousand by mortgaging your house."

I'm truly lost for words.

"I need you to do this one thing for me," he pleads. "I'm running out of time."

He then takes out his phone and taps away at the screen.

"I've just emailed you my bank details," he continues. "I'll also email you details of a broker who can liquidate your shares and a company who guarantee to provide mortgage funds within seven days. I've done all the hard work, Kelly. You just need to set the wheels in motion."

Open-mouthed, I glare down at him.

"You really are desperate … desperate and deluded. Did you honestly believe I'd be willing to sell my shares and mortgage my home just to bail you out of a mess you created?"

"Yes, I did. I'm legally entitled to half your assets so my proposal is a gift. Help me out of this hole and you'll never hear from me again."

"How about I leave you in that hole and never hear from you again?"

"Don't turn your back on this opportunity, Kelly. You owe me and I'm trying to be reasonable."

"You arrogant shit," I hiss. "You stole eleven years of my life and denied me the chance of becoming a mother. I owe you nothing. Nothing!"

Without another glance in his direction, I grab my bag and make for the door.

Once I'm back on the street, I use the residual anger as fuel; taking long, purposeful strides to get away as quickly as I can. There's still ample fuel remaining when I turn into Juniper Lane.

Arriving home, I kick off my shoes and contemplate which stimulant I need the most: wine or coffee? I decide on coffee, and head to the kitchen.

I put the kettle on and snatch a mug from the cupboard. A red mist descends and the remaining fuel ignites. The mug sails across the kitchen before exploding against the far wall. A rage-fuelled scream then builds and builds until I can no longer contain it.

The scream doesn't end until I run out of breath. Shaking, and panting hard, I lean up against the counter. I'm not prone to uncontrolled outbursts but in this instance there's ample justification. It may have come at a cost — a now-sore throat and the sacrifice of my favourite mug — but the restorative value outweighs both.

The kettle reaches its own boiling point and clicks off.

I reach for another mug but decide against coffee; never a more appropriate time for a soothing dose of chamomile tea.

Composure restored and tea made, I sit at the table and close my eyes. Exactly one week ago today, Hannah called to whine about loft insulation. As much as she irritated me, little did I know what comparative chaos lay ahead. This week has been exhausting, exasperating, exhilarating, and probably a host of other adjectives beginning with 'ex', which I can't currently recall.

However, it's an altogether different kind of ex which prompted my outburst.

There's no sense letting my anger fester — it'll do me no good. The best way to deal with it is to process it, and pack it away.

Accordingly, my mind turns to Nathan's plea.

I never had much interest in his career but he frequently complained about some seven-figure deal or other, and the stress he was under. With such huge sums of money at stake and influential clients to please, perhaps he cut corners or stretched the rules from time to time. If he did, more fool him. In my limited experience, people involved in high finance are a lot like politicians — they're happy to make brazen promises when working with other people's money.

If Nathan did cut corners to fulfil his promises, he has to face the consequences. Whatever he's done and whatever threat pushed him to seek my help, his only way out is to speak to the police. He created the problem so it's his to own, and his alone.

However, his actions have leaked into my life and those video files are a worry.

If there's any consolation, it's that Nathan insisted we turn the lights out whenever we had shenanigans, as he called it, and we were always cloaked in a duvet. I should probably be more concerned about photos of me in the buff but I'm struggling to give a shit — perhaps it's the calming influence of the chamomile tea. Untrimmed pubic hair aside, I'm not ashamed of my body. Besides, what's the worst Nathan's blackmailers can do now they've sent a photo to my best friend's husband? If Mum and Dad were still around or I had any other close family, I'd be mortified if they received such photos, but sadly it's not a concern.

Sitting back in my chair, I take a moment to reflect. With the processing now complete, I think all my Nathan-related woes are now safely packed away.

Time to move on and restore some order to the rest of my life. I grab a notepad and compile a to-do list.

At the top of that list is a reminder to contact the IT

department at work so no more random emails can be sent from my address. It's probably a sensible idea to change all my other online passwords too, so I add that task to the list.

Next on the list is the lunchtime meeting with Richard at Ramsey Rowe & Associates tomorrow. Once I sign his proposal, it'll be one significant weight off my mind and I'll be one step closer to my goal.

As for the clinic, I'm assuming they'll want me to go in for an initial consultation which means booking a day off work as they're in London. I make a note to ask if Martha fancies joining me when I know the date. I'd like a bit of moral support, and maybe we could hit Oxford Street afterwards. Knowing my friend, we're more likely to end up necking cocktails at a bar near the river.

List complete, I puff a contented sigh. Sometimes in life, the simple act of working through your issues and consigning them to a to-do list works wonders. Only then can you determine what matters and what doesn't. I'm going to focus on the former — the latter can fuck right off.

My throat is still sore and I own one less mug than I did half-an-hour ago, but at least I no longer feel like I'm being blown around like an autumn leaf.

It's only a mug of tea, but I raise a toast.

"To the future."

17.

Having shifted a ton of weight from my mind yesterday afternoon, it's equally nice to wake up without a fat ginger weight on my chest.

Ten minutes before the alarm is due to sound, I climb out of bed and stretch. A quick peek beyond the curtains confirms the weather is also in a good mood.

I make straight for the bathroom to deal with my bloated bladder before trotting downstairs. I'm not able to put my finger on why, but there's a different atmosphere in the house today. I know it's most likely just my mind-set but, as I wander into the kitchen, I'm feeling thoroughly chipper. Today is going to be a good day — I can sense it.

There's no sign of Frank at the back door.

With the radio turned up loud I feast on a breakfast of coffee and croissants. I then shower, get dressed, and leave the house ahead of schedule.

Despite missing out on the bus queue gold medal by only seconds, I'm happy to take silver. One by one the others arrive, and the bus eventually trundles into view.

I secure a prime seat, and after an uneventful journey, follow the well-trodden path from the bus stop to Starbucks to my office.

Far from a typical Monday morning, I open my inbox with a degree of anticipation. It's too early to expect a response from the clinic but that doesn't stop the butterflies. They soon flutter away when I'm met with the usual deluge of work-related tedium.

"Patience, Kelly," I whisper to myself.

The first item on my to-do list is a call to the IT department. I ring their extension and explain the email password issue to Andy — leaving out a confession about what Stuart received in his inbox.

Barely two minutes later Andy arrives at my office. A further minute to update the password on my computer and phone, and he's done.

"I wish everyone else in this building worked with the same efficiency," I remark.

"Early bird and all that," he smiles. "If you'd left it another half-hour, I doubt I'd have got here so quickly."

"Well, thank you, Andy. I feel better now it's sorted."

A tick to my list, and a pat on the back for the IT department.

With limited enthusiasm, I return to my now-secure list of emails and start slowly working through them. Only when I hear chatter from the main office do I notice the time.

Ben then pokes his head around the door; his hipster beard particularly well-groomed today.

"Morning, boss. I thought you might want to know I've just received an email from Natalie — she won't be coming in again."

"What's today's excuse?"

"Have you already had breakfast?"

"Err, yes."

"Good. Apparently, she puked up in her car so violently she shat herself. Didn't even make it off the driveway."

"How unnecessarily graphic."

"I agree, but I think she's telling the truth."

"What leads you to that conclusion?"

"She sent a photo of her dashboard. I can show you."

"Christ, no. Will she be in tomorrow?"

"Probably."

"Okay. When she does finally grace us with her presence, tell her I'd like a word."

"Will do."

Ben disappears but the mental image of Natalie's dashboard lingers on. If it were anyone else I'd believe them, but it wouldn't surprise me if she staged the photo. A simple can of vegetable soup would do the trick I reckon.

I remind myself I'm due a good day, and I shouldn't let a skiving subordinate spoil it. God-willing, Natalie won't be my problem much longer.

For the next hour I work on a report while intermittently

checking my inbox in case an email from the clinic has slipped through unnoticed.

Then, my mobile rings. I answer while continuing to type with my free hand.

"Kelly Coburn."

"Good morning, Miss Coburn. This is Samantha Barclay from the Demeter Clinic. Have I called at a good time?"

I stop typing.

"Oh, absolutely. Sorry, I was expecting an email rather than a call."

"I can email if you'd rather?"

"No, I'm very happy to talk. Just give me one second."

I dart over to my office door and ensure it's firmly shut.

"Sorry, Samantha. Ready when you are."

After checking my details and asking some routine questions, Samantha launches into a detailed overview of the clinic and its services. I sit and listen with all the intensity of a child gripped by a fairy story; not daring to interrupt as my narrator builds to what I hope is a happy ending.

The moment of truth arrives.

"Based on what you've told me, Kelly, it's definitely worth your while coming in for an initial consultation."

"It is? I mean ... that's great news."

"Please keep in mind it's just the first stage. On paper, you appear a good candidate for our treatment but we won't know for sure until we've conducted tests. It's not necessarily a long road, but it would be amiss of me not to stress there might be unforeseen obstacles."

"Okay. Understood."

My excitement takes a knock when we get on to the subject of dates; the earliest available appointment being three weeks away. I counter that disappointment with some advice Dad once offered. He said: if you call a restaurant at seven o'clock on a Saturday evening and they've got tables free at eight, book elsewhere. I guess high demand is a good sign.

Samantha wraps up the call with a promise to email confirmation later today, along with a medical questionnaire I need to complete before my visit.

I sit quietly for a moment; just staring into space.

I've waited so many years and endured so many false dawns, but it finally feels like I'm on the right path. As Samantha stressed, I'm sure there will be obstacles but I've overcome enough of those in the past and I'm still standing. Whatever shape they take, I'll be ready to face them.

Buoyed by a new-found positivity, I crack on with my report and finish it twenty minutes before I'm due to meet Richard. I leave the office and take a slow walk through the streets, all the while hoping another significant piece of my jigsaw is in place by the time I make the return journey.

Unlike my last visit, I arrive at the offices of Ramsey Rowe & Associates without incident. The receptionist is particularly polite and sees me through to Richard's office where the man himself is waiting.

"Hello, Kelly. Good to see you again."

We shake hands and I'm invited to take a seat.

I've never understood why, but every meeting I've ever attended seems to begin with a smattering of small talk. Every day, countless hours are wasted with idle chit-chat about the weather, social lives, and each participant's general wellbeing.

I smile through Richard's diatribe as he recounts his son's university graduation. I'm sure it was wonderful but I wish he'd hurry the fuck up so we can talk about the reason I'm here.

"Anyway," he says, finally drawing breath. "Shall we get down to business?"

"That'd be great."

He places a document on the desk in front of me.

"That's our standard instruction agreement. I can talk you through it but there's nothing in there which should worry you."

"Okay," I reply, scanning the first page.

"Basically, we have sole rights to sell the land for twelve-months and if we fail to find a buyer who proceeds to completion, you don't owe us a penny."

"Twelve months?"

"If you were selling a house, it'd be a month or two but land transactions are a whole different level of complicated. We need that time to find the right buyer at the best possible price, and to conclude the deal."

"Fair enough. And how confident are you, about finding a buyer?"

"Well, finding a buyer won't be an issue. It's a case of finding a buyer who'll have most sway with the local planners … presuming we go for a deal conditional on planning."

"Err, meaning?"

"We find a buyer and agree a price. Then, contracts are exchanged subject to the necessary planning permission being granted. Once that permission is granted, the buyer has a set period of time to complete the deal — usually four weeks but it's up for negotiation. If they don't get planning, the contract is simply voided or they may make a revised offer."

"Right, that makes sense, I think."

"Don't worry; we'll explain every stage as we go. And keep in mind my company doesn't earn a commission unless we complete a deal, so it's in our interest to see this through as quickly as possible."

"And dare I ask, Richard: how quickly is as quickly as possible?"

"I'd hope you might see the money by early spring next year."

"Oh."

"However, if you need cash sooner, we could revisit the non-conditional option."

"For much less money?"

"That's the choice."

"I'd love to see the money sooner but I'm not in such a hurry I'm willing to sell the land for half its potential value. That option was put to me last week, and I dismissed it."

"It was?" he asks, unable to mask his concern.

"Don't worry. Just something my ex-husband tried to force upon me. It's not happening."

"But the land is in your name only, right?"

"Correct. Forget I mentioned it."

He breathes easy and starts talking me through the contract. It proves as dull as his graduation anecdote.

"And there we have it. So, if you're ready to sign …?"

He hands me a pen.

I sign and date the contract, and hand it back to him.

"Thank you. I'll send you a copy along with the sales particulars as soon as they're prepared."

"And when will that be?"

"No time like the present. I could pop down to the site this afternoon and complete the survey."

"Can you give me twenty-four hours? I need to speak to the tenant."

"Of course. Email me once you've cleared it."

With no subtlety whatsoever, I check my watch — just in case Richard wants to bookend our meeting with more small talk.

"I'd better get back to work. Lot's to do."

"I'll see you out."

By the time I leave Richard's office I've still got half my official lunch hour remaining. I rarely take the whole hour but I'm peckish. A short walk to my favourite sandwich shop is in order so I set off with a spring in my step.

My good fortune continues as there's no queue when I arrive. Once my order is ready, I decide to eat it at one of the tables outside rather than at my desk. It'll give me ten minutes of uninterrupted peace to consider what I discussed with Richard.

I can't say I fully understood everything from our meeting but he clearly knows what he's doing. One part made perfect sense, though, and if his estimate is correct, I could have the money in my bank account by March next year — only nine months away, ironically. My initial appointment at the clinic is the first of July and from what Samantha said, it could take a month or two before any treatment starts.

Despite promising myself I wouldn't, potential birth dates start tumbling through my mind. If I fell pregnant in September, I'd be due in May next year. Like the woman in the store, I'd have to suffer an alcohol-free Christmas but at least I wouldn't have to carry the baby through the heat of the summer months — hellish, I'm told.

The only issue is cost. I presume the clinic will require the cost of the treatment in advance so I might need to get a short-term loan.

I'm about to grab my phone and start searching loan options when an invisible force grasps my wrist. Not for the first time, I've set my mind free and allowed it to wander too far into the future. This is a habit I've got to break or I'll drive myself insane over the coming months. This plan has so many moving parts; some of which I barely understand yet, let alone have control over.

Patience. Patience. Patience.

I finish my sandwich and switch back into work mode. Better to focus on events I can influence rather than those I can't.

A quick time check and I realise I've only got eight minutes of my lunch hour remaining. Needing to get a wiggle on, I set off on a post-lunch power walk back to the office. By the time I reach the lifts I'm in desperate need of a moist towelette and a swig of Gaviscon.

I reach my floor with a minute to spare. There's little chance anyone is keeping tabs on my time-keeping but it's a matter of principle. I can hardly bollock members of my team for being late if I don't set a good example.

Still flush from my exertions, I enter the open plan office and slow to a standstill. Only a third of my team are at their desks dealing with calls. The rest are gathered around Ben's desk; staring at his monitor with their backs to me. I don't like to be presumptuous but I suspect they're not gathered to view the company's latest shareholder report. Pound to a penny they're looking at some childish crap on YouTube or the like.

Quietly as I can, I edge towards the back of the pack so I can catch them doing what they're not supposed to be. The company frowns upon employees viewing social media websites on their work computers. I'm okay with them having a quick look while on their lunch break but not when it involves two-thirds of my team being away from their desks.

I get within a few feet and they're so engrossed with whatever is on the screen, not one of them notices my approach. Most are also sniggering which only confirms my suspicions. Ideally, I need to see what they're looking at before I administer a group bollocking. I take a step to the right and crane my neck to catch a glimpse of the screen. It's enough to confirm they're looking at Facebook; the layout and colour scheme now ingrained in our collective psyche.

I duck and crane in an attempt to see what's so entertaining but I'm too far away and the view too fleeting to tell. It doesn't really matter as I've seen all I needed to see.

Taking a few steps back, I clear my throat.

They react like a mob of meerkats. Postures straighten and every head abruptly turns in my direction; the prey realising a fraction too late the predator is upon them.

"Get back to your desks!" I bark. "Now!"

They do as instructed but their initial surprise at being caught quickly gives way to more sniggering and smirk swapping. I turn my attention to the main culprit, just in time to catch Ben switching browser tabs.

He turns and looks up from his chair as I stride towards him.

"Switch that back," I demand.

"Err, it was nothing, boss."

"Seeing as you're so keen to share it with everyone in the office, wouldn't it be rude to exclude me?"

"I'm sorry, honestly. It won't happen again."

"I know it won't, but I still want to see it."

There's only one way to ensure it won't happen again, and that's for the whole team to realise I'll willingly use shame to make my point. Unfortunately for Ben, the bulk of that shame is heading his way; not least because he should know better as team leader.

"I need to get on," he whines. "Can we just let it go?"

"No, we can't. Show me what you were all watching."

"Please, boss …"

"Last chance, Ben. Show me, or it'll be a verbal warning."

He deflates, and with obvious reluctance turns to face the

screen. A click of the mouse and the Facebook page reappears.

"I'm really sorry," he repeats.

I lean over to get a closer look. Only then do I realise it isn't Ben's Facebook page, but mine. The last post on my news feed is at the top of the screen but I don't recognise the dark image.

"What's so fascinating about my Facebook page, Ben?"

He turns to me; his face scarlet red.

"You really need to view it in the privacy of your office."

"Why?"

"Just trust me. I'll take whatever punishment I'm due but I guarantee you'll be better off checking it in your office."

"Fine. I'll do that, and then we can have a little chat."

I turn on my heels and make for my office. I'm tempted to slam the door for extra effect but resist.

Flopping down in my chair, I open a web browser and click the shortcut to Facebook. My news feed pops up on the screen and I lean in to study the image that everyone found so fascinating. On closer inspection, it's not an image at the top of my news feed, but a video.

Perturbed how it even got there, I click the play icon.

18.

Within a second, the dark screen brightens a fraction to reveal a scene I've already seen one too many times in recent days.

"Ohh, fuck," I blurt.

Worse still, I'm not looking at a photo of myself lying naked in bed at Kensall Gardens, but actual video footage. Just like the photo, the resolution is poor, as is the lighting, but anyone who knows me would recognise the face which is now looking towards the ceiling.

The scene triggers a long-forgotten memory. As it arrives, my blood runs cold.

Horrified, I watch on as a pixelated hand glides slowly down my naked body. It comes to rest between my legs, and there it stays.

Living in a sexless marriage, I occasionally indulged in a spot of self-gratification but always in the shower or beneath the duvet — except this one time. The reason I remember it so well is that it happened on a sweltering summer night and I'd been out to a friend's hen night. Nathan was away on business and I returned home with a belly full of prosecco and a head full of male strippers; our entertainment for the evening.

The figure I don't want to be me rolls on to her side. She opens a drawer in the bedside table.

"No ... no ... no."

I've seen enough. I pause the video just as the figure rolls onto her back, brandishing a bright pink vibrator.

My eyes skip to the timer and my stomach turns; I've only watched two minutes of the twenty-minute video. Without being reminded, I know what follows — eighteen minutes of graphic footage I wouldn't wish to share with my best friend, let alone my work colleagues.

I can't move. I remain trapped in a state of denial; just staring at the screen.

This can't be happening.

The sound of laughter bleeds under the door from the main office. It lights a fuse which in turn detonates enough anger to break my trance.

With a shaky hand, I snatch at my mouse and drag the cursor to the video. Two clicks and it's deleted. Easy enough, but no amount of clicking will delete the humiliation waiting for me beyond these walls.

My mobile rings.

I can't think of a single living soul I want to talk to right now — except the one ringing me.

Still shaking, I accept Martha's call.

"Hi," I whimper.

"What the fuck is that on your Facebook page?" she screams down the line.

"It's gone now. I've deleted it."

"Oh, my God, chick. I … Jesus … what were you thinking?"

"What? You think I posted it?" I reply, incredulous.

"Sorry … of course not. Who did?"

"I don't know who or how, and I didn't even know I was being recorded."

"Shit. Seriously?"

"I don't have time to explain the full story but someone got hold of security camera footage from the house in Kensall Gardens."

"Bloody hell, that's awful. You need to contact the police."

"I will, but for now I've got a bigger issue to contend with."

I then explain how I discovered the new addition to my Facebook page, and that I'm currently imprisoned in my office behind bars of shame.

"You've only got one option," Martha suggests. "Face it full on."

"Easy for you to say. On the opposite side of my door are two-dozen colleagues who just watched me enjoying a drunken wank."

"So what? It's only as humiliating as you allow it to be but the longer you hide, the harder it'll get."

"What do you suggest I do?"

She offers her advice. I don't know if I can pull it off but, faced with no other option, besides taking up permanent residence in my office, I reluctantly confirm I'll give it a go.

"Trust me," she adds. "This will blow over by the end of the day."

"God, I hope you're right."

"But before you face them, change your bloody Facebook password."

"I will."

"And contact the police. Whoever posted that video has broken the law."

I'm not sure the police will be able to help, but Martha is right — as embarrassing as it might be, I have to report it.

"One other thing," she adds.

"Yes?"

"I love that duvet cover. Where did you get it?"

As always, Martha makes me laugh when I really feel like crying.

We agree to chat on the phone this evening when we'll both have more time. I let her get back to work and end the call.

I immediately go through the motions of changing my Facebook password and just as I complete the process, another round of laughter booms from beyond the door. It's all the motivation I need.

Closing Facebook, I log-in to our call management system and set it to divert all incoming calls to voicemail. I also block all outgoing calls as I need my entire team's undivided attention. I wait a few minutes to ensure any existing calls are over; using the time to prepare myself.

I get up and stride across my office. One deep breath and I open the door.

Immediately, every set of eyes is upon me.

"Listen up, folks," I call out. "I need your attention for two minutes."

Silence.

I clear my throat and summon my inner-Martha.

"There will be no repercussions, but please put your hand up if you saw the illegally filmed video of me on Facebook?"

At first, they all just glance at each other until I make eye contact with Ben and he leads the way. Others soon follow until nearly every hand is in the air.

"Thank you for your honesty. Now, I need you to keep your hands raised for a second."

I pause for a moment and offer a silent prayer no one from senior management walks in.

"Keep your hand raised if you've never masturbated. And I mean, never."

More than a few red faces stare back at me but one-by-one, every hand comes down.

"Great," I smile. "So, we've all knocked one out, right?"

I'm met with a ripple of embarrassed sniggers.

"Would any of you be happy if someone posted a video of you enjoying a … private moment?"

Heads shake and a few of them appear genuinely appalled at the thought.

"So, I'm sure you can appreciate I'm far from happy. I can't do anything about it but I'm not ashamed about what I do in the privacy of my own bedroom. With that, can we all agree to forget it and move on?"

Murmurs of agreement.

"Thank you. Any questions?"

I scan the room but nobody bites.

"Okay, let's get back to work, and if anyone wants to know the make and model of that vibrator, drop me an email. As you probably gathered, it's bloody good."

My parting remark is met with universal laughter, and perhaps relief I never asked them to share their own wank-related anecdotes.

I return to my desk and switch the phones back on.

There's no doubt I'll remain the butt of staffroom jokes for a while yet, but I've salvaged enough pride I can still face my colleagues. Now I can begin the post-mortem. It begins by accepting my own culpability. Why didn't I find time this morning to deal with the second item on my own to-do list? If

I'd changed all those bloody passwords, this never would have happened.

Belatedly, I spend the next half-hour updating the password on every website I regularly use. I know I'll have to update every app on my phone but that can wait until tonight.

Once that task is complete, I turn my attention to the root cause — Nathan.

As much as I'd like to call him and vent, it'll do no good. Besides, when I said I didn't want to speak to him ever again, I meant it.

Rather than waste my breath on Nathan, I decide to take Martha's advice and speak to someone with the power to address my problem. I call the non-emergency number for the police.

I'm put on hold for several minutes before choosing which constabulary I wish to talk to. A man then answers, confirming his name as PC Walker. I explain the situation.

"It's your ex-husband being blackmailed?" he confirms.

"Correct."

"In which case, he really should contact us and report it."

"That's what I told him, but he claims there's no point because the blackmailer is virtually untraceable."

"I'm afraid your ex-husband makes a valid point. Cybercrimes of this nature are notoriously difficult to deal with as the perpetrators are usually in a different country and hidden behind a complex maze of anonymous IP addresses."

"Surely there's something you can do?"

"I'm not making excuses but there are more than three million cybercrimes reported every year, and that number is growing. We simply don't have the resources to investigate all of them."

"Great. So what can I do?"

"You did the right thing in updating all your passwords, but I'm afraid there's not much else anyone can do; particularly if your ex-husband is unwilling to report the crime."

"But you think he'd be wasting his time?"

"I never said that — we take all reported crimes seriously. If I were in his shoes, I'd ignore the threats but that's just my view."

"He's concerned they'll publish confidential material they downloaded from the computer."

"To what end? If they do, they no longer have any leverage. Take your video for example: now they've aired it, there isn't much they can do with it. Because of the content, Facebook, and all other social media platforms would have removed it pretty sharpish even if you hadn't deleted it."

"They could email it to people I know."

"Possibly, but if your husband is the target and you're now divorced, they'll be wasting their time."

"I'm not sure they know we're divorced."

"Then your ex-husband should tell them, just before he tells them he won't be paying a penny. If he makes it abundantly clear he doesn't have the money, they'll likely move on to someone who has. To them, it's just business and they don't want to waste time chasing money that isn't there."

"Some business."

"The joys of the Internet," he sighs. "But again, I would stress your ex-husband needs to call us so we can discuss his options. I'm only talking in general terms."

"Noted."

"And one final point: if the threat to you or your ex-husband develops beyond a demand for money, you must call us. I understand what happened to you with the photo and video must have been horrendous, but physical threats are a different matter."

"You think they might start making physical threats?"

"As I said, it's highly unlikely they're in the country so I wouldn't worry too much."

PC Walker then adds my details to the system and puts a note on the file outlining our conversation.

"Your call has now been logged and if you've any concerns about your physical safety, or the incidents escalate in any way, please call us again — same goes for your ex-husband."

"Right. Thanks for your time."

He ends the call.

I hate to admit it but perhaps Nathan was right — there's little the police can do. However, PC Walker has confirmed my view he should just tell them he's skint, and they'll move on. I can't imagine there's anything else on that computer worse than my solo antics in the bedroom, so it's not even my problem.

I check my Facebook page again, just in case I've received any messages from concerned friends who might have seen the video. I've no idea when it was posted but it wasn't there when I checked Facebook on the bus this morning. Fingers crossed the audience only extended as far as Ben and Martha. It's a shame one of them shared it with all my colleagues but Ben will get his comeuppance soon enough.

Just to be sure, I also check my phone for messages. Nothing.

I'd like to breathe a sigh of relief but I'm not feeling it. At best, I've limited the damage but it'll take several days for my cringe-switch to stop tripping. I need to keep my mind distracted, and a good starting point is a conversation with my tenant.

The initial reception is frosty, and Donald's tone doesn't get any warmer when I tell him a surveyor will visit the yard tomorrow. He objects until I remind him he hasn't had a single rent review in all the years he's been using the yard. The threat of tripled rent for the remaining three months of his lease is enough to gain his cooperation, albeit begrudgingly.

I email Richard to confirm he can conduct his survey tomorrow, and not to expect a sunny reception.

With my to-do list complete I return my attention to the work I should be doing. An email from Justin arrives, requesting my thoughts on a number of key issues he has identified for our department. It's a series of questions which all lead down the same path: how can we increase productivity and profits, while spending less? Nothing is static in the corporate world — there are always new opportunities to gain and efficiencies to make. A constant demand for more, for less.

Still, Justin's request is the perfect way to dull my mind. More than any report I've previously compiled, I throw myself into it and the rest of the afternoon passes in a blur of spreadsheets and statistics.

By the time I switch off my computer, the office is silent.
It's Monday, and I shouldn't, but God, I need a stiff drink.

19.

Like most kids, I have to thank Disney for creating my favourite childhood movie. On my ninth birthday, I unwrapped a VHS cassette of *Flight of the Navigator* and watched it so many times the tape eventually wore out. However, my first experience of a Disney movie left less of a positive impression.

I must have been four or five when I first watched *Fantasia* and I probably enjoyed it until the scene where Mickey Mouse casts his first spell and brings a broom to life. Mickey then falls asleep and wakes up to an entire army of brooms; marching relentlessly with buckets of water in hand.

Coupled with the slightly sinister musical score, it scared the living shit out of me. Nightmares followed.

Perhaps it was the two bottles of wine, but I relived those nightmares last night; my subconscious mind swapping brooms for giant pink vibrators.

Lying in my sunlit bedroom, I can still picture them. Terrifying, yet strangely erotic.

Best I get up.

In the kitchen, I open the back door.

"Fancy a headache, Frank? I've got one going spare."

He trots in and jumps straight up onto the table.

"Suit yourself."

Feeling a bit queasy, I fork tuna into a bowl while holding my breath. I then make a coffee and sit down just as Frank finishes. He looks at me expectantly.

"Forget it. The kitchen is closed."

I turn my attention to the laptop which is still open on the table. Memories of an email I sent last night return. There really should be some kind of mechanism which stops people using electronic communication devices when they're under the influence.

I blame Martha.

We had an hour-long chat during which I brought her up-to-speed with Nathan's situation. Martha has never been his biggest fan and by the time I told her how the moron set-up security cameras without my knowledge, and then facilitated the contents of our computer hard drive being stolen, she was positively enraged.

I think we may have then discussed a revenge plan which included her popping round his flat and pissing through the letterbox, but we agreed it would involve a level of physical dexterity my friend isn't blessed with, and a scathing email might be easier.

With a degree of trepidation, I wake the laptop to see exactly what we composed.

Nathan,

Firstly, Martha sends her love. Not really, she thinks you're a massive bellend.

Thanks to your stupidity, I had a humiliating experience at work today as your blackmailing friends posted a video of me on Facebook. I called the police and told them what a tool my ex-husband is, and they agreed. They say you shouldn't pay those arseholes another penny (told you so). They also said you should report it — I don't care one way or another but I won't be bailing you out.

You need to make it 100% clear we're divorced and targeting me won't get them anywhere. If I have any more nasty surprises, including visits by your creepy friend, I'll hire a lawyer and sue your arse. I've got the money and I'll gladly spend it taking you to the cleaners.

Kelly — your gratefully ex-wife.

PS: Martha still thinks you're a massive bellend.

PPS: So do I. Don't bother replying.

"Oops," I chuckle to myself.

Unsurprisingly, he hasn't replied.

Maybe I could have worded it a little better but I'm glad Martha convinced my tipsy self to send it. Nathan brought this on himself so why should I suffer? Now there can be no doubt he's on his own.

Frank completes his clean-up and pads across the table. A change from my shins, he rubs his forehead against mine.

"Never get married, Frank" I whisper.

On reflection, I don't think he's the settling-down type.

I waste five minutes enjoying my ginger friend's affections before I notice the time. I'm running late.

"Sorry, mate. Some of us have got work."

By the time I return, Frank has gone. I'm relieved as I hate shooing him out of the house.

I've just got time to swallow a couple of painkillers before darting out the door.

As I make my way to the bus stop, I make a pact with myself. Now I've set the wheels in motion with the yard, and the clinic, I should pour all my energies into work and not get carried away by distractions; good or bad. Hopefully, my drunken email has dealt with the bad, but I don't want to tempt fate by obsessing over baby plans. I've done all I can and now I need to be patient.

I arrive at the bus stop just in time and filter on in last position. There's a free seat near the front, next to a pension-age woman who looks the type who enjoys nattering with strangers. I plug my headphones in before sitting down but flash her a half-smile, just to be polite.

As the bus pulls away, I dare to check Facebook and jab the phone screen.

It's exactly how I left it — full of inane crap I posted when either bored or drunk, or both. I close the app and question if it's even worth having a Facebook account. If yesterday taught me anything, it's that my so-called friends pay no attention to anything I post. The more I think about it, what is the point of Facebook at all?

By the time I disembark, I still don't have an answer.

I'm greeted by more inane crap as I sit down at my desk and survey the list of emails. Frankly, I'm grateful. If life for the next few weeks continues on the same mundane path, I'll be a happy girl. I just want normality.

I spend a contented half-hour answering emails when there's a knock at the door, and Ben appears.

"Um, morning," he says coyly.

"Yes?"

"Three of the team have called in sick today, including Natalie. I thought you'd want to know."

"Email me the names."

"Sure."

"And we need to have a chat."

"Yeah, I thought we might."

"No time like the present. Sit down."

The last time I saw anyone approach a desk so unenthusiastically it was for a religious education lesson in secondary school. Ben flops down in the chair and looks everywhere but at me.

"You okay, Ben? You look a little peaky."

"No, I'm fine."

His cheeks flush red.

"Are you uncomfortable, after yesterday?"

"A bit, maybe."

"Which part are you uncomfortable with? Seeing the video, or being caught showing it to the entire team?"

"Both."

No one has gawked at his genitalia so I've little sympathy.

"Why do you feel uncomfortable?"

"It's, err … you know, just a bit embarrassing."

"Nope, I don't know. Tell me why it's embarrassing."

If I'd asked him to visualise his parents having sex, he couldn't cringe any more.

"I, um … I shouldn't have shown the others. I am sorry, honestly. It was stupid, and childish."

"Yes it was, and you accept I have to issue a reprimand, right?"

He looks to his lap, and slowly nods.

"Ignoring my humiliation, that video was wholly inappropriate material for the workplace. If I speak to HR, they'll almost certainly insist I fire you."

"Eh? Oh, please. I can't lose this job."

I ignore his pleading and slowly tap the desk with a pen while I consider his fate.

"Okay, Ben, here's what I propose."

"Yes?"

"When I was a teenager, my Dad caught me and my best friend smoking behind the garden shed one evening. As a punishment, he made us both smoke three cigarettes, one after another. We were sick as dogs, and even now the smell of cigarette smoke turns my stomach, but his lesson worked because neither of us touched a cigarette again."

"Err, okay."

"So, I'm prepared to teach you a similar lesson, rather than report you to HR."

"And how will that work?"

"Every morning for the next month, I'll expect you in my office at eight-thirty sharp. You'll then watch that video in its entirety."

I stare at Ben impassive, while he picks his jaw up from the floor.

"Are … what? You're joking, right?"

"Do I look like I'm joking?"

The cogs whir. What a choice: the sack, or watching a homemade porno featuring his middle-aged boss, every morning.

He puts his head in his hands.

"Well, Ben. What's it to be?"

He looks up. Remarkably, his face is even redder than before.

"Shit, boss. I'm so sorry, but I don't know … Jesus, how awkward will it be … I can't …"

I let him squirm and stammer a few seconds longer before putting him out of his misery.

"Enough," I interrupt. "Of course I'm bloody joking."

"Oh, sweet Jesus," he pants, holding his chest. "Thank you."

"Consider yourself reprimanded, and I hope you've learnt a lesson."

"Trust me, boss, I have."

"Good. Now, get back to work."

He can't get out of my office quick enough.

Ben is typical of twenty-something men in that his laddish bravado is paper thin. Scratch away at the surface and you'll usually expose a layer of insecurity and inexperience. This is a subject Martha and I have discussed at length and we concluded young men are like puppies. They might be cute, full of energy and willing to please but they require way too much training. At our age, we don't have the time or patience for that shit.

No, give me a wily old hound any day.

Still sporting a wry smile, I get on.

For the next three hours, phones ring, emails arrive, and I shuffle paperwork around my desk. All in all, a blissfully uneventful morning. I decide to celebrate with a stroll to the sandwich shop.

As I leave my office, a few of the more juvenile team members can't help but look in my direction and smirk to themselves. I return a glare and they quickly look away. We'll see if they're still smiling next time they want to book a day off.

A minute into my stroll, I pass a clothes store and a particularly hideous outfit in the window catches my eye. It serves as a reminder I need to buy a few outfits for our girl's weekend in September. I'm led to believe it's customary to dress up in nineties attire but that presents a problem. Unlike the sixties, seventies, and eighties, I'm not sure the nineties had a distinctive style. There was plenty of stonewashed denim early in the decade but by the time Britpop came along, fashion moved to the middle of the road.

An alarming thought occurs.

She hasn't mentioned it but I guarantee Martha will suggest we dress as the Spice Girls. She'll bag Scary, on account of her wild hair and wilder mouth, Jennie will want to be Baby because she's cute and blonde, and Rachel will undoubtedly choose Posh because she's stick thin and loves a little black dress.

I'd bet my last quid Martha has me down for Geri, for no other reason than my hair colour. And if I'm to be Ginger Spice, that means wearing a Union Jack dress which will barely cover my lady parts. I know I'll have to face the same question from dozens of pissed-up idiots: do the collar and cuffs match?

Sod that. I'm going to be Sporty. At my age, jogging pants and a vest top are a far more sensible, and forgiving, option.

I arrive at the sandwich shop and place my order. With their usual efficiency, a tray soon arrives and I head back outside to nab one of the few remaining tables.

The bacon and Brie sandwich is delicious, as is the blueberry muffin I scoff for dessert. It's a shame they never had a Tubby Spice as I reckon I could pull that off by September; particularly if I don't temper my wine intake.

Stomach full, I sit and sip my coffee while browsing fancy dress outfits on eBay. There's slim picking for the nineties unless I fancy going as MC Hammer.

Out of the corner of my eye, I notice a hand grab the chair opposite. It's not unusual for solo diners to share a table when it's busy so I keep my eyes on the phone, knowing I'll be leaving soon and they can have the table to themselves. I definitely don't wish to start a conversation with a stranger.

"Hello, Kelly."

My head snaps up but I already know who the voice belongs to. Kenneth.

20.

"You again?"

"Yes, it's me."

I put my phone away and stand up.

"Why won't you leave me alone?" I hiss.

"Please, sit down. All I ask of you is five minutes of your time."

"Why?"

"Because it is imperative you hear what I have to say. Again, I mean you no harm."

I weigh up my options: walk away, call the police, or hear him out. If I walk away he'll likely reappear again, and if I call the police what can they do? He hasn't threatened me and as we're in a public place, I can scream for help if needs be. My gut instinct is to walk away but this might also be an opportunity to put an end to this.

I sit down.

"Listen to me, Kenneth, or whatever your name is, I've already told Nathan I'm not bailing him out so you're wasting your time."

"Nathan Thaw?"

"Yes, Nathan Thaw. Who else?"

"Your former husband, I believe?"

"You know full well who Nathan is … considering he told you to stalk me."

"No, that's inaccurate."

"Which part?"

"I've never met Nathan Thaw, but I do know you were once married to him."

"I didn't say you'd met him. I said he told you to … I don't know … freak me out."

"I've never had any communication with Mr Thaw and it certainly isn't my intention to freak you out."

His warm tone of voice adds credibility to his statement.

"What do you want then? Wait … are you hitting on me?"

"Hitting on you? I'm not sure what that means."

"You know ... trying to chat me up."

"Oh, I see. You want to know if my intentions are romantically inclined, correct?"

"Actually, I'm not sure I do."

"Rest assured, Kelly. My interest in you is purely platonic."

"Interest? Meaning?"

My question hangs as he takes a sip from the cup I hadn't noticed until now. His face puckers and the cup returns to the table.

"Coffee must be an acquired taste," he remarks. "I'm not sure I understand the mass appeal."

"Screw the coffee. What did you mean by 'interest'?"

Sitting forward, he takes a furtive glance at our fellow diners as if he's about to share state secrets.

"The last time we met, in the shopping centre, I imparted some advice. Do you recall?"

"Advice? I took it as a threat."

"Really?" he frowns. "Perhaps I need to work on my social skills. I apologise."

"You said fate has sent me on a path I mustn't follow, and I should change direction."

"My intention was to warn, not threaten."

"Warn me of what exactly?"

He moves his coffee cup and rests his arms on the table.

"I had hoped we'd never have this conversation, Kelly, but now we are, I'll attempt to explain in the simplest terms I can."

"Thanks. Being a mere woman, I love it when a man makes things simple for me to understand."

"You're most welcome."

My sarcasm appears to have missed its target. He continues.

"Why do people walk their dog on a leash?"

"Eh? What a strange question."

"Humour me, please."

"To stop the dog running off, I suppose."

"Potentially running into harm's way, correct?"

"I guess so."

"Let's imagine a chap is walking his dog without a leash. The dog sees a cat on the opposite pavement and, despite being commanded to stay, it instinctively runs across the road, putting its life in danger. You can train a dog to obey certain commands but they don't have the mental capacity to understand why those commands are important — it simply follows its instincts."

"Are you going somewhere with this?"

"My point is: I cannot explain why you shouldn't follow a certain path because you wouldn't understand or accept my reasoning. However, I can put you on a metaphoric leash so you follow the right path. Do you understand?"

"I understand that's one of the most offensive analogies I've ever heard. You're comparing me to a dog?"

"No, I'm just confirming the situation. If I don't guide you in a certain direction, the consequences could be dire."

"Right, we're back to threats again? If you've got something to say, how about not guiding me but telling me straight?"

"I wish I could tell you but such candour would likely cause problems for us both."

I could ask for the specifics of those problems but they're of less relevance than the purpose of this discussion; a purpose I still don't understand.

"As interesting as this is, Ken, I'm ..."

"My name is Kenneth," he interjects. "Not Ken, nor Kenny. Kenneth."

"Whatever. You said it's imperative we talk but all I've heard are veiled threats and a highly offensive analogy. I think we're done here."

"Excellent," he says brightly. "We're in agreement."

"I ... what?"

He then delves a hand inside his jacket and extracts a small box wrapped in silver paper. He places it on the table in front of me.

"What's that?" I ask.

"It's your leash."

"My what?"

"It'll ensure you follow the right path."

He then gets to his feet.

"Goodbye, Kelly. I sincerely hope our paths never cross again … for both our sakes."

Before I can shake off the confusion and react, he strides away. I'm caught in two minds whether to follow him or run away in the opposite direction. Ultimately, I do neither and watch him disappear around the corner on the opposite side of the street.

My attention turns to the box he left on the table.

For a second or two I contemplate leaving it where it is and heading back to work. However, Kenneth's denial of any involvement with Nathan is even more worrying than my initial assumption — at least I understood his motivation then. He's already left me with too many unanswered questions and unwrapping his gift is likely to add more. Reason enough to leave it on the table.

But what if it contains answers?

One thing is for sure: just staring at it won't help. Open it, or leave it?

I compromise and snatch it from the table. It's light, about the size of a cigarette packet, and the wrapping precise; no misaligned edges or stray sticky tape. Shaking it doesn't offer any clue to the contents.

Sod it.

I tear the wrapping away to reveal a nondescript white box with a folded slip of paper attached to the lid. After carefully peeling it away, I unfold the note to reveal a single sentence written in blue ink: *If you want to know, come find me — Kenneth.*

Know what?

My curiosity now piqued, I remove the lid.

"What the …"

I lean in to double-check I'm looking at what I think I'm looking at: a coin-sized medallion atop a blue satin cushion. The simple piece of jewellery is unremarkable in every way, except the mermaid-like figure etched on to the medallion — Amphitrite: the goddess of the sea.

The only reason I know who Amphitrite is, and that I'm looking at her image, is because I spent weeks looking for a present for my dad's fiftieth birthday. The perfect gift for a man who loved the ocean proved to be a silver medallion featuring the goddess of the sea — the exact-same silver medallion I'm now staring at.

I swallow hard and remind myself this cannot be Dad's medallion. It's in pristine condition and Dad wore his every day for three years — up until he, and the medallion, disappeared in the middle of the English Channel. The question is: how in God's name would Kenneth have known Dad owned an identical medallion, or that I gifted it to him? And why give me a copy?

I put the lid back on the box and drop it into my handbag; keeping hold of the note. I read the sentence over and over again: *If you want to know, come find me.*

Before I opened his gift, I had questions. Now, I have a savage yearning for answers. Whatever Kenneth is playing at, he's tapped into a vein which leads to the very core of my heart. He has made it impossible for me not to follow his instructions, but why, and what happens if and when I find him? Surely if he wanted to tell me something, he could have told me five minutes ago. What possible reason is there for dragging me into this ridiculous quest? Is it even a quest, or a game? Am I being played? Is this some sick joke with my Dad's death the punchline?

"Are you nearly done?" a voice asks.

I turn and look up at two women; one holding a tray.

"Oh, um, yes. Sorry."

I grab Kenneth's note and vacate the table.

A million questions chase me all the way back to the office; snapping at my heels in the foyer, tugging at my skirt in the lift, and whispering in my ear as I seek sanctuary in my office. No matter what I do to avoid them, they keep coming. I stare at spreadsheets, compile emails, make calls — every action haunted by a chorus of voices in my head.

By mid-afternoon, I've got a fair idea how insanity feels. I need to talk to someone.

I text Martha, asking if I can drop by after work for a chat. She replies within ten minutes and suggests I join them for dinner as I haven't seen the girls in a few weeks. I'm only too glad to accept the invite.

Knowing I'll be able to share the weight of the questions later, I'm just about able to keep them at bay for the remainder of the afternoon. It's not so easy on the bus, even with music blaring in my headphones.

I arrive at my friend's house just after six and ring the bell. Excited screams echo down the hallway, growing louder until the door swings open.

"Auntie Kell! Auntie Kell!"

Ella and Millie are miniature doppelgangers of their mother; the same fizzing energy and wild blonde hair. I'm almost knocked off my feet as they both throw their arms around me.

"Your new hair is lovely," Millie says. "Really cool."

"Thank you, poppet. I'm sure you two have grown a foot since I saw you last."

"No, we've still got two each," Ella replies, looking down just to be sure.

"Your height," I chuckle. "It won't be long until you're both taller than me."

"Does that mean we can borrow your clothes?" Millie asks.

"Only if I can borrow yours."

"Yes!" they scream in unison. "We'll go choose some."

Before I can argue, they dash off upstairs. I've no idea what's in fashion with eight-year-old girls at the moment but I suspect I'll find out soon enough.

My co-host appears at the end of the hallway.

"Oh, um. Hi, Stuart."

"Hey, Kelly."

I've been so preoccupied thinking about Kenneth's gift, the photo which landed in Stuart's inbox had completely escaped my mind. Now recaptured, I can't ignore it.

"I, err, owe you an apology."

"Do you? What for?"

"That email."

"Oh, right," he smiles. "It's forgotten, honestly. Martha explained."

I suppose I should be grateful Stuart doesn't have a Facebook account. The nude photo was bad enough but if he'd seen the video, I'd never have been able to set foot in this house again.

"Thank you, and if you need me to pay for counselling, just ask."

He laughs, and Martha appears in the doorway before the situation becomes awkward.

"Hey, chick. Come on through."

Stuart heads upstairs to see what carnage the girls are creating while I follow Martha into the kitchen. My handbag has barely touched the work surface when a glass of wine is thrust at me.

"I'm supposed to be cutting back," I plead, half-heartedly. "But one glass won't hurt, I suppose."

"Are you still suffering from last night?"

"A bit. I don't know how I got through two bottles on my own."

"You were a bit squiffy. Have you heard anything from knobhead?"

"Not a peep. I can't imagine why."

"You remember the email then?"

"I didn't until I read it this morning. You're a terrible influence."

"Hey, I only helped a bit."

"Hmm ... it had your fingerprints all over it."

"It was a collaborative effort. We were like Elton John and Bernie Taupin."

"I don't think any of Elton's songs mention a massive bellend, do they?"

"There's still time."

It's such a relief to giggle but I know it's only a temporary release.

"Dinner will be ten minutes. It's just lasagne, I'm afraid."

"I love a good lasagne."

"I never said it was good. Just pray it's edible."

I help Martha lay the table while we swap small talk. She asks what I wanted to chat about but the girls come bursting into the kitchen before I get the chance to answer. Probably no bad thing as it won't be a five-minute conversation.

Stuart manages to corral his offspring to the table where they argue which one will sit next to me. I drag a chair around the table and sit between them.

"There. Now you can both have the pleasure of my company."

"What's your favourite colour, Auntie Kell?" Ella asks.

"Oh, err, I'll have to think about that. What's yours?"

"Minty buff."

"Gosh, that makes a change from pink."

"Mine is gingerbread dreams," Millie declares.

"They've been studying a paint colour chart," Stuart adds. "We're thinking about redecorating the hallway."

"Not thinking," Martha frowns. "Doing."

"Yes, honey. Doing."

We settle down to eat although the chatter and the chuckling continues. I adore Martha's little family and although I'd never tell her, I'm deeply envious. For all the squabbling and the mess and the general dysfunction, their home brims with love and laughter. I'm blessed to be part of it, and spending time with them reinforces how much I want a slice of family life for myself.

After a double-helping of chocolate ice-cream for dessert, I spend half-an-hour in the lounge with the girls while Martha and Stuart clear up the kitchen. Unsurprisingly, none of their clothes fit me so they restyle my make-up instead.

Martha enters.

"It's nearly pyjama time, girls."

They groan and complain but eventually slope off upstairs.

"I'm loving the new look," Martha giggles. "Kind of street prostitute chic."

"Always best to keep your career options open."

"I'll get you some wipes once they're in bed."

"Thanks."

The girls return and we chat about school and dance club and a million other subjects they haphazardly bring up. Just after eight-thirty, Stuart bribes them with the promise of a bedtime story and I kiss them both goodnight.

They leave behind a mess, and a frazzled mother.

"I should probably have told them to tidy up," Martha puffs.

"Why didn't you?"

"Because you're here, they'd take forever. They'd still be pissing around at midnight."

"Cunning."

"That, they are."

She tosses me a pack of make-up wipes and I remove the girl's handiwork.

"So, how's your day been?" she asks. "Any more video-related incidents?"

"Mercifully not. I think my porn career started and ended yesterday afternoon."

"What a nightmare, eh? I can't imagine anything worse than my colleagues watching me enjoy a good old fuddle."

"I wouldn't wish it on my worst enemy but your advice limited the damage. Unfortunately, I've got yet another bloody issue to contend with."

"Oh, Christ. Now what?"

I explain what happened outside the coffee shop, and show Martha the medallion, and Kenneth's note. Her immediate response is to recommend more wine. She dashes out to the kitchen and returns with two glasses.

"Are you sure he's nothing to do with Nathan? It's the kind of twisted mind game he'd play."

"At first, I was positive he was behind it but for the life of me I can't understand why he'd go to such lengths to unsettle me. There's no obvious end game and I don't recall ever mentioning Dad's medallion to him."

"So, not Nathan?"

"Probably not."

"And you're sure this Kenneth guy isn't just some random pervert?"

I pull out my phone and show Martha the photo I snapped in the lift.

"What do you think? Does he look like your average pervert?"

She takes a long, hard look at the photo.

"Was he on his way to a wedding?"

"If you're referring to the flower in his buttonhole, I think it's just his thing. I've met him three times now, and on each occasion he was wearing a fresh lily."

"He looks like a character from Jeeves and Wooster."

"That's not a bad call. He is properly polite, and just … friendly. That's what makes the whole situation so weird. Despite all that nonsense about taking the wrong path, he doesn't come across as threatening."

"Okay, so are you going to find him?"

"That's the thing — how?"

"Is he on Facebook?"

"No idea. I don't know his surname."

"That's you fucked then. How do you find someone without their full name?"

"I could hire a detective."

"You could, and what would they have to go on?"

"Err, not sure."

"Precisely. With the best will in the world, how can you expect a detective to help when you know absolutely nothing about this guy, other than his first name?"

"I guess that also rules out the police."

"I wouldn't have ruled them in to start with. What are you going to say? I'm being stalked by a polite guy in a suit who likes giving me gifts?"

"Hmm … fair point."

We're so in tune with each other's thinking, we simultaneously take a moment to sip wine and ponder.

"Here's a thought," Martha pipes up. "You could just carry on as normal. Pretend you never met the guy."

"I suppose so, but then I'll never know."

"Know what?"

"How he knew about the medallion."

"Does it matter? Is it going to change your life in any discernible way?"

"He said I'm on the wrong path, and by finding him, I'll be back on the right path."

"He said that?"

"More or less."

Martha rolls her eyes and groans.

"What?"

"Don't you see it?" she replies, shaking her head. "He's one of those religious nutters. I bet that path leads to Jesus. Follow it, and the next thing you know you're banging a tambourine and singing *Kumbaya* every weekend."

"It's an unorthodox recruitment strategy, wouldn't you say?"

"Sure, but they've gotta think outside the box these days. They can't just knock on doors or pester folks in the street like they used to."

"I'm not sure …"

"Trust me, chick. Look at that photo again and tell me Kenneth doesn't look like a God-botherer. If I were in your shoes, I'd forget him."

It's clear Martha has made her mind up, and I know from experience she won't back down. To prove my point, she moves the conversation along.

"Anyway, let's discuss a more positive subject."

"Err, like?"

"Our weekend away in September," she grins. "I've been thinking about outfits, and I reckon you'd look amazing in a Union Jack dress."

Ahh, shit.

21.

Four glasses of wine proved just the right amount. Not enough to deliver a hangover but just enough to take the edge off any residual awkwardness when Stuart drove me home.

I went to bed a teeny bit tipsy but this morning I feel the right side of okay.

Martha and I spent the rest of the evening discussing our weekend away: what outfits we'll wear, which acts we absolutely had to see, how much booze we should take. She was as excited as I've ever seen her, and I've seen her at a Robbie Williams gig. Her enthusiasm swept away any further thoughts about Kenneth.

But while my friend might have dismissed the conundrum, I can't shake it off quite so easily.

"What do you think, Frank? Should I persist, or do as Martha suggests and forget it?"

Having already wolfed down his tuna, my guest is preoccupied; licking various parts of his anatomy.

"I'm glad I don't have to wash like you."

He continues without comment.

"Then again, if I could lick certain parts of my body with such ease, I'd never leave the house."

Martha would have laughed. Frank doesn't.

My humour wasted, I leave him to it and get ready for work.

I return to an empty kitchen and lock the back door. With my own advice still rattling in my head, I leave the house intent on having a productive and distracting day at work. Dealing with Natalie's poor attendance, if she's in, might give me something to get my teeth stuck into.

On the bus, I dig into my handbag looking for a compact to check my rushed makeup. The first item I come across is the box containing Kenneth's gift. Before I know it, I've opened it up and I'm staring at the silver medallion; glinting in the morning sunlight as the bus bumps along. The questions I hoped might still be slumbering wake up.

What occurred to me last night, just before I fell asleep, is that it's not a question of whether I follow the advice on Kenneth's note, but how I follow it. Martha's dismissive attitude felt a little harsh, but it wasn't without foundation — I might as well be searching for Jesus.

I put the lid back on and drop the box back in my handbag. The questions can continue to heckle but without a single clue to Kenneth's whereabouts, they're yelling at an empty stage.

An Espresso Frappuccino helps to ease my troubled mind and the awaiting inbox adds another distraction. I'm only halfway through it when Ben knocks at my door.

"Thought you'd want to know, Natalie is back."

"Okay, thanks."

"Better get on," he says hurriedly.

He scoots away before I can muster a reply; perhaps worried I might change my mind and enact the daily video punishment.

I let Natalie sweat by emailing her a request to come and see me at eleven o'clock. She'll already have a meticulous excuse prepared but the wait will test her nerve.

As it is, she knocks at my door five minutes early.

"You wanted to see me?"

"I did. Come in and close the door."

I offer her a seat which she accepts without a word. The tone set, I waste no time on pleasantries.

"I wanted to have a chat about your attendance record."

"What about it?"

"You've had twice as many sick days as the department average."

"Maybe I've been twice as sick as the average team member."

My sweating tactic has failed; Natalie's attitude indifferent.

"Is there something I should know about your health?"

"No."

"So, the company should just allow your less-than-acceptable attendance record, without question?"

"If I'm unwell, I can't work. What would you like me to do?"

"I'd like you to be honest. If there's an underlying reason you're unable to work, we have to know about it."

"That would be a breach of my personal privacy. My contract of employment states I have to follow a set procedure if I'm unable to come in. I only have to explain the reason, but it says nothing about discussing my general health with a line manager."

I find myself at the end of a contractual cul-de-sac.

"Fair enough," I sigh. "It's your life, your career, but at some point the company will require an explanation if your attendance doesn't improve."

"Will that be all?"

"Yes."

She gets up and marches out of my office.

Left to dwell on our short meeting, I can only conclude Natalie probably hates me. It's not the first time I've inspired such a negative emotion.

Back in infant school, I accidentally knocked a glass of water over a painting one of my classmates had spent all afternoon working on. Tina McMahon — spiteful little cow — said I was a clumsy idiot, and she hated me. I was so upset I cried all the way home. Dad tried to comfort me through the medium of pickled onions. I detested pickled onions, and still do, but he told me I'd find them on the shelves of every supermarket because plenty of people loved them. To further his point, he said lots of people hated jam roly-poly; my favourite pudding. He made me realise that people hate and love for different reasons, and sometimes those reasons make no sense to us.

I don't like pickled onions and Natalie Barnett doesn't like me. Neither of us are likely to change our position so it's senseless fretting about it.

Putting the encounter to the back of my mind, I make a start on the pile of paperwork stacking up in my in-tray. I loathe dealing with paperwork but I've no one to blame but myself for getting behind. Too many distractions over the last week.

Another one pulls me away before I've even made a start. I answer my mobile.

"Hey, chick."

"Morning, Mrs Miller."

"Just a quick call to check you're okay?"

There's a hint of concern in her voice.

"I'm fine."

"Sure?"

"Spit it out. What's worrying you?"

"I might owe you an apology. I shouldn't have been so dismissive about your mystery stalker."

"An apology?" I snigger. "It's not a leap year, is it?"

"Sarky cow."

"It's okay, honestly. Now I've had time to sleep on it, I think you were probably right."

"I wasn't. Stuart told me off."

"He did?"

"Yep. We had a chat about your predicament in bed last night. He asked how I'd feel if some random guy presented me with a copy of my granddad's old war medal. It kinda freaked me out when he put it like that."

"I won't deny it freaked me out ... I'm still freaked out ... but you were definitely right about trying to find Kenneth. It's a lost cause."

"Maybe it isn't."

My pulse quickens.

"You think? Why?"

"Because men think differently, or at least my husband does. You'll kick yourself when I tell you."

Silence.

"Don't be a tease. Tell me!"

"Calm your tits," she chuckles. "So, I described your stalker to Stuart and after we got into a heated discussion about brown suits, he picked up on the flower."

"What about it?"

"You said he had a fresh lily in his buttonhole each time he confronted you, right?"

"Yes."

"Which means he's either a regular customer at one of the local florists, or he's actually a florist himself. I checked, and there are only two in town."

It's so obvious I have to kick it around my head for a few seconds to be sure.

"Well?" Martha urges. "What do you think?"

"I think we're idiots, and your husband is a genius. The lily never crossed my mind."

"In fairness, chick, your mind has had a lot to contend with of late."

"True."

"Anyway, I hope it's something to go on."

"It's all I've got to go on, but maybe that's the point — it's so subtle, yet obvious when you think about it. Please, thank Stuart for me."

"Will do."

I end the call with a promise to let her know how my investigation goes.

The paperwork is shoved to one side.

I open a web browser and search for florists. As Martha suggested, there are just two in town: Avalon and Daisies. Both are within a shortish walk of the office.

By nature, I'm not prone to making rash decisions; I should formulate a plan before making my next move. Alas, I'm also a born worrier and the greater concern is losing this lead if I don't act in haste.

Before I can talk myself out of it, I inform Ben I'm taking an early lunch and head for the lifts.

Out on the sunlit pavement, I have a decision to make. Both florists are on the High Street, but at opposite ends. Daisies is furthest away and the extra yards will allow me a little thinking time. I turn to my left and stride purposefully towards the first point of call.

With only minutes to think, I consider what might happen when I walk through the door. Will I find Kenneth behind the counter, or will there be a helpful member of staff willing to confirm they sell him a single lily every morning? If it's the latter, I need a back story of sorts to explain why I'm trying to locate their customer.

By the time I approach Daisies Florists, I've a vague notion of what I'm going to say.

I wander in through the open door.

I'm immediately hit with the sweet scent of a summer meadow, and vivid colours burst from every direction. How wonderful it must be to receive this greeting every morning when you turn up for work. I'm used to the scent of stale coffee, cheap aftershave, and a dull palette of corporate greys.

It's such a heady combination I forget myself for a moment.

"Morning."

I turn to the source of the voice.

"Oh, good morning."

I wander over to the counter in the corner, and smile at the woman behind.

"What can I do for you, love?" she asks, her tone and expression both warm.

"I've got a bit of a situation, and I'm hoping you might help?"

"I'll do my best."

"Thank you. I'm trying to find someone, and all I know is they have a soft spot for white lilies. I wondered if he might be a customer — can I show you a photo?"

"By all means."

I dig out my phone and show the woman Kenneth's photo.

She dons a pair of spectacles and looks at the screen for a second or two.

"He loves a lily in his buttonhole, you see?"

"I do."

"Which is why I hoped he might have popped in here at some point over the last week or two. Does he look familiar?"

"I'm afraid not."

"Oh, okay. Might any of your colleagues recognise him?"

"There's only two of us, love, and Maggie is out most of the day doing deliveries. If your chap had called in, I'd have been the one who served him."

"Ah, I see."

"I'm sorry."

"It's okay. I appreciate your time."

171

My back story unused, I leave the woman to get on with her day.

One down, one to go.

I wind my way up the High Street towards Avalon Florists with less than half the confidence I had when I left the office. Surely the woman in the first shop would have recognised Kenneth if he worked for the competition?

Who knows?

I arrive at Avalon Florists and push the door open. A bell clangs above my head.

I'm greeted by a similar scent to the first shop, although Avalon's premises are smaller, and their displays not as colourful. On first impression alone, I'd guess Daisies is the more popular of the two businesses.

There's a counter directly ahead of me with an open door behind. A male voice calls out.

"Be with you in a sec."

My heart sinks a little. The voice has a gruff edge, nothing like Kenneth's.

It's no great surprise when the man who subsequently steps through the doorway looks nothing like Kenneth. He doesn't look much like a florist either. I notice the Avalon logo embroidered on the chest of his dark-green polo shirt. Without that shirt, I might have assumed he's a tradesman; here to fix the boiler or put up some shelves.

"Hi," he says, wiping his hands on a cloth.

"Oh, hi."

"What can I do for you?"

I approach the counter.

"Sorry, I'm not after flowers."

"Story of my life. What is it: directions or you need to use the loo?"

"Neither. I'm looking for someone and I think they might be a customer of yours."

"It's an exclusive club."

Despite a half-smile, his tone errs towards bitter.

"Can I show you a photo?"

"Fill your boots."

As I fumble in my bag, he leans across the counter. I try to avert my eyes but a spotlight above lights up his bald pate like a bulb.

"A gift, from my dad," he says.

"Sorry?"

"Male pattern baldness. It's hereditary."

Unsure what to say, or if I've maybe caused offence by glancing at his head, all I can do is smile. I sense a fluster building.

"Photo?" he reminds me.

"Yes, right."

I unlock my phone and hold it out.

"I don't suppose you recognise him?"

He takes a quick look but his face gives nothing away.

"Maybe."

"Sorry to be blunt but you either do or you don't. Which is it?"

His dark brown eyes narrow as he scratches a stubbled chin with his right hand.

"Seeing as you appreciate bluntness," he replies, flatly. "Why are you looking for him?"

"It's complicated."

"Give me the non-complicated version."

"With respect, it's none of your business."

"It wasn't, but then you walked into my shop and made it my business."

Checkmate. I don't know why I'm being so prickly with this guy but I suspect it's a lot to do with the way certain male arseholes have treated me of late.

"Sorry," I concede. "Can we start again?"

"Guess so."

"This guy has some information on my late father I'm desperate to discover. All I know is his name, Kenneth, and that he has a thing for lilies."

"So, you're not the police, or Inland Revenue?"

"Definitely not."

"Fair enough. Yes, he is a customer."

"Oh, thank God," I pant. "When did you see him last?"

"Yesterday, but he's been in three or four times before — always waiting at the door when I open up."

"What time is that?"

"Eight. My deliveries arrive early so I'm usually here by seven. This isn't the ideal job if you like a lie-in."

My scant plan doesn't extend to the next step. Kenneth wanted me to find him, and although I've discovered one of his regular haunts, I'm still some way off the actual finding part.

"Can I ask a favour?"

"You can ask."

"Would you mind if I dropped by tomorrow morning, just before you open up?"

"I don't know if I like the idea of you accosting one of my customers the minute they walk in the door."

"I understand, but let me show you something."

I put my bag on the counter and rummage through it. I find what I'm looking for and hand it to the man.

"That's the note Kenneth gave me. As you can see, he asked me to find him."

"Seriously?" he frowns. "Is this some kind of weird hide and seek competition?"

"Possibly. It's all a bit … complicated."

He hands me the note back but doesn't answer my question. I've tried prickly, and that didn't work. Time to deploy the carrot.

"I'll bring coffee," I coo. "And fresh croissants."

Seconds tick by before I get an answer.

"Get here ten minutes before opening and you can wait."

"Thank you so much."

"A word of warning, though. I can't afford to piss off even one customer so if there's any kind of scene, I'll need you to leave. Understood?"

"You have my word."

"I'll see you tomorrow then."

"Yes, you will."

He makes for the doorway but pauses before he gets there.

"I'm Liam, by the way."

"Kelly."

For the first time since I walked in, the edges of his lips curl upward. Not quite a smile, but an easing of tensions, I'd hope.

"Right. Seeya, Kelly."

He disappears back through the doorway.

22.

Too early for Frank. Too early for me.

Six-fifteen in the morning and I'm plodding around the kitchen in a near-coma state. I pour a coffee so strong it would likely stain fence panels.

As I sit down at the table, I'm too tired to even question the ridiculous reason I'm awake at such an ungodly hour.

Caffeine provides a lubricant and the cogs slowly turn. Only then do I question what the hell I'm doing. Just when I think my life can't get any more complicated, there's another unexpected twist in the road. The trouble is, that road is more like a steep hill and I'm barrelling down it without brakes. Any moment, I fear I'll hit a bend so sharp I'll completely lose control.

What am I doing?

I spent most of yesterday evening pondering what might happen when, or if, Kenneth turns up at Avalon Florists and finds me waiting. Will he answer my questions, or will I discover he's really the nutjob Martha warned me about? If my friend is correct, I wonder if I could bribe Liam into giving Kenneth a good hiding — he looks capable of administering one.

Besides his physical appearance, there are other reasons Liam doesn't seem to fit the typical profile of a florist. For one, his demeanour — a stark contrast to the lovely woman I spoke to at Daisies. If I were to guess, I'd say he's not a man happy in his work.

Then again, how many of us are?

I glance at the clock. No more time to dwell if I'm to catch the early bus. The bathroom beckons.

The shower finishes what the coffee started, and I leave the house jaded, but awake. The bus is due at seven-fifteen which will allow me enough time to pick up the promised breakfast before a short walk up the High Street to Avalon Florists.

There's no queue at the bus stop, and when it arrives I've all but four seats to choose from. Although it's already setting up to be a glorious summer morning, you wouldn't know it based on the glum faces of my fellow passengers. The British, on the whole, don't do early morning bonhomie. We have, however, perfected that expression which says we'd rather be anywhere other than where we currently are.

Zombie like, we all get off the bus in the town centre and go our separate ways.

I nip into the bakery first and, like the florists yesterday, my senses are made to feel most welcome. Having skipped breakfast, the scent of freshly cooked bread is as divine as it is tortuous. I order two of their largest croissants.

Starbucks is in the opposite direction so my next stop is an independent coffee shop. I take two Americanos to go and, slightly ahead of schedule, continue my journey up the High Street.

Avalon Florists is in darkness when I arrive. Trying to juggle my handbag and two coffee cups, I rap on the door. As I wait, the scent of coffee and croissants taunts.

"Come on," I mumble under my breath.

I'm about to juggle again when the lights come on. Liam then appears from beyond the counter and wanders over to the door with no sense of urgency. Much like the passengers on the bus, his expression isn't one of unbridled joy.

"Morning," he sighs, as the door swings open.

"Good morning," I chirp back, hoping to inject a little sunshine into his day.

Without so much as a smile, he turns and makes for the counter. I follow, at a safe distance.

"As promised, coffee and croissants."

I place the cups down on the counter and reach into my bag for the croissants.

"You're early."

"Yes, the bus was on time, remarkably."

He peels the lid from one of the coffee cups and looks at it like it's a urine sample.

"Sorry. I didn't know what you liked, so I went with the safe option. I figured everyone likes an Americano."

"Like is a strong word. Thanks, anyway."

177

Christ, this guy is a miserable sod. If Kenneth is to make an appearance, it better be soon.

I offer him a croissant in the hope it might cheer him up.

"I'll fetch some plates."

"Honestly, there's no need."

"Yes, there is. I've just swept the floor."

"Oh."

He nips out the back and returns with two tea-plates. I'm handed one with several chips and a dubious brown stain on the rim.

"I don't entertain much," he says, by way of an apology.

With nothing to do other than wait, I lean up against the counter; sipping coffee and nibbling my croissant. Liam finishes his in four bites before gulping back half the coffee.

I check my watch: ten to eight. As much as I'd like to, standing here in silence for ten minutes isn't an option.

"How long have you been a florist?" I ask.

"Eighteen months."

"And I'm guessing this is your business?"

"Yep."

It seems quite a gamble, setting up a shop with only eighteen months experience.

"How's it going?"

"Badly."

"I'm sorry to hear that."

"Everyone is," he shrugs.

"What did you do before you became a florist?"

"Do you really want to know, or are you just killing time until your hide and seek partner arrives?"

"Honestly? A bit of both."

"I joined the army straight from school. Left after fifteen years and set up my own little business as a handyman. Did that for seven years before taking this place over."

"That's quite a change of direction."

"Circumstances."

He takes a long gulp of coffee. I detect a reluctance to explain what those circumstances might have been.

"What do you do?" he asks, validating my detection skills.

"I run a department for Marston Finance. You heard of them?"

"You could say that. I owe them a few quid."

"As will a lot more people by the end of the day. It's relentless work."

"As long as someone's getting rich, eh?"

"Not me, that's for sure."

He finishes his coffee and crushes the cup.

"You'll have to excuse me. I've got a few bits and pieces to be getting on with."

"Sure. No problem."

To my surprise, I'm a tad disappointed being left on my own. Liam might not be the most cheerful host but the conversation helped the minutes tick by. I glance at my watch again to see I'm five minutes closer to Kenneth's possible appearance.

I wait, and those five minutes pass by, followed by another five. It's nearly ten-past eight before I'm joined in the shop by another person, albeit the same person who's been here all the time.

"Been stood up?" Liam asks.

"You tell me. Has he turned up on the dot of eight every time?"

"Afraid so."

"Great," I huff.

I don't know what to do. I could wait a little longer although it seems I'll be waiting in vain, or I can give up entirely on this charade. In lieu of the answer I wanted, I seek some answers from Liam.

"What did you make of him? Kenneth?"

"In what way?"

"Did he say anything peculiar, or tell you anything about where he works, or lives?"

"Nope. He came in, asked for a white lily, paid, and left."

"How did he pay?"

"Always cash."

"So, you never had a conversation with him?"

"At that time of the morning, I avoid conversations."

"I gathered."

He doesn't react to my jibe.

"What's the deal with this guy, anyway? Why are you so keen to track him down?"

"As I said yesterday, it's complicated."

"I know. Yesterday I wasn't curious, but now I am."

"Curious?"

"Yeah. Wouldn't you be if the roles were reversed?"

"Probably."

"Come on, then — spill the beans."

"Do you really want to know, or are you just killing time?"

"Touché," he replies with a wry smile. "I'll give you that one."

He should smile more often; it fits his face better than the permafrown he's worn since I walked in.

"Okay, I'll spill."

I delve into my handbag, retrieve the box containing the medallion, and place it on the counter.

"Kenneth gave it to me."

I then explain the events which led up to the meeting at the sandwich shop. With my explanation delivered, Liam picks up the box and examines the medallion.

"And you say this is an exact replica of the one your dad wore?"

"Yep."

"I've heard some weird-arse tales in my time but yours ... no wonder you're keen to find the bloke."

"Does that sate your curiosity?"

"Quite the opposite. I think you should come back tomorrow."

His invite takes me by surprise. I hadn't even thought about coming back, and even if I had, I wouldn't have expected Liam's cooperation.

"I'm not sure it's a good idea."

"Why?"

"This has all the hallmarks of a wild goose chase. Whatever

game Kenneth is playing, I don't think I want to participate anymore."

"Game or no game, I'd want to know."

"Would you? Why?"

"Because … I just would," he replies, his expression and tone almost sympathetic. "If you come back tomorrow, I might tell you why."

"Now it's my turn to be curious."

"It's nothing like your situation."

Despite his absence, Kenneth has added further intrigue. I don't know why I should care about Liam's story but I sense he wants to tell it.

"Will you provide the coffee?" I ask.

"Proper coffee, yes."

I place the medallion back in my handbag and flash him a smile.

"Guess I'll see you tomorrow then."

I'm in no hurry to get to work and wander back down the High Street at a snail's pace. I catch sight of several suited men on the opposite pavement but every time the suit is dark grey, navy, or black — never brown.

Maybe Kenneth never considered I might track him down so quickly, and maybe he will turn up tomorrow. Or maybe, I'm past caring either way.

I arrive at my desk with those possibilities no closer to being resolved.

My work day begins with the pile of paperwork I never completed yesterday. I make a promise to myself: to clear the backlog by the end of the day. If nothing else, it'll keep my mind busy; in much the same way having your pubic hair smothered with hot wax and ripped out at the roots helps you forget about a headache.

It's just after five when I file away the very last piece of paper. On the one hand, it's a huge relief to clear my in-tray but on the other, it's been a day of mind-numbing tedium. I vow never to get so far behind with my paperwork again.

Mentally exhausted, I call it a day. A weary traipse to the bus stop follows.

When I arrive home, there's a large envelope waiting for me on the doormat. I open it in the hallway, and it contains a set of sales particulars for the yard, together with a copy of the contract. In his covering letter, Richard confirms he's already had tentative discussions with two interested parties and he'll report back next week. It seems he conducted his survey without Donald causing a scene. All in all, positive progress.

I file the paperwork and then change into something comfortable while the microwave gets to work on a chicken risotto.

With every intention of spending the evening on the sofa, I finish my dinner and then scan Netflix in search of a new box set to keep me entertained. My phone has other ideas and trills loudly from the coffee table.

"Hey, Martha."

"Evening, chick. Is it a good time?"

"It's always a good time."

"I thought I'd see how your investigation went. It's a measure of how dull my life is; you're my only source of entertainment."

"Gee, thanks," I chuckle. "Although I wouldn't call it entertaining."

"I know, but you get my drift."

"I do."

"Come on then. Tell me how you got on."

I recount the visit to the florists yesterday, and the wasted early morning.

"You could be right. If this florist guy … what was his name?"

"Liam."

"Right. If this Liam guy says Kenneth doesn't turn up every morning, it's got to be worth another visit."

"Well, I've agreed to try again tomorrow."

"Agreed? With whom?"

"Liam."

"You've lost me. Why would you agree with him?"

"I was all for giving up but he suggested I go back tomorrow morning."

"Ohh," she purrs. "Did he now?"

"Martha. Stop it."

"Stop what?" comes the innocent reply.

"I know exactly what you're thinking."

"And what might that be?"

"You're wondering if he's boyfriend material."

"I resent that allegation."

"Hmm … really? Remember that poor waiter at Prezzo? Just because he smiled at me a few times, you gave him my phone number. And then there was Stuart's colleague who came to your barbecue last summer — remember that incident?"

"I honestly didn't know he was gay."

"But even when you did, you asked if he'd ever been curious about sleeping with a woman, and that I might be a willing participant if his curiosity ever got the better of him."

"Yes, in hindsight that was an error of judgement."

"It was humiliating, and I was still married at the time."

"I'd had a few, and I apologised."

"You did, and you also promised never to interfere in my love life again."

"Did I?"

"Yes."

"I lied."

"Anyway, I don't think Liam is my type."

"Why? Is he fugly?"

"Fugly?"

"Yeah, fuck ugly?"

"Oh, not really. He's got this broody, Bruce Willis thing going on."

"Bruce Willis is in his sixties and bald."

"Okay, perhaps not the best comparison. Liam is bald, but he's definitely not in his sixties. I'd say he's more like a younger version of Jason Statham."

"Jason Statham is hot. I'll tell you who else is hot, that …"

"Martha," I interject.

"Yes?"

"Remind me: how did we get on to this subject?"

"You fancy Liam."

"I do not fancy Liam. He's simply allowing me to hang around his shop tomorrow."

"Thinking about it, it's an odd profession for a guy, don't you think? Maybe he's gay."

"I don't know, and I don't care. Can we change the subject?"

"You're in denial," she giggles. "Admit it."

Someone has definitely had a few glasses of wine and it isn't me.

After another twenty minutes of nonsense, I eventually get her off the phone. I return to my Netflix browsing and settle on an American comedy which is unlikely to tax anyone's mind.

By the fourth episode, my eyelids begin to droop.

I don't quite make the fifth episode.

23.

If I ever decided to switch religions, I think I'd lean towards Hinduism.

Hindus believe that when we die, our soul lives on through reincarnation in the form of an animal. They're vague about the details but if you've led a good life, you'll likely come back as a gorilla or lion; but if you've been a bit of a shit, you'll come back as a wasp or some other loathsome creature.

I'd put myself somewhere towards the good end of the scale, and given the choice, I'd definitely come back as a cat.

For starters, they straddle the line between cute and majestic, and they're blessed with extreme agility. They also lead virtually independent lives, relying on humans only when they're hungry or fancy a bit of attention.

It's the perfect existence.

"I don't suppose you used to be an accountant from Surbiton?" I ask Frank, as he waits at my feet for his breakfast.

"Actually, that would be disappointing. And, as you've been in my bed, a bit creepy."

I fork tuna into his bowl.

"God, what if you were someone awful, like Harold Shipman or Jimmy Savile?"

I put the bowl on the table and he jumps up with the usual effortless ease.

"I'm going to assume you were a nice person, otherwise you wouldn't now be living such a privileged existence. You spoilt moggie."

I leave Frank to his breakfast. Despite ten hours of sleep, I still overslept and I've only got half-hour before the early bus departs.

A quick shower, a dab of makeup, and I throw on the first outfit I find. I then suffer a mild panic attack when I can't find my keys. After searching high and low, I find them on the kitchen table; a few feet away from an empty bowl.

I lock up and leave.

185

I'm met by the same glum faces on the bus. My face is probably pink and clammy on account I had to jog most of the way to the bus stop.

Having already suffered a frenetic start to the day, it's a relief I don't have to rush once I arrive in the town centre. Although Liam promised coffee, he made no reference to breakfast, and I'm hungry. I return to the bakery and order two bacon rolls; safe in the knowledge they'll both go to a good home if my host doesn't have an appetite.

Even though I plod slowly up the High Street, I reach Avalon Florists fifteen minutes early. Unlike yesterday, the lights are on and Liam is at the counter. I knock on the door and he beckons me in.

"You're keen," he remarks.

"Sorry. Am I too early?"

"No, it's fine. Coffee?"

"That would be great."

"Give me a minute."

He heads out the back, leaving me alone with his stock. I put my handbag on the counter and browse the displays while I wait. I'm no expert on floristry but Liam's merchandising skills leave a lot to be desired. Either he doesn't have the creativity to produce eye-catching bouquets, or he doesn't know what he's doing. As much as I love receiving flowers, I'd be disappointed if any of these sorry efforts arrived at my door.

"One coffee."

He holds a cup in my direction. I approach the counter and take it.

"Thank you. I took the liberty of buying breakfast. Fancy a bacon roll?"

"I could force one down."

I hand him the bag and, as he opens it, delicious but opposing scents collide: crispy bacon, and the sweet perfume of flowers.

With twenty minutes to kill, we lean up against the counter and demolish the rolls while slurping equally moreish coffee. I make several attempts at small talk but it's difficult while eating. We settle into silence until we've finished.

"Cheers. That was good."

"You're welcome."

With no option but to talk, Liam shuffles awkwardly.

"I think I owe you an apology."

"Do you? Why?"

"My moody behaviour on your previous visits. I don't mean to come across as a stroppy dick but …"

"But?"

"This is awkward."

"Go on."

"Okay," he puffs. "I went from an all-boys school straight into the military so I didn't get to mingle with many women. As you probably noticed, my communication skills need work."

"That must be difficult in this business. I'm guessing at least half your customers are female?"

"They are, and it's bloody hard. I try, but it isn't me."

"That then begs a question: why on earth did you decide to open a florists?"

"I didn't."

"I'm not with you."

He stares at the floor, as if there's an invisible line and he's deciding whether or not to cross it.

"This was my sister's business," he eventually answers in a low voice.

"Was?"

"She died."

"Oh, I'm so sorry. I didn't mean to …"

"It's okay. I'm a big boy and I should be over it by now."

"Talking from experience, I know how long grief lingers after a family bereavement. Christ, it's the reason I'm here this morning."

"True."

"So, what made you take this place over?"

"I thought I'd be honouring my sister's memory if I kept it going but … I've made a right hash of it."

I glance at a bucket of ten quid bouquets on the floor to my right. They're still tragic but in a completely different way.

"For what it's worth, Liam, I think you've done an amazing job."

"Yeah, right," he scoffs. "My accountant has a different view."

"It's not about the money — it's about you trying. You've tried your absolute best, and what more can anyone do?"

"You sound like my old English teacher. He said in my report: not blessed with intellect, but he's a trier."

"Your English teacher sounds a right twat."

I didn't mean to speak so bluntly but it's met with laughter.

"Yeah, he was."

"Mine wasn't much better. She used to make us stand in a waste-paper basket if she caught us chatting when we were supposed to be reading."

"Don't think a teacher would get away with that these days."

"Probably not."

He glances at his watch.

"Your man of mystery should make an appearance any minute."

"Possibly."

"And if he doesn't?"

"I guess it's the end of the road. I can't keep turning up here every morning."

"Says who?"

"Me. I'm not keen on leaving the house at stupid o'clock."

"Tell me about it, but it's no reason to give up."

"Isn't it?"

"Nope, but then again, I am a trier."

My turn to laugh.

"I'll see what the next ten minutes bring."

"Sure. I'll be out the back if you need anything."

He picks up his cup and disappears through the doorway.

A wave of déjà vu breaks as I glance at my watch and wait. Five to, eight o'clock, five past. Predictably, Liam returns at ten past and looks at me like a parent mourning their child's poor exam results.

"No show again?"

"Yep."

"Sorry."

"Life is full of disappointments. Unanswered questions and disappointment."

Unintentional bitterness but it landed with ease. My host looks for an appropriate response.

"Try again tomorrow? Could be third time lucky."

"I'm not sure. Maybe I've got this wrong and I've missed another clue to Kenneth's whereabouts. Or maybe this situation is as ludicrous as it currently feels and I'm just wasting my time."

"You haven't wasted your time."

"Beg to differ," I huff.

"You made me laugh before lunchtime — very few people have achieved that feat."

I muster a smile.

"Third time lucky, you reckon?"

"Sometimes in life you've got to take a punt, even when the odds don't stack up."

"I'll see you tomorrow, then."

He nods as I grab my bag.

"Tomorrow."

As I walk to the office, I open the photo of Kenneth. I might as well be staring at a blank piece of paper. Apart from the lily, it's just a photo of a nondescript man in a brown suit. I could stare at the photo all day but there isn't anything else to go on. And it's not as though I can trawl every menswear shop in town and ask if they've sold any brown suits or black sweaters lately.

Frustrated. I put my phone away.

The frustration takes a back seat once I sit down at my desk. One of the first emails I open is from Justin, my boss, requesting a meeting at eleven o'clock to discuss how my department can implement the board's latest efficiency drive. The last time we had a conversation on cost-cutting measures, he banned staff from charging their mobile phones in the office, arguing it would save hundreds of pounds every year.

As usual, Justin didn't factor-in the negative effect on staff morale, and for two weeks they were unmanageable. Our productivity levels dropped, costing the company tens of thousands of pounds. The ban was eventually lifted and Justin told my team in person, delivering a union-grade speech in which he implied he'd been instrumental in having the ban overturned. He neglected to mention it was his stupid idea in the first place.

I dread to think what half-arsed ideas he's got up his sleeve this time.

At half-ten, with the meeting looming, I decide my caffeine levels need a top up. I wander into the staffroom and put the kettle on. Ben enters a few minutes later, brandishing an oversized greetings card.

"Got a sec, boss?"

"Sure."

"It's Kate's thirtieth birthday tomorrow. Did you want to sign her card?"

"Of course."

He rests it on the table and hands me a pen. I get halfway through penning a generic message when the sting arrives.

"We're having a whip round, for a present."

Having signed the card, I can't refuse a contribution.

"I haven't got my purse on me but nip into my office later."

"Will do. Thanks."

"What are you getting her?"

He extracts his phone and holds it up for me to see the screen.

"What do you think?"

The photo is of a silver necklace with a Celtic-inspired pendant. Presumably a nod to Kate's Scottish roots.

"Very unusual. It looks expensive."

"Two hundred quid, but Steve's other half works in the jewellers on the High Street and he sorted out a decent discount."

"I should have a word with Steve when I'm in the market for a birthday gift."

"Yeah, you should. They've got some lovely stuff in there."

"I'll bear it in mind."

I glance at my watch.

"I've got a meeting with Justin in twenty minutes so I'd better get on."

Ben leaves me to make my coffee. As I pour the water into the mug, a thought sparks. I hurry back to my office. The trip takes only seconds, but it's sufficient time to realise I've been a complete idiot.

I have a game on my phone — similar to a crossword. The aim is to guess interlinking words from a selection of letters. I've spent too many hours stuck on a particular word, and when I finally work it out, it's nearly always blindingly obvious and I spend ten minutes kicking myself for not realising sooner.

I've been so obsessed with Stuart's theory, I missed the obvious. Kenneth's clue must have been the medallion itself.

I open a web browser and google jewellery shops — there are four in town, and perhaps Kenneth purchased the medallion from one of them.

I'm pleased to have finally made a possible connection but the timing sucks. I'm supposed to be at the opposite side of the building in ten minutes so any further investigation will have to wait until Justin is done with me.

I shut the browser and leave.

When I arrive, Justin's PA asks what sandwiches I'd prefer for lunch. She replies to my quizzical expression with an explanation — the meeting will probably stretch well into the afternoon. There goes any chance of touring the jewellery shops on my lunch break.

Justin appears and beckons me into his office. Like a condemned woman taking her final walk along death row, I trudge in behind him.

Two hours and forty minutes later, I emerge like a condemned woman; albeit a condemned woman taken to the electric chair, lightly fried for a while, and then made to sit through four lengthy PowerPoint presentations.

My brain actually aches, almost as much as my buttocks.

If losing two hours and forty minutes of my life wasn't bad enough, Justin wants an action plan put together before the end of the day. Never has the term 'thank fuck it's Friday' been more apt.

I return to my office and make a start.

Minutes feel like hours as I try to focus on the action plan, rather than the four jewellery shops which are all tantalisingly close by. I had hoped I might get to a couple of the shops before they close but as five o'clock comes and goes — the end of the action plan does not.

It's almost six by the time I email it to Justin.

I'm about to shut down my computer when I realise there's another email I need to send. With a more obvious lead to follow, it seems pointless turning up at Liam's shop again tomorrow morning. I find his website and send a quick email thanking him for his time but confirming I won't be bothering him tomorrow.

Breathing a deep sigh of relief, I shut the computer down.

By the time I boot it up on Monday morning, hopefully I'll have tracked Kenneth down and put this situation to bed, one way or another.

For now though, I need a glass of something chilled.

24.

I caught the tail end of the news before heading to bed, just as a smarmy presenter delivered the weekend's weather forecast. He used words like 'uncomfortable' and 'sticky'; neither of which do justice to the furnace I find myself trapped in.

Last time I checked, it had just gone one in the morning. The window is wide open and I've stripped down to just a pair of knickers, but to no avail — I'm still sweating in places I didn't know it was possible to sweat.

I detest nights like this.

Roll to the left, roll to the right, lie on my back. No matter how many times I reposition myself, sleep evades me.

After what feels like hours, I drift into a semi-conscious doze but then a fox screams outside; dragging me back to the start line. I roll over and try again.

Finally, my body accepts the inevitable and I drift away.

I've no idea how long I slept for but I'm suddenly dragged back as Basil-fucking-Brush screams for the umpteenth time. I roll over and will myself back to the land of nod. Again, the fox screams although it sounds higher pitched than before, and closer.

My brain — still in standby mode — can't compute.

Every fibre of my being wants to sleep but the sound repeats again and again; every time sounding less like a fox and more like a ...

I open my eyes.

"You've got to be kidding me!"

Inches from my pillow, Frank squeaks another high-pitched meow.

"How did you ... oh, shit."

Did I forget to close the kitchen window again? In my sleep-deprived stupor I can't remember my date of birth, let alone whether I completed every step of the nightly routine.

I slip my nightshirt back on and pick Frank up.

"You and me are going to fall out if you keep turning up in

my bedroom, Mister."

Cradling my feline intruder, I shuffle out the open bedroom door to the landing. I make five steps towards the stairs and stop. There's a slightly odd odour to the humid air. I try to decipher what it might be but the scent is too faint. I plod down the stairs and along the hallway to the kitchen. By the time I step through the door, the odour is pungent enough to be unmistakable.

"Shit!"

I drop Frank to the floor and reach for the light switch. Right at the very last second, my hand freezes in mid-air.

"Stupid cow."

Stumbling my way through the dark, I make for the hob and locate the source of the odour — one of the rings pumping gas into the kitchen. I turn it off and carefully open the back door. Unsure what to do next, beyond escaping a potential explosion, I step outside and lean up against the back wall of the house.

A second later, Frank emerges. He stops, looks up at me, and trots away into the darkness. I glance across at the kitchen window, expecting it to be open but it looks firmly shut. I've no idea how Frank got into the house but one thing is clear, that fat ginger cat might have just saved my life.

That terrifying thought established, I struggle to process how the situation even came about. Two questions circle around and around: how did Frank get in, and how did the hob turn itself on?

Those questions will have to wait. My priority is to clear the house of gas.

I venture back inside and open the front door, and then the window in the lounge. The breeze is feeble but given sufficient time, hopefully strong enough to displace any lingering gas which hasn't already escaped via the kitchen door.

The odour slowly ebbs away but I'm still not willing to risk switching on any lights. As for sleep, that's a non-starter until I'm absolutely sure every molecule of gas has gone.

For now, there's nothing else I can do but return to the garden and sit at the table. There, I notice the time: four-fifteen.

My thoughts turn back to the two questions and a potential answer to both. Perhaps Frank came in through the window yesterday evening, and unbeknown to me, made himself at home in a quiet corner of the house where I wouldn't notice him. If he did, it's not beyond the realm of possibility he jumped up on the kitchen side looking for food. Could he have inadvertently stepped on the knob and switched the gas on? An unlikely explanation but the only explanation which makes any sense.

It seems Frank might have caused the potential catastrophe he then saved me from — as much a villain as a hero.

With my phone upstairs and no other point of reference available, all I can do is guess how much time to allow before I can safely remain in the house. I decide on half an hour, then settle back in the chair and wait.

I guess if there's one consolation, at least I don't have work in the morning. Nor do I have to worry about the early visit to Liam's shop. It's also a relief I only had two glasses of wine last night. Typically, on a Friday evening I'd sink a bottle or two and that usually knocks me out for the night. The clear head and broken sleep were probably the only reasons I stirred at Frank's meows.

Despite the humid air, a cold shiver arrives. If the gas had been on all night, and the boiler — on the wall in the kitchen — had fired up at seven o'clock, they'd have been collecting bits of me from every street within a half-mile radius.

I feel a bit sick, and not because I've inhaled a few lungfuls of gas.

Mother Nature then provides a timely distraction as the sun slowly creeps above the horizon; tingeing the low streaks of cloud a shade of purplish-gold. It's accompanied by the first chirps of birdsong and a cool breeze. Utterly distracted from my ordeal, I could almost thank Frank for gifting the opportunity to witness such a beautiful sunrise. Almost, but not quite.

I sit and watch the sun wake up for another fifteen minutes before heading back inside. Sniffing like a bloodhound I can't detect gas but, just to be on the safe side, I avoid switching on the lights. I lock both the doors but leave the kitchen window open a few inches — enough to let any final traces of gas escape but not wide enough for a mischievous ginger cat to enter.

An overwhelming need for sleep hits hard. I trudge back upstairs and collapse on the bed.

I must have fallen fast asleep but, after what feels like three minutes, I'm woken up by my alarm. On any other Saturday, I'd turn it off and go back to sleep, particularly as I can ill-afford to be losing several hours of beauty sleep, but I've got a lot on my to-do list today. The first and most pressing task involves a bucket of strong coffee.

Still sniffing the air, I plod slowly down the stairs to a gas-free kitchen.

I put the kettle on and open the back door. There's no sign of Frank which is probably just as well; if I were in his paws, I'd want to avoid a cantankerous, sleep-deprived human who isn't best pleased with me.

Two cups of coffee and three toasted bagels later, I reckon I've consumed enough caffeine and calories to face the day. I plod back up the stairs and get ready for my foray into town.

Weekend bus trips have a different vibe from the morning commute. Most of my fellow passengers are taking a journey through choice rather than necessity, and that's reflected in their general perkiness. Those passengers include giggly teenagers and nattering pensioners; plus a few loners like me, content to sit and watch the world beyond the grimy windows go by.

A few minutes before we reach the town centre, I pull out my phone and plan a route around the four jewellery shops. Unlike the florists, there's no reason to think Kenneth works in one of those shops but they could be a significant breadcrumb on the trail to finding him. Either way, I've decided today is the end. If I don't find him, I'm giving up. I'll toss the medallion in the nearest bin and vow never to think about Kenneth again.

The bus pulls up and I let my fellow passengers disembark first. I then follow and wind my way through the streets to the first jewellery shop on the list.

Being a typical chain store, the two women behind the counter offer a scripted, lukewarm greeting.

"Morning," I smile. "I'm wondering if you could help me?"

"We'll do our best," the older woman replies, less-than-convincingly.

I extract the box containing the medallion from my handbag and open the lid.

"Do you stock this medallion?"

In unison, the two women lean forward to inspect it.

"I don't think so," the younger woman replies.

"May I take a closer look?" her colleague asks.

I hand her the box and the sales assistant fingers the medallion for a few seconds.

"No, definitely not one of ours," she then confirms.

"You're sure?"

"This looks almost brand new. Medallions haven't been in fashion for a good few years so we only carry a few — this definitely isn't one of them."

"Okay. I appreciate your help. Can I ask one other question?"

"Sure."

I swap the box for my phone. It's clear Kenneth never purchased the medallion here but it might save some time if they recognise him from one of the other shops. It's the longest of long shots but there's no harm in asking.

"Do you recognise this man?"

Both women lean in again, and squint at the photo of Kenneth. I'm met with head shakes and apologies.

"Never mind. Again, thanks for your help."

"You're welcome. Have a nice day."

For the next hour it feels like I'm reliving that famous old Yellow Pages advert. Drifting shop to shop, I'm met with similar disappointment as the old boy who can't locate a copy of *Fly Fishing* by JR Hartley. Lots of sympathetic smiles but a negative response to both the medallion and the photo of Kenneth.

It's late morning by the time I leave the last of the four jewellery shops. Rather than disappointed, I'm annoyed with myself for taking the bait, in what has proven to be a wild goose chase. With the sale of Dad's yard in hand, and the appointment at the clinic booked, I should be focusing on what really matters, and that excludes this bullshit.

"Screw you, Kenneth," I mumble under my breath, as I stride

away from the last jewellery shop.

I reach the entrance to the shopping centre and spot a bin. I'm about to change course when an elderly guy in a blazer steps across my path; six medals pinned to his chest.

"Excuse me, love," he wheezes. "I'm collecting for the local British Legion. Could you spare a few coppers?"

He holds up a collection tin.

"Don't you have a charity shop on the other side of town?"

"We do," he replies. "But times are hard and we're struggling for donations."

I snatch the medallion box from my handbag and place it in his hand.

"There's a silver medallion in this box, and it's probably worth more than you'll collect all day. I hope it helps."

He carefully removes the lid and his face lights up.

"Blimmin' hell. That's … too kind. Are you sure, love?"

"Absolutely."

I deliver a quick kiss to his cheek and wish the old soldier luck.

As I stroll into the cool confines of the shopping centre, I decide my good deed deserves recognition in the form of a treat. I make my way to the food court and order an iced smoothie with cherries and berries. After an hour of pounding hot pavements, my feet could also do with a treat so I find a table and take the weight off them for a while.

Slurping away, I ponder what I'm to do with the rest of my day. I suspect Martha has plans with the girls but maybe she'll let me gate-crash.

I call her.

It rings eight times and I'm about to give up when she finally answers.

"Hi," she says, breathless. "Sorry … I was … tied up."

"Oh, have I called at a bad time?"

"No, Stuart and I were just … um, changing the bed."

"Is that a euphemism?"

"Yes."

"Oops, sorry. I'll call back."

"Nah, you're okay. We're done."

"That's a romantic turn of phrase," I chuckle. "But, I'm impressed you're getting jiggy on a sweltering Saturday morning — still can't keep your hands off each other after all these years, eh?"

"Not quite, chick. The girls are at their grandparents for the day and the only chance we get is when they're out of the house."

"Err, why?"

"You'll find out one day. When they're little, you can tell them mummy and daddy are having a pillow fight but as they get older, that excuse doesn't wash. A few months back, we were at it one night when Ella banged on the door and yelled at us to keep the sex noises down."

"Oh, God. Awkward."

"You're telling me. We had real problems with Little Stuart after that."

"Who's Little Stuart … oh, wait. Don't answer that."

"I'm sure you can guess."

"Yes, and moving swiftly on, I was calling to see if you had any plans this afternoon?"

"Why, what did you have in mind?"

"I'm sat in the shopping centre at the moment. Thought you might fancy a mooch around the shops."

"Not much."

"Right. Okay."

"But, I wouldn't mind sitting in a beer garden for a few hours."

"You're such a bad influence."

"I know, but I'm in the mood for a lazy afternoon with something chilled in my hand."

"Stuart won't mind?"

"Are you kidding? A spot of lunchtime sex and then an afternoon watching cricket without the wife and kids bending his ear — that's his idea of the perfect day."

"Great. Shall we meet at The Three Horseshoes in an hour?"

"Sounds good. Shortly, shorty."

My afternoon sorted, I finish the smoothie and make for the bus stop.

Alcohol beckons.

25.

It's all about the circumstances.

Last night, I'd have given anything to escape the summer heat. Relaxing in a beer garden on a Saturday afternoon, it's a different matter. Despite its semi-urban location, the beer garden at The Three Horseshoes is a little oasis of tranquillity. I snare a table tucked away in the corner beneath a wooden gazebo entwined with climbing plants. Of the eight other tables, only one is occupied; a middle-aged couple talking in hushed tones. Martha is typically late but I'm content just sitting on my own with a cold wine glass in hand.

I'm close to nodding off when the blonde whirlwind bursts through the door leading from the public bar. Incapable of a discreet entrance, she's wearing a bright orange dress and sporting a pair of huge Bardot-style sunglasses.

I wave from the corner and she sashays over, glass of wine already in hand.

We hug and she collapses into the chair opposite.

"God, I need this," she puffs.

"One of those mornings?"

"Exhausting."

"Don't be looking for sympathy; not from someone with the sex life of a Benedictine nun."

"I wish that was the reason I'm knackered. When you only get the chance to do it once or twice a month, it doesn't last long enough for exhaustion to become an issue."

"That's more info than I strictly needed."

"Just saying, chick," she grins. "No, it's the girls. They were up at seven this morning, causing chaos."

"Not cooking Play-Doh sausages again?"

"Worse and it's kind of your fault."

"My fault? How?"

"They loved your new hairstyle so much they decided they'd like shorter hair."

"Oh, no … they didn't?"

"They did. I wandered into the kitchen to find Ella cutting lumps out of Millie's hair."

"Shit. The little sods."

"Yep, so I had no choice but to drag her to the hairdressers at nine — damage limitation. It cost me twenty-five quid."

"At least she didn't ask for a colour."

"I wish I could laugh about it but every day they find new and inventive ways to drive me insane."

"The joys of parenthood, eh?"

"Unplanned parenthood."

"Yes, but you wouldn't be without them, would you?"

It was a throwaway question but Martha's pause is a sign she's thinking about it.

"I think it's the peanut butter curse," she says flatly.

"The what?"

"I've never told you this … never told anyone … but a few weeks after we brought them home from hospital, Stuart had to go back to work. There I was, left at home on my own with two tiny humans. I thought I knew what hard work and stress felt like. I had no idea."

"You never said anything. I thought you were coping brilliantly."

"Pride, I guess. The whole motherhood role should come naturally, shouldn't it? I thought there had to be something wrong with me as I just wanted to go back to work and pretend they didn't exist."

"I'm so sorry, hun. If I knew you felt like that, I'd have helped more."

"It was my problem," she shrugs. "And I tried my hardest to work through it. At one point, I thought I'd cracked it … and then came the peanut butter curse."

"You'd better explain."

"One night they kept us both awake until the early hours. Stuart had an important meeting at eight o'clock and overslept so I offered to make him a sandwich to eat in the car. I hadn't had a chance to go shopping and all I could find was peanut butter. Anyway, I send Stuart on his way and the second he leaves, Ella screams from her crib. So, I go back up to their bedroom and it's like walking into a wall of shit. She'd obviously crapped herself so I laid her on the changing mat and removed the offending nappy — it was like an explosion in a toffee factory."

Her graphic description is perhaps too graphic. She continues.

"Still half-asleep, I clean up the mess and put her back in the crib. Then, I head back down to the kitchen to make myself a coffee. While I'm waiting for the kettle to boil, I wipe down the sides and notice a blob of peanut butter on my wrist. Of course, I lick it off."

"Rather you than me. I can't stand peanut butter."

"I'm not a huge fan," she says dismissively. "But that didn't matter because, turns out, it wasn't peanut butter after all."

"Ohh …"

"Yep. I licked a blob of baby shit from my wrist."

I have to bite my lip.

"I thought morning sickness was bad," she continues. "But I couldn't leave the bathroom for half-an-hour."

"That's … terrible. I feel queasy just thinking about it."

"It was terrible, and in some way I think it was a curse. Ever since that day, motherhood has always had a slightly shit taste to it. I love those girls more than anything but some days I really don't love being a mum."

She sits back in her seat.

"There," she says. "I've finally said it."

"Christ, hun — no wonder you wanted a drink. Have you told Stuart how you feel?"

"You know what men are like. He thinks it's a phase and one day I'll just wake up feeling like Mary Poppins."

"I wish I had some worthwhile advice, but it's beyond my area of expertise. What I do know is you can't possibly be the first and only mother to feel this way."

"Maybe, but it doesn't stop me feeling bloody awful about it."

I reach across the table and squeeze her hand.

"Do you remember that boy you dated at college … what was

his name?" I ask.

"Jamie."

"That's the one. Do you remember how you felt when he dumped you?"

"He didn't dump me. We mutually decided to separate."

"After he shagged Melissa Trueman in the girl's loo?"

"Well, yes."

"Ignoring the details, I remember you telling me afterwards you could never love another guy as much as you loved Jamie."

"Did I?"

"Yes. You were absolutely convinced, and I don't think you dated again for almost a year."

"That's young love for you. What a silly little twat I was."

"Possibly, but in the end, you eventually met the true love of your life in Stuart."

"This sounds a lot like advice and I'm terrible at taking advice. You know that."

"I do, but here's some more. Love isn't binary, hun — it ebbs and flows like a tide. Christ, at one point I thought I loved Nathan … turned out to be more ebbing than flowing. My point is: I think one day you will wake up and you'll find yourself in love with motherhood, just as you woke up one day and realised you could love a man more than you loved Jamie."

She squeezes my hand back.

"This is why you're my best friend, Kelly Coburn — you're so bloody sensible."

"Is that a compliment because it sounds like you think I'm a bore?"

"Just a bit," she sniggers. "But I wouldn't change you for the world. Thank you for at least taking the edge off my neurosis."

"Anytime."

"You're gonna make such a brilliant mummy. I know it."

"Stop it. You'll have me crying into my wine in a minute."

"Just one thing, though."

"What's that?"

"Never ask me to change a nappy."

"Deal, as long as you agree never to make me a peanut butter

204

sandwich."

We clink our glasses together; our empty glasses.

"Same again?"

"Need you ask?"

"Silly me."

I head into the bar and return with a bottle of Chardonnay.

"To the brim," Martha requests, as I top up our glasses. "And then you can tell me how you got on tracking down your stalker."

"Kenneth?"

"How many stalkers have you got?"

I swallow a large mouthful of wine before explaining my theory about the jewellery shops, and my wasted morning.

"I think your original theory was right," I conclude. "Maybe he is a religious nutter, but I reckon he's like one of those Internet trolls. You know the type who get their kicks from causing distress to strangers. Either way, I gave the medallion away and drew a line under the whole stupid thing."

"Probably for the best," Martha concludes. "But aren't you still just a teeny bit curious how he knew about the medallion?"

"Of course I'm curious, but not so much I'm prepared to play silly buggers. Kenneth had ample opportunity to tell me whatever he needed to tell me, but instead he messed with my head. Whatever it was, I've decided I no longer want to hear it."

"Good for you."

"So, we can admit Kenneth in to the club of manipulative arseholes we never have to discuss again — members: two."

"Three."

"Who's the third?"

"Jamie from college, the two-timing wanker."

"Three it is."

With our mutual issues put to bed, we spend the next two hours discussing and debating our weekend away. Over the course of the conversation, it becomes clear just how much Martha is looking forward to getting away and I can't help but wonder if the destination is almost secondary. Somewhere amongst her enthusiasm for nineties nostalgia, there's perhaps a greater enthusiasm for three days of long lie-ins and no parental responsibility.

Considering what we discussed earlier, I decide not to push the subject until the subject itself is brought up in the form of a phone call from Stuart.

With a seismic sigh and a roll of the eyes, Martha takes the call. I can hear the tinny voice at the end of the line but not what's being said. Whatever Mr and Mrs Miller are discussing, it doesn't sound like good news if the groans and mumbled expletives are anything to go by.

Martha ends the call and tosses her phone on the table.

"Problem?"

"Yep. Ella is down at A&E."

"Christ, what's happened?"

"She fell out of a tree and hurt her wrist — the same tree we've warned her not to climb a hundred times."

"Please tell me she's not been seriously hurt?"

"Do you think I'd still be here if she had? No, Stuart thinks it's probably just a sprain but my beloved daughter is refusing to have an x-ray."

"Why?"

"Because she doesn't want to become The Hulk."

"I … what?"

"Do you remember how David Banner first became The Hulk?"

"Err, you'll have to remind me."

"Gamma radiation, and Ella spotted a sign in the x-ray room which warned of radiation."

"Oh dear. Young minds."

"Apparently, she's convinced an x-ray will turn her into a green monster the next time she loses her temper."

"Knowing Ella, I'd have thought she'd consider that cool?"

"She does. It's the ripped clothes she's not keen on. Anyway, it seems I'm the only one who can talk her around so Stuart is on his way to pick me up."

"So much for a relaxing afternoon, eh?"

"I rest my case. Parenthood is overrated."

With obvious reluctance, Martha gets to her feet.

"I'm sorry to leave you like this, chick. I was looking forward to drunken oblivion."

"Me too but never mind. I'll come and wait with you."

We make our way back through the bar to the front of the pub and lean up against the wall.

"I can get Stuart to drop you home," Martha suggests. "His mum is with Ella at the hospital."

"No, don't be silly — Ella needs you, and I could do with walking off at least one bottle of Chardonnay."

"You'll be okay?"

"Don't worry about me."

Stuart's black Audi approaches and pulls up to the kerb. I give Martha a hug and ask her to pass one on to Ella. With that, she gets into the car and they set off with a parting toot of the horn.

I glance at my watch: not yet four o'clock. I'm stuck in the mid-afternoon no-man's-land where it's too early to settle down for the evening, and too late to make other plans.

Would it be wrong to turn one-eighty degrees and head back into the pub? Probably, yes. I've already passed tipsy and it'll only take a few more glasses to reach properly pissed. I should go home.

I delve into my handbag and retrieve a pair of headphones. With my best friend stolen away, I can at least listen to some other friendly voices. It takes five minutes to untangle the headphones and select a playlist suitable for my level of inebriation — cheesy pop hits. Thirty yards of pavement later, I'm humming away merrily to *Tragedy* by Steps.

By the time I reach the end of Kiln Road, my humming has developed into mumbled singing. I can't remember all the words but improvise as I cross the road. A woman pushing a buggy approaches and gives me a wide berth. I suspect to avoid being in direct earshot.

The stroll becomes a bit of a skip when the next track begins: *Relight My Fire* by Take That, featuring Lulu. Martha and I both agreed it's a modern classic, although my drink-addled brain is no more inclined to help me remember the lyrics. I make do.

Despite my intoxication, the music provides a boost to my pace and the third track begins as I approach the corner of Juniper Lane. It brings the widest of smiles.

Martha doesn't get out much in the evenings but when she does, we occasionally like to indulge in a bit of karaoke. Neither of us can sing but we make up for it in sheer enthusiasm, particularly when murdering our favourite songs. Martha's is *I Should Be So Lucky* by Kylie, and mine is Adele's *Chasing Pavements;* the current tune on the playlist.

As I turn the corner, I warble the opening lines to Adele's classic while staring down at the pavement in a misguided attempt to chase it. I've never quite understood the lyrics but I like to treat it as a game and avoid the cracks between the slabs. It results in a jerky stroll as my stride is too short to cover two slabs, but a fraction too long to place a step on every slab. To anyone watching on, it must look like my first day of hopscotch practice.

I get halfway up the lane and begin searching my handbag for the house keys as I walk. They prove elusive and I still haven't found them by the time I reach the front gate. I stop to continue the search.

Just as I spot them lurking at the bottom, I'm torn from my stupor mid-chorus as a hand grabs my right arm and yanks hard. My legs have no chance of responding in time to the sudden force and before I can work out what's happening, I'm being dragged beyond the front gate.

I look up just in time to see a flash of white to my left — a van tears past, only inches from the pavement where I stood a second ago. As my momentum continues pulling me in the opposite direction, I turn towards the front door hoping to identify who has hold of my arm.

I collide into him before I get the chance.

It takes a few seconds to shake off the shock and find my legs. I look up; straight into the frowning face of a man I thought I'd never see again.

Adele's voice is still ringing in my ears, and for a moment I can't work out why. I then tug the headphones from my lugs.

As I do, I catch the end of a gruff voice yelling over my head.

"… you blind prick."

The insult meets with the loud scream of an engine at high revs.

"You okay?" Liam then asks in a slightly less aggressive tone.

I look him up and down as if I'm in some kind of surreal dream. He's swapped his florist's polo shirt for an almost identical one without the logo on the chest.

"That nutter only just missed you," he adds, shaking his head.

I glance over my shoulder but the white van is now long gone.

The Chardonnay acts like syrup in my veins, clogging thoughts and instructions. All I can do is stare blankly at Liam while I wait for the obvious question to reach my mouth. It eventually arrives.

"How … what are you doing here?"

I then notice a tool bag on the doorstep.

"Apart from saving your life? No need to thank me."

"I … thank you."

"You're welcome. Is your road usually such a drag strip?"

"It, um, happens now and again," I mutter. "Van drivers don't realise it's a dead end and then tear up the lane in frustration when they do."

He still hasn't answered my question, but it appears a moot point.

"Shall I get on with it then?"

"Get on with what?"

"Changing your lock."

"My lock? Why does it need changing?"

He adopts a puzzled scowl and scratches his chin. Then, he sniffs the air.

"Are you drunk?"

"Tipsy, maybe."

"That explains it. You've forgotten, haven't you?"

Irritation arrives on the scene.

"Just wait a sec," I strop, hands on hips. "My state of inebriation is none of your business. What the hell are you doing here and why are you so fixated with changing my lock?"

"Your friend told me to be here at four o'clock, because you urgently needed your lock changed."

"What friend?"

"That Kenneth bloke. He came into the shop at lunchtime."

26.

Not one part of Liam's claim makes sense. In fact, not one part of this situation makes sense; not helped by the afternoon's overindulgence.

"I need a black coffee."

"I think you do."

"And an explanation, if you've got time?"

"Nothing else in my diary," he replies with a shrug.

I unlock the front door and Liam trails me in to the kitchen, tool bag in hand. He looks around as I put the kettle on.

"Nice place," he remarks. "You've done a good job on the kitchen."

"Thanks, but I can't take the credit. That'd be the previous owners."

"How long have you lived here then?"

"Five or six months."

Pleasantries out of the way, I invite Liam to take a seat at the table. If I were sober, I might have thought twice before inviting a stranger into my home but seeing as I'm not sober, and Liam isn't a complete stranger, I find myself grabbing two mugs from the cupboard.

"It's just instant, I'm afraid. I don't think I'm capable of using the percolator at the moment."

"No worries."

I spoon coffee granules in the vague direction of the mugs. Most of it makes it.

"Sugar?"

"Just the one, ta."

Somehow, I produce two mugs of coffee. I even manage to transport both of them to the table without spillage.

"If it tastes like crap," I say apologetically, while taking a seat, "feel free to tip it down the sink."

"I was a handyman for seven years. Trust me, I've had more than my fair share of crappy coffee."

I smile back and take a sip from my mug; the bitterness acute compared to the sweetness of the Chardonnay I've been glugging all afternoon.

"You mentioned Kenneth?"

"I did, and I presumed you knew I'd be here."

I shake my head.

"Shall we start at the beginning?" I suggest.

"Well, he turned up at the shop at lunchtime and I mentioned you'd been in, looking for him. He said he knew, but you had a more pressing issue."

"He said that?"

"More or less. He somehow knew I used to be a handyman and asked if my experience extended to changing door locks. I said it did, and he asked how much I charged. He then handed over the full amount in cash, plus an extra fifty quid, and told me to be here not a second later than four o'clock — he was insistent about that and said I should wait if you're not at home."

My face puckers, but it isn't the bitterness of the coffee. Liam's ability to read body language is better than his floristry skills.

"You knew nothing about it?"

"No, and I've no idea why he'd ask you to change my lock."

"Can't help you with that. Did you have your locks changed when you moved in here?"

"Why would I?"

"Because it's sensible. You've no idea who the previous owners lent a key to: friends and relatives, neighbours, tradesmen, all manner of people might have a key to this house."

"I never thought of that."

"So, do you want me to change it?"

"Who'd have a key?"

He dips a hand into his tool bag and plucks out a box.

"This is a new lock barrel I bought from the DIY store an hour ago. It includes two keys, and as you can see, it's still sealed so you and you alone will have the only keys in existence."

"And Kenneth has already paid?"

"Yep."

"I guess there's no harm then."

Whilst it might be sensible to change the lock, I've no idea why Kenneth even considered it, let alone organised and paid for it. Nor do I know how he discovered my address.

Liam gets to his feet and grabs his tool bag.

"It'll only take ten minutes."

"Great. I'll stay here and try to sober up."

"You do that."

He turns and disappears back towards the hallway.

Left alone, I tap through to the photo of Kenneth on my phone, as if looking at his face will suddenly reveal a motive for his unfathomable actions.

"What are you playing at, Kenneth?" I whisper to myself.

Even if I had a starting point for an answer, which I don't, the sudden scream of a drill shatters any chance of concentrating. I turn my focus back to the task of sobering up and sip at the coffee while staring into space. The drilling ends but it's replaced by a series of loud bangs; presumably a result of the old lock barrel being evicted from its long-term home.

A text message arrives from Martha: *Mission accomplished, and it's just a sprain. Doctor prescribed painkillers, rest, and pizza xx*

I thumb a reply with a couple of suitable emojis and a kiss. A satisfactory resolution to the afternoon for one of us, at least, but I wish she hadn't mentioned pizza. I haven't eaten since breakfast and I've now got a savage yearning for a Hawaiian. As always, I find an excuse — a generous helping of starchy pizza dough might help soak up the alcohol.

Liam wanders back into the kitchen.

"All done."

"That was quick."

"Believe it or not, I'm pretty good with my hands … unless they're arranging flowers."

"Practice makes perfect."

"I wish that were true."

Silence then fills the kitchen and before thinking through the ramifications, I open my mouth to fill it.

"I'm about to order a pizza. Do you fancy joining me … my treat to say thank you?"

"Err, okay."

"You sure? Don't feel obliged if you've got somewhere else you'd rather be."

"No, I … pizza would be great. Thanks."

"Sit yourself down then."

He shares a half-smile and takes a seat at the table; his expression nervy. Perhaps the prospect of an hour in my company is worse than dealing with a spray of roses or an enemy combatant.

"Are you okay, Liam?"

"Yeah, yeah. Just a bit warm."

"Me too. I'll open the door."

I get up and unlock the back door. Within a second of opening it, a ginger feline slinks in.

"Hey, Frank."

He trots over to the table and jumps up.

"Liam, meet Frank."

The cat stands motionless for a second and eyes my invited guest. Then, he wanders over to Liam. For some reason, I think of Nathan and how much he detested pets of any kind.

"Sorry, I should have checked. Are you okay with cats?"

He answers with a nod and runs his hand over Frank's thick fur.

"My mum's got three," he replies. "Some of the best conversations I've had have been with those cats."

"Tell me about it," I snigger. "Although Frank isn't my cat."

"No?"

"I've no idea who he belongs to, but he turns up here almost every day."

"Must be the warm welcome."

"Or the tinned tuna. Speaking of which."

I get to my feet.

"How do you know his name if he's not yours?"

"I don't. I just thought he looked like a Frank."

"I can see that."

With my guests playing nicely, I prepare dinner for one of them and then place it on the table. Frank forgets his manners and immediately turns his back on Liam.

"He's got his priorities right," Liam jokes, as Frank attacks his dinner.

"He has, and on that note: what kind of pizza do you fancy?"

"I'm a simple man. Ham and mushroom."

"Thin base or regular?"

"Thin, please."

I open the takeaway app on my phone and order our pizzas, together with garlic bread, and a pot of chocolate ice cream. If Liam can't find space for it, I sure as hell will.

"Sorted. It'll be here in forty-five minutes."

Thinking back to our conversation the other day, I'm conscious the wait might be forty-minutes too long for a man uncomfortable chatting with a woman he barely knows. His face says as much so I return to our earlier conversation.

"So, shall we talk about Kenneth?"

"If you like, although I'm not sure what more I can tell you."

"Did you get my email?"

"Cancelling your visit this morning? I did."

"Sorry about that but I thought the medallion itself might be the clue, so I trawled jewellery shops instead."

"I'm guessing it didn't pan out?"

"Nope. None of the four shops stocked the medallion and no one I spoke to had ever seen Kenneth."

"Looks like you're stuck with me then. For whatever reason, he seems to enjoy popping into my shop."

"I am sorry."

"For what?"

"Dragging you into this … whatever it is."

"It's fine. I just don't get what his motive is. You have any ideas?"

"Not really. My friend, Martha, had a theory he might be a religious nut and I'm being lured into some kind of sect."

I expected Liam to dismiss Martha's theory, but it's met with a thoughtful silence. Frank — having eaten — takes the silence as his cue to leave. He's not the only one to feel a sudden discomfort.

"What are you thinking?" I ask.

"Doesn't matter," he says dismissively. "You'll think I'm crazy."

"I'm past caring about crazy. Shoot."

"I watched a documentary a few weeks ago about that American medium, Taylor McCabe. Did you see it?"

"Afraid not, but go on."

"The bloke conned hundreds of people into believing he could communicate with the dead. At first, I just assumed they were gullible idiots willing to believe any old tosh but McCabe was a pro. He had a team of investigators who dug into every detail of a victim's life before he made his move. He knew so much about the deceased and their family, people believed him."

"What a devious arsehole."

"It gets worse. He used his influence to con money out of the families … millions of dollars over the years. He set himself up as a charity and encouraged people to make sizable donations so he could continue his work. He also organised afterlife retreats at two grand a ticket. People flocked to them in their droves because McCabe was so convincing."

"Those poor people."

"They got justice in the end. The FBI took him down and he's currently enjoying a thirty-year sentence."

"I'll have to watch it, but what's it got to do with Kenneth?"

"Maybe your friend, Martha, wasn't too far off the truth."

"I don't follow."

"What if this Kenneth bloke is looking to exploit your grief, like Taylor McCabe? The medallion is a pretty twisted way to get your attention, but it worked."

"To a point, but what it doesn't explain is why, let alone how."

"Same motive as McCabe: money."

Before the revelation about Dad's yard, I wouldn't have considered myself a worthwhile target for a scam artist. I presumed they play a high stakes game, and if you're putting your liberty at risk, the reward has to be worthwhile. The potential value of the yard would definitely be a worthwhile reward.

"As for how he knew," Liam continues. "There are plenty of ways."

"Name one."

"Are there any photos of your dad on Facebook or elsewhere online — photos where he's wearing that medallion?"

"Err, probably yes. I set up a memorial page to mark the tenth anniversary of their passing. I read somewhere it might help if I celebrate their lives rather than dwell on their deaths."

"Did it?"

"Kind of."

"And it's a public page? Anyone can see it?"

"I think so."

"So, it's not such a stretch to imagine a con artist stumbling across that page and using the information about your parents to wrangle their way into your life, and your bank account."

Even in my semi-drunken fog, Liam's theory finds a way home. It's a theory which at least makes sense, but also suggests either I've been supremely naïve or he's supremely cynical. I then find an obvious hole.

"What about his visit to your shop today? I see how the medallion fits with a con, but why on earth would he pay you to change my lock?"

"You ever play chess?"

"Nope, but I understand the basics."

"I used to play a lot, and your opponent's moves don't always make sense until they suddenly declare checkmate."

I sit back and let Liam's words sink in.

"If you want my advice," he adds. "I'd steer well away from the bloke. If he calls into the shop again, I'll tell him where to go."

"I don't know if you're right about his motive, but you're right about steering clear."

I reach the bottom of the mug.

"Can I get you another one?"

"I'm okay."

"I'm not. I need more caffeine."

I get up and return to the kettle.

"You said your dad died in an accident. Do you mind if I ask what happened?"

It's a well-worn tale and one I hoped I'd never have to tell again. As I stir the coffee, I'm undecided whether I want to share it with a man I barely know.

I return to the table and swallow hard. The silence and the alcohol prove adequate levers, and before I can stop myself, the words begin to flow. I'm so used to being interrupted with token platitudes and sympathy, I'm relieved when Liam just sits quietly and listens without comment.

His silence continues beyond my final words.

"You don't know what to say, do you?" I mumble. "That's how most people react when I tell them how I lost my parents."

"I don't know what to say because … well, there's nothing anyone can say."

"Nope, there isn't."

"But, for what it's worth, I know how you feel."

"I doubt it."

He leans forward and rests his elbows on the table.

"My sister, Louise, died in an accident."

My cheeks are already aglow before I have a chance to backtrack.

"Oh, I'm so sorry … I didn't mean …"

"It's okay," he interjects. "As you say: most people don't know how to react."

"Do you, um, want to talk about it?"

"Another time, maybe."

Perhaps just throwaway words but I'm not sure if there will be another time. It was only Kenneth's plotting which threw us together, and as we've both committed to steering clear of him, it seems unlikely our paths will cross again after today.

"Sure. Another time."

I glance up at the kitchen clock — still another twenty minutes before the pizza is due.

"Tell me about the shop."

"What about it?"

"You said it was becoming a struggle. How bad is it?"

"Not sure," he sighs. "But I don't think I'll make it through to Valentine's Day."

"Could you not hire a trained florist?"

"Lou employed a girl and she was great but a month after I took over, she left."

"Why not replace her?"

"It's not that easy. Kids don't want to train as florists these days, and those with training don't seem keen to work with a misery like me."

"I'm sure you're not that bad."

"I'm not, but I'm not exactly a people person either. It was okay when I was putting up shelves and fixing leaky taps, but I'm so far beyond my comfort zone I can't find a way back."

"You could … sell the business."

"That's what my mum said."

"Well, why don't you?"

"I can't imagine there would be a queue of buyers for a failing florists. And, it'd be the end of Lou's dream. All she ever wanted to do was run her own shop."

The obvious response would be to point out his sister's dream wasn't for the shop to become Liam's nightmare. Then again, who am I to pass judgement when I couldn't bear to be apart from boxes of my parents' junk?

"You could find a business partner."

"Same problem as finding a buyer. Who'd want a share in a business dying on its arse?"

"Maybe someone with experience who's looking to start their own business but can't afford to start from scratch. Even if they only pay a few grand, it'll help steady the ship, and they could run it day-to-day while you pick up your old business."

It's already clear Liam is a thinker and when he does his thinking, it's in silence.

"That's not a bad idea," he finally admits. "Although I wouldn't know where to find someone."

"Do you know if there's a trade magazine for florists?"

"Lou used to subscribe to one, but I cancelled it."

"I'd start there. Run an advert and I'm sure you'll get plenty of offers."

Even with just the seeds of a solution sewn, his dark brown eyes appear a shade brighter and his scowl less pronounced; like a weight has shifted.

"I'm glad I popped by now," he smiles. "Even if I wasn't invited."

"You see. It does help to talk."

"Depends who's listening, I suppose."

"Very true."

The doorbell rings.

"That's probably our pizza."

I scoot up the hall and collect our dinner from an impatient delivery driver. Barely halfway up the hallway and I'm tempted to dig in.

"Can I get you a plate, or cutlery?"

"Um …"

"I'm a slob I'm afraid. Happy to eat it out of the box."

"That's a relief."

I sit down and slide one of the boxes across the table. We simultaneously flip the lids open.

Liam then looks at me a little awkwardly.

"I've got a confession to make."

"Please don't tell me you're gluten intolerant."

"No, it's just … I'm not much of a social diner. I've never got the hang of eating and holding a conversation at the same time."

I chuckle in response.

"What's so funny?"

"You're in luck. I much prefer eating in my own company so don't expect conversation."

"Thank God for that."

"I'll put the radio on so you don't have to hear how unladylike I am."

I get up and switch it on.

We both make short work of our pizzas. I can't deny it makes a pleasant change eating with someone who doesn't talk between every mouthful. On the odd occasion I eat with Martha she never shuts up, and Nathan did nothing but critique the food whether we were eating at a restaurant or at home.

"Thanks for that," Liam says, as he closes the lid on his box.

"You're welcome."

I follow suit and close the lid of my box.

"You've got a big appetite," he then grins. "For a …"

The next word catches in his throat and the grin vanishes. I let him stew for a second or two.

"I, um … sorry. Ignore me."

"I've got a big appetite, for a small woman. Is that what you were about to say?"

He dips his head forward and cusses under his breath.

"I warned you," he then mumbles. "I'm bloody hopeless in female company … always putting my foot in it."

"Well, Liam," I reply calmly. "It's true: I am a small woman, and I do have a big appetite."

"Yeah, but only a lumbering idiot like me would point it out. You can now see why I'm single."

"You just haven't met someone who appreciates your qualities."

"What qualities?" he scoffs.

"You're a good listener, you're refreshingly honest, and what woman wouldn't want a handyman on demand?"

He returns my smile.

"Thank you."

"Anytime. Fancy some ice cream? It's double-chocolate."

27.

The trouble with drinking in the afternoon is the same-day hangover. By nine o'clock I felt like that van had actually run me over, and I slipped into a coma-like sleep.

The evening wasn't all bad, though.

Liam stayed for another hour and despite the gathering hangover clouds, it made a pleasant change to chat with a man, who, despite his lack of tact, had no pretences and no agenda. Once he relaxed, there were flashes of humour and glimpses of an intelligent, principled human lurking beneath the surface. I can kind of understand why some women might not consider Liam their cup of tea, but personally I've always favoured coffee.

As we said goodbye on the doorstep, we swapped phone numbers and he said I should call if I have any odd jobs, or free pizza going spare. I'm sure I can find a few odd jobs but spare pizza hasn't ever been an issue.

I roll over and check my watch: half-nine. It looks like I've already made a good start to a lazy Sunday but it's too warm to stay in bed. I get up and, after visiting the bathroom, trudge downstairs.

Much to my annoyance, I find a handful of leaflets scattered on the doormat. Littering is rightly illegal, but it seems perfectly acceptable for takeaways, double glazing companies, and various estate agents to shove a never ending torrent of crap through my letterbox. I snatch the leaflets up and scan each one so I can make a mental note never to use any of the littering perpetrators. The first is a menu for an Indian restaurant, the second a discount voucher for a car valeting company, and the third a flyer promoting a summer craft fair being held this afternoon.

I drop all three in the recycling bin on my way to the kettle.

Just over an hour later, having showered, dressed, and eaten, I'm already bored. The problem with being lazy in the summer is that we Brits appear genetically obliged to venture outdoors whenever the sky is blue and the mercury high. In spring, autumn, and winter, it's perfectly acceptable to hunker down in front of the television or to find a cosy nook to read, but we feel guilty wasting a day of fine weather.

I do my best to ignore the calling; browsing the web, watching television, and generally faffing around. In the end, I sit in the garden and read. It's only when I reach the end of a chapter do I realise nothing is sinking in. I can't concentrate, and I know why. At the back of my mind, a niggling voice keeps asking the same question: why did Kenneth ask Liam to change my lock?

Yesterday, there was enough alcohol in my bloodstream to drown it out but this morning it won't shut up. It's fine deciding not to take part in any of Kenneth's games but that doesn't stop me wondering why he staged them in the first place. I need to find a distraction before the voice drives me crazy.

Closing the book, I get up, return to the kitchen, and begrudgingly extract a flyer from the recycle bin — the craft fair starts at noon. The map on the back confirms the location is only a twenty-minute stroll away, and the promise of homemade cakes and pastries provides the decisive incentive.

With bag shouldered and sunglasses donned, I set off.

I've barely reached the end of Juniper Lane when the niggling voice catches up. Not to be outdone, I plug my headphones in and drown the bastard out. I don't hear another peep all the way to the recreation ground where the fair is being held.

At the gate, I hand over the entrance fee in return for a programme listing all the various stalls and events. I tuck it into my bag and, with no plan or preference, idly wander towards the first stall. That stall turns out to be the first aid tent. I flash an embarrassed smile at the two women in St John's uniform and move on.

The adjacent stall does have some handcrafted goods for sale. I approach the table to inspect rows of pebbles painted in a variety of colourful designs; badly, as it happens. It feels rude just glancing and then walking away but I don't want to give the impression I'm interested in the stallholder's tat. I can sense her stare as I politely browse her dreadful wares. She might predict a sale but I can predict buyer's remorse. Fortunately, I'm then joined by another potential customer who goes as far as picking up one of the pebbles. My escape is swift.

The next few dozen stalls I visit offer an eclectic range of goods from jewellery to candles, sculptures to clothes. They stretch the definition of craft with some of the wares, but there are a few stallholders who've created genuinely beautiful goods. In particular, I can't resist a handmade bracelet beaded with leather and turquoise gemstones. At forty quid it's not exactly a bargain but I reckon I deserve a treat after my recent wrangles.

The next stall is the one I really wanted to visit, although it's more a marquee than a stall. I wander in.

At the rear there are four tables laden with cakes and staffed by a bevy of white-haired women. A fifth table houses a large stainless steel urn and two more women serving hot beverages. I make my way over to the first table and peruse the wide range of homemade cakes. There's almost too much choice but I settle on a slab of carrot cake so moist-looking it would be madness tackling it with fingers alone. I grab a fork and make my way over to one of the cheap patio tables laid out around the perimeter of the marquee.

I've barely forked the first mouthful when I feel a tap on my shoulder. I turn around.

"Oh, wow. It is you," a beaming woman shrieks in my face.

Just my luck to choose a table right next to Hannah and Rupert; the insufferable couple who live in my former home in Kensall Gardens.

"Hi, Hannah. Rupert."

"I love the new hairstyle. It's so chic," she coos.

"Thank you."

"Why don't you join us so we can have a catch up?"

She then turns to her husband.

"You can ask Kelly about that plant in the garden."

"Oh, yes," Rupert replies, before turning to me. "Please, come and sit with us."

Hannah pats the empty chair next to her.

My mind scrambles for an excuse but comes up empty. I've no choice but to transfer my arse to the chair and my cake to their table.

"How have you been, Kelly?"

"Well, thanks. You?"

I regret asking as she details every tedious moment of their lives since moving to Kensall Gardens. Hannah is one of those people who talks at you, rather than to you. On the upside, I'm free to pick at my cake.

She runs out of steam, and then Rupert takes over.

"I've been struggling to identify some plants in the garden. Do you know what that large shrub in the north-west corner is?"

"Sorry, but Nathan hired a landscape gardener just after we moved in so I couldn't tell you."

"Could you ask Nathan for the gardener's number? I'd like to plant another one in the opposite corner."

It seems neither Rupert nor his boring wife know the reason they're now living in our home. I assumed the estate agents might have mentioned it, but obviously not. I'm not in the mood to prolong our conversation by airing my dirty laundry.

"I don't think he'll remember."

"I should have asked him when I had the chance," he says, shaking his head.

"That might have been a better idea," I remark, a little too smugly.

"He was a tad preoccupied when I bumped into him — quaffing champagne with colleagues."

Nathan rarely ever drunk enough to become tipsy and never drank champagne in all the years we were together.

"He was drinking champagne? Are you sure?"

"Yes, having a merry time in a bar near Waterloo station."

"When was this?"

"I'm not sure exactly, but I remember it was bitterly cold so it must have been back in January, or possibly February."

That was around the time our divorce papers were being served. Perhaps the cause for his celebration.

"I suspect he's not so pleased now, though," Rupert adds,

struggling to disguise his smirk. "After what happened with Epsom Pharma."

"Epsom Pharma?"

"Yes, that's why he was celebrating. He took a fraction too much pleasure bragging about the fortune he and his colleagues were set to make. Pride comes before a fall, they say."

"You'll have to excuse me, Rupert. What is Epsom Pharma, and what happened?"

"He didn't tell you?"

"We rarely speak about work."

"It's probably best you ask him. I don't wish to tell tales out of school."

"Makes no odds to me. We're divorced now."

The couple stare at one another in mild shock. There's a sudden atmosphere at the table.

"I wish we'd known," Rupert frowns.

"Why?"

"Because of the negative aura."

"Err ..."

"I have to say," Hannah interjects. "I'm really disappointed you didn't tell us, Kelly. It would have influenced our decision to buy the house."

Her tone is accusatory, and unwelcome.

"I'm not aware we had any legal obligation to inform you, Hannah."

"No, but you had a moral obligation. You knew we were planning to raise our children in that house."

"So what? I don't see what bearing our divorce has on your offspring."

"As Rupert said, the negative aura created by a toxic relationship will linger in a house for years, and that does affect our children."

Gobsmacked, I stare back at her.

"I think you're being a bit over-dramatic. It's not as though we decorated with asbestos wallpaper or stored nuclear waste in the loft."

"Over-dramatic?" she huffs. "You wouldn't be so dismissive

if you discovered your children were being raised in such an environment. Oh, and now you mention the loft, we had to have it completely re-lagged, didn't we, Rupert?"

"Yes, at significant cost. I'm minded to contact our solicitor to seek recompense."

My appetite has gone. I drop the fork on the plate.

"Good luck with that," I reply, getting to my feet. "And if you've got any more questions about the house, can I suggest you stick them where the sun doesn't shine. Goodbye."

I stride away.

My annoyance is so severe I stomp on for another hundred yards until I reach the boundary of the recreation ground. Conveniently, there's a bench for me to sit and stew.

After ten minutes I conclude I loathe Hannah and Rupert, and I pity their kids. Every parent wants to protect their child but not to the point of suffocation. If, God-willing, I'm blessed with a child next year, I want him or her to have the same kind of childhood I did — to feel loved, not smothered. The world can be an amazing place, and a shitty place, and life plays out at both ends of that spectrum. Kids need to learn that themselves. Hannah and Rupert are doing their offspring a disservice by pretending otherwise.

I'm no longer in the right frame of mind for browsing craft stalls, and I'm definitely not in the right frame of mind for a second round with Hannah and Rupert should I bump into them again. I get up and make my way home.

An hour later, I'm back in the garden browsing nursery furniture on my laptop. I shouldn't, I know, but it's the only method of distracting myself from negative influences.

I make a list of my favourite items but stop short of ordering anything. I've not long to wait until my first consultation at the clinic and then I can go crazy with the credit card. Hopefully.

With the list complete, the conversation with Hannah and Rupert creeps back. I've no desire to focus on their ridiculous accusations but one subject is worth my curiosity. With nothing else better to do for the next five minutes, I search for Epsom Pharma.

Negative news stories dominate the results page. I click on one from the BBC to see why.

There's a brief introductory statement about the company and their woes, followed by a graph which displays Epsom Pharma's share price over the last six months. In January, the shares were worth just over eleven pounds and then they shot up to almost thirty pounds by late February. The graph continues to rise sharply upwards past fifty pounds, and then suddenly, in April, there's a severe and immediate drop to just over two pounds. Last month, the shares were suspended altogether.

I know next to nothing about the stock market but even I can see something catastrophic must have occurred for a company to lose so much value so quickly. Curious, I read on.

The answer comes in the next paragraph. In February, Epsom Pharma released a new wonder drug for treating dementia. Then, in March, the police launched a criminal investigation into the company's development team. That investigation would have certainly hit their share price, but the reason they tanked so badly was due to a confession from a whistle-blower within Epsom Pharma's development team. He provided indisputable evidence they had used data hacked from their competitor's computer system to tweak their own dementia treatment — a treatment they rushed to market six months ahead of their competitor.

As a result, Epsom Pharma ceased trading and their shares are now worthless.

I think back to the conversation I had with Nathan in The Three Horseshoes. He claimed to have a cash-flow issue, and that's why he couldn't pay off his supposed blackmailer. One minute he's celebrating, the next he's being blackmailed and can't muster two hundred grand. Admittedly, it's a significant sum but not to a man of Nathan's means. When we divorced, and he reclaimed the money from the sale of our marital home, he must have had close to a million in the bank.

With all the jigsaw pieces suddenly dropping into my lap, a picture emerges.

"Oh. My. God."

The picture is fuzzy, but there's enough clarity to draw a

conclusion. When Rupert bumped into Nathan at the beginning of the year, my then-husband must have known Epsom Pharma were about to release their new drug. If he knew about the tweaked formula, he and his clients stood to quadruple their investment. Cause for celebration.

Could it be that Nathan risked his entire wealth on a dead cert which turned out to be a dead duck?

It also explains why he insisted we avoid attaching a financial settlement to our divorce. If he had, I'd have been entitled to half his multimillion-pound windfall. If my theory is correct, he's now potless so there's nothing to lose if he tries staking a claim on my assets.

The devious arsehole.

The more I stare at the picture, the more it bleeds into focus. When it comes to money, this is exactly the devious, deceitful tactic I'd expect of Nathan, but I doubt he ever thought I'd unearth the truth. That truth offers me leverage. He mentioned some documents on our computer he couldn't afford anyone to see, and I'd bet those documents relate to the data theft by Epsom Pharma. It's not too much of a leap to assume Nathan knew something about the stolen data before he made the investment, which is possibly why he bet everything.

Whoever hacked our computer must have thought all their Christmases had come at once when they realised they had inadvertently found evidence of corporate espionage. They're not alone.

If ever there was an example of silver linings, it's my chat with Hannah and Rupert. They may have irritated the hell out of me, but Rupert's casual gloating about Epsom Pharma has gifted me a potential way to silence my ex-husband once and for all, should the need ever arise. Saying that, I've not heard a peep from him since I sent that email five days ago so maybe he's given up or found the money to pay off his blackmailers.

Either way, it's cause enough for a slice or two of celebratory cake; not that I need an excuse.

I should go buy some.

28.

The faces of my fellow waiting passengers are painted with a Monday morning expression. The lack of a bus isn't helping. It's now five minutes late; the tutting and sighing spreads like a virus.

A further five minutes pass before the bus trundles into view. I'm irritated because I'll have to endure staffroom coffee but others will miss a train or arrive at work to a disgruntled boss.

We shuffle on board. Fortunately for the driver we're all seasoned travellers and know complaining will only add to the delay. The journey is slow and tense, and it's a relief to disembark before someone finally loses their shit.

By the time I wander into the staffroom, I'm fifteen minutes behind schedule. It's late enough I'm not the first to arrive — Natalie is at the table, sipping what smells like green tea.

"Good morning," I cough.

"Morning," she replies, without looking up from the table.

"Feeling better today?"

No answer, but the look she returns isn't too dissimilar to those on the bus.

"Suit yourself," I mumble.

A few more of my team arrive to break the awful atmosphere. I don't wish to hear their weekend tales and escape to the sanctuary of my office.

Flopping down in my chair, I boot up the computer. I notice the photo of my parents has moved a few inches from its usual position. The cleaners, no doubt. I turn it back so I can see their smiling faces.

"Sorry," I mouth.

If there's one day I don't want to be behind schedule, it's a Monday. With hundreds of loan applications which have stacked up over the weekend, I'm bound to face more hassle than any other day, and that's before I've dealt with the lengthy list of emails currently tumbling into my inbox.

No sense complaining, even if there was anyone willing to

listen, which there isn't.

I gulp back a mouthful of coffee and crack on.

By mid-morning I've made some headway. Time to reward my endeavours with another cup of bland coffee but I'm thwarted when my mobile rings. It's Richard from Ramsey Rowe & Associates.

I answer, and we swap pleasantries before he gets down to the reason for the call.

"I had a meeting on Friday with the Land Director of a company called Redwood Homes. Have you heard of them?"

"Can't say I have."

"They've just completed on the land which abuts yours so they were always likely to be interested. It seems they're extremely keen to do a deal."

My heart beats a little faster.

"That's great to hear. How keen exactly?"

"£1.25 million keen."

"I ... err ..."

Until this moment, we'd only ever discussed value in a hypothetical sense. For that reason, the offer steals my breath.

"I hope you're speechless in a good way," Richard chuckles.

"I ... yes, um. That's amazing."

"It is. There are some caveats, however."

"Uh, huh?"

"The offer is conditional on planning, although they don't foresee any issues, and they want a seven-day lockout so they can prepare their option agreement."

"What's ... sorry, I'm still shell-shocked. What's a lock-out agreement?"

"It simply means we won't actively market the land for a week, or entertain any other offers. It's a common practice. All things considered, it's a very good offer but if you'd like me to push them a little higher, there's no harm in trying."

"Um, I don't know. What do you think?"

"Most developers leave themselves some wriggle room so I'd suggest we go back and ask for £1.35 million. The worst they can say is no but I suspect they'll meet us in the middle at £1.3

million. It's an extra fifty thousand, which isn't to be sniffed at."

My gut reaction is to snatch the first offer. It's such a vast sum of money and I'm too scared to risk losing it, but Richard's casual tone makes it sound like we're haggling over a restaurant bill.

"If you think that's the best strategy, I trust your judgement."

"Excellent. Leave it with me and I'll come back to you as soon as I've spoken to them."

With a cheery goodbye, Richard hangs up. I keep the phone pressed to my ear as I stare, open-mouthed, at the far wall.

Did that just happen? Did I just receive a £1.25 million offer for the scrubby patch of land Dad bought on a whim?

My computer pings a notification — an email from Richard. Finally, I lower the phone and open the email. Confirmation of what I'm still struggling to believe; all there in black and white pixels. It really happened.

The shock soon gives way to elation. Surely the developer would only have made the offer if they're confident they'll secure planning permission. Even the pessimistic part of my brain can't deny this is a significant milestone. Like a marathon runner passing the twenty-mile mark, I think I'm closing in on the home straight.

The elation reaches a point I'm almost fit to burst. So much so, I have to get up and pace the eight feet of carpet beyond my desk.

The pacing helps to bring some measure of calm and a clear head. The offer is a significant milestone but I need to keep in mind the conversation with Samantha at the clinic: there might be unforeseen obstacles blocking my path.

Before my mind has the chance to wander off again, I head to the staffroom to make the coffee I promised myself.

When I return to my desk I'm met with a new raft of emails to answer and issues to resolve; a dent in the headway I made earlier. I need the distraction and strike a deal with myself: if I catch up before lunchtime, I'll treat myself to a calorific snack at the sandwich shop.

The next two hours are a battle and not helped when Justin

pops in for a chat. Despite my phone ringing off the hook and email notifications pinging every thirty seconds, my boss doesn't take the hint and loiters like a particularly noxious fart. I suspect he's just killing time between meetings and trying to portray himself as the friendly, approachable director he isn't. When he asks how Nathan is, I flatly remind him for the second time I divorced months ago. With a red face, he finally buggers off.

Despite Justin's interference I'm still able to get on top of the workload. At one o'clock, I make my escape.

On the way to the sandwich shop, I pass a toy store and linger outside to look at the window display. Martha will tell me off but I'd like to buy a little something for Ella to mark her bravery at the x-ray department. The problem with twins is it feels cruel giving one of them a gift and not the other so I nip in and buy a charm bracelet kit they can use together. The gift assumes one of my goddaughters isn't now a hulking green abomination with wrists like bollards. I'm sure Martha would have mentioned it.

I arrive at the sandwich shop and place my order: a tuna panini, a chocolate-chip flapjack, and an orange juice. After a wait for the panini, I'm handed a tray and then step outside to one of the two free tables.

I'm about to take the first bite of my lunch when a figure steps into view.

"Hello, Kelly."

Kenneth sits down in the chair opposite. I reach for my phone.

"You've got thirty seconds to explain what the hell your game is, and then I'm going to call the police."

"Thirty seconds seems a little unrealistic," he replies. "Would you settle on four minutes and nineteen seconds?"

"I'll add pedantry to the growing list of reasons I'd rather call the police. But before I do, I want some answers."

"I had a feeling you might. Please, go ahead."

"Why the wild goose chase? I wasted hours racking my brain trying to work out how the hell I might find you and then wasted more of my time trawling florists and jewellery shops."

"You found what you needed to find. That's all that matters."

"Are you serious? That's not an answer."

"It is, and one day you'll hopefully realise it."

"And what about Dad's medallion? How did you know about it?"

"Let's just say I have a keen interest in genealogy."

"Again, not an answer."

"I can't tell you."

"Can't, or won't?"

"Aren't they the same thing?"

"Okay, seeing as you won't answer that question either, it begs another: why?"

"Why did I give it you?"

"Yes."

"To set you on the right path."

"What is it with you and paths? If you want something from me, just spit it out."

"I want nothing from you, apart from your trust."

"Bullshit," I spit. "You're trying to mess with my head. Why?"

He checks his watch.

"Can I ask you a question, Kelly?"

"You've got some bloody nerve."

"It's a simple enough question. Do you believe in fate?"

"I … yes, no … what a ridiculous question."

"Perhaps, but hear me out. There is a saying: fate doesn't care about your plans. Have you ever heard it?"

"No."

"In your case, it couldn't be more relevant. Fate really doesn't care about your plans."

"That's ridiculous."

"Please, just bear with me."

"Jesus wept," I mutter. "Get on with it, then."

Undeterred by my impatience, he presses on.

"Imagine a relatively innocuous event occurred; one which sent you on a path you were never supposed to take."

"Such as?"

"Such as breaking the heel of a shoe."

"What's that ... wait. How do you know I broke a heel?"

Ignoring my question, he sits forward and rests his arms on the table.

"I have done all I can to re-correct your future but there are events I cannot control. The only way to resolve the future is by dealing with Nathan Thaw. He requires money, urgently, and you're his only hope."

Now his motive is clear, my exasperation forms a coalition with anger. I'm about to reach for my phone when my brain retrieves one question Kenneth has failed to answer: how he knew about Dad's medallion.

"Ahh ... I get it now."

"I'm not with you?"

I'm so annoyed with myself for not spotting the connection sooner.

"I thought you were in cahoots with Nathan. It never crossed my mind that you're the one blackmailing him."

"I can assure you, Kelly, you're a long way from the truth."

"Am I? It makes perfect sense. You realised you can't get any money from Nathan so now you're targeting me."

"How have you reached that conclusion?"

"Here's the thing, Kenneth. I'm not telling you, but I will tell the police. This is harassment ... no, this is intimidation; demanding money with menace."

"Kelly, it's the only way we can outwit fate. If you continue on this current path, the consequences are grave."

I get to my feet.

"We'll see how grave they are for you once I've spoken to the police."

"If I thought their involvement would change your path, I'd offer you every encouragement but it won't make one jot of difference."

I've lost my appetite but, as a point of principle, I'm not willing to walk away from a lunch I've paid for. I return the panini to the paper bag and toss it into my handbag along with the flapjack and the unopened bottle of orange juice.

"We'll see about that. Next time I see you, Kenneth, I expect it to be across a courtroom."

I glare down at him and storm away; heading back to work at a brisk and determined pace.

My thunderous expression acts as a deterrent so none of my team dare approach me as I stride towards my office. I slam the door and my phone is in hand by the time I'm at my desk. Scrolling through my history I locate the last time I called the police to report the video being posted on Facebook — exactly a week ago. I jab the screen and go through the same process.

I'm not connected to PC Walker this time, which is no great surprise or disappointment. As sympathetic as he was, I'm relieved when a female officer answers my call. She introduces herself as PC Johnson and I bore the poor woman witless for five minutes as I explain my history with Nathan and Kenneth. I conclude by telling her about his threat if I didn't hand money to Nathan.

After a short silence, PC Johnson poses a question.

"Mr Thaw is your ex-husband?" she asks.

"Thankfully, yes."

"And this Kenneth character?"

"I have a theory he's the one who tried to blackmail my ex-husband, and now Nathan is refusing to play ball, he's coming after me."

"And what do you base this theory on?"

"Kenneth gave me a medallion — an exact copy of one I purchased for my late father years ago. It kind of freaked me out and I guess that's why he did it … to get under my skin."

"Right, so, this Kenneth character gives you a medallion similar to one your father owned?"

"Exactly."

"I can see how that would upset you but I'm not sure how that makes him a blackmailer."

"Because it links Kenneth to the hacked computer Nathan and I shared."

"How so?"

"I purchased the original medallion from an online gift store, and I'm positive I logged in to that gift store several times on the same computer the blackmailer hacked. It only occurred to me twenty minutes ago. If Kenneth is the blackmailer, all he had to do was log in to the account and he'd have access to my purchase history."

"But how did he know you bought it for your father, specifically?"

I relay Liam's suggestion about the photos on my parents' Facebook memorial page. The same photos which show Dad wearing the medallion.

"So, you're suggesting Kenneth hacked your computer, found this gift store account and realised you bought a medallion. He then stumbles across a memorial page on Facebook where he sees photos of your father wearing that medallion. Based on those two pieces of information, he purchases the same medallion and lures you into some kind of scam which has now escalated into a demand for money. Have I got that right?"

Hearing my theory relayed to me, I have to accept it sounds a stretch.

"Err, yes. That's about right."

"And did Kenneth directly ask you for money?"

"No, he said I should give money to Nathan."

There's a brief moment of silence on the line.

"Can I level with you, Miss Coburn — I'm struggling to understand what's going on here? I can see from the notes on your file my colleague recommended your ex-husband contact us but we've heard nothing from him. I need to make that same recommendation."

"We're not exactly on speaking terms."

"Okay, but you can see my problem here? Your ex-husband is apparently being blackmailed but won't report it, and you've got an admittedly odd situation where a guy is giving you gifts but not directly asking you for money. As for that medallion, your theory is a little tenuous."

Without emotion blighting her analysis, I have a feeling PC Johnson is having difficulty seeing the same picture I am.

"I understand this is all a bit … confusing."

"It would be a lot less confusing if you and your ex-husband spoke to one of my colleagues in person. I appreciate you might not be on speaking terms but it's realistically the only way we'll sort this situation out."

"I'll have a word with him, and then what should we do?"

"I'll give you the number to ring. You must come in together and bring any evidence you have relating to Kenneth."

"Evidence?"

"Like the medallion."

"Ah, I gave it away."

"Do you have any other evidence, or clues to this man's identity?"

"I've got his photo, but I'm afraid that's it."

"You don't know his full name or any other information which might help us locate him?"

"Sorry, no, but it's not through want of trying."

"Well, take what you have to the station and they'll do what they can."

I'm no longer convinced this was such a good idea. PC Johnson stresses I should call 999 if I feel threatened or fear for my safety but I hang up not entirely happy with the outcome. It looks like I'll need to speak to bloody Nathan.

I retrieve the flapjack from my handbag as a shitty consolation prize. The sugar rush provides just enough motivation for me to call Nathan's number. It connects straight to answerphone but a female voice states the inbox is full so I can't leave a message.

It leaves me with just one option. I send him an email suggesting he calls me in the office as soon as possible, or I'll go to the police without him.

My lunch break ruined and no prospect of progress until I hear from my dick of an ex-husband, I take my frustration out on the keyboard with some heavy-fingered keystrokes. Therapeutic, in a way.

The rest of the afternoon passes by in a whirlwind of phone calls, emails, and firefighting. By half-five I've just about had enough and quit for the day. The bus turns up on time and the faces of my fellow passengers are brighter than those on the inbound journey.

I arrive home, change, and retreat to the kitchen to finish the panini I started five hours ago. It's a lazy excuse for dinner but I hate wasting food.

Before I sit down, I open the back door to let the stifling air escape. I should have known the scent of tuna would attract a certain someone to my feet.

"Evening, Frank."

He doesn't bother with his usual shin rub and leaps straight up onto the table.

"Are we hungry by chance?"

He meows to demonstrate just how hungry he is.

I turn and open the cupboard. Then, as I grab his bowl, the silence breaks with a scratching sound, like fingernails across a blackboard. I spin around and almost drop the bowl. Frank is stretching his body and dragging both front claws across the table.

"Frank! No!"

He stops, and then casually sits down.

I dart across the tiles to examine my beautiful, nearly new, bloody expensive table.

"Nooo!"

A series of prominent lines, about two inches long, scratched in the waxed oak surface. If I wasn't an animal lover, I could easily throttle the creature looking up at me with all the innocence of a choirboy.

Today is the gift that just keeps on giving.

"Why did you do that?" I snap. "Bad cat!"

He yawns at my outburst. I'm on the verge of depositing him outside when a pang of guilt stops me. I must be a mug, but instead of barring the vandal, I serve him dinner on the table he's just ruined.

"Any more scratching, Mister, and that'll be your last supper. Understood?"

I then turn my attention to the damage. The gouges look too

deep to polish out, and I don't trust myself to attempt a DIY fix as it'll probably look even worse by the time I've messed around with it. Bloody cat. Bloody, bloody cat.

"I wish I knew who owned you, Frank. I'd send them a repair bill."

I then recall the conversation with Richard earlier. In the bank of good luck, I'm well in credit, and Frank has never done anything like this before. Cats will be cats, I suppose, and it's my fault for inviting him into my home.

Besides, I can't stay angry at the ginger fuzz ball and it won't fix the damage. Fortunately, I now know someone who might be able to fix it.

I call Liam.

"Hello," he answers gruffly.

"Hey, Liam. It's Kelly."

He clears his throat.

"Oh, hi, um, Kelly."

"Have I called at a good time?"

"Yeah, I'm good. Just finished dinner."

"Anything nice?"

"Seared scallops, risotto, and lemon salsa."

"Oh, wow — sounds delicious. You need to tell me where you buy your meals."

"You can get the ingredients at any supermarket."

"You made that from scratch?"

"It comes with being a bachelor. You learn how to cook, or starve."

"I'm impressed. I wish I had the same motivation to cook nice meals."

"In fairness, you do order a mean pizza."

"True," I chuckle. "Anyway, I was wondering if I could call upon your handyman skills."

"Sure. What's the problem?"

I explain what Frank did to the table.

"I'm sure I can sort it, although it might mean re-waxing the whole table top to blend it in."

"That's such a relief. How much, and when can you do it?"

"Materials won't cost more than twenty quid, and if you throw in a bite to eat, I won't charge for labour. I can pop round early evening tomorrow if that works?"

"That's so kind of you, thanks. Shall we say half-six?"

"No worries. I'll see you then."

I hang up and place my phone on the table.

"Did you hear that, Frank? Liam's coming over tomorrow evening … and you're cooking."

29.

"No way," I declare. "It's not happening."

"Don't be such a fun sponge."

"Martha, I am not dressing up as Ginger Spice."

"You'll look amazing, and you've almost got the body for that dress."

"Maybe fifteen years ago … wait. Almost?"

"Don't worry. It's nothing a push-up bra won't fix."

"Oh, for Christ's sake …"

"Gotta shoot, chick. I'll see you tomorrow."

"But …"

She hangs up.

My Tuesday morning was crappy enough before Martha called. Her reason for calling appeared innocent enough to begin with; the pretence of meeting at Rachel's tomorrow evening to discuss plans for our weekend away. Just after confirming she'll pick me up at seven, the bombshell arrived — she's taken delivery of four Spice Girl outfits and I might like to wear something easy to change out of. When that woman gets an idea in her head, it's near impossible to talk her around.

I check my email inbox for the tenth time this morning to see if Nathan has replied. Still nothing, so I open a web browser window and begin searching for push-up bras.

My online shopping is short lived as Ben wanders in and asks for help with an angry customer. I only ever get to speak with angry customers. Once they've lost it with whoever took their call, they demand to speak with a manager; namely me.

Nine times out of ten, complaints relate to a failed credit check and the customer thinks I'm able to overturn the decision. Sometimes their arguments are sound but there's no way to circumnavigate the credit algorithm. Unsurprisingly, few customers give a shit about the algorithm and their anger spikes. If I'm really lucky, this customer won't end the call by calling me a 'fucking whore' or suggesting I should die in some gruesome manner.

Twenty minutes later, I put the phone down after being screamed at by another unsatisfied customer. I'm a 'credit Nazi', apparently. Full marks for their originality.

I close their file and get on.

As the morning turns to afternoon, I panic about what I'll feed Liam tonight. Unless he fancies a bowl of flaked tuna, I've nothing in, which means a dash to the supermarket on my lunch break. It's bad enough cooking for someone who appears to be highly competent in the kitchen but I face the additional challenge of not knowing what he likes, or doesn't like. Add in the time constraints and my options are limited to something with salad.

I'm about to head out and begin the quest when my mobile rings. My heart beats a little faster when Richard's name flashes on the screen. I'm guessing he's got a response about the offer on Dad's yard.

"Hi, Richard."

"Afternoon, Kelly. Have you got a moment?"

"Sure."

"I'll keep it brief. Redwood Homes have just confirmed an increased offer of £1.3 million."

The last six syllables hang in the silence. I try to remain calm. Internally, fireworks are going off like New Year's Eve on the banks of the Thames.

"Oh. That's … nice."

"Would you like me to accept it?"

"Um, yeah. Why not?"

"Excellent. I'll ask my secretary to prepare a memorandum of sale once you've confirmed your solicitor's details."

"My solicitor?"

"Well, yes. You'll need a solicitor to handle the legal side of the transaction. Do you have one?"

"Not one I'd be happy using again, no."

"Can I recommend Simon Byfield of Pitman and Partners? They're a local firm, and Simon has a wealth of experience in land transactions."

"Sure. How do I contact him?"

Richard quotes Mr Byfield's phone number which I scribble down on a notepad.

"Have a chat with Simon and if you're happy to appoint his firm, just drop me a short email to confirm. We'll then put him in touch with the developer's solicitor."

"Will do."

"Perfect. We'll speak again soon."

He ends the call and I remember to remove the phone from my ear this time.

I'm about to punch the air when Samantha's voice echoes over the fireworks: obstacles to overcome. It's enough to stymie the excitement, and the urge to charge through the main office whooping and hollering. Even so, I wish there was someone around I could share my news with. There are plenty of bodies in the building but not one I want to celebrate with. Instead, I pick up the photo of my parents and kiss the glass.

"I'm getting there," I whisper. "… Nanny and Granddad."

A lump dances in my throat. Choked by my own words, I carefully place the photo back on the desk.

Suddenly in need of air, I grab my bag and head to the lifts.

As hard as I try to focus on menu options, a reflective haze shades the walk to the supermarket. If I bump into a casual acquaintance and they ask how I am, I don't think I'll be able to offer a cohesive reply. The morning's events have left me a little punch drunk, emotionally. I've journeyed through irritation, anger, and elation, stopping by at regret, and hope. Come to think of it, that pretty-much sums up the entirety of June thus far.

I never thought I'd say it but I'm looking forward to twenty minutes of food shopping, and a dose of normality.

The town centre supermarket is only a third the size of its sibling on the outskirts of town. Less shelf space means fewer options so, after snatching one of the few remaining bags of Caesar salad, I grab a sandwich for lunch and move on to browse the scant selection in the chiller aisle. Four garlic and herb chicken breasts are duly dropped into my basket. I complete the shop with a packet of wild rice and a not-so-healthy summer fruits trifle. It's not exactly a MasterChef-winning menu, but it's the best I can do in the limited time. At the self-service checkout I can't help but chuckle to myself when I'm warned there's an unexpected item in the bagging area.

Back in the office, I deposit everything in the staffroom fridge and trudge back to my desk to eat. Two mouthfuls are reminder enough why I rarely eat supermarket sandwiches.

Once I've finished my underwhelming lunch, I've got one more personal task to deal with before I'm back on the clock. I grab my phone and call Simon Byfield's number. It's answered by a woman who sounds like she's suffering with hay fever, if her nasally tone is anything to go by. She puts me through to the man I need to speak to.

"Simon Byfield."

"Hello, Mr Byfield. My name is Kelly Coburn and I've been dealing with Richard at Ramsey Rowe — he gave me your number and suggested I speak to you regarding a land transaction."

"That's very kind of him. What can I do for you?"

I relay a synopsis of where I am with Dad's yard, and the impending sale. He then asks more questions than I anticipated, and insists I call him Simon. Despite his acute public-school accent, he sounds user-friendly enough.

"I'd be delighted to act on your behalf, Kelly, and I can email over our fee structure and terms of business. Ideally, I'd like to meet so we can discuss your specific needs in detail."

"My needs?"

"Beyond the land transaction itself. Had you considered what you'll do with the money?"

"Kind of. I'm looking to invest it so I can give up work but I didn't want to tempt fate by planning too far ahead."

"In which case, we can discuss your options along with a few other legal issues I'd recommend we address. It's a sizable amount of money so it would be prudent to look at estate planning, tax liabilities and mitigation ..."

He keeps talking, but the subject matter is duller than a bowl of Bran Flakes. My mind switches off.

"... I've got a slot available Monday of next week if that

works?"

"Oh, err, sure. What time?"

"Shall we say one o'clock?"

"Great. How long do you think we'll need?"

"No more than three hours."

The thought of spending three hours in a solicitor's office holds no appeal whatsoever. But as much as I'd love to offer an excuse why I can't make it, I'll only be postponing the tedium. I'll have to book a day's holiday.

"Thanks, Simon. I'll see you on Monday."

"I look forward to it."

You and you alone, mate.

I hang up and make a note in my diary, adding a reminder to take a pillow. I then ping a quick email to Richard to confirm I'll be using Pitman and Partners so he can issue whatever paperwork needs issuing.

Another tick on a list but it took longer than I expected. I need to get on.

Being a typical Tuesday, the afternoon is quiet enough I can stay on top of my workload. I'm so on top of it, I'm able to leave on the dot of five and scamper to the bus stop; arriving just in time to catch the quarter past five departure. Although the house is fairly tidy, I want to run the hoover around and give the kitchen a once over before Liam arrives.

The bus drops me off and, after completing a sweaty dash to Juniper Lane, the kitchen isn't the only thing that could do with a once over.

Shopping away, hoover deployed, and kitchen cleaned, I hop in the shower. There is nothing quite as therapeutic as washing away the day's stresses, and after slipping into a pair of knee-length denim shorts and a vest top, I return to the kitchen in a far more relaxed state than when I left it.

I switch the radio on, and while jiggling my hips to a One Direction song, remove all evidence dinner came pre-prepared: the salad tossed into a bowl, the chicken breasts arranged on a baking tray, and the rice deposited into a small frying pan. Just as I'm working out how to decant the trifle without it looking like I dropped it from a third-floor window, the doorbell rings. So nearly the perfect crime.

I return the trifle to the fridge and scoot down the hallway; opening the door to the man who'll hopefully save my table.

Liam has arrived in full handyman attire: a paint-splattered black t-shirt, jeans, Timberland boots, plus his trusty tool bag.

"Evening."

"Hey, Liam. Come in."

He follows me back through to the kitchen and makes straight for the table.

"What do you think?" I ask, as he runs his fingers over the scratches.

"The good news is your mate has only taken off the top layer of wax; the wood itself looks intact."

"So, you won't have to sand it?"

"Don't think so."

"Cool. Dinner will be about forty minutes."

"I'd better crack on then."

Liam delves into his bag and removes a pot of wax and a packet of sponges. My cue to start dinner, which is just shoving the chicken breasts in the oven and frying the rice for five minutes. I put the chicken in and find myself suddenly redundant.

"Can I get you a drink?"

"Something cold would be good, thanks."

I pour him a glass of orange juice and place it on the table. Not wanting to get in the way, I hop up onto the kitchen side. It's unlikely any tradesman wants a customer watching over them while they work but I can't help myself. I used to spend hours watching Dad fixing Kellybelle or patching up some scrappy old piece of furniture to sell on, and I've always found it mesmerising. Nathan always considered himself above any kind of manual task so he'd call someone in, even for minor jobs like putting up a shelf or mowing the lawn.

Liam suddenly looks up and catches me watching.

"I'm not inspecting your work," I blush. "Honestly."

"No?"

"I used to love watching my dad work. It's kinda nice reliving that feeling."

He smiles back at me and carries on.

"Oh, did you get anywhere with that advert?" I ask. "You know, for a partner?"

"I did," he replies, concentrating intently on the table surface. "It'll be in next month's edition."

"That's great news. I'm sure you'll get plenty of offers."

"Let's hope so."

Ordinarily, watching a man I barely know at work would be deeply awkward, for both of us, but Liam seems happy for me to watch and I'm too content to care. If I try hard enough, I could be that ten-year-old girl again; watching Dad polish the chest of drawers he rescued from a skip, or scraping rust from a cast iron Victorian fireplace he won in a card game. Here, now, I'm almost as contented watching Liam; although that contentment bristles with an altogether different feeling.

I hadn't really paid much attention before but his forearms are like the trunk of an old chestnut tree; pronounced veins running from his wrists to his biceps, and knots of muscle twitching at every movement. And although his jeans have seen better days, he fits them well.

I have to snap myself out of the trance. The kitchen is suddenly a shade too warm.

"Do you, err, like trifle, Liam?"

He glances up again, looking slightly perplexed.

"Trifle?"

Shit. I knew I should have gone for the cheesecake.

"It's my favourite pud. How did you know?"

"Let's put it down to women's intuition. And the piss-poor choice of desserts in the supermarket."

A snort of laughter escapes, and then he returns his attention to the table.

The oven beeps to confirm I need to fry the rice.
Disappointing as it is, I jump down from the side and get on with my own tasks.

Five minutes later, with the salad and chicken breasts neatly plated, I spoon the rice on.

"Grubs up."

"Good timing. I'm just about done."

I put the plates down at the other end of the table and inspect his work.

"That's amazing," I gush. "I can't even tell where the scratches were."

"That's the idea."

"You're wasted in a flower shop, Liam."

"Thanks, I think."

I offer him a seat.

"Sorry dinner is nothing special. I didn't have time to be creative."

"No need. It looks great."

I sit down opposite and, much like Saturday, we eat with the bare minimum of conversation as tunes on the radio fill the dead air.

Liam finishes first.

"Hungry, were we?"

"I enjoyed it — thank you."

"No problem."

He then gets up, grabs his plate, and moves towards the sink.

"What are you doing?"

"Washing my plate up."

"Don't be silly. You're my guest."

He stands motionless for a moment.

"Sorry. I'm so used to eating on my own and then washing up, it's just a habit."

"A fully domesticated man," I state with a grin. "Who knew such a mythical creature existed."

"My upbringing," he smiles back. "Mum is a stickler for keeping the house tidy. As for the army … I'm sure you can imagine."

"I can, but you're excused on this occasion. Just pop it on the side and I'll deal with it."

He does as instructed and sits back down. I can almost hear his mind whirring as he searches for a topic of conversation. I throw him a lifeline.

"I had another encounter with Kenneth yesterday."

"Really?"

I explain what happened outside the sandwich shop.

"I reported it to the police."

"Good for you. What did they say?"

"Not much, but in fairness the situation is a mess; my ex-husband being the primary cause of it."

"Your ex-husband?"

"Long story but I think his current financial plight had led Kenneth to my door. Unfortunately, or fortunately I suppose, Kenneth hasn't actually made any direct threats, nor has he broken any laws. As frustrating as it is, there also isn't a great deal for them to go on until I visit the station with Nathan."

"When are you going?"

"No idea. I can't get hold of him."

I finish my last mouthful of chicken as Liam stares at the table. He eventually shakes his head.

"If you … um, you know, have any more problems with this bloke, I'll happily have a word if he resurfaces. You shouldn't have to put up with this crap."

"That's very sweet of you, and I might take you up on that offer if he keeps turning up uninvited."

"You've got my number. I'm only a phone call away."

I get the feeling Liam's words to Kenneth would not be as sweet as his offer. It's nice, though, to think he'd do that for me. Almost gallant.

"Thank you. I appreciate that."

I get to my feet.

"On a more positive note, can I tempt you to a bowl of trifle?"

"Definitely."

There's no point hiding the fact it's shop-bought so I transfer the packaged trifle from the fridge to the table with two bowls.

"My apologies. Even if I knew how, I wouldn't have had time to make a trifle from scratch."

"If you ever want a recipe, I've got a great one."

"You can make trifle?"

"It's Mum's secret recipe, really, but yeah."

I spoon our pudding into the bowls and hand one to Liam.

"Does your mum know you're offering up family secrets?"

"I'm sure she wouldn't mind. She used to love making it with Lou, and probably hoped she'd pass it on to her kids one day."

"She never had kids?"

"No, which was kind of a blessing in a way."

"How so?"

"She always planned to have them, but only after she got the shop up and running. It was bad enough … after we lost her … without having to explain to a young child why mummy wouldn't be coming home."

For a fleeting moment, I try to imagine such a conversation. It's so awful I splutter a random question just to move the thought along.

"You never came close to having kids?"

"Nah," he shrugs. "Guess it wasn't meant to be."

"Would you have wanted them?"

"Christ, yeah," he gulps. "What bloke wouldn't?"

I can think of one.

"I'm no different," he continues. "I used to daydream about, you know, doing the usual things dads do: teaching them how to ride a bike, reading bedtime stories, kicking a ball around the park … that kind of stuff."

"I know what you mean."

"You never said: do you have kids?"

"Nope, but I haven't given up hope."

"You married just the once?"

"Yep. We divorced earlier this year."

"Sorry to hear that."

"I'm not. The only thing I'm sorry about is I wasted eleven years married to a man I didn't really love."

Perhaps picking up on the unintentional bitterness in my words, he casts an awkward glance towards the bowl of untouched trifle.

"But hey-ho," I continue in a chirpier tone. "I've concluded life is too short to dwell on the past. Fate doesn't always play nicely so you've got to learn how to deal with it and move on."

"Easier said than done, sometimes."

His words are now bitter.

"Your sister's accident?"

A slow nod.

I've had twelve years to deal with my parents' passing but for Liam, he's only had eighteen months so I guess the wounds are still raw.

"Can I ask what happened? You don't have to tell me."

He puffs a long sigh and sits back in his chair.

"It was all because of a stupid New Year's resolution."

I say nothing in response. From my experience, I know it's best just to sit quietly and if he wants to talk about it, he will.

It seems he does.

"I didn't want to spend another year on my own so I joined one of those online dating websites. It was Lou's idea, and she helped me set it up. I went on a handful of dates and met a few nice women. Not one of them asked for a second date. I think they all wanted a bloke with a proper career, or at least a bloke who could hold a conversation. They all said I was too quiet."

"Some women would kill for a man willing to listen — it wasn't a quality my ex-husband possessed."

"Yeah, well, these women didn't. Anyway, I was about to give up when I got a message from this woman called Julia. She looked nice, and said she preferred the strong, silent type so I gave the dice a final throw and we arranged to meet up. Trouble was, she wanted to meet at this pub out in the sticks and the weather was bloody awful on the night … freezing fog and sleet."

"You still went?"

"Yeah. I convinced myself Julia might be the one but let's just say the date didn't go well. When she said she liked the idea of a man willing to listen, I didn't realise she'd moan about men for two solid hours."

"I know a few women like that."

"It got to about ten o'clock and I made my excuses. I walked

Julia to her car and said goodbye but after she'd gone, I couldn't find my keys so I went back into the pub and checked around the table — they weren't there. I enlisted three members of staff and half-a-dozen other customers to help with the search but no joy. That's when Lou called, to see how the date went. I told her it hadn't gone well, and I'd lost my bloody keys so I was stuck in the middle of nowhere. She offered to drop off the spare set."

He closes his eyes for a few seconds.

"I should have said no," he then says in a low voice.

"Why?"

"After an age and God-knows how many calls, there was still no sign of her. When the pub shut, I decided to walk back in case she'd broken down and couldn't get a phone signal. About a mile from the pub, I caught the first flash of blue lights off in the distance."

I already know Liam's tale won't have a happy ending. There's an urge to reach across the table and squeeze his hand but I resist. All I can do is offer the same pitiful look of sympathy I've seen too many times on too many faces.

"Long story short, she lost traction on a patch of black ice and the car hit a tree. The accident investigator said Lou's death was a one-in-a-thousand stroke of bad luck as she wasn't speeding and had her seat belt on … the only reason it proved fatal was the obscure angle the car hit the tree."

"That's … I'm so sorry."

"Julia texted me the next day to say she'd found my keys in her handbag. She couldn't explain how they got there but I reckon she took them out of spite because I turned down a second date."

"Christ. If only she'd known the consequences."

"Life's like that, isn't it?" he sighs. "Every day we make decisions, never really thinking about where they might lead. I could have cancelled the date, kept my keys in my pocket, told Lou not to come … I've wasted countless hours thinking about every decision I made that evening, and which ones might have led to a different outcome. A waste of time and energy."

I lean forward and again fight the instinct to reach out; at least physically.

"From what I understand, it's a perfectly rational response to grief. I almost drove myself insane wondering if I could have done something, said something which might have stopped my parents setting off that day."

"You couldn't have known."

"And neither could you."

He forces a rueful smile.

"Funny, isn't it? It's easy enough telling someone they shouldn't shoulder blame, but with your own guilt, it's not so easy to shift."

"I had counselling, and it helped a bit but there's no fix, not really."

"Time, apparently."

"For sure. And as much as I hate to admit, talking helped."

"That's what Mum says: it's not healthy keeping it all bottled up."

"You should always listen to your mum."

"I don't have much choice. She could talk for Britain."

It seems an appropriate time to nudge the conversation in a lighter direction. In between mouthfuls of trifle, Liam tells me all about his parents. There's another sombre lull when he confesses his dad was also in the armed forces but sadly died in the Falklands War when Liam was just a boy. I sense that wound has long since healed, or at least bandaged with fond memories and pride.

We finish dinner with a coffee and without even noticing the time pass, it's suddenly nine o'clock.

"I'd better be going. I've got an early start tomorrow."

"Oh, of course. I'll see you out."

Liam grabs his tool bag and I follow him to the door. He opens it and turns around.

"Thanks for dinner, and for listening. I hope I didn't depress you too much."

"Not at all. And it's me who should thank you for fixing the table."

"To be honest, it felt good doing a job I know how to do.

You did me a favour."

"Did I? In which case, you now owe me a dinner."

"Err, sure. How about Saturday?"

The realisation arrives like a slap to the face — Liam has misinterpreted my jokey response. I wasn't angling for a dinner date.

"Oh, right … um …"

He grimaces and then quickly mumbles a goodbye. Before I can get another word out, he's got a hand on the gate. As the gate swings shut, my brain finally reengages. Do I want to have dinner with Liam? Really? Do I? The internal argument continues as he strides away.

I finally blurt a response.

"Seven o'clock?" I call after him.

He stops dead in his tracks and turns around.

"Seriously? You're sure?"

"Definitely. Text me when you decide where."

He nods, and a proper ear-to-ear smile breaks across his face. I wave a goodbye and close the door.

My own smile lingers a little longer than I would have expected.

30.

Once bitten, twice shy they say. True, although I'm more concerned about scratches than bites.

Frank jumps up on the table and freezes as his paws meet the tablecloth. He then takes four wary steps towards the bowl.

"It's staying, like it or not, Mister."

I don't think Frank likes the thick, linen tablecloth but after a few mouthfuls of tuna it becomes a non-issue. I sit down and sip at my coffee.

It's half-seven in the morning, and twelve hours since I fed another male at this very table — this one has more hair but he's not so great with conversation. Both, however, have wormed their way into my affections.

I'm not sure how I feel about Liam. I like him, and he's got more going for him than he knows, but I've kind of removed myself from the market, romantically. I'm not sure any man would want to date a woman through a pregnancy in which he played no part. Then again, is our dinner a date, or is it just two friends having a bite to eat?

I'm over-thinking. Perhaps he just wants a friend and I'll settle on that for the moment. I've got enough on my plate without trying to predict the future, or how a man's mind works.

I finish my coffee and head upstairs to get ready for work.

There's no podium place at the bus stop but neither is there a late bus, thankfully. I arrive in town with enough time to grab a coffee from Starbucks and I'm at my desk by half-eight. On every level it's a routine morning until Ben pokes his head around the door.

"Morning."

"Morning, Ben."

"Guess what."

I avert my eyes from the screen.

"Ben, I haven't imbibed nearly enough caffeine to play guessing games. What is it?"

"Natalie emailed. She's not coming in today."

"Why not?"

"Migraine."

"Okay. Thanks for letting me know."

"No problem."

As Ben returns to his desk, I rest my elbows on mine, and ponder — what am I going to do about Natalie? Our chat last week appears to have fallen upon deaf ears, to the point she can't even be bothered to offer an original excuse for her absence.

Migraine? I call bullshit.

I return my attention to the screen and log-in to the system where the personnel records of my team reside. I'm hoping Natalie's record will confirm her address isn't too far away as I have a plan.

I'm in luck — Google confirms her address is only a ten-minute walk from the office.

I wouldn't usually stoop to checking up on my staff but I'm prepared to make an exception for Natalie. It's not fair the rest of the team have to pick up the slack whenever she fancies a day off. Her blatant skiving has to be called out, and I intend to do the calling.

I open my day planner and shuffle a few tasks around so I've got an hour free at eleven o'clock. I'm hoping I'll arrive at her house and find her putting the washing out or hoovering the lounge. More likely, she'll be lying on a sun lounger in the garden. Whatever she's doing, I just need to catch her anywhere but cocooned in a dark room.

As I sit back in my chair, I'm suddenly struck by a jolt of nervous excitement; a measure of how badly I want to catch Natalie out. If nothing else, a spot of light investigation will add some spice to the otherwise mundane day ahead.

I press on with that mundane schedule until half-ten when I call Ben into my office. I tell him what I'm up to and warn him he'll be joining Natalie on the dole queue if he shares the details of my plan with any of the team. Ideally, I'd have rather kept the entire plot to myself but if Justin drops by, I need someone to confirm my absence is work-related.

Phase one complete, I grab my bag and set off.

A few minutes into my journey, it dawns on me I know very little about Natalie's domestic set-up and she might still live at home with her parents. If she is still living at home; I need to tread carefully. The last thing I want is to enrage an over-protective parent.

A minute earlier than the route planner estimated, I turn into Beechnut Road.

I should have guessed from the house number the road would be fairly long. I'm looking for number thirty-five and the first house I pass on the left is number sixty-two. The road bends sharply to the right a hundred yards ahead, and the immediate view is just boxy semi-detached houses lined up on both sides. I suspect it's just the kind of cookie-cutter housing development Redwood Homes intend to build on Dad's yard, not that I care as long as they conclude the deal in a timely manner.

I reach the bend, passing number thirty-eight, and prepare to cross over once I pass a large van parked on the kerb. As I draw level with the van's passenger door, a dark blue hatchback approaches from the opposite direction. With sunlight reflecting off the windscreen I can't be certain but the female passenger looks a lot like Natalie.

Not wanting to make my move until I can be sure it's her, I edge back a few steps and shelter behind the van. The car then slows and turns onto the driveway of a house maybe thirty yards short of my location.

I watch on as the car idles to a standstill.

The driver's door opens first and a tall, youngish man gets out. He closes the door and makes his way around the front of the car as the passenger door opens. A female figure eases herself out, and when she turns to face the approaching driver, I can see her face.

"Gotcha," I whisper.

Rather than lying in a dark room suffering a migraine, it appears Natalie has been out and about with her other half. Doing what, I don't know, but as I suspected, she lied. I just need to capture the evidence.

I open the camera app on my phone and zoom in on the

couple as they stand on the driveway and embrace. I snap a couple of photos before they part with a kiss; the man returning to the car and Natalie stepping toward the front door of the house. I capture a few more photos before she disappears inside. The car then reverses off the driveway and heads off in the same direction it appeared from.

The street quiet again, I have a decision to make.

I so badly want to knock on the door and confront Natalie; to see the look on her face when she realises the game is up. However, satisfying as that might be, I don't want to risk saying something which might render my evidence unusable from a legal perspective.

Reluctantly, I conclude this needs to be by the book. I turn around and retrace my steps back to the office.

Once I'm back at my desk, I call the HR department and explain I have evidence an employee has been feigning illness and taking time off. As is corporate sensitivity to lawsuits, they confirm the exact steps I need to take, which they then confirm in an email. Alas, their procedure will remove some of the glee as I'm only able to confront her with the evidence and take a statement, but it should still result in the termination of her employment. In turn, it'll free up a wage for a more reliable individual to join my team.

A productive morning, worthy of a trip to the sandwich shop.

The excitement doesn't last long into the afternoon as I play catch up. In fact, it's a stark reminder just how dull and repetitive my job really is. Now I've got a formal offer on the table for the yard, I'm tempted to create a countdown clock so I can mark off the days until I can escape this drudgery. It's a nice idea, but I've no way of knowing when that countdown will end exactly. Besides, counting the days will make them feel even longer than they already do.

At five o'clock, I wind down so I can get away on time. I've got the humiliation of a Union Jack dress fitting this evening, and Martha is picking me up at seven so I don't want to be at my desk a second longer than I have to be.

Five minutes before I'm set to leave, Justin wanders into my office.

"Hi, Kelly. Have you got five minutes?"

"Literally five minutes. I need to be away on time tonight."

"It won't take long. I spoke to Joanne in HR earlier and she mentioned you've got an issue with one of your team. Is that right?"

"Yes, but it's under control."

"From what I gather, it sounds like there are sufficient grounds to terminate her employment?"

"It looks that way."

"So, you'll be looking to recruit a replacement?"

"Naturally."

One minute he's standing, the next he's in the chair on the opposite side of my desk. This does not bode well for a five-minute conversation.

"This is probably a good time to discuss resource streamlining, then."

"Resource streamlining?"

"Yes. Let me explain."

He does, at length, and it turns out resource streamlining is management-speak for reducing the numbers in my team. Should we terminate Natalie's employment, we won't be recruiting a replacement, or for the next four members of my team who leave. If four more haven't left by Christmas, we might encourage them to leave. In a nutshell, they want to cut my staff budget while also increasing productivity.

As Justin continues to drone on, my mind turns to the bible. I'm sure there's a passage about Jesus feeding hundreds of people with a few loaves of bread and a couple of kippers, probably. I'm being asked to perform a similar miracle.

There are two reasons I don't fight against his proposal as vehemently as I once might have. Firstly, I'm late. Secondly, I don't give a shit. All being well, this will be someone else's problem by Christmas, or at least the countdown timer will be edging close to a definitive end date for my time at Marston Finance.

"I understand," I lie.

"Great. I knew you would, and if anyone can rise to the challenge, it's you, Kelly."

"Always willing to go the extra mile. That's me."

Satisfied with his work, Justin then relays some lame quote from an American businessman, and leaves.

"Twat," I mumble under my breath.

I thought he was out of earshot but Justin suddenly pokes his head around the door.

"Sorry, Kelly? Did you say something?"

"Hat," I reply. "I can't find my hat."

"Oh, right. Do you want me to help look for it?"

"Err, no. Thanks."

"Okay. Goodnight, then."

This time, I make sure he's definitely gone before mumbling more profanities.

I glance at my watch.

"Shit."

I've no chance of making the bus and the next one isn't due until six-thirty. By the time I get home, I'll have less than ten minutes to eat, shower, and change before Martha is due. Thanks to bloody Justin and his five-minute chat, I'll now have to fork out for a cab.

I gather my things and make for the lifts. Fortunately, there's one waiting with the doors open. I hop in and impatiently jab the button for the ground floor several times.

"Come on."

The doors close.

The lift finally descends but as it passes the sixth floor, the lights flicker and it lurches to a sudden halt.

I press the button for the ground floor but nothing happens. I press it again and again but the lift stubbornly refuses to move. With panic mounting, I try hitting the nine other buttons, and even the eleventh one; reserved for building maintenance.

Futile.

There's just one button left to try — the emergency call button. I press it and the adjacent speaker crackles with static.

"Hello?"

I listen intently for a good ten seconds before trying again.
"Hello? Can anyone hear me?"

Again, I'm met by the crackle of static. I might as well be talking into a badly tuned radio.

Becoming desperate, I delve into my bag and search for the last chance of rescue. I eventually find my phone and pluck it out.

"You're fucking kidding me."

Right at the top of the screen in a space usually occupied by signal bars, there are two words: no service.

Left with no alternative, I resort to yelling for help. I shout and scream and bang the doors until my throat is raw and my fists throb. My efforts result in silence. I'm out of ideas and the reality hits home — I'm stuck in here. I don't like confined spaces but I've never found myself trapped in one before. The reality is deeply disconcerting and my body responds accordingly: a thumping heart, jelly-like legs, and beads of sweat building on the back of my neck.

My only hope is the emergency button triggered an alarm somewhere, and an engineer is on their way. If not, I could be here all night.

That thought does little to ease the panic, and my body ups the ante by highlighting just how full my bladder is. Christ-knows why, but the potential humiliation of being found in a puddle of my own piss serves as a distraction. I take a few deep breaths and slump to the floor.

"Just relax, Kelly. Help is on the way."

Minutes pass, and I know exactly how many because I keep checking my watch every sixty seconds. It doesn't help. I slip into a routine of getting up, pressing every button, and swearing into the speaker. Frustrated, I sit down again, only to repeat the process ten minutes later.

Seven o'clock comes and goes. Martha will no doubt be banging on my door and calling my phone, to no avail. My friend is not a patient woman so I doubt she'll persist for long. My worry is she'll assume I'm stuck in a meeting at work — that's happened several times before when we've made plans. If that is her assumption, it's fair to say she won't be raising the alarm.

No one knows I'm here and unless the lift company send an engineer, this is my home for at least thirteen hours.

I need a piss, badly. Thirteen minutes seems a stretch; thirteen hours an impossibility. Desperate, I suddenly recall a blog post I read some time ago. It offered advice about what to do if you're stuck in traffic and need the loo. Apparently, it helps to think about sex. I can't remember the rationale but I'm willing to try anything.

Despite my best efforts, it soon becomes clear that even a nymphomaniac would struggle to think sexy thoughts while hot, sweaty, stressed, and trapped in a space no bigger than a walk-in wardrobe.

Discomfort edges towards pain. If I don't go within the next five minutes, I risk ruining another pair of shoes.

"Jesus," I whimper, dancing on the spot.

I've no choice.

The only consolation is I'm wearing a dress rather than a trouser suit. I tug my knickers off and drop them in my bag. All that remains is to decide where to unleash the impending tsunami of piss. The lift is seven feet long and barely five feet wide so I'm not spoilt for choice. The corner seems the logical choice.

I choose the corner opposite the panel of buttons and as far away from the doors as is possible. In reality, it doesn't make one iota of difference in such a tiny space. There will be no escaping the flood, or the smell.

Lifting my dress, I slowly squat down.

Assuming the position, there's a brief moment of stage fright. As much as I want to go, this isn't normal. Whilst men are used to peeing wherever and whenever they fancy, we women prefer to be sitting on a porcelain throne, or at least hovering slightly above it.

I reposition myself and try to relax. At the exact same moment, the lights flicker and the lift judders into life. I look towards the ceiling.

"Thank you, God. Thank you."

As the lift descends, I stand up. The urge to pee returns with a vengeance but, barring further delays, I'm seconds away from escape.

The lift stops, and the doors edge open. I don't wait for them to part fully and squeeze through the gap, squinting at the bright evening sunlight flooding the reception area.

If Usain Bolt had raced me to the loo, he'd have lost. I lurch into the nearest cubicle and sit down. Then, I omit a sigh of relief so loud the door rattles.

Bodily functions dealt with, I reinstate my knickers. After washing my hands my next priority is to vent at the security guard.

Unfortunately, there is no security guard at the reception desk. I then panic I'm trapped in the building but one of the main doors is mercifully unlocked. Just as I make the final dash to freedom, my phone finds a signal and beeps to signify incoming messages. Both are from Martha, the first asking where the hell I am, and the second stating she's bored with waiting and is heading to Rachel's.

I call her number to explain but it just rings out. Seeing as it's gone seven-thirty, she's probably at Rachel's now, trying to squeeze herself into a pair of leopard-print leggings.

All I want to do is go home, shower, and eat, but I'll never hear the end of it if I don't turn up. Reluctantly, I call Rachel to confirm I'm on my way and I'll be there as soon as I can get a cab.

She answers almost immediately.

"Come on then," she says, before uttering any form of greeting. "Let's hear it."

"My excuse?"

"Yep."

"It's a long story. I'm just about to jump in a cab and I'll tell you when I get there."

"Why are you getting a cab? I thought Martha was picking you up."

"Eh? Isn't she there?"

"No, but you know how hopeless she is with time-keeping."

"But she texted me half-an-hour ago to say she was on her way to your place. I've been … held up at work."

"Half-an-hour ago? Are you sure?"

"Yes. She should have got to you twenty minutes ago."

"Maybe she stopped off for petrol."

"Or there's been a problem with the girls and she's gone home. You know Ella hurt her wrist last week?"

"So I heard. They're proving a right handful at the moment so it wouldn't surprise me."

This evening is turning out to be a disaster.

"Shall we take a rain check?" I ask. "There's plenty of time between now and September for my humiliation."

"Yeah, you're probably right. Shame, though — I was looking forward to a visit from Ginger Spice."

"Hmm … I'm glad you were. Another time."

"No worries. Let me know when you track Mrs Miller down, won't you?"

"Sure."

I end the call to Rachel and make another to the cab company. Wednesday evenings are patently quiet as only minutes later I'm in the back of a cab heading home. I try calling Martha a couple more times but it rings out on both attempts.

An hour later, once I've had a shower and eaten, I try again — three times over a half-hour period. There's still no answer so I try the home number but after a dozen rings the answerphone kicks in. It's getting on for nine o'clock and even taking into account Martha's lackadaisical time-keeping, the radio silence is worrying.

My mobile rings. I snatch it up, hoping to see Martha's name. The name Miller is present, just the first name is different.

"Stuart? What's up?"

"It's … it's Martha," he says, his voice close to breaking. "She's …"

31.

Stuart takes a sharp intake of breath but appears unable to find the final word. The pause is excruciating.

"Stuart?"

"Sorry, my head is all over the place."

"What's happened?"

"Martha … she's been in a road accident."

His revelation isn't as bad as it might have been, but awful enough to stoke panic.

"My God. Please tell me she's okay."

"I … I don't know. She's conscious but …"

He breaks off as I hear the twins chattering in the background. He says something to them I don't catch.

"Sorry. My parents have just arrived."

"Where are you?"

"The hospital. The medics are treating Martha now."

"I'll be there as soon as I can."

"You don't have to. I only rang as I know you were going out with her this evening."

"Stuart, I want to be there."

"I know," he concedes after another pause. "We're in the A&E waiting room."

"Okay. See you soon."

I make another call to the cab company. It's only ever times like this I wish I could drive as the ten-minute wait is a living hell. The journey is no less fraught as my mind replays the conversation with Liam on Saturday evening; specifically the confession about what happened to his poor sister. Just an innocuous car accident but a devastating outcome.

I offer a silent prayer for my friend as the cab pulls up into the drop-off area outside the hospital. After throwing a tenner at the driver, I get out and dash to the main entrance. Over my shoulder, I catch sight of an ambulance tearing past with sirens and lights blazing. Such a common day-to-day sight but in the current situation, it provokes a cold shiver.

The A&E department is poorly signposted and I lose my way after following the sign in the main reception. By luck rather than judgement, I barge through a set of double doors to a room with bright orange plastic chairs fixed to the perimeter wall. The dozen-or-so sombre faces confirm I'm in the right place.

"Kelly."

I spin around. Stuart steps towards me, his expression unreadable. As much as I want to ask how Martha is, he looks like he could do with a hug almost as much as I could. I throw my arms around him.

"Have you heard anything?" I ask, as we break apart.

"Not a thing. They just told me to wait, and they'd call me in when …"

"When?"

"They know something, I guess."

I glance around.

"Where are the girls?"

"My parents have taken them back to their place. When the police called around to tell me about the accident, I had no option but to drag them down here."

"Are they okay?"

"I told them Mummy had a little bump in the car and the doctors are just fixing her up. Dad promised them ice cream, and that seemed to take their minds elsewhere."

"Have you told Graham and Sue yet?" I ask, referring to Martha's parents.

"Not yet. I didn't want to panic them into a two-hour car journey before knowing how she is."

"Makes sense."

I'm not sure what else to say. I flash a feeble smile and suggest we take a seat. Stuart looks exhausted; high stress and fear does that to you, as I know.

"Did the police say what happened?"

"Not really. All they told me is a truck crashed into the side of her car."

"Jesus … please tell me it was the passenger's side?"

He nods.

"Was the truck driver okay?"

"He must have been as he did a runner from the scene. The truck was stolen, apparently."

Martha's little pink Mini wouldn't have stood a chance against a truck. Thank God it hit the passenger's side otherwise we might be waiting to identify Martha's body, rather than for news of her injuries.

Another cold shiver duly arrives.

"Mr Miller."

Our heads both snap towards a nurse scanning the room. Stuart is on his feet in a heartbeat and I'm not far behind.

"I'm Stuart Miller. You've got news on my wife?"

"Yes, you can see her now."

"She's ... she's okay?"

"A bit battered and bruised but no major injuries."

Stuart gulps hard and then clamps a hand to his mouth. He's a blokey kind of guy but there's no masking the gut-punching signs of relief. I don't know whether to stay here or follow as he sets off behind the nurse. He turns back and beckons me with a wave.

We follow the nurse silently through a set of double doors and along a stretch of corridor into an open ward; each bed shrouded with a pale blue curtain.

She stops by the second bed and pulls the curtain aside.

"After you."

Stuart passes through first and I bring up the rear. He then dashes forward and wraps his arms around his wife. They cling to each other and I can hear Martha's sobs, but I can't see beyond Stuart to assess just how battered and bruised she is. I feel like an intruder and I'm about to suggest I give them some space when Stuart breaks their hug.

"My God," I blurt.

My friend looks like she's done ten rounds in a boxing ring and lost every one of them. There's a large, angry bruise running from her right cheekbone to her temple, and at least a dozen small cuts dotted across her face. The bandage around her head completes the forlorn picture.

Martha bites her bottom lip and waves me across to the bedside. I dash over and throw my arms around her; so tight she winces.

"I'm sorry," I weep. "I'm sorry."

Much blubbing ensues.

I finally let her go, to find Stuart has positioned two chairs next to the bed. There's no debate — I sit down in the chair furthest from Martha's side. Stuart mouths a thank you and sits down.

"How are you feeling?" he asks.

"Funnily enough, like I've been hit by a truck."

Typical Martha, but the snort of laughter causes her to wince. Stuart grabs her hand.

"Easy, babe. Are you okay?"

"They gave me some painkillers but … put it this way: I'll never complain about a hangover again."

"Is that a promise?"

"Absolutely not."

Superficially, Martha appears fine, bar the cuts and bruises, but I know my friend. Behind the smile she'll be in shock, and at some point it'll smash its way through the brave front. There will be more tears and later tonight, when she's alone, the realisation will arrive — her girls are damn lucky Mummy isn't lying cold on a mortuary slab.

The smiles ebb away and Stuart poses an obvious question.

"Can you remember what happened?"

"Kind of."

"You don't have to talk about it."

"It's okay. The police want to question me shortly so it's probably best I try to remember the details while I still can."

In preparation, she tries to sit up but her battered body is having none of it.

"Shit," she hisses.

Stuart stands and helps her get comfortable.

"Guess you won't be doing much housework this week?" he jokes.

"No, but you flippin' will."

There are more chuckles before Stuart sits down and Martha adopts her serious face. She starts by throwing a question my way.

"Where were you, chick? I can't believe I turned up on time for once and you weren't even there."

"I'm so sorry, hun. I'll fill you in on the details another time, but I got caught up at work."

"I guessed as much. I gave it five minutes and … well, you know me. I got bored waiting and made my way over to Rachel's, thinking you could jump in a cab if you got away at a reasonable hour."

"That was my plan, but I called Rachel just after half-seven and she told me you hadn't arrived."

"Did you go over?"

"No, the dress will have to wait, I'm afraid."

"It's only a temporary reprieve," she frowns. "Anyway, I digress. So, I was heading along Glazier Lane towards the junction with Shortheath Road when I come up behind a cyclist dithering along in front of me. We get within fifty yards of the junction and he slows to a crawl but as he's in the middle of the road, I can't overtake. I must have looked at the stereo or something as the next thing I recall, I return my attention back to the road and the cyclist is sprinting away like Bradley bloody Wiggins. Just as I shift up a gear to pull away, I catch a flash of blue in the corner of my eye. The next thing …"

Martha's voice breaks into a dry cough. Stuart passes her a glass of water from the nightstand.

After a few sips, she waves away Stuart's suggestion of rest.

"I remember turning to my left and the truck was maybe twenty feet from the junction, but going way too fast to stop. He just carried on and before I could react, the idiot smashes into the side of my car. It was like a bomb going off … glass and dust and shards of plastic flying everywhere, but the worst part was the sound when it hit. God, I've never … I'll never forget that sound."

"The police said the car is a write-off," Stuart says.

"I'm not surprised, but that little car saved my life. The truck hit so hard it forced the car sideways and it smashed into a wall … so hard the side airbags went off."

"How the hell did they get you out of a car sandwiched between a wall and a truck?" I ask.

"They didn't."

"Eh?"

"I remember banging my head and must have lost consciousness for a moment. When I came around, the windscreen had gone and the entire cabin stunk of petrol. I crapped myself, thinking the car would burst into flames any second so I panicked. Somehow, I crawled out of a small gap and across the bonnet. I staggered a dozen yards along the road and just collapsed on the road. It was like … like an out-of-body experience."

A silence descends as all three of us take a few seconds to contemplate just how lucky one of us was. It's a minor miracle Martha is still alive to recount her experience. She then turns to me.

"Whoever organised your meeting at work, you owe them a drink."

"It wasn't actually a meeting. The lift broke down and I was trapped in the damn thing for over an hour."

"You were bloody lucky then, chick. If I'd picked you up as we'd arranged …"

In all the concern for Martha, it hadn't crossed my mind I was supposed to be in the car with her.

"I was fucking lucky," she continues, gulping hard. "But not as lucky as you. If that lift hadn't broken down, you'd have been in the passenger seat, and … shit, it doesn't bear thinking about."

Too late. I'm already thinking about it.

"You okay, Kell?" Stuart asks, putting a hand on my shoulder. "You're as white as a sheet."

"I … Christ. I'll, um, be okay in a second."

He passes me a glass of water. Just as I reach out to take it, a police officer pokes his head through the curtain.

"Sorry to intrude," he says. "Are you feeling up to giving a statement, Mrs Miller?"

Martha nods. I think this might be my cue to leave, not least because I'm feeling a bit nauseous.

I hug Martha a goodbye.

"Hopefully, I'll be home tomorrow. They want to keep me in overnight for observation."

"If you need any help when you get home, you only have to ask."

"I know," she replies, squeezing my hand. "Are you okay?"

"Yeah, yeah. Just a little tired."

"Go on, get yourself out of here."

I give Stuart a quick hug and leave them to it.

As I wander back through the corridors, I pass the ladies' toilet. With a tightening knot in my stomach and bile burning my throat, the timing is impeccable.

I make it into a cubicle just in time. I won't be going home just yet.

32.

What ifs are pernicious little bastards.

Lying in bed this morning, they've gathered en masse to squeal and gnaw like rats in a hay barn.

What if Justin hadn't delayed my departure yesterday afternoon?

What if I'd taken the other lift?

What if the fault had occurred five minutes later?

On and on, the questions keep coming. They all journey in the same direction, to the same damning conclusion: I could have been killed last night.

It's only just gone six but there's no chance of going back to sleep. In total, I've managed just five restless hours all night. The tiredness isn't helping as I try to reverse my thinking: I wasn't in the passenger seat and Martha is relatively unscathed, therefore we should both count our blessings.

Perhaps my situation isn't so different from folks who've recovered from a serious illness, and once the last remnants of shock pass, I might be less inclined to take life for granted.

"Carpe diem," I sigh, as I clamber out of bed.

I think several mugs of strong coffee are in order before I'm ready to seize the day.

The coffee, followed by a bowl of cereal and a long shower, occupies the first hour of my day. I then eke out another twenty minutes getting dressed and dealing with my hair and makeup. At half-seven I decide a break in my routine might be in order. It's a glorious morning and with ample time on my side, a stroll to work should silence the last remaining what ifs.

Forty minutes later I push open the door to Starbucks feeling immeasurably better. Glowing pink and a little out of breath, but better. I need a drink to quench my thirst so order an iced green-tea lemonade.

I reach my desk earlier than usual but with a degree of disappointment. The change of routine ends here. After booting up my computer I consider calling Stuart to see if he knows what time Martha will be discharged. I dismiss the idea as he's probably trying to corral the girls for school; a test for anyone.

Besides, I've my own drudgery to deal with.

As I sift through the tasks on my to-do list, it's with the mind-set I activated earlier. Is this really living life to the full? If I hadn't inadvertently discovered the value of Dad's yard, I do wonder how long I'd have continued plodding along on this treadmill. Worryingly, despite the offer, there's still no guarantee I'll ever get off it. What if there's a sudden change of planning policy at the council? I might not have a choice but to continue plodding along for the foreseeable future, the dream of motherhood ripped from my grasp once again.

I reach into my handbag and rifle around. There, deep inside one of the pockets, is the babygrow I purchased — my good luck charm. I pull it out and brush my fingers across the soft fabric.

I need a contingency plan.

The last few weeks have shone a light on how little I now enjoy my work and how badly I want to be a mother. It's a yearning I don't think many would understand, unless they'd experienced the same denial. I can't explain it but it tears at my very soul; leaks into every thought of the future. I hope to God I don't need a contingency plan, but yesterday's events served as a reminder how quickly life can veer off course when you least expect it.

However, knowing I need a plan and developing one are two different matters. Sitting here now, Martha's advice doesn't seem as ridiculous as it once did. A quick bunk-up in a back alley and Bob's your uncle. But then what? Months and years of financial insecurity. It scares me.

I could ignore the fear and just go for it, but I'd have no control, no way of knowing how I'd support the resulting child. Some women take a less pragmatic approach and put their trust in a flaky man or the State. Their choice, I suppose, but it's definitely not my preferred choice, or a choice at all. I'm not willing to enter my child into a lottery lifestyle. Does that make me a bad person, too judgemental? My parents weren't exactly financially secure when I arrived, but they had each other. I'd be alone, with no family or partner to support me. The only way I can do this alone is with a financial safety net.

I've come full circle; a conclusion which does me no good at all. I'm supposed to be thinking positively.

I re-read the email from Richard, confirming the offer from Redwood Homes. It helps bolster my hope, and I get on with the bill-paying grind.

Half-hour later, I'm interrupted by Ben.

"Morning, boss."

"Morning. I'll indulge the guessing games this morning. No Natalie again?"

"Correct."

"Never mind. It's in hand."

He doesn't ask what's in store for Natalie when she returns.

I make it through the rest of the morning courtesy of several trips to the staffroom and an unhealthy amount of caffeine. I'm about to grab some lunch when my mobile rings. Seeing Martha's name, I sit back down and eagerly prod the screen.

"Hey, Mrs Miller," I answer cheerfully. "How are you doing?"

"I'm home, which is good, but I've also had access to a mirror, which is bad."

"Aww … you'll look gorgeous again in no time, I'm sure. How are you feeling otherwise?"

"Better than I have any right to feel, considering what happened."

"You're one lucky lady."

"I know, but I'm trying not to think about it. I barely slept a wink last night."

"Me neither, and probably for the same reason as you. I couldn't help but fret over what might have happened if I'd been in that car with you."

"Yes, that kept me awake, but it wasn't the only reason."

"No?"

"The woman in the bed next to me had chronic flatulence. Honestly, chick, it was like sleeping next to an open sewer."

Despite her ordeal, Martha is back on form.

"Trust you," I giggle. "A near-death experience and you moan about some poor woman's wind."

"It was awful. I can still smell it now."

"Eww! Enough."

"I'll never be able to eat creamed spinach again."

"Martha!"

She laughs at my disgust.

"Joking aside, are you really okay? Nobody comes out of an experience like that without a few mental scars."

"I'm not going to lie to you — there were a few tears shed last night, but I'm lucky I've got Stu and the girls. They create enough chaos I don't have time to feel sorry for myself or dwell on what might have been."

"True. Did they cope okay without you?"

"No," she chuckles. "One morning my husband had to do the school run … one bloody morning. The way he talked about it, you'd think he'd just returned from a tour of duty. He reckons he's got PTSD."

"That bad?"

"In his defence, he's fussed over me since I walked in the door."

"I guess you should enjoy it while it lasts."

"I intend to."

She then holds the phone away from her face and yells a request for more grapes.

"If he doesn't peel them properly," she says. "I'm gonna lose my shit."

I know she's only kidding and I also know Stuart won't take her for granted again. Seeing him last night, and the way he reacted to the nurse's news, I think Mr Miller will be quite happy peeling grapes for as long as his wife demands.

"Anyway, hun, I'd better get on but I will pop round in the next day or two."

"Please do. I've got the in-laws coming this evening and as lovely as they are, I can't wind them up like I wind you up."

"Glad I serve a purpose."

"Part of my convalescence process, chick. You wouldn't deny me that, would you?"

"Hmm … no. In the meantime, look after yourself and enjoy those grapes."

"Will do, and you know I love you, really."

"I know. Love you too."

I end the call and a wave of relief washes over me. Martha, thank God, appears to be okay both physically and emotionally; aided by the supportive, loving family around her. She has all she needs and all I ever wanted.

The prickling heat of envy returns. It appears now and then; usually served with a side order of guilt. On this occasion, it also awakens the what ifs.

I'm not having it. I grab my bag and make for the door. I've already wasted most of the morning going around in circles, only to end up at the same point. I doubt there's a Latin equivalent, but basically I should follow one of my own proverbs: don't dwell on shit you can't control.

What I can control is my hunger. Lunch beckons.

After stocking up on sugar and carbs, I return to work determined not to endure another ride on the emotional rollercoaster. Head down, focused, I plough on through the afternoon without a thought for anything other than the next task ahead of me. It's kind of mindless but sometimes that's a good thing.

The mantra continues beyond the office walls: waiting at the bus stop, on the bus, and for the final walk back to Juniper Lane.

I open the front door and pat myself on the back. I've made it through a challenging twenty-four hours and my reward will be an evening of uneventful laziness; just me, the television, and a pot of salted caramel ice cream.

Before I get down to business, I've got the usual homecoming routine to deal with. Upstairs to change followed by a meeting with the fridge and microwave, and possibly a ginger feline who didn't show up this morning.

Once I'm decked in suitably comfortable slobwear, I pad through to the kitchen and open the fridge. I'm met with a depressing sight. I still haven't come to terms with cooking for one so microwave meals have become my staple diet at home. It's a habit I need to break, and I will when my appetite for more hearty, wholesome meals arrives in the autumn.

For now, it's spaghetti bolognese served in a plastic tray.

I throw it into the microwave and jab a few buttons. Dinner in hand, I then unlock the back door and pull it open, half-expecting to find Frank waiting but there's a distinct lack of ginger on the patio slabs. I'm sure he'll return when he's hungry.

"Hello, Kelly."

My heart attempts an escape and the contents of my bowels almost follow suit.

"What the …"

In a dizzying panic, I grab hold of the door frame for support. I can't believe both my ears and my eyes are playing games, but I can confirm with the latter. Yes, I did see … can see … Kenneth seated in a chair at the bistro table, in my garden.

"You … you broke into my house."

"Technically, I'm not in your house," he replies calmly. "And I didn't break in."

Shit! Where's my phone? It's in my handbag. Shit! Where's my handbag?

"I was hoping we could have a chat?"

"Are you insane? Get the hell out of my garden."

"I will, however, it is rather important we talk."

"I told the police about you. They know you've been threatening me."

"Again, I've not threatened you. I've merely warned you."

He pats the empty chair.

"Please. I promise, all I want from you is five minutes of your time. Give me that, and then I will leave. You have my word."

The following silence isn't entirely silent. The sounds of a summer evening in suburban Britain: muted chatter in a neighbour's garden, the hum of a lawn mower, and the faint beat of music in a nearby street. People are outside, and that's where there's some measure of security. If I turn and bolt for the front door, Kenneth could catch me in the hallway. I can scream inside the house but no one will hear.

I take a dozen tentative steps across the paving slabs. Reaching the chair, I grab the arm and drag it to the opposite side of the table.

"If you're still here in six minutes, I'll scream until my lungs bleed. Clear?"

"Understood."

I sit down.

"Thank you, Kelly. I appreciate your cooperation."

"Cut the pleasantries. What do you want?"

"It's quite simple, really. You need to pay Nathan Thaw the money he asked for."

"You … what?"

"I believe you own company shares. If you were to liquidate those shares tomorrow and transfer the funds to Nathan Thaw's bank account, it would be enough to alter your path."

His tone is so measured, so benign, it's completely at odds with the words coming out of his mouth.

"You are insane," I cough. "Why on God's earth would I do that?"

"I guessed you might ask, and I've given a lot of consideration to how I might answer. There really is no easy way to say it, Kelly — if you don't, you'll be dead by Monday lunchtime."

If I scream, there are probably a dozen people within earshot who might come to my rescue. The problem is, I can barely force a whimper.

"I'm so sorry," he adds. "I understand this must be an awful shock."

Finally, I'm able to form words.

"Get … out."

"Please, Kelly. You must do as I say. It's the only way. I've checked every possible permutation, and it's almost impossible to see any other path forward."

There is no ambiguity in this threat; no way I'm misreading his intent.

"Get out. Now," I growl.

A flicker of frustration shows in the lines across his forehead.

"Are you aware there have already been three attempts on your life?"

"What?"

"You should have died in a gas explosion, and then a van attempted to run you down outside this very house. And most recently, you avoided fatal injuries in a car struck by a truck. I have tried to keep you safe but there is only so much I can do."

If I wasn't already sitting down, I'd be on my backside — Kenneth's claim knocking the wind and the words out of me. Unable to speak, disorganised memories slowly coalesce into a damning timeline. The night I awoke to find the hob on, the Saturday afternoon when Liam dragged me from the path of a delivery van, and most damning of all, the truck colliding with Martha's car.

Individually, all explainable events. Here, now, looking at the three events as a collective, there's no ignoring the obvious — the threat to my life is real.

"Are you okay, Kelly?"

My hands grip the arms of the chair; knuckles white and, I'm sure, my face whiter. No, I'm far from okay.

"I'm so sorry I had to tell you but there was no other choice. I had to make you realise the seriousness of the situation."

I swallow hard, fighting to catch my breath.

"Get … away … from … me …"

"As you wish, but please heed my advice. Time is short and this is the last opportunity to change your path."

He gets to his feet, nods, and calmly walks into the kitchen. A few seconds later, I hear the front door click shut.

I remain seated until the shock-induced paralysis passes. Then, I scramble to my feet and dart back into the house.

"Where the hell is it?"

I can hear the panic in my voice as I try to remember where I left my bloody handbag. There's little chance of thinking straight so I just tour the house until I return to the kitchen and find it hung on the door handle. With a shaky hand, I snatch my phone out and dial 999.

"Police, please."

Barely six minutes later there's a knock at the door. I check the spyhole and open the door to two burly policemen.

"Oh, thank God."

"Miss Coburn?"

"Yes, yes. Come in."

Sergeant Perry introduces himself, and his colleague, PC Foley. They follow me through to the lounge and sit down on the sofa while I try to compose myself; not helped by a reminder of the last time I faced two police officers on a sofa.

Fortunately, they get straight to the point and request Kenneth's description so they can alert other units in the area. Once that task is in hand, both officers listen patiently as I bluster my way through an explanation of what happened, and my previous encounters with Kenneth.

Sergeant Perry then asks the questions.

"He said you'll be dead by Monday?"

"Yes."

"Did he elaborate on that statement in any way?"

"Not really, no."

"And he said there have already been three attempts on your life?"

I relay the details of each event, as best as I can remember.

"I see why you didn't make a connection," Sergeant Perry confirms. "On their own, you could consider each incident just a random stroke of misfortune. However, the fact he knew about all three incidents is reason enough to suggest the threat is credible."

"You think?"

"I do, but what I don't understand is the incident with the van. You say this Kenneth sent someone to change the lock on your front door?"

"Yes, Liam Bradley."

"And who's he?"

"We met a few weeks ago. He's actually a florist, but he used to be a handyman. If it wasn't for Liam dragging me away from that van, I wouldn't be here now."

"I'll need Mr Bradley's details so we can speak to him."

"Why?"

"Doesn't it strike you as odd, that Kenneth would send someone to witness the attempt on your life, particularly as that witness saved your life?"

"I, err, I hadn't considered that."

"It muddies the water, but that's our problem to solve. Maybe he wanted a witness present but anyway, let's focus on the here and now. Do you have any idea how he got into your garden?"

"Not a clue."

He turns to his colleague and nods. By some method of telepathy, PC Foley accepts an instruction and gets to his feet.

"PC Foley is going to have a look out the back. If this man got in via a neighbour's garden, someone might have seen him."

"Okay," I mumble.

While PC Foley checks out possible access points, I show Sergeant Perry Kenneth's photo.

"Can you send that to me via an email?"

"Of course."

I prod the screen a few times and enter the sergeant's email address. He checks his phone and confirms receipt.

"If you give me a moment, I'll get this photo over to the control room and they'll forward it on to all the units on shift."

"Sure. Sorry it's not a lot to go on, I know."

"I doubt there will be many men wandering the streets in a brown suit with a lily in the buttonhole. It's a great help."

"Actually, I don't think he had a lily in his buttonhole on this occasion."

"Right. Noted."

For the next hour the two policemen do all they practically can. They speak to all my neighbours, check the house top to bottom, inspect all the windows and doors, and ask me a myriad of questions; many of which I can't really answer. I do, however, tell them about Nathan's blackmailer.

"Considering what this individual asked you to do, there's clearly a connection," Sergeant Perry suggests. "And when you phoned in on Monday, my colleague confirmed your ex-husband hasn't reported the blackmail attempt?"

"I told him to, but he's a stubborn arsehole ... pardon my French."

"No apology needed," he chuckles. "My ex-wife probably uses a similar phrase when she's talking about me."

He scribbles a few illegible lines in a notebook.

"Do you have your ex-husband's phone number and address?"

"I've got his phone number, but I've tried calling numerous times and it goes straight to voicemail. He previously told me he was living in a rented flat down by the river but he never gave me the address."

"Do you know where he works?"

"He's a consultant for a company called Firgrove Investments, up in the City. And I don't know if it's any help, but his mother is in Oakland Nursing Home across town. He visits her three or four times a week so he's bound to show up there at some point."

There's more scribbling before Sergeant Perry snaps the notebook shut.

"Right, we've got plenty to go on, Miss Coburn. You've been incredibly helpful."

"I don't feel like I've been helpful, but you two have. Thank you so much."

"All part of the service," he smiles. "But there's one final issue we need to address before we go."

"What's that?"

"Your safety. Is there a relative or friend you can stay with, or failing that, someone who can stay here with you?"

"I'm sure I'll be fine."

"And I'm sure too, although it's best to play safe in these situations. Your house is perfectly secure and your neighbours are now on high alert, but I think we'd both sleep a little easier tonight if you weren't on your own."

"I'll phone around when you've gone."

"Promise."

"Cross my heart."

"Fair enough."

The two policemen get to their feet and I follow; although I preferred it when we were all sitting down and they weren't towering over me. Still, it's reassuring, in a way.

After confirming what will happen next, they say their goodbyes on the front step.

I watch them wander vigilantly back up Juniper Lane and close the door once they're out of sight; activating the dead-lock, sliding the bolt, and fixing the chain. I've never felt so vulnerable, but at least it's still light outside. That won't last, though.

Returning to the kitchen, I catch the faint whiff of the spaghetti bolognese still festering in the microwave. With no appetite, the food recycling bin is the best place for it.

After surveying the garden through the window, I open the back door. There, in his usual position, is Frank. Being the closest thing to a reassuring hug on offer, I gather him up in my arms.

"Nice of you to think of me, Mister, but I don't think you're quite what Sergeant Perry had in mind when he suggested I ask a friend to stay."

He nuzzles his head under my chin as I stroke the back of his neck; his contented purr a partial antidote to my unease.

"Fancy something different tonight?"

I lower him down on the side where I'd put the tray of cold spaghetti bolognese. He sniffs it a few times and then tucks in.

"Don't be getting used to that. This is a one off."

Frank dealt with, my own urgent needs come to the fore: wine. I scour the cupboard and snatch the largest glass I own. Once it's brimmed, I sit down at the table. The exhaustion and emotional fallout soon join me. In turn, the what ifs all pull up a chair.

"Don't you dare cry, Coburn."

I pant a few heavy breaths instead. It takes the edge off, just enough to avert a meltdown. Now is not the time for tears; now is the time to be practical.

Sergeant Perry was right in that I can't see myself getting any sleep tonight if I'm here on my own. I hate feeling vulnerable in my own home but I also hate the idea of dumping my problems on friends who've all got their own issues to contend with.

I work through my shortlist.

Martha and Stuart are an obvious option, but they've got enough to contend with at the moment with Martha's recovery. Besides, they don't really have the room. There's Rachel, but being a nurse I don't know if she's on shift tonight, or sleeping before her next shift. Either way, I don't want to impose. Jennie lives miles away, and the last time I spoke to her she confessed her and Gavin were having marital issues. My presence is probably the last thing she needs.

There is one person I could ask. A man who doesn't have a partner or shift work or kids to worry about. He'd also be more than capable of defending me from Kenneth, should he return.

I pick up my phone and locate his number, only to stop myself from calling at the last second. I don't know him well enough to ask such a huge favour. My finger hovers for an age.

Truth is, he really is the only other person I can turn to.

I prod the call icon, just below Liam's name.

33.

We all have to compromise in life, and I compromised with myself. I told Liam what happened with Kenneth and asked if he wouldn't mind coming over so we could revisit his meetings with my stalker. I figured I'll be able to judge the situation better when Liam is here. Fingers crossed his previous gallantry wasn't a one-off.

The doorbell rings.

A check in the spyhole confirms yet another burly man is at my door. If the circumstances were different, I'd be counting my blessings.

"Thank you so much for coming over, Liam. I know it's getting late."

I usher him in.

"No worries. I wasn't exactly busy."

He follows me through to the kitchen.

"Can I get you something to drink? I'm on the wine."

"I'll just have a juice, thanks, if you've got some in."

"Sure."

I pour a glass of orange juice and place it on the table. As I do, a hand lands gently on my shoulder. Surprised by his sudden tactility, I turn around and look up at Liam.

"How are you feeling?" he asks.

"Have you got a pen handy? I've got an entire list."

"I've got a good memory and a sympathetic ear … so Mum tells me."

"I'm tired and angry and scared. I'm also grateful, and maybe a little embarrassed."

"Why embarrassed?"

"Dragging you over here. I'm sure the last thing you need in your life is a neurotic nuisance throwing problems your way."

"I don't think you're neurotic, and as nuisances go, you're a hell of a lot easier to deal with than a bouquet of freesias."

"Thank you. That's very sweet of you to say."

"You're welcome," he mumbles, shuffling awkwardly on the

spot. "Shall we, you know, deal with your list then?"

"Lets."

We sit down at the table and I begin by relaying the evening's events and then move on to a less-than-glowing tribute to my ex-husband and his hapless predicament.

The words continue to pour like October rain and before I know it, I've gabbed my way through an entire life story, warts and all. Not what I intended but perhaps what I needed.

"And there you have it," I conclude. "The life and times of Kelly Coburn. The end."

"Christ," he says, rubbing his chin. "You've been on quite a ride."

"You could say that. Life hasn't exactly gone to plan, but I never envisaged a stalker and death threats."

"Yeah, about that."

"Yes?"

"You shouldn't be here on your own. Don't you have friends you can stay with?"

"Not really. They've all got husbands, kids, and complications of their own. Besides, Sergeant Perry checked all the locks and said the neighbours are on high alert. I'm sure I'll be fine."

"I, err, I've got a suggestion."

"Oh. What's that?"

"I've got a tent and a sleeping bag in the back of the van. I could pitch it in the garden."

"Err, do you always carry camping gear around with you?"

"I go night fishing once or twice a week, usually a spur-of-the-moment thing depending on the weather."

"Right, but I can't ask you to camp in my garden just because I'm Billy No-Mates."

"You didn't ask, did you?"

"Well, no, but it's not fair to ..."

"I won't take no for an answer."

"Um, you could always kip on the sofa. It'd be more comfortable."

"Thanks, but that's not an option."

"Why not?"

"Because the whole point of having someone here is so you can sleep soundly. Having a bloke in the house you don't know so well won't help, will it?"

"I trust you, Liam."

"And I appreciate that, but I'm thinking about you. You said you feel vulnerable, and I don't want to make you feel unsafe … even just the slightest bit."

"But …"

"Please, Kelly. I want to help, not hinder."

In hindsight, maybe I was too willing to grasp any lifeline, even if that lifeline is anchored to a man I only met a few weeks ago.

"If you're sure?"

"Positive. I'll go grab my gear before it gets too dark. I'll be five minutes."

He's up on his feet and out the door before I can re-open the debate.

I sit back in my chair and take a sip of wine. As I do, the same thoughts I pondered yesterday morning resurface. This time, however, those thoughts carry the influence of alcohol. When I woke up yesterday, I didn't know how I felt about Liam, but now I'm erring in a direction I hadn't envisaged. The more I get to know him, the more I feel at ease in his company. There's an indescribable aura about him which resonates with me on so many levels. Hard to explain, impossible to ignore.

Perhaps it's just the swill of emotions I've experienced of late, but I think I like Liam. I think I like him a lot. Such a shame the man who instigated our chance meeting is the same man who seems intent on killing me. Probably not the ideal foundations for a relationship.

The doorbell rings. I empty my glass and trudge back down the hall.

"Everything okay?" he asks, as I open the door.

"Well, I'm still alive, which is a bonus."

"I prefer you that way."

He picks up the hessian rucksack at his feet and slings it over his shoulder.

"Show me to my bedroom then."

Liam is happy enough to let me watch as he erects his tent on the patio. It doesn't take long.

"You've done that before," I comment.

"Once or twice."

"Years ago, I went to a festival with a friend. It took us four hours to put the tent up. Even then, it collapsed in the middle of the night."

"This thing is designed to be put up quickly. No pegs."

"Ahh, that's where we went wrong. However, I'm much better at serving wine and as you're not driving, can I get you a glass?"

"Yeah, why not?"

I disappear into the kitchen and return with two full glasses.

"Do you want to sit outside? Seems a shame to waste what's left of a lovely evening … well, weather-wise."

"Sure."

"To be honest, I could do with the fresh air. I'll probably fall asleep at the kitchen table."

"If you're tired, go to bed. Please don't stay up on my account."

"No, I'm okay. Besides, I fancy some mindless chatter. I want to try and forget what happened earlier; even if it's just for a few hours."

Forgetting becomes a whole lot harder as Liam sits in the same chair Kenneth occupied three hours ago.

"I'll do my best," he says. "But chatter isn't my strong point."

"No problem. I've got more than enough for both of us. And, didn't your mum say you're a good listener?"

"She did, and I am."

I put that theory to the test and despite his denial, Liam contributes his fair share to the conversation. We work our way through a couple of bottles of wine, and as evening turns to night, I'm close to forgetting the threat hanging over me. Almost.

As midnight approaches, my eyelids start to droop.

"I think someone is heading to sleepy town," Liam grins.

"Sorry to be a lightweight. I was having such a lovely evening, too."

"Really?"

"Ignoring the death threat earlier, yes. You've been a real friend."

He replies with a faint smile, not mirrored in his eyes.

"I'll give you a key to the back door."

"You trust me with a key to your house?"

"Do you trust your bladder to hold out all night?"

"Um, probably not."

"I appreciate you offering to sleep out here but I can't deny you access to the loo."

"If you're sure."

"I am. What time will you be up in the morning?"

"Sixish."

"Ah, right. I'll still be in the land of nod so just lock the back door and let yourself out."

"Will do."

I gather up the empty bottles while Liam grabs the glasses. He then follows me into the kitchen and puts the glasses in the sink. Once I've put the bottles in the recycling bin, I hand him a key for the back door.

"I'll say goodnight then."

"Night, Kelly."

He turns and makes for the door.

"Liam."

"Yes?"

"Sorry, I've completely forgotten my manners — I haven't really said thank you. Few people would have stepped in to help like you have."

"Honestly, it's nothing."

"No, it means a lot. I can't imagine being alone tonight. I'd have been ... well, I don't think I'd have got much sleep."

I stand on my tip-toes to plant a kiss on his cheek. Tired limbs and too much wine combine to steal my balance. Just as I totter backwards, Liam reaches out his trunk-like arms to offer support.

"You okay?"

A bit dizzy, a lot tired, but being held by a pair of strong arms causes the butterflies to flutter.

"I'm … I'm fine, thanks. This is becoming a habit; you coming to my rescue."

I look up into his dark brown eyes.

"No bad thing," he replies, his voice low. "It's a habit I'm growing quite fond of."

34.

I wake up with a thickish head and a dry mouth.

"Kelly," a voice bellows from the bottom of the stairs. "You awake yet?"

Liam's voice stokes an immediate sense of relief. I'm not alone. I put on my dressing gown and scamper down the stairs to find him holding a mug of coffee.

"What are you doing here? I thought you had to be away by six?"

"I did, but I messaged the delivery guy and told him I couldn't get there until nine."

He hands me the mug.

"I didn't want you to wake up in an empty house. I hope you don't mind."

"Mind? I'm ... thank you, again."

He nods and retreats back into the kitchen where his rucksack is lying on the floor. I follow, to find Liam isn't my only guest.

"Morning, Frank."

I step over to the table where Frank is waiting patiently for his breakfast.

"He's been here for over an hour. I didn't want to root through your cupboards but I think he's hungry."

"He's always hungry. Talking of which, can I make you some breakfast?"

"I don't want to be any trouble."

"Trust me: you're not, although I don't have much in, I'm afraid. Would toasted bagels suffice?"

"I'll eat just about anything, except spinach. I hate spinach."

"So does my best friend now," I giggle. "Although for different reasons, I suspect."

He looks at me quizzically.

"I'll tell you once we've eaten. Pull up a chair."

"Do you want me to feed Frank while you sort out breakfast?"

"Err, okay, sure," I confirm, nodding up at the cupboard.

"His bowl and the tuna tins are up there."

Something approaching a domestic situation then ensues. No husband or child, but a random bloke I met a few weeks ago and a ravenous cat. Still, there's definitely a slight fuzzy feeling as I slide bagels into the toaster while Liam feeds the not-so-little one.

I do like Liam, and I definitely like this kind of start to my day.

"Did you sleep okay?" he asks.

"Really well, thanks to you. How was the patio?"

"It was all right, actually. All those years in the army, you get used to sleeping whenever and wherever you get the chance."

"I feel bad, you sleeping outside while I was tucked up in a comfy bed."

"There's no need. As long as you got a decent night's sleep, that's all that matters."

I turn to face him, just as he sits down at the table.

"Your mum did a good job."

"What do you mean?"

"There aren't many men who'd have done what you did, and the few who might would only have done so hoping to get something out of it."

"I was someone's big brother once. I'm just doing what I hope someone would have done for Lou if she ever got herself in trouble."

"She'd be very proud of you, and I'm sure your mum is too."

"I'm sure," he nods, his low voice indicating a change of topic might be in order.

The toaster suddenly pops, breaking the silence.

"Breakfast."

I switch the radio on and we both make light work of the bagels. I'm about to make another coffee when I notice the time.

"Shit. I'd better get my skates on otherwise I'll miss the bus."

"You're going to work?"

"Why wouldn't I?"

"I thought the police might have said it's too risky."

"They gave me a long list of precautions I can take to stay

safe, and one of those precautions is to avoid being in this house on my own."

"I could stay here, if you like?"

"Thanks, but you've got a shop to run and I need a distraction. Besides, it's not likely any harm will come to me while I'm behind a desk and surrounded by dozens of colleagues."

"No, I guess not. I'll drop you off."

"You've already done more than enough for me."

"It's no problem. I'm going to the shop so it's not exactly out of my way."

"If you're sure?"

"I am."

Forty minutes later, we pull up at the kerb outside the Marston Finance building.

"Thanks again for everything, Liam. You've been an absolute godsend."

"Anytime, and if you want me to meet you after work, just ask."

"I was actually planning to visit my friend, Martha, after work."

"If you need a chauffeur, I don't have much in my diary."

"I'll bear that in mind, thank you. I want to hear what the police have to say so I'll let you know later."

"Sure."

I lean across and peck him on the cheek. As I pull back, I realise I've left behind an impression of my lips in rose lipstick.

"Oops. That colour doesn't suit you."

I rub it off with my thumb; my palm resting on his cheek.

"You're a godsend, too," he smiles. "I'm glad you wandered into the shop that day."

I feel my face flush. Returning his smile, I splutter a goodbye.

Sergeant Perry stressed it's unlikely I'll come to any harm in public spaces but I don't feel comfortable going to Starbucks. Instead, I wander into the reception area with the prospect of staffroom coffee ahead of me. Before that, I need a conversation with the security guard — one I should have had yesterday.

"Are the lifts working okay this morning?"

He looks up from behind the desk. Judging by his sunken eyes, he's at the end of a long night shift.

"They are."

"Well, they weren't on Wednesday night. I was stuck in one for over an hour."

"Were you? No one else reported any problems and I used them both after I came on shift at eight o'clock."

"Are you saying I'm lying?"

"No, I'm saying no one else has reported any problems. I will ask the maintenance team to have a look, though."

"Thank you."

I take the stairs again, just in case.

With a mug of muddy-brown liquid in hand, I sit down at my desk. The door firmly closed, my poky office feels like a safe haven this morning. It won't be long before I'm surrounded by people and there's safety in numbers. With security staff in the reception area, I can't see Kenneth even getting into the building, let alone trying anything while I'm here.

For today at least, I'm content to get on with my work and happily suffer the many pains in the arse I'll no doubt encounter.

One such pain in the arse comes to the fore as Ben wanders in just before nine.

"Natalie is back."

"Ah, good. Tell her I'd like a word."

"Now?"

If ever I needed a distraction, it's this morning.

"Five minutes."

"I'll tell her."

He heads off to give Natalie the news.

I open the email HR sent over and double-check the list of things I can and cannot say. Gone are the days when you can just fire someone on the spot so I won't have that pleasure but at least I get to load the bullet.

There's a knock on my door.

"Come in."

Natalie enters.

"You wanted to see me?"

"Yes. Take a seat, please."

She does but her body language suggests she's far from happy about it.

"Before we get started, I need to confirm this is a disciplinary meeting. If you want someone present, it's your right."

She shrugs her shoulders.

"Anything you say in this meeting might be used in further disciplinary action, which could lead to possible suspension or termination of your employment contract. Do you understand?"

"Yep."

"Good. I'll use my phone to record our conversation, just to avoid any misunderstandings."

As is her way, she appears non-plussed. If I thought I were about to lose my job, I'd be a damn sight more worried than Natalie appears to be.

"Can I confirm why you were absent on Wednesday and yesterday?"

"As I told Ben, a migraine."

"Right. Would I be right in saying the usual way you deal with a migraine is to lie in a dark room?"

"I guess so."

"Is that how you dealt with your migraine after you reported your absence on Wednesday?"

"Yes."

"All morning?"

"Yes," she huffs.

"That's not true, Natalie, is it?"

"What? Says who?"

Rather than answer, I pick up my phone and open the image gallery. I try not to let the glee reach my face.

"On Wednesday morning, you were out and about, weren't you?"

I hold the phone out so she can see the photo I snapped of her arriving home.

She leans forward and glares at the screen.

"You … you were spying on us?" she snaps, obviously flustered.

"Not spying, Natalie — confirming the reason for your absence. Are you willing to admit you lied?"

I put the phone back on the desk and wait for a reply.

Her body language shifts towards discomfort but there's no admission.

"Natalie, did you lie?"

She sniffs and looks to the ceiling before closing her eyes for what feels like an age. When she opens them, a solitary tear rolls down her cheek. Crocodile tears won't wash with me.

"Natalie?"

"Yes," she finally replies in barely a whisper.

"Can you repeat that, please — you're confirming you lied about the reason you were absent?"

"Yes."

Her face now pale, I keep the pressure up. She's a sneaky cow and I don't want to leave any loopholes open for her to exploit down the line.

"Where had you been on Wednesday morning when I saw you getting out of that car?"

She wipes the tear away with her sleeve.

"An appointment."

"An appointment?" I parrot, raising an eyebrow. "Hair salon? Nail bar?"

"Hospital."

Here we go. Her first lie exposed, she's already got another one lined up.

"If you had a genuine appointment at the hospital, why lie?"

"Because … because you wouldn't understand."

"Understand what exactly?"

"Pregnancy," she gulps. "I went for a scan."

"You're pregnant?"

"I am."

Her excuse throws me, and my carefully crafted plan, off course.

"What? I … what do you mean I wouldn't understand?"

"You're a career woman. I knew you wouldn't have any sympathy for my position, or why I've been off sick."

Her statement stirs a confusing cocktail of feelings. I don't know if I'm shocked, insulted, saddened, or all three.

"Why on earth would you make that assumption?"

"You've never had children, have you?"

"Well, no."

"It shows. Look at the way you treated Claire last year, after she announced her pregnancy. You were really standoffish towards her."

"I wasn't … was I?"

"Noticeably so. It was like you couldn't bear to be in the same room as her."

Perhaps subconsciously, I couldn't, but not for the reason Natalie assumes. It was pure envy.

"And you're not exactly my number-one fan, are you?"

There's no answer to that question.

"I figured it made more sense to lie, rather than have you make my life hell."

I sit back in my chair.

"Bloody hell, Natalie," I sigh. "I don't know what to say."

"You're fired? Isn't that what you've wanted to say for months?"

"Possibly, but I'd rather we started again with a blank sheet of paper, and the truth."

"Why? So you can use it against me?"

"No, so I can help you. You might think I'm some career-obsessed ogre who hates children but … God, you are so, so wrong about that. Just talk to me, please."

She sniffs a few times and pulls a deep sigh.

"I had a miscarriage a few weeks into the New Year," she says, her voice close to breaking. "The second in a year."

I can't think of any suitable platitudes to fill the stunned silence. Seconds pass until I have to say something.

"Oh, my. I'm so sorry. Why didn't you say anything?"

"I didn't tell anyone because I couldn't face talking about it. It was so much easier just saying I had a bug. Then, when I fell pregnant again back in March, I was diagnosed with hyperemesis gravidarum."

"Err, what's that?"

"Extreme morning sickness. Although it's not limited to mornings."

"That's what Kate Middleton suffered from, isn't it?"

She nods.

"I remember a doctor on the radio discussing the condition. It sounded awful."

"It was … still is, some days. I can deal with that, though. What I'm struggling with is the worry I'll miscarry again, and that's why I've been off so much. Every twinge, every ache … I'm terrified something will go wrong, and all the doctor says is I just need to rest."

If the sudden guilt wasn't bad enough, I also have to contend with a sizable portion of concern.

"But, everything is fine with this one, isn't it?"

"So far," she replies with a nod. "We've had the eighteen-week scan."

"How'd it go?"

"I can show you … if you like?"

"Sure."

Her face lights up as she reaches into her pocket. I'm then presented with a monotone photo of a tiny human — the kind of photo I've craved for so long.

I study the photo. It summons bittersweet emotions.

"She's a little girl," Natalie coos. "We're going to call her Amy."

In one of my weaker moments, I've browsed baby-name websites and Amy was a name I'd long-listed.

"It's a lovely choice," I reply, swallowing hard.

"Thank you. It was Jack's choice."

"Jack? The guy I saw you with yesterday?"

"Yes, my fiancé. He's even more excited than I am, and probably just as terrified."

The last emotion I expected in this meeting arrives. I should feel guilty for knowing so little about one of my team.

"How long have you been together?"

"Nearly three years, and he's been my absolute rock. There's no way I'd have coped without his help."

"People do, though, don't they? Some women have a baby without a man on the scene."

"True, and I really admire them. I don't think I could do it, though. It's not just the support — I want to share all the magical moments with someone."

Our conversation is now venturing into uncomfortable territory.

"Yes, I, err … anyway. What are we going to do with you?"

The last remnants of her smile wither away.

"I know I lied, and I guess I deserve whatever is coming my way."

"You do."

"But can I just say one thing?"

"Go ahead."

"We've got so much we still need to buy, and I know I don't deserve a second chance but I can't afford to lose this job. I am sorry, Kelly. I really am."

I reach across the desk and tap my phone screen.

"Shall we pretend this never happened?"

"Seriously?"

"Seriously, but please do me one favour."

"Anything."

I get to my feet and step around the desk.

"Keep me updated on your progress, please. That baby is the most precious of gifts and far more important than any job, mine included. If I can do anything to help or you need time off, you only have to ask."

"I … I honestly don't know what to say."

"You don't have to say anything. However, if you wanted to show your gratitude, I could murder a coffee from Starbucks."

35.

Natalie and I will never be the best of friends but that's on me. Now she's returned to her desk, I'm left alone to lick my wounds. All these months that poor girl felt it was easier to lie than open up to her boss. I feel genuinely ashamed one of my team harboured such a negative opinion, and it was my behaviour which helped cultivate that opinion.

Not exactly my proudest moment but as Dad used to say: if you make a mistake, don't run away from it, own it and fix it. This one might take some fixing, but I will try.

If there's any consolation, at least we got to the truth before I instigated her dismissal. I'll have to explain to Justin why our departmental wage bill won't fall next month but I owe it to Natalie to fight her corner. In the meantime, a large bunch of flowers might go some way to making amends. Fortunately, I have a florist on speed-dial so I won't have to venture out.

I return to a spreadsheet and wrestle with a formula. It keeps me occupied until lunchtime when I ask Ben to grab me a sandwich from the supermarket as he heads out to get his own lunch.

One unfulfilling sandwich later, my concerns over managerial ineptitude step aside to make way for more worrying thoughts. Bloody Kenneth. No matter how hard I try to block him out, no matter how hard I focus on my work, his face keeps breaking through.

Inevitably, our conversation replays on a loop in my head. Like everything about the man, it's perplexing. Irrespective of what he said, the way Kenneth delivered his threat felt almost apologetic. Looking back on it with a clear head, rather than through a prism of fear, his tone suggested a warning rather than a direct threat.

Saying that, everything Kenneth has ever said to me has been in that same measured tone. Why should a death threat be any different?

I give up. I can't concentrate.

Maybe an hour of helping out on the phones and dealing with Joe Public will help keep Kenneth out of my head, and quite possibly mend a few bridges with the team, too. I'm about to get up when my phone rings. A local landline but I don't recognise the number.

"Kelly Coburn."

"Afternoon, Miss Coburn. This is Detective John Royce — I believe my colleague told you I'd call?"

"Oh, hi. Yes, he did."

"Is it convenient to talk?"

"Sure."

He runs through a few details to confirm what I told Sergeant Perry last night and then moves on to discuss what progress they've made.

"Regarding this gentleman who keeps turning up."

"Kenneth."

"Yes, him. The good news is there's a traffic camera fifty yards along Hillman Road, and it just about covers the entrance to Juniper Lane. My colleague spent an hour this morning checking the camera footage to see if any vehicles came or went. A number plate would have potentially led us to a name and an address."

"Would have?"

"That's the bad news. Apart from a Royal Mail delivery van, not a single vehicle came or went all day."

"Maybe he walked?"

"That was our assumption but he doesn't appear on the camera an hour either side of the time you said he left your house."

"Eh? But, Juniper Lane is a dead end — there's no other way in or out."

"Not an obvious way, no, but he patently left the area somehow. We're looking at other cameras so maybe he'll show up on one of those."

"Right."

"The main reason I called was to check a few details on your ex-husband, if that's okay?"

"Sure."

"We contacted Firgrove Investments to get his home address, and they confirmed Nathan Thaw's contract was terminated back in March. He hasn't worked there in over three months."

"Oh, that's strange. I've seen him a few times recently, and he never mentioned leaving."

"Maybe he was embarrassed … male pride and all that. They didn't go into detail but I got the impression from the chap I spoke to at Firgrove Investments that your ex-husband left under a bit of a cloud."

"Hmm … you're probably right. Knowing Nathan, I doubt he'd have wanted me to know."

"There's something else," the detective then says, leaving a slight pause.

"Oh?"

"You told Sergeant Perry that Mr Thaw visits his mother at Oakland Care Home several times a week."

"Religiously. They're very close, and his mother isn't in the best of health."

"That's an understatement. I'm sorry to inform you, Miss Coburn, but Beatrice Thaw died six weeks ago."

"What … are you sure?"

"I'm afraid so."

I hated the old cow but still, the news of her death is a shock, particularly as Nathan told me she was alive and well.

"God," I gulp. "Do you know how?"

"Suicide."

"Bloody hell. They're positive it was suicide?"

"That's what the preliminary report states. Mrs Thaw had been prescribed a potent medication to help her sleep, but it looks like she may have saved her nightly pill and taken two-week's worth in one dose. A fatal dose, unfortunately."

"That's awful. I know she was in pain and far from happy, but I had no idea things were that bad."

"Sorry to say but it's more common than you'd imagine. In any event, her passing doesn't help us track down Mr Thaw."

"No, I guess not."

"We checked with the resident's association of the development down by the river and they've no record of him having ever lived there. There's no mention of his name on the electoral role, either.

I don't know what to make of the detective's revelations, and my silence says as much.

"Do you have any other means of contacting your ex-husband, Miss Coburn?"

"Apart from an email address, no."

"What about mutual friends, or his relatives? Would they have a contact number or an address?"

"Nathan didn't talk to his family, not that there were many to talk to. He only invited a handful of guests to our wedding, and that was twelve years ago. Apart from Beatrice, I never saw or heard from any of them again."

"Friends?"

"Nathan didn't have friends, or a social life. He was a workaholic."

"Well, he hasn't been a workaholic for the last three months, that's for sure. Your ex-husband appears to have slipped off the radar."

"But if you can't speak to Nathan, there's no way of determining who's been blackmailing him."

"I'm afraid not, which makes it even more difficult tracking down the chap in the brown suit; presuming he's involved somehow."

"Great," I sigh. "Am I supposed to just sit around and wait for him to turn up then?"

"We can install a panic button in your home. I'll get on to that as soon as I put the phone down."

"Thank you."

"Can I ask you one final question?"

"Sure?"

"The lady I spoke to at Oakland Care Home told me Mr Thaw was two months behind with his mother's fees. Do you know if your ex-husband has money problems?"

"He did say he had temporary cash-flow issues, but I

assumed those issues were related to the blackmail. We had a conversation about me selling a piece of land I inherited and giving him half the proceeds."

"When was this?"

"A few weeks back. He asked, I said no, and then I told him he should contact the police."

"Very wise."

"Now you've mentioned money problems, I bumped into the couple who bought our marital home, and the guy told me something which might be relevant."

"Go on."

"He saw Nathan in a bar back in January or February, and they talked briefly about some investment Nathan was celebrating — apparently in a company which went bust back in the spring."

"Can I get that gentleman's name and address?"

"Sure. Do you think it's relevant?"

"Everything is relevant until it isn't, Miss Coburn. At the moment, all we've got is a long list of questions and two men we can't find. I really don't know what to make of it."

"Join the club."

"I'll leave you in peace now, but if you think of anything else, please call me."

"That's all?"

"For now, yes."

"But what about the threat to my life?"

"Your safety is our top priority so please don't think we're not taking this seriously. We've covered a lot of ground in a very short space of time."

"I know, and I appreciate it. I'm just ... I'm worried."

"Please try not to worry. If this Kenneth character shows his face again, we'll have a unit with you in under five minutes."

"That might be four minutes too late."

"It's perhaps cold comfort, but if this situation is linked to your ex-husband's blackmail, then there's nothing for them to gain by following through on that threat. Dead people don't pay up."

"So, why the three prior attempts on my life if not to kill me?"

"Please don't think we're not taking those threats seriously but we've only got one man's word they were genuine attempts on your life, and that man is the one demanding money. My gut instinct is that this is all smoke and mirrors — it's the money he wants."

"About that. Why did he tell me to pay my ex-husband? Why didn't he just demand I pay him?"

"That's a good question, and one which ties into a theory we're working on."

"Can I ask what that theory is? I need some hope."

"It's nothing more than guesswork at the moment, and there's way too much guessing here for my liking so you'll have to bear with me. Try to remain positive. We're throwing all available resources at this."

"I'll do my best."

Once the call is over, my poky office doesn't feel quite such a safe haven. For all the police's efforts, they've found precisely nothing on Kenneth. As for Nathan, I don't have the first clue what he's up to. I can understand why he didn't mention losing his job, but to lie about his mother is just plain sick. Even though we never got on, what reason is there for not telling me Beatrice had passed away?

"Where the hell are you, Nathan?"

Until I know his whereabouts, and more importantly, Kenneth's, it'll take more than a bloody panic button for me to feel safe.

However, there is one man who might be able to help with that. I make some calls.

First, I text Martha to say I'll be arriving with a plus-one. I then make a call to Liam; a call I should probably have made first.

After suggesting he might like to come visit my best friend with me after work, his response edged on nervy. I get the impression he's a bit of a loner; not at his most comfortable in social situations. However, I reassured him Martha doesn't bite, much, and Stuart is definitely a man's man, so they should get on just fine. If anything, I reckon Stuart will be glad of some male company.

Social life settled, I do my best to plough through the list of tasks I've neglected most of the day.

It proves difficult enough keeping one strain of shitty thoughts at bay, but avoiding two proves impossible. I can either dwell on my mortality, or my conversation with Natalie. Neither fill me with joy but I choose the least depressing option. The more I analyse what my colleague said, the closer it drifts towards dispiriting shores.

Natalie's experience has flagged two flaws in my perfect plan for motherhood. She's only twenty-eight and the poor thing has suffered two miscarriages. At my age, there's already an increased risk of miscarriage, so what if I'm destined to suffer that same heartbreak? How many times can you go through that before you give up? I don't want to think about it; no more than I want to think about Natalie gushing over her fiancé.

Beyond the practical and financial challenges, I haven't given a single thought to the reality of being a single parent. There will be no rock in my life. No one to share the moments of pride; to hear the first words or witness the first steps. No one to share the sleepless nights, or to bear the worries of a temperature or a rash.

The child, my child, won't have a daddy.

My eyes are suddenly drawn across the desk to the photo of my parents. How would I have fared if that photo featured just a mother? The last twelve years have been bad enough; the worst moment being a walk down the aisle without a father on my arm. How would I have coped without a father in my formative years?

Unbelievably, I've poured cold water on the beacon of hope which has kept me sane through the last few weeks.

"Nice one, Kelly."

I need to step out from under the gathering clouds. It's not a healthy place to remain, and perhaps once this Kenneth-themed nightmare is over, I might be able to rekindle the positivity. Negative thoughts cause negative feelings — another gem from the therapist, but not without some basis in fact.

My phone rings and I snatch it from the desk, welcome of the distraction.

"Kelly Coburn."

"Miss Coburn, it's Detective Royce again."

"Oh, hello. I didn't expect to hear from you so soon."

"We've had a development."

"Have you found Nathan?"

"No, but we have found Kenneth."

"Oh, thank God for that. Where did you find him?"

"We didn't."

"Sorry, I'm not with you. I thought you said you'd found him."

"Not quite — he found us. He wandered into the station an hour ago."

36.

One less cloud, albeit the biggest and blackest.

"Has he been arrested?" I ask.

"We've cautioned him so he won't be going anywhere for twenty-four hours. At that point, we have to charge or let him go."

"But you will charge him, right?"

The detective replies with a prolonged silence.

"There's a problem with that, Miss Coburn. He's refusing to give us any information: no full name, no address, no date of birth. Just to complicate matters, he's also refused legal advice."

"Do you need him to confirm his details to charge him?"

"It's not just his personal details he's refusing to provide. He won't answer our questions so it'll be difficult building any kind of case against him; not one the Crown Prosecution Service will entertain, anyway."

The cloud floats back.

"Surely there's something you can do?"

"There is, hence my call."

"Go on."

"He has agreed to speak to us, but only if you're present."

"Me? No way ... I've got nothing to say to him."

"I fully understand, however, we're in a spot here, Miss Coburn. If he doesn't talk, there's nothing in the way of physical evidence we can use to detain him. We're working on the theory he wants you there so he can confess. Seeing as he came into the station voluntarily, it's not beyond the realm of possibility."

"Even if I don't want to hear his confession?"

"It's entirely your choice. I would stress that if you were to come in, the interview would be in a secure room and he will be handcuffed. I'd also be present."

"It's not the physical threat I'm worried about. It's what he'll say."

"And that's why this has to be your choice. If you want to sleep on it, we've got until mid-afternoon tomorrow but I must stress we won't be able to hold him on what we've got, which is basically nothing other than what you've told us."

"Can I let you know in the morning? I've got plans for tonight anyhow."

"Of course. If you decide to come in, we can set it up within an hour's notice."

"Understood. Thank you for updating me; at least I'll sleep a little easier tonight knowing he's locked in a cell."

"No problem. I'll await your call."

Once I've put the phone down, I don't know whether to laugh or cry, cheer or scream. I'm also torn between curious and concerned by Kenneth's request to see me. There's no doubt in my mind I'd rather not see him ever again but conversely, I want answers; the most significant also being the simplest — why?

That question stays stuck in my head until it's time to leave. I'm hoping a few hours with Martha and her family will help shift it. In the meantime, maybe Liam might help me understand it.

After avoiding the lifts again, I stride through the reception area and out the front door. Liam's van is parked in the same spot he dropped me off this morning.

As I make my way over, he gets out and opens the passenger's door.

"How chivalrous," I remark. "Thank you kindly, Sir."

I hop into the seat.

"I wasn't sure if it's still the done thing."

"What makes you say that?"

"I went on a date once and opened a door for the woman. We hadn't even got our coats off when she called me a chauvinist, turned around, and left, just like that."

"Oh dear. I'm guessing you didn't get a second date?"

He shakes his head and closes my door.

Her loss, I reckon.

"Are you sure your friend is okay with this?" he asks, getting behind the wheel. "I don't want to intrude."

"Martha is the loveliest person you could hope to meet. She's got a heart of gold."

"Right."

"And the mouth of a scaffolder."

"Err …"

I put my hand on his shoulder.

"You'll be fine. I promise."

He doesn't look convinced.

As we wind our way through the rush-hour traffic, I decide to bring Liam up to speed on my conversation with Detective Royce.

"Kenneth wandered into the police station this afternoon and handed himself in."

"He did what?"

"If that wasn't baffling enough, he won't speak to anyone but me."

"Why?"

"Beats me, but unless he makes a confession, they'll have to release him tomorrow."

"Are you going in?"

"I'm still considering it, but if I do, it won't be until tomorrow. I've had one hell of a day already."

"Fair enough."

"The police also unearthed some troubling information about my ex-husband."

"Like?"

"I don't know where to begin but the last time I saw Nathan, he told me his elderly mother was doing okay. Detective Royce discovered she died four weeks before I had that conversation. God knows why, but he lied to me."

"He didn't mention his mum had died?"

"Nope. He acted as if she was alive and perfectly well."

"That's twisted."

"It gets worse. Beatrice, his mother, committed suicide."

Liam shakes his head.

"I've never met the bloke, but it sounds like you made the right call divorcing him."

I nod, not wishing to waste another breath on Nathan. Whatever rock he's crawled under, I hope he stays there for good.

"Do you mind if I open the window?"

"Sure. I keep meaning to get the air-conditioning looked at."

I open the window but it makes little difference; the air outside is as baked as it is inside the van.

Once we escape the traffic and get up to speed, the noise of the wind rushing in prevents further conversation, but it's preferable to being slow-roasted. We arrive in Grange Close just after six.

I peel myself from the vinyl seat and step onto the pavement. Liam joins me.

"Ready?"

"You know, now they've got that Kenneth bloke safely locked up, you probably don't need me hanging around."

"Need? Probably not. Want? Yes."

"Really?"

"Yes, really."

"I don't want to embarrass you."

"You could walk into that house with a tea cosy on your head and I wouldn't feel embarrassed. Quite the opposite, in fact."

"I might have one in the van. Want me to check?"

"Nah, you're okay. Come on."

He digs his hands into his pockets and I take his arm; partly because it makes me feel safe but also to stop him running back to the van.

As we walk up the path of chez Miller, the front door swings open and two excitable girls beam from the hallway.

"Auntie Kell!"

"Hey, girls."

I release Liam's arm and gather the twins into an embrace.

"How's that arm?" I ask Ella.

She doesn't answer. Both twins adopt a curious frown and stare up at Liam.

"This is my friend," I announce.

Cautiously, the girls take a step forward. I've got a horrible feeling Liam isn't familiar with the inner workings of eight-year-old girls.

"Hello," he says. "I'm Liam."

The girls remain mute.

"I know what you're thinking. You're wondering if I'm related to Shrek."

A slight chuckle. Liam squats down so he's facing them eye-to-eye.

"Can I let you into a little secret, girls?"

They both nod.

"He's my brother."

"He's not," Millie says, defiantly.

"He is, and I can prove it."

"How?"

"This isn't my real voice — my real voice is exactly the same as my brother's. Would you like to hear it?"

The girls, both now grinning, nod enthusiastically. Liam clears his throat.

"Listen, little donkey," he bellows in a broad Scottish accent. "Look at me. What am I?"

Millie and Ella turn to each other, open-mouthed, before scampering forward. They then jump up and down while throwing question after question at Liam. Does he live in a swamp? Does his cat have boots? Has he met Princess Fiona?

Still in character he answers every question, much to the girls' delight. Their excitement builds until they have to dash off and share their news with Martha and Stuart — Shrek's brother is with Auntie Kell.

"Wow," I blurt. "Where did that come from?"

"I spent too long with an old army mate from Aberdeen. I guess the accent rubbed off."

"Well, you've certainly impressed my goddaughters."

"Kids are easy to get on with. It's adults I struggle with."

"Not this adult. You're a constant source of surprise, Mr Bradley."

I've learnt Liam doesn't do compliments; always responding with a sheepish grin and an awkward shuffle.

"Hey, chick."

I turn around, straight into Martha's arms. We hug, and then I

313

do the introductions.

Liam squirms as Martha chooses a hug over a handshake.

"We've got the barbecue on the go," she then confirms. "And wine, obviously."

"Should you be drinking?"

"It's medicinal wine."

We follow Martha through to the back garden where Stuart is tending the barbecue and the girls are slurping neon-coloured slushies.

Martha introduces Liam to Stuart and the two men shake hands. I'd already briefed Martha about Liam's military career and with Stuart having a brother in the Parachute Regiment, the two men have enough in common to spark a conversation.

What I haven't briefed Martha about is today's events with Kenneth. She's a natural-born worrier with enough on her plate.

"How are you feeling, hun?"

"A bit sore but otherwise I'm okay."

"Your face looks a little better."

"Liar."

"Your bruise isn't as … um, purple today."

"No, more yellowy-green, wouldn't you say?"

"It's a lovely shade. Brings out your eyes."

"Thank you."

We giggle and inevitably gravitate towards the fridge in search of wine.

"Does Liam want a beer?" Martha asks, as she fills two large wine glasses.

"I'll check. Hold on."

I poke my head out the back door and call across the patio. Liam declines a beer and asks for a glass of whatever the girls are drinking, much to their glee.

"He'll have a slushie."

"Interesting choice."

"He's an interesting man."

"Is he? He seems quite shy."

"Once you get to know him, he's lovely."

Martha's eyes light up.

"Ohh … sounds like someone is smitten."

"Stop it. He's just a friend."

"And is that all he's ever likely to be?"

"I've only known him five minutes."

"But you like him, don't you?"

"There's so much going on at the moment, I don't know if it's the right time to even think about relationships."

"You're still planning a date with that turkey baster?"

"Yep."

"Wouldn't you rather have a date with a penis?"

"God's sake," I splutter. "Can we change the subject?"

"Seriously, chick. What if this is fate?"

"Fate? Since when did you start believing all that crap?"

"Just hear me out."

"Go on," I groan.

"Has Liam got kids?"

"No."

"Does he want them?"

"I think so."

"So, you want kids, and now you've met someone you like who also wants kids. Are you telling me that isn't fate?"

"We barely know each other. I'm not willing to wait around in the hope something might happen."

"Don't wait then. He's a decent-looking bloke with no baggage so just crack on with it."

"Martha!"

"You're the one who moaned about wasting all those years with knobhead Nathan. Now, I'm not one for all this second chance bullshit but if I learnt anything from my scrape with that bloody truck, it's to grasp whatever opportunities life gives you while you've got the chance."

My defence has run out of road.

"I'll play it by ear," I concede.

"Good, and don't wait too long. You're no spring chicken."

"You cheeky cow. You're only two months younger than me."

"Yeah," she grins. "But I've aged so much better."

It feels so good to laugh with my friend; to forget about all the grief we've both been through this week, despite how much I still face.

"Come on. Let's go check how cremated those burgers are."

Outside, Liam and Stuart are deep in conversation. I hand Liam his slushie.

"Everything okay?"

"Yeah. Stuart was just telling me about his brother's antics."

"I can only imagine."

Martha sidles up to Stuart, and he puts his arm around her waist.

"You're supposed to be sitting down, Miss," he chides.

"I'm so bored with sitting down."

"Fair enough. Go fetch me a beer then."

She playfully slaps his backside before they share a quick kiss.

I glance across at Liam and our eyes lock for just a second. I wonder if he's thinking what I'm thinking — how much I envy Mr & Mrs Miller's relationship, and how long I've hankered to have the same connection with someone.

Martha then says something highly inappropriate about hot dog buns. Impossible not to laugh, and it sets the tone for the rest of the evening.

When I arranged our visit, I only intended to nip in for an hour to check on Martha. As it is, it's gone nine o'clock by the time we say goodbye on the doorstep. Despite the circumstances, I had such a fun evening, particularly once Liam relaxed. When he did, I think Martha saw glimpses of the man I'm coming to know. As for the girls, they adored him, although they insisted he comes back in full ogre gear next time. I've got a feeling he'll willingly oblige — he's a natural with kids.

"You were right," Liam says, pulling his seatbelt on. "They're a really nice family."

"They are. I love them all to death."

"I can see why. The girls are adorable."

"I think you've got yourself a little fan club there. I've never known them warm to a stranger so quickly."

"That'll be my inner-ogre," he quips in his now well-worn Scottish accent.

He slips the van into gear and pulls away. I wave to Martha and Stuart until they're out of sight.

With his hand resting on the gearstick and my head a little fuzzy with alcohol, I do something without thinking. I place my hand on top of his.

"Thank you, Liam."

"For what?"

"For helping me have a lovely evening. For a few hours I didn't have to worry about Kenneth or death threats or errant ex-husbands."

"It should be me thanking you. I haven't enjoyed myself like that in … well, it's been a long time since I had reason to smile."

I squeeze his hand.

"Your face suits a smile. You should do it more often."

"I'll try. In the meantime, I might need to change gear."

"Oh, sorry," I chuckle, removing my hand. "You can see why I failed my test so many times."

He laughs, and I concur with myself — he does look so much more handsome when he's smiling.

"Fancy some music?" he asks.

"Absolutely."

He reaches across and switches the stereo on. I recognise the tune playing within a few beats.

"God, I love this song. Reminds me of being fifteen."

"Were you a big fan of Take That?"

"Wasn't every teenage girl?"

"Err, I don't know. I never had much to do with teenage girls … when I was a teenage boy, obviously."

"Obviously," I giggle. "Didn't you date much when you were younger?"

"No, I was hopeless … a complete lack of confidence."

"Aww."

"I remember there was this girl at the local youth club I fancied like crazy. For months, I tried to pluck up the courage to ask her to dance, and when I finally did, she walked right past me like I wasn't there. Never saw her again, although I sometimes think about her and what might have happened if we'd dated. I might not have joined the army and who knows how my life might have changed."

"Those pesky what ifs, eh? I've had a few of those myself of late."

"Anything you want to talk about?"

"Thanks, but some other time. I just want to enjoy the rest of this song, and the evening."

We both hum along to *Back for Good* until we're within a few streets of Juniper Lane. Liam plucks up the courage to ask an inevitable question.

"I know your stalker is safely locked up, but do you want me to come in and check the house?"

"Would you mind?"

"Course not."

"I know I'm being paranoid but I think I've earned that right."

"You have."

With nowhere in the lane to park, Liam pulls into one of the side streets around the corner. With twilight now upon us, we exit the van to an indigo-blue sky with an almost full moon shining down.

I take Liam's arm again as we wander home.

We reach the front door and I scramble in my bag for the front door key.

"Ah, here it is."

I unlock the door, and a question slips from my lips with no forethought.

"No tent tonight?"

"Oh, I didn't know if you wanted me to stay. I'll go fetch it if you want me to?"

Martha's advice returns to focus, albeit tinted with a hue of Pinot.

"Carpe diem," I whisper, grabbing his hand.

"Eh?"

I drag him into the hallway and kick the door shut. Before I can find a reason not to, I reach up and clasp my hands on the back of his head. He doesn't resist as I pull him towards me; our lips meeting in a slow, lingering kiss. I haven't kissed a man since Nathan, and that was a long time ago. It might be the same physical act but this experience could not be more different; a first kiss that fits like the five-hundredth.

Reluctantly, I ease back.

"That was Martha's fault."

"Was it?"

"She said I shouldn't waste opportunities."

"Is that what I am? An opportunity?"

I nod.

"For?"

"That remains to be seen."

I flash a grin before pulling him into another deep kiss, more intense than the first. There's a connection I don't understand; don't want to understand. Don't care. I just want it to go on and on.

If only we had gills.

Still breathless, I take Liam's hand and lead him to the bottom of the stairs.

"You can turn around and leave if you want to. It's entirely your choice."

"No, it's not."

I gaze up at him, quizzically.

"From the moment you walked into my shop, I never had a choice."

"How so?"

"You don't say no to fate."

37.

A hand on my shoulder and a weight on the edge of the bed.

"Kelly? You awake?"

I force my eyes into slits.

"Sleep well?" Liam asks.

"I'm still asleep," I rasp. "What time is it?"

"Half-six."

I'm about to shuffle into an upright position but modesty intervenes — beneath the duvet, I'm naked.

"But, it's Saturday."

"I know, but some of us have a shop to open. I didn't want to leave without saying goodbye."

"Oh."

He nods towards the bedside table.

"I made you a coffee."

"Thanks."

I lean over and grab the mug, managing not to let an errant boob escape the duvet.

"You okay?"

A loaded question. What I think Liam really wants to know is how I feel, in the cold light of day, after last night's sudden turn of events.

"I'm good," I reply, sipping at the coffee.

"Any regrets?"

"Just one."

"Ahh," he frowns. "Dare I ask?"

"I regret being awake at half-six on a Saturday morning."

"I'll accept responsibility for that one," he says with a chuckle. "Sorry."

"But besides that, no, not a single regret. Last night was … wonderful."

"It was. It really was."

"I would stress, I don't make a habit of dragging men up to my bedroom."

"Good to know, but I'm glad you did."

"So am I, despite feeling just a little awkward this morning."

"Why awkward?"

"Because I've just woken up and I'm naked. You look like you've been up a while, and you're dressed. You have me at a disadvantage."

"Well, I could make amends later, if you like?"

"How?"

"I could cook you dinner," he replies, with a glint in his eye. "Wearing nothing but a pinny."

"Did Martha suggest that?"

"No. Why?"

"Um, no reason," I cough. "But count me in."

"Great. I'll bring over everything I need so you can put your feet up."

"And watch."

"And watch," he grins.

Liam then leans over and kisses me gently.

"Are you going to be okay on your own?" he asks.

The bubble bursts as Kenneth gate-crashes my thoughts.

"Until four o'clock."

"Saturday afternoons are usually dead. I'll shut-up early so you're not alone when they let him out."

"*If* they let him out. I've decided to go in this morning."

"You sure?"

"Nope, but as Detective Royce said, they've nothing else to go on. If I sit and hear what he's got to say there's a chance he'll incriminate himself."

"Do you want me to come with you?"

"I'll be fine. You go do your flowery thing and I'll call you later."

"Okay. I'd better get going."

"Do I get a goodbye kiss?"

He duly obliges and leaves with a promise of many more kisses later.

Kicking Kenneth to the back of my mind, I lie back on the pillow and bask in a contented glow. Last night really was wonderful, and for a man who claimed limited experience with the opposite sex, Liam certainly knew his theory. I'd honestly forgotten what it felt like to be desired, to lose myself in the throes of wanton lust. It was so good my pink vibrator may have had its last outing, public or otherwise.

I get up and head for the shower before my mischievous mind wanders too far — a cold one might be in order.

Once the devilish thoughts have been washed away, I skip down to the kitchen and open the back door. Too early for Frank, it seems. It's probably also too early to be calling Detective Royce, so I ping him a message saying I'm willing to come in and listen to Kenneth.

Twenty minutes later, just as I'm about to make another coffee, he replies, asking if I can come in at nine. What I'd really like is to spend a lazy Saturday morning doing as little as possible but Kenneth remains a significant blot on my relaxed landscape. This has got to end, and the sooner he's erased from my life, the better. I message Detective Royce back, saying I'll be there.

My date with destiny confirmed, I'm unable to think about anything else; particularly food. With no stomach for breakfast I try watching television and browsing Facebook but neither are distracting enough. By half-eight I give up and decide a slow walk to the police station might help settle the growing sense of unease. I wish I hadn't been so quick to dismiss Liam's offer. Too late now.

I don my headphones, select a suitably upbeat playlist, and leave the house.

By the time I step through the police station doors, my unease has evolved into acute nervousness. As I indicated to Detective Royce, I'm not concerned for my physical safety, but I am worried about what Kenneth wants to say, and why he'll only say it in my presence. I spent so long living with a controlling, manipulative man, this situation has too many similar hallmarks.

I approach the reception desk and ask the officer on duty for Detective Royce. A call is made and I'm invited to take a seat. I don't want to sit and prefer to pace up and down the reception area. When that becomes tedious, I turn to reading crime prevention leaflets fixed to a pin board. Anything to distract from the reason I'm here.

A door swings open and a suited man wanders in. Early fifties I'd guess and carrying all the baggage of a high-pressure job involving too many desk hours.

"Miss Coburn?"

"Yes, hi. Detective Royce?"

We shake hands and he beckons me to follow him back through the door. He makes an attempt at small talk as we wander along a dreary corridor but, now I've passed the point of no return, not a word sinks in.

I'm guided into the detective's office and take a seat in front of a desk so loaded with paperwork, I'm glad it's not mine. Detective Royce takes a seat opposite.

"I appreciate you coming in," he says. "I know this isn't easy."

"No, it's not. Necessary, though."

"Our friend hasn't uttered a word since last night's meal so yes, it is necessary if we're to make any headway."

"He's not said anything at all?"

"Not a peep. He smiles, and nods politely, but that's it. He's an odd one, I have to admit."

"Tell me about it."

"But hopefully he'll open up to you."

"I hope so. I just want this over."

"Understood. We'll be interviewing him under caution so anything he says will be recorded and we can use it in evidence."

"And if he admits to threatening me, what will happen?"

"It really depends on what he says, specifically. If he makes that same claim about you being dead by Monday, we might have grounds to charge him."

"Christ," I groan. "Ironic I now need him to threaten me."

"Evidence is evidence."

A phone rings on the desk.

"Excuse me."

He picks up the handset, mumbles a few words, and then puts it down.

"They're ready for us."

"Right," I puff.

"If at any point you're uncomfortable, please just tap my arm and we'll have you out of there in a heartbeat. Okay?"

"Okay."

"Remember, this is on your terms. He's the one who'll be wearing handcuffs and facing a criminal charge."

I nod, and the detective gets to his feet.

"Let's get this over with."

We return to the corridor and head away from the reception area. Twenty paces later we come to a stop outside a nondescript door. A sign above confirms we've arrived at Interview Room One.

Detective Royce opens the door and steps inside. He then turns and offers a reassuring smile.

A deep breath and I follow.

The room is larger than I envisaged but just as sombre; charcoal-coloured carpet tiles, pale grey walls, and lit by a single fluorescent tube overhead. As Detective Royce steps aside, two men peer in my direction. The first is a uniformed officer stood against the side wall. He nods. The second man, wearing a brown suit, is seated at a table which abuts the rear wall.

Kenneth looks up at me and smiles. I'd rather turn away but I don't want to set a submissive tone for our conversation. I glare back at him.

Detective Royce ushers me towards two plastic chairs on the opposite side of the table. I snare the nearest one and slowly sit down; my eyes drawn to the handcuffs on Kenneth's wrists. The detective takes the chair to my left, closest to the wall and directly opposite Kenneth.

He presses a button on a chunky recording device and rests his arms on the table.

"This is a taped interview with a suspect identifying himself as Kenneth; his full identity is unknown. Those present are myself, Detective Sergeant John Royce, Constable Jack Collier, and Miss Kelly Coburn. The time is 9:04am on Saturday 22nd June."

He turns to Kenneth.

"For the tape, please confirm we have offered you legal representation, and you declined."

"That is correct."

"Good, now the formalities are out of the way, perhaps you'd like to explain to Miss Coburn why she's here."

Kenneth shifts in his chair to face me.

"Hello, Kelly."

I don't respond.

"How is Liam?"

Straight out of the gate, the randomness of his first question throws me.

"None of your business."

"You're right. I apologise. For what it's worth, I'm sure you'll have many happy years together."

"Get to the point," Detective Royce suggests. "Namely, the threat you made against Miss Coburn."

"It seems I haven't made myself clear. It was not a threat but a warning."

"That she'll die Monday lunchtime?"

"No, that she'll die *before* Monday lunchtime."

"And how do you know this?" the detective asks.

"That's not really relevant."

"Would you care to tell us something that is relevant?"

Kenneth switches his focus back on me.

"I told you there had already been three attempts on your life. The fourth will be successful."

"That sounds like a threat to me," Detective Royce says.

"It would only be a threat, Detective, if I were the one making an attempt on Miss Coburn's life. As I'm not, your statement is inaccurate."

"Who is the threat then?"

"The individual responsible is Nathan Thaw."

I turn to Detective Royce at the exact moment he turns to me.

"Nathan?" I scoff. "He might be many things, but it's ludicrous to even suggest he's capable of murder."

"You might think that, Kelly, but Nathan Thaw instigated the three attempts on your life."

"I don't believe you."

"That is a pity. How would I change your mind?"

"Try offering me some proof."

"Surely that is Detective Royce's role? I can only relay the facts."

"In which case, tell me one fact … just one."

"Very well. I can tell you that on Tuesday 4th June, you met with Nathan Thaw at a public house. I believe he proposed marriage during your meeting."

"I … what? Have you been following me?"

"No."

"How could you possibly know I met Nathan that evening, then?"

"How I know is immaterial. However, what is material is the fact you left the table to visit the bathroom, correct?"

I don't answer. I'm too busy trying to picture the bar at The Three Horseshoes that evening; searching for a stalker in a brown suit.

"While you were away," he continues. "Nathan Thaw removed a set of keys from your handbag. Using a key duplication mould, he took an impression of your front door key in order to create a copy. He would later use that duplicated key to enter your home."

"You witnessed him doing it?"

"In a way."

"In what way, specifically?" Detective Royce asks.

"It would not be wise for me to say."

"How about you start cooperating before I shut this down?"

"I am trying to cooperate, Detective."

"In which case, you can at least answer one fundamental question: what is Nathan Thaw's motive for wanting to kill his ex-wife?"

"Predictably, money," Kenneth replies matter-of-factly. "Miss Coburn has recently discovered she owns a piece of land which is worth a considerable sum of money. Beyond that land, there is her property in Juniper Lane, a company pension, and shares."

A knot tightens in my stomach.

"And then there's the significant life insurance policy Mr Thaw neglected to cancel after their divorce. All told, Miss Coburn's death would have resulted in a pay out in excess of three million pounds."

"But why?" I blurt. "Nathan is …"

I stop mid-sentence because I know I'm about to mumble a sentence I know to be untrue. Nathan *was* a wealthy man, but my chance meeting with Hannah and Rupert at the craft fair revealed the truth. I'm now beginning to wonder if that meeting was down to chance.

"Nathan Thaw is on the verge of bankruptcy," Kenneth confirms. "A failed investment, I gather. Unfortunately, he shared that investment with several unscrupulous individuals who are keen to discuss their losses with Mr Thaw, if they can find …"

"Wait," I interject. "Are these the same individuals who are blackmailing Nathan?"

"No one is blackmailing him, Kelly. Mr Thaw concocted the blackmail plot as a means to extract money from you. He orchestrated the email to your friend, Martha Miller, and the unfortunate video which appeared on … what's the name of that website?"

"Facebook?"

"Yes, that's the one. If you'd paid him as per his original request, he'd have used that money to flee the country and that would have been the end of the matter. However, once it became clear you weren't willing to pay the supposed blackmailer, Mr Thaw took a different approach. He went to ground and formulated a plan to end your life. I'm afraid desperate men will often resort to desperate measures."

"Why keep insisting I pay him off if he's still trying to kill me, as you suggest?"

"He has enacted a high-risk strategy; putting his liberty at stake. If he had the original funds as requested, there is no longer the need to take such a risk — he'd simply use that money to disappear. I recommended you pay him off to avert his current plan, but, unfortunately, you haven't followed my advice which is why we are here this morning."

The detective scribbles a series of lines on a notepad and then poses another question.

"Assuming what you're telling us is true, are you claiming Nathan Thaw will make another attempt on Miss Coburn's life?"

"Yes, and that attempt must be instigated before Monday lunchtime?"

"Why Monday lunchtime?"

"Because Miss Coburn has an appointment with a solicitor at one o'clock."

Detective Royce seeks my confirmation about the appointment. I nod.

"What's the significance of the meeting?"

"Perhaps you'd like to answer that question, Kelly?"

"Eh?"

"What is the purpose of your meeting?"

"To, um, discuss the sale of the land, and the solicitor mentioned something about tax, and estate planning."

"Estate planning would include the writing of a will," Kenneth continues. "One which would supersede your marital will, which is still in force, and exclude Nathan Thaw from the list of beneficiaries. For that reason, it is imperative you die before that meeting on Monday afternoon."

The pale grey walls darken as they close in on me. It takes a real effort not to tap Detective Royce on the arm. I glance at Kenneth. Outwardly, he appears every bit as calm and collected as he did when we first entered the room.

"I need you to explain something," Detective Royce says. "Namely, how you came to know what you've told us so far?"

"Really, Detective?" Kenneth sighs. "Do I have to repeat myself again?"

"I'm afraid you do."

"It isn't relevant."

"Oh, but it is. You've levied some serious allegations at Mr Thaw but you haven't offered us a single shred of evidence to substantiate those allegations. For all we know, you could be making it all up, or worse, somehow involved in this alleged plot against Miss Coburn."

"Miss Coburn's safety is the reason I'm here. My sole purpose is to ensure she follows the right path."

"Why? And please don't say it isn't relevant because it damn well is."

"You wouldn't understand."

"Try me."

"I don't think so."

The detective's eyes narrow.

"Listen to me, Kenneth," he growls. "I'll ask you one more time, and if I don't receive a satisfactory answer, you'll find yourself back in that cell for another twenty-four hours. Understood?"

Kenneth nods.

"Well? How do you know about this supposed plot against Miss Coburn?"

"Because I know who's behind it."

"What the hell is that supposed to mean? You said Nathan Thaw was behind it."

"Nathan Thaw is just the tool. Fate has decreed Miss Coburn will die and my challenge is to counter fate's plan."

Detective Royce turns to me and rolls his eyes towards the ceiling. I share his conclusion; Kenneth is unhinged. A simple question will demonstrate just how unhinged.

"Tell me then, Kenneth. If fate is out to get me, how do I die?"

"That is a very good question, Kelly."

"Yes, it is. Are you going to answer it?"

"I can't."

"Yep, that's more or less what I thought you'd say."

"You misunderstand. I can't give you an answer because I don't know."

"Convenient."

"Fate is like the weather: the further ahead one looks, the harder it is to forecast. The reason I'm here is because I don't know when or where the next attempt on your life will be. I had to make you and the police aware because I cannot predict what fate has in store for you with any certainty."

"Good grief. You're now implying you can predict the future?"

"No, because it's incredibly difficult to predict which path any individual will take. I cannot control your free will, or that of Nathan Thaw, or anyone else for that matter. I can only react to the ever-changing paths you all take. As it stands, your current path leads towards an early grave."

"Give me strength," Detective Royce mumbles, before nodding towards the uniformed officer.

"Interview terminated at 9:26am."

38.

The uniformed officer steps over to the table.

"Take him back to the cells," Detective Royce orders. "We'll decide what to do with him once I've had chance to process his … allegations."

As Kenneth gets to his feet, he looks down at me, his expression close to earnest.

"You know the truth now, Kelly, and I implore you to use that knowledge wisely. Pay Nathan Thaw enough money to flee the country and I promise you'll thank me one day."

I've nothing to say and the policeman leads him away. The silence in the interview room lasts but seconds.

"Well, that was … bizarre," the detective says.

"What do you think? Do you believe him?"

"I believe he's a complex character with a vivid imagination. However, he seemed to know an awful lot about you and your ex-husband."

"A worrying amount. Putting his allegations to one side for the moment, I can't begin to work out how he knew most of it."

"You don't need to be a detective to work that out — someone must have fed him that information."

"Who?"

"The only contender is your ex-husband. If I'm correct, it ties into the theory I mentioned on the phone yesterday.

"And that theory is?"

"The short version: your ex-husband owes Kenneth money."

As I see it, it's not even the first step towards an explanation.

"I think you might need to give me the long version."

"Okay, here's my theory. I hope you're sitting comfortably."

"I'm not, but go on."

"I say it's my theory, but really it's yours."

"Eh?"

"You had a theory Kenneth was blackmailing Nathan, and I think you were on the right lines."

"Really? Good to know I'm not completely losing the plot

because it feels that way."

"Your ex-husband claimed he didn't know who was blackmailing him, but I think he lied. Based upon what he's just told us, I suspect Kenneth was one of the original investors who lost money in Nathan's dodgy deal with Epsom Pharma. I also suspect Kenneth hacked that computer; possibly looking for evidence Nathan's investment advice was based on illegally obtained data. I think he found it."

"Nathan did say there were documents on our computer which he couldn't afford anyone to get hold of."

"Precisely. So, Kenneth then demands his investment back otherwise he'll take that information to the police. Trouble is, Nathan doesn't have any money. We know he's skint because he couldn't pay the fees for his mother's nursing home."

"That's why he asked me to bail him out."

"But you said no."

"Repeatedly."

"And how did Nathan react?"

"He pulled out a solicitor's letter, saying he intended to pursue me through the courts for fifty percent of my assets."

"What did you say to that?"

"I told him I'd drag it out as long as I possibly could; months, years, if necessary."

"At which point, Nathan concedes defeat and tells Kenneth there's no hope of getting his money back."

My mind races ahead; trying to piece the jigsaw together. The detective, being a detective, is quick to note my pondering.

"That's when Kenneth started showing up, isn't it?"

"More or less."

"And did you mention that to Nathan?"

"I did, because I thought Nathan sent him to get under my skin."

"That was probably Kenneth's intention — a way of showing Nathan he wasn't ready to give up so easily."

"And Nathan, being the coward he is, didn't do anything to stop him."

"Perhaps he didn't have a choice. How many times did you

suggest he report the blackmail to the police?"

"Plenty," I huff. "He either ignored me, or said it was a waste of time."

"When, in reality, he couldn't. Kenneth had him over a barrel with evidence of his involvement with Epsom Pharma."

"But what about the threats to my life?"

I don't receive an immediate answer as Detective Royce scribbles some notes on a pad.

"How long were you married?" he then asks.

"Eleven years."

"And during those eleven years, did Nathan ever physically threaten you?"

"No."

"Did you witness him threaten anyone, physically?"

"No."

"And did you ever feel unsafe, or concerned about patterns of aggressive behaviour?"

"Not that I recall."

"That's the reason I'm having difficulty believing Kenneth's allegations. I'm not saying people like your ex-husband don't commit serious crimes, but when they do, it's usually down to a bad decision made in the heat-of-the-moment. They don't tend to embroil themselves in complex murder plots, and I've checked Nathan's record — he doesn't have so much as a speeding fine to his name."

"Christ, are you suggesting Kenneth was behind those attempts on my life?"

"Probably, possibly, or maybe they weren't even genuine attempts on your life. The van for example: why did Kenneth send Liam Bradly to change your door lock?"

"That's a question I've never been able to answer."

"I think Kenneth wanted him there to pull you out of the way, and that's assuming the van would have even struck you. As I said before: dead people can't write cheques."

"I guess not."

"Based upon all we know, I think he was trying to scare you into paying Nathan. It all fits."

"Let me get this right. All I've been through over the last few weeks is because Nathan owes Kenneth money?"

"In a twisted nutshell, yes."

"In which case, why the hell did Kenneth wander into a police station with this cock and bull story?"

"There's a fairly straightforward explanation, and Kenneth made a critical mistake right at the beginning of the interview."

"Did he?"

"I think so. Can I ask a personal question?"

"Sure."

"Your relationship with Liam Bradley: are you close?"

"Um, I've only known him a few weeks but ... I guess you could say we've become friends. Why?"

"What was the first question Kenneth asked when you entered the room?"

"He asked how Liam is."

"An odd question, right? Some might consider it a veiled threat, if you and Mr Bradley are close. It explains why Kenneth wouldn't talk to us unless you were present."

"God, do you think Liam is in danger?"

"No more than you, and I don't think you're in danger as long as Kenneth is in custody."

"Right, but you didn't answer my question: why is he even here?"

"It sounds to me like he's trying to frame Nathan. As he came in voluntarily, it appears he's cooperating but I think his motive is revenge. If Kenneth can't get his money back from Nathan, what better punishment than implicating him for attempted murder?"

"Bloody hell."

"He probably thinks we'll switch our attention to finding Nathan and release him without charge because he hasn't done anything wrong; other than warn you, supposedly. However, the fact he made that veiled threat against Mr Bradley suggests he might try a different lever once he's out of the spotlight."

I slump back in my chair; head throbbing. Much like my recent meeting with Justin, the detective has dumped too much information to process.

"I'm confused, Detective. What makes you think he's trying to frame Nathan?"

"He's just told us your ex-husband instigated this plot to kill you but he won't tell us how he knows. Anyone can wander into a police station and make allegations, but we work on facts and hard evidence — neither of which Kenneth is able or willing to provide. In my opinion, these supposed attempts on your life are just a ruse to get you to pay up; hence his insistence you pay Nathan. I think Kenneth has tried to frighten you into paying but he underestimated your resolve."

"Sorry to keep throwing questions, but why the whole charade with my Dad's medallion?"

"I've no idea but my best guess is just to unsettle you, in the same way he sent that email to your friend's husband, and posted the video on Facebook. He doesn't realise it but basically he just confessed by admitting he knew about it."

"Did he?"

"How could he have known unless he was the one behind it? If he hacked that computer, he would have had access to your company email account, Facebook, and the online gift store you purchased your father's medallion from."

The jigsaw nears completion, but the detective has another question.

"Can I ask: what mobile phone do you use?"

"A Samsung Galaxy."

"Android, right?"

"Yes."

"Did you ever sign-in to any Google account on that computer?"

"I can't say for sure but almost certainly, yes."

"In which case, he'd have had access to the Google tracking app. These supposed chance meetings where he suddenly appeared; I don't think they were chance meetings at all. I think he knew your exact location because he was tracking your phone."

"I … Jesus, I hadn't thought of that. I changed so many of

my passwords after the Facebook incident but I don't recall changing the Google password on my phone. What an idiot."

"Sorry to add to your concerns but Kenneth is clearly an intelligent individual so I wouldn't be surprised if he installed an app to record your calls. I'd strongly recommend re-setting your phone back to the factory settings."

It's deeply disconcerting to think Kenneth might have bugged my phone, but it does explain how he knew so much.

"I'll do it as soon as I get home."

"Good. It's best to be on the safe side."

In ten short minutes, Detective Royce has provided a convincing theory, and one which answers virtually every question. I should be pleased, or at least relieved, but I'm not feeling either.

"What happens now?" I sigh.

"We really need to find your ex-husband, and that computer. If we can trace the hack back to Kenneth, we've got him."

"Any idea where Nathan might be?"

"That could be the issue. If I were in his shoes, I might be inclined to leave the country."

"Great."

"Try not to worry. Now we've got something to work on, I'm going to secure an extension to Kenneth's custody so we can build a case against him. If you hadn't come in, we wouldn't have his statement on record so you've been a great help."

After further assurances about Kenneth's detention and a conversation about restraining orders, Detective Royce escorts me to the main entrance.

Although he's delivered a plausible explanation to Kenneth's claims, and his general behaviour, I'm not sure if that explanation provides any real sense of closure. Still, as long as he's locked up, I can put fear on the back burner.

Half way home, while I'm trying to ignore a pounding head and a rumbling stomach, my phone rings.

"Hello," I answer wearily.

"Is that Miss Coburn?"

"It is."

"Hi, it's Darren from The British Heart Foundation."

"Err, okay. What can I do for you Darren?"

"Just a courtesy call to say we'll be with you shortly."

"Sorry, you've lost me."

"You arranged a collection of some boxes. A donation?"

"Ahh, right. My apologies — it completely slipped my mind."

"Is it still okay to collect them?"

"They're all still up in the loft, if that's okay?"

"We're not supposed to go up into lofts; for health and safety reasons."

"Right, we have a slight problem, then. I live on my own and I don't think I'll be able to carry them down a ladder without help."

"Tell you what: if you can stack them near the hatch, we can grab them from there. Technically, we won't be in the loft."

"I can do that, I suppose."

"In which case, we'll see you in forty minutes."

"Sorry? I was told you'd give me at least an hours' notice. I've had a hectic morning and I haven't even had breakfast yet."

"We're a bit behind schedule with collections and we're trying to get through as many as we can."

As annoyed as I am, I can't say no, otherwise I fear those boxes will remain in the loft forever if I don't deal with them now.

"Fine. I'll see you in forty minutes."

I really don't need this hassle.

My mind drifts to four o'clock. Knowing Liam will arrive with his pinny I evade the call of more negative thoughts.

"Home stretch, girl," I mumble to myself.

39.

I reach my front door and open it to a pile of envelopes on the mat. I gather the mail up and bump the door shut with my backside.

After dumping my bag and the mail on the kitchen table, I turn the radio on, hoping for some cheery tunes. As George Michael's voice fills the kitchen — repeatedly insisting he's my man — I open the back door.

"You're a sight for sore eyes, Mister."

Frank brushes up against my shins, purring loudly: a familiar comfort blanket.

I pick him up and hold him close to my chest. The purring deepens.

"Are you hungry? I am."

After lowering him gently to the table, I serve his breakfast while keeping one eye on the clock. I could murder a coffee but, like breakfast, it'll have to wait until I've moved the bastard boxes.

The only benefit of my impromptu task is the distraction. I suppose I'd rather be doing something rather than nothing, and head up to the spare bedroom where I keep a stepladder; a necessity for getting into the loft. Being vertically challenged, it's also a necessity for changing bulbs or dusting cobwebs.

I carry the ladder to the end of the landing; just below the hatch. Once erected I clamber up, slide the metal latch across and let the hinged slab of timber boards swing open. I'm no fan of lofts — it's home to too many things with too many legs, or worse still, wings. I switch the light on and climb up in to the musty void.

I've only been in the loft once before and it's bigger than I remember. A broad chimney breast splits the space into two sections: the part I'm stood in, and a section beyond the chimney breast where there's little light and many spiders, no doubt. I'm relieved to see the removal men stacked the boxes this side of the chimney breast, although they're still a dozen steps away from

338

the hatch.

With the slate tiles on the roof absorbing the sun's heat, it's also uncomfortably warm.

I stand for a moment and face the wall of boxes; the boxes which won't move themselves. It isn't likely to get any cooler up here, either. Why didn't I just cancel the collection?

"Just get on with it," I mumble.

The first box isn't too heavy but the second one weighs a ton. Rather than break my back, I drop it onto the floor and slide it across the dusty boards towards the hatch, hoping the cardboard doesn't give way. I then deploy the same strategy to move the rest. When they're all stacked next to the hatch, I clamber back down the ladder; panting and a little sweaty.

A quick glance at my watch confirms I've got five minutes to snatch the overdue coffee and beat some eggs for an omelette. I make it as far as the top stair when the doorbell rings. Darren clearly has a different understanding of forty minutes to me.

I stomp down the stairs and open the front door.

"Miss Coburn?"

I'm met by two men wearing bright red t-shirts emblazoned with the British Heart Foundation logo. Their van, parked on the lane, also bears the same logo on the side.

"Darren, I presume?"

"Yeah, and this is Micky."

He nods towards the weedy young man by his side. Micky doesn't look strong enough to lift his own trousers.

"Come on in."

The two men follow me up the stairs to the landing.

"I've just finished moving the boxes and they're all within reach of the hatch."

"Thanks. It'll take us five minutes to load."

Sufficient time to make a coffee.

"Can I leave you to it?"

"Yeah, no problem."

As promised, I leave them to it.

Back in the kitchen, Frank is loitering by an empty bowl. I put the kettle on and spoon copious amounts of coffee into a mug. As the kettle rumbles away, my feline friend sniffs the empty bowl. He then turns his head and fixes me with expectant eyes.

"Forget it, Mister. You're chubby enough."

Voices echo from the hallway. I don't quite catch the conversation but the tone implies typical blokey banter; the kind you might expect to hear in a backstreet pub or outside a betting shop.

The kettle boils. I pour water into the mug along with a generous glug of milk to cool it to a drinkable temperature.

My first sip is sublime. It might only be instant coffee but I don't care — I need the caffeine.

I'm just about to grab a couple of eggs when Frank pads across the table and sits down near the edge. He then looks up at me and meows.

"Aww, is someone in need of attention, eh?"

I step over to the table. As I stroke the fur behind his ear, he closes his eyes, and the purring begins.

"This relationship of ours is a bit one-way," I whisper, not wanting Darren or Micky to overhear my conversation with a cat. "When is it my turn for a stroke?"

Maybe I'll receive a stroke later, although I don't think Frank will be the male administering it. That prospect is enough to raise a smile and, coupled with Frank's therapeutic purring, my spirits lift a notch.

They say stroking a pet helps to lower blood pressure, even if that pet isn't strictly yours. I close my eyes and savour the moment.

"Hello," Darren yells. "We're done, Miss."

Peace fractured, I plod through to the hallway. Keen to be on his way, Darren is at the front door with a clipboard.

"Would you mind signing the collection note?" he asks.

"Sure."

I take the clipboard, scribble my signature, and offer it back to him.

"You need to add the time of collection."

"Oh, right," I smile through gritted teeth.

Form completed, Darren returns to the van. A rev of the engine and they speed away to the next collection.

One task down, two remaining. I return to the kitchen where Frank is waiting patiently on the table for more attention, or food, or both.

"You're a demanding one this morning."

I grab my phone and multitask; stroking the back of Frank's ear while tapping through the phone's menu to re-set it. Having been through the tortuous procedure before, I know it can take an age so I might as well start it while attending to my uninvited guest's needs. It's times like this I wish I were ambidextrous as it's akin to rubbing your tummy and patting your head at the same time.

Finally, I reach the point of no return — a stark warning my data and apps will be permanently erased from the phone's memory with one final tap of the screen. With everything I want to keep backed up in the cloud, I initiate the re-set. As the phone goes through the motions, there's a mild sense of relief my device will shortly be re-born; free from Kenneth's digital skulduggery.

I place the phone down on the table and return my full attention to Frank, much to his delight.

"I've got to get on, Mister. You're not helping."

My needs appear irrelevant as he tilts his head to the side to encourage more stroking.

"One more minute, and that's it."

A few seconds in to that minute, he suddenly snaps his head to the left; body stiff, eyes wide. Then, over the radio, I catch the creak of a floorboard. Instinctively, I spin around, and freeze.

"Shit!" I gasp. "What the hell, Nathan?"

My ex-husband is in the doorway; his usually neat hair overdue a cut and chin dark with stubble.

Slapping my hand to my chest, I draw a few deep breaths to quell the shock.

"For crying out loud. How did you get in?"

"Those chaps in red t-shirts kindly left the door open," he casually replies. "I thought I'd wait in the lounge until they left."

My mind scrambled, I can only stare back at him, mute.

"I didn't mean to startle you," he says apologetically.

"You have no right wandering into my home."

"Don't be like that, Kelly."

My shock gives way to anger as the red mist descends.

"Screw you, Nathan. Do you have any idea what I've been through over the last few weeks because of you?"

"I beg your pardon."

"I've had … no, forget it. There aren't enough words to explain how much grief you've caused me; how utterly sick I am of your shit."

"I can only apologise."

"I'm not interested in your apologies."

I reach for my phone, intending to call Detective Royce. Rather than the usual screen, I'm greeted by a spiralling icon and a message: *Installation at 12% — please wait.*

I turn back to Nathan.

"You need to speak to the police."

Rather than respond to my statement his eyes wander around the kitchen.

"Functional," he comments. "Not a patch on the kitchen in Kensall Gardens, though."

"Don't change the subject, Nathan. Call the police and ask for Detective Royce."

Ignoring me, he turns his attention to Frank.

"I see you finally got that cat you were after."

I'm about to reassert my demand for a third time when Frank suddenly bolts from the table. In a flash of ginger fur, he scarpers out the back door.

"Anti-social creature," Nathan mumbles.

"I don't think he likes you invading his territory, any more than I do. Either call the police or leave."

"Do I detect a little hostility in your tone?"

"No, Nathan. I'm absolutely delighted you showed up, uninvited. I'm also delighted you saw fit to lie to me."

"I haven't lied to you."

"You lied about your mother?"

"What are you talking about?" he snaps, his eyes narrowing.

"You said she was doing okay … weeks after she died."

"Who told you that?"

"The police."

"It's none of their damn business and they had no right telling you."

"Well, they did. In fact, they're keen to talk to you about this blackmail plot."

"Right," he snorts. "As if there's anything they can do. I'm not willing to waste my time, thank you."

"It's not as though you're strapped for time, is it?"

"What's that supposed to mean?"

"You never told me you lost your job."

"Someone's been a busy beaver, haven't they? What gives you the right to poke around in my affairs? We're divorced, remember?"

"Actually, I didn't. The police spoke to someone at Firgrove Investments."

"Good grief. Is there anything else you've gossiped to the police about?"

"Seeing as you've raised the question, I thought you were living in that new development down by the river but the residents' association told the police otherwise."

"Not that it's any of your business but I was staying with a friend."

"Bullshit. You don't have any friends."

There's a brief pause; no immediate retort.

"That, Kelly," he then sighs, "is painfully close to the truth."

He slumps against the door frame and visibly deflates.

"I've had the worst run of bad luck," he says in a low voice. "I've lost close to everything: my marriage, my job, my savings … and my poor mother."

"Oh, boo-fucking-hoo," I snap. "I might have been sympathetic if you hadn't spun so many lies. Why the hell did you lie about your own mother's death?"

"I don't know, denial maybe. Surely you of all people know how it feels, and how it messes with one's mind. I suppose I just blocked it out."

"Whatever, Nathan. I'm sorry for your loss but I've had a gutful of your problems. Just call the damned police."

"When did lying to your ex-wife become a crime? What is it they think I've done?"

"You know what you've done, and they have a suspect in custody for this bloody blackmail plot."

"Do they?"

"Yes, and don't lie to me again. You know who it is — Kenneth."

I know my ex-husband well enough to tell when he's genuinely taken aback, and this is one such instance. The clock on the wall ticks a dozen times before he responds.

"Are they going to charge him?"

"Hopefully, yes, but they want to check the computer to prove he was the one who illegally accessed it. Where is it?"

"Somewhere safe, but I don't want to speak to the police."

"And I didn't want the nightmare I've had to endure over the last few weeks, but that's life."

"I'm willing to compromise, though. I need a favour."

"A favour?" I choke. "You've got some nerve."

"I'm willing to tell you where the computer is, but I need some money. Just a few thousand."

"What for?"

"I've secured an opportunity overseas. I've got some cash stashed away but not enough."

"You're unbelievable, Nathan. After all you've done, you expect me to bail you out?"

"Needs must. I just want a clean break, to start afresh."

"I'm not giving you any money."

"I understand why you're angry with me but you need to think strategically. If you give me the money, I'll be out of your life for good. You'll never hear from me again, and that promise extends to any claim on your assets."

He's almost right about one thing: I'm harbouring more anger than I've ever felt, for anyone. However, if that money ensures we'll never cross paths again, and he tells me where the computer is, it could be a sensible investment.

I glance at the phone. *Installation at 24% — please wait.*

"Tell me where the computer is first."

"It's in the boot of my car."

"Which is where?"

"Parked around the corner."

"Go fetch it."

"No."

"Pardon?"

"I don't have time to play games, Kelly. I'm booked on a ferry which leaves in a little under two hours. If you want the computer, transfer the cash now and we'll go to my car together."

The red mist returns.

"Your days of dictating what I do are over. Go get that fucking computer or I'll call the police."

He shakes his head and tuts repeatedly like a schoolmaster chastising a troublesome pupil.

"Deary me," he snorts. "Some things never change."

"What?"

"You always were a testy mare when hungry."

"Don't you dare …?"

"Money first," he interrupts. "Then we'll go retrieve the computer. It won't kill you to wait another ten minutes for breakfast."

Seething, I look down at the phone. *Installation at 31% — please wait.*

At this point I can't fulfil my threat but I sure as hell don't want to give in. I consider my options but Nathan's patronising retort has raised the temperature of my fury from simmering to boiling point. How dare he dictate when … my thought process comes to an abrupt halt.

"How do you know I haven't had breakfast?"

"Sorry?"

"Simple question: how do you know I haven't had breakfast yet?"

"We were married for eleven years, Kelly. I know all your

345

little quirks and irritations."

"Do you also know how to read my mind, because I definitely never mentioned breakfast?"

The tick-tock of the clock signifies the passing seconds, and with each of those passing seconds we both step closer to a realisation.

"How did you know I haven't had breakfast, Nathan?"

"I really don't have time for this. Do you want that blasted computer, or not?"

"What I want is for you to answer my question."

He just glares across at me. I know the expression well — he's weighing up his options, deciding on his next move. My mind is ablaze; trying to work out how he knew. I know for absolute sure I never told him I haven't eaten yet. In fact, the only time the word 'breakfast' has passed my lips was during the telephone conversation with Darren earlier.

The realisation steals my breath.

"Oh, my God … you've been listening to my calls."

40.

My eyes flick back to the phone. *Installation at 33% —
please wait.*

I'm in such a state of paralysed shock, there's no chance of
reacting when Nathan suddenly leaps forward and grabs my arm.
I try to snatch a lungful of air to facilitate a scream but I'm too
slow. He kicks the back door shut while maintaining a vice-like
grip on my arm.

To keep my scream captive, he then positions himself behind
me and slaps a hand across my mouth. I feel the pressure release
on my arm but it's of no help with his hand rigidly clamped
across my face.

"It seems I've put my foot in it," he growls in my ear. "Plan-
B, it is."

With his right hand free, he reaches towards the counter top. I
can't turn my head but I shift my eyes to follow his hand as it
settles on the knife block. He then withdraws a boning knife with
a six-inch, serrated blade.

"It's just a precaution, Kelly," he says. "I don't much care for
your new-found feistiness."

His statement isn't relevant. What is relevant is how much of
what Kenneth said earlier is actually true. I scorned his
suggestion Nathan might be capable of murder but my current
predicament suggests I may have leapt to my ex-husband's
defence too readily.

"I'm going to move my hand from your mouth. If you so
much as whimper, I won't hesitate to use the knife."

To enforce his point, he presses the knife into the small of my
back; not enough to hurt but enough pressure I know it's there.
The hand falls away and I gasp for air. The hand doesn't stay
unemployed for long and it's quickly dispatched to my jacket
collar.

"It's all true, isn't it?" I blurt.

"What is?"

"You want me dead."

"What I wanted was enough money to get away, but you refused and that's why we're here. Whatever happens from this point onwards, you brought it on yourself."

He then pushes me towards the hallway. I try my best to resist but the knife is a strong motivation to keep moving forward. Once we're in the hallway, he kicks the kitchen door shut, trapping me in the claustrophobic space. Fifteen feet ahead, the front door offers an escape route.

"Don't even think about it," he warns. "I've got a perfect plan-C if you try anything."

"I, uh …"

"Aggravated burglary," he adds. "Some random youth breaks into your home looking for money. He doesn't realise anyone is at home and then walks into the kitchen. You escape into the hallway but after a brief scuffle, he stabs you repeatedly with your own kitchen knife. Tragic, and plausible, wouldn't you say?"

"You … you wouldn't."

"Trust me, Kelly. Any qualms I had about ending your life left town long ago. I'd rather not see you suffer but if you don't do as I ask, you'll leave me no choice."

It's one thing to know you married a controlling narcissist, but knowing you walked down the aisle and shared a bed with a man capable of murder is on a whole different level of stupefying. It turns my stomach to think anyone, let alone the man who might have fathered my children, considers money more important than human life. Then again, Nathan's entire world revolved around money, and it became his drug of choice — however large the fix, he always wanted another. He was an addict, and addicts will stoop to any depths to feed their habit.

He partly pushes, partly drags me towards the bottom of the staircase.

"Get up there."

Panic mounts as I work through the reasons he might want me upstairs. Too many thoughts and questions are already hogging the limited resources and I give up on guessing.

"Move."

Slowly, cautiously, I climb the twelve steps. The panic heightens and it becomes increasingly difficult to focus on a way out of this nightmare. I step onto the landing with a knife in my back and nothing worthwhile in my head.

"Go to the end," he orders.

There's one door at the end of the landing — the bathroom door, and it's shut. Just in front of that door, the loft hatch is still hanging open with the stepladder beneath.

"Eh?"

"You heard me."

With little choice I shuffle forward until we reach the stepladder.

"Up you go," he then orders.

"What?"

"Do I have to keep repeating myself? Get up the damn ladder."

The tip of the knife presses into my skin with enough force, I yelp.

I reluctantly place my hands on the stepladder but I will not go willingly into the loft. I don't even know why he wants me up there.

"That's better," he says in a gentler tone. "More like the compliant Kelly I used to know and love."

His calmer demeanour and reference to love sets my mind on a path to an idea. A stomach-churning idea but one which might lower his defences long enough I can get to a door or window.

"Whatever you're planning, Nathan," I say calmly. "There has to be another way, surely?"

"What do you suggest?"

Releasing one hand from the stepladder, I turn to face him.

"I ... I don't know, but surely we can work it out if we just sit down and talk. Maybe I should have taken your marriage proposal more seriously."

"Ahh, I see," he says, mockingly. "Is this an epiphany? You now realise you still love me and deeply regret shunning my marriage proposal?"

"I'm not saying that, but ... don't you care about me at all?"

"Perhaps I did, and perhaps we could have avoided this, but you destroyed any chance of a reconciliation last night."

"What happened last night?"

"Once you're up in the loft, I'll show you."

"I don't understand … show me what?"

"The disgusting video footage of you and that Neanderthal in bed."

The revelation winds me like a punch to the stomach. I fight the urge to gag as I recall the copied key Kenneth referred to. Nathan *has* been in my home.

"You … you put a camera … in my bedroom?"

"In the interest of transparency — not that it matters now — your kitchen and sitting room, too."

"Why the hell would you do that?"

"With so much at stake, I had to monitor what you were up to. Shame I had to watch you degrade yourself in such a base manner, though. You really have let your standards slip."

Raging indignation engulfs the fear. I can't help myself.

"Fuck you, Nathan," I spit. "He's ten times the man you are, in every department."

My dig lights a fuse and the explosion goes off before I've chance to retreat to a safe distance. Nathan flashes out an arm and a backhand slap connects with my cheek.

My face ablaze with a burning sting I stumble sideways, bounce off the wall, and fall to the floor.

"Get up, you filthy whore."

Still smarting, I ignore his demand and pull deep breaths.

"Now!" he hisses, jabbing the knife within inches of my head.

I cower down on to all fours. As my hands brush the carpet, I glance up; my line of sight at the same level as Nathan's crotch.

A forgotten memory offers a slither of hope.

Once, I wandered into the staffroom and a gaggle of my male colleagues were debating if a punch to the bollocks hurts more than childbirth. I've no experience of either but maybe I have a tiny window of opportunity to test the theory on my ex-husband.

Balling my right fist, I prepare; tensing my right shoulder and switching my weight to the left. I risk another glance towards Nathan's crotch to confirm the best trajectory. Only then do I notice the rectangular object outlined in his trouser pocket. Initially, I presume it's just his mobile phone but the top end of the object protrudes above the pocket hem, revealing the rectangular object to be bright yellow. So too is the cap which sits on top. I can only think of a few products which come in a bright yellow container and I've never seen a mustard tin with a nozzle. By a process of elimination I'm left with one possibility — lighter fuel.

"Get up."

I remain rigid with fear. There's not one good reason for Nathan to have a can of lighter fuel on his person. Plenty of bad ones, though.

"Why ... why have you got a can of lighter fuel?" I stammer.

"That was for plan-A, and it's now an integral part of plan-B. Get up."

Now or never. I either implement my own plan in the next few seconds or I'll discover exactly what Nathan intends to do with his can of lighter fuel. I ball my fist again and prepare to throw the punch. If I miss the target or he reacts quickly enough, he'll have no problem thrusting the knife into my exposed back. It's an all-or-nothing gamble, with my life being the prize.

I adjust my balance an inch.

"Stop fucking around."

One, maybe two heartbeats before I get the chance to swing my arm, Nathan grabs a handful of my hair and yanks me to my feet. It happens so fast the pain receptors in my brain lag. When I'm pinned up against the wall, they catch up and the tears follow.

"Please, Nathan," I sob. "Let me go."

With his forearm pressed hard across my chest, he waves the knife inches from my eyes with his free hand.

"You won't feel a thing if you do this my way," he says, without a hint of emotion in his voice. "In nearly every house fire, the victim dies of smoke inhalation long before flames consume their body."

"Please … please … no."

"I'm sorry, but this is the best way. As you know full well, fire destroys evidence."

"I … I'll give you anything … everything. However much money you need, it's yours."

"You're forgetting something, Kelly. When you're gone, everything you own will be mine."

"The police know … they already suspect you're involved in some shady deal."

"They can suspect what they like. They have no evidence and I'll be on the other side of the world when I claim your assets."

Somewhere in my chest, the organ which has kept me alive for thirty-nine years hammers like never before. I try to breathe but I can only gasp shallow breaths.

"Your choice, Kelly. Get up in the loft and take your chances, or I'll kill you slowly here and now."

He presses the tip of the knife against my cheek.

"Eyes first, then maybe I'll slice away for an hour. I can always get a later ferry if that's your preferred choice?"

I can't speak and Nathan takes my shocked silence as an answer.

"Now, get up the ladder. I won't tell you again."

I look up to the black square in the ceiling. It's no different to a terminally ill patient staring into their own grave. The same harrowing sense of terror as you stare in to the dark void with absolute certainty your life is nearly at an end.

"Get up there."

I don't move. I can't move.

Is this how my parents went? Did they know they were about to die; certain cremation long before a crematorium service? Did they hold each other in that final moment and share the same last breath before slipping away peacefully? Or did they cry and scream as the flames scorched their flesh?

The doorbell rings.

Nathan reacts instantly. He reaches around and clamps his hand across my mouth. The knife leaves my back and then digs into my ribs.

"Not so much as a squeak," he says in barely a whisper.

In the silence, all I can hear is Nathan's heavy breaths and the rapid thump of my heart. Mind racing, I try to picture who might be at the door. Chances are it's a parcel delivery driver and they'll give up after a second ring; my parcel abandoned on the doorstep.

Silent seconds pass until the doorbell rings again. This time, it's a much longer press of the button, as if the caller is growing impatient — all the hallmarks of a delivery driver.

The ringing ends and the silence returns. If my theory is correct, it'll be the last time I ever hear that doorbell. Time ticks by and the tension in Nathan's hand eases a fraction. His guess perhaps not too far from mine.

Any fleeting hope I had has just walked away.

"Shall we get on?" he hisses. "I've got a busy afternoon."

Suddenly, a thumping sound booms from the hallway, all the way up the stairs. A fist banging the door?

Nathan's hand stiffens again, and he curses under his breath. The thumping sound booms again, then repeats seven or eight times in quick succession. Someone wants to gain the homeowner's attention and someone isn't going quietly.

But then the thumping stops. Long seconds pass.

"Kelly?" a voice yells from the doorstep. "Are you in there?"

I recognise it in an instant — the sweet sound of a gruff voice.

Unable to answer, I can only hope Liam hears my silent prayers.

41.

The line between hope and despair is paper thin. Hearing Liam's voice offers hope but the pessimistic part of my brain won't let that hope linger. I don't know why he's outside my house when he should be at the shop, but he won't hang around if I don't answer the door, surely?

Perhaps it's a surprise visit while he's out on a delivery. He'll walk away soon, disappointed. No one is home.

"Kelly! Kelly!"

His voice is definitely louder, verging on frantic. The front door receives more thumps; so hard it rattles in the frame.

The tortuous silence returns. I count the seconds in my head. One, two, three, four, five, six, seven. I reach twenty and give up. Too long, and the hope fades to nothing. The tears flow again; the sting mirroring the one Nathan applied to my cheek minutes ago.

"Enough of this," he hisses in my ear. "Get up that fucking ladder, now."

He digs the knife in the soft flesh on my hip, enough to pierce the skin. I try to scream but with his hand still covering my mouth; it comes out a muffled grunt.

Another thump suddenly echoes up from the hallway. Hope? One, two, three … again, the same dull thump. I don't have a chance to re-start my count. The tense silence suddenly breaks; an ear-splitting crack and the clatter of the front door slamming against the hallway wall.

"Kelly?"

Liam is inside the house.

Nathan tightens the clamp across my mouth and edges the blade an inch closer to my kidney. I can hear heavy footsteps stomping across the floorboards downstairs. The hallway, then the lounge and into the kitchen. The footsteps return to the hallway and stop.

"Kelly?"

I can't scream, can't shout, can barely breathe with Nathan's hand in the way but I need to make Liam aware I'm up here. My eyes dart left, right, and then stop on the ladder directly in front of me. It's old, aluminium, and close to rickety. I flick out my right leg and kick the bottom rung. The clattering rattle reverberates in the silence, bouncing off the walls and signalling someone is definitely home.

Heavy footsteps stomp on the treads. Nathan responds by twisting me around one-eighty degrees so we're both facing the top of the stairs.

Liam's head appears beyond the wooden banister. He turns and catches sight of the once married couple; the former husband with a knife digging into the ribs of his former wife; his hand covering her mouth. He appears confused and stops dead for a second.

"Who the fuck are you?" he barks.

I can almost hear Nathan's brain processing his options. My saviour might be steps away but on the narrow landing, there's no space to make a move.

Nathan remains silent.

"I asked you a question," Liam growls, edging a step forward.

"Back off," Nathan replies over my head. "Or I will kill her."

"No, you won't. The police are on their way so you've got three or four minutes to make a decision."

"I don't believe you."

"We'll all just stand here and wait then. They're bound to send a firearms unit so you can negotiate with them."

I can feel Nathan's heart pounding against my shoulder, and the stench of sweat on his palm. In his chess game, surely he knows there's only one move available.

"You've still got time to let Kelly go, and you can walk away," Liam says in a level voice. "As long as she's safe, I won't stop you."

Nathan's hand slips half-an-inch lower on my mouth.

"But I'll tell you something for nothing," Liam continues. "If you harm a single hair on her head, I'll take that knife and cut you to ribbons."

"I'd like to see you try."

"I doubt that," Liam snorts. "Unless you're willing to pit my fifteen years of combat experience against whatever the fuck it is you do?"

I sense checkmate is close. Both men glare at each other, waiting for the other to blink. Nathan blinks first.

"Stand in the bedroom," he snaps. "I'll move to the top of the stairs and you can have your whore. You try anything and I won't think twice about using the knife."

Liam does as instructed and takes three steps back into my bedroom. Nathan then removes his hand from my mouth and grabs my jacket collar again.

"Move slowly. No sudden movements."

With a knife digging into my back there's no chance I'm willing to risk a sudden movement.

I edge forward in slow, mechanical steps. Nathan is so tight behind me I can feel every breath on the top of my head. Together, we shuffle forward until I'm level with the top of the stairs. Liam watches on helplessly; his expression pained.

Using my collar, Nathan pulls me around so I'm facing the wall opposite the stairs. I can't see, but I'd guess I'm being used as a human shield while he backs down the first few stairs. I only hope at that point he withdraws the knife and bolts for the front door.

"Don't think this is over," he then spits. "You owe me, Kelly."

I turn to my right and lock on Liam's face. He mouths a few words of reassurance and just as I nod back, Nathan suddenly releases the grip on my collar. Footsteps hammer down the stairs a fraction of a second later.

I glance over my shoulder — he's gone.

Liam dashes towards me. All I want to do is wrap my arms around him but he has other ideas.

"Who is he?" he asks, urgently.

"Nathan, my ex-husband."

He charges down the stairs.

"Wait," I yell after him.

He disappears without a reply.

I'm left alone, shell-shocked and emotionally shattered. My first instinct is to curl into a ball and sob my heart out but with Liam now in pursuit of my deranged ex-husband, self-pity will have to wait.

I scamper down the stairs and out past the battered front door.

There is only one way Nathan could have gone, and that's left. I step beyond the front gate — Liam's van abandoned at the kerb — and look up the lane towards the junction.

"Oh, no!"

The rush of adrenalin arrives just in time. It stiffens my jelly-like legs and sweeps the shock to one side. I break into a sprint and cover the fifty-odd yards of pavement with no idea of what I'll do when I reach the two men.

As I jog to a stop, they both seem oblivious to my presence. Stood five feet apart and facing one another, Nathan is waving the knife around in an attempt to bypass Liam's blocking manoeuvre; the younger of the two men having quickly caught up with his grossly unfit foe.

"Give it up," Liam barks. "You're not getting past."

"Get out of my way."

"No chance."

They've reached an impasse, and neither man appears willing to yield. The problem for Nathan is the clock is ticking and the longer he's prevented from leaving Juniper Lane, the greater the chance the police will arrive before he can escape.

He continues to step left and right, looking for an opportunity to skirt past Liam and run. It's a futile tactic as Liam mirrors every step; careful to remain just out of jabbing distance.

"Fucking move!" Nathan pants, his face now crimson red.

I so badly want to tell Liam to step aside but I daren't distract him, even for a second. It's enough time for Nathan to thrust the knife forward while his adversary's eyes are elsewhere. One second, one decisive strike, and he'll be free to run.

"I'm not moving."

Nathan responds with a wild lunge but the tip of the knife

doesn't come close to its target.

The dance continues and then I hear it — the faintest wail of a siren. It offers hope, but I fear I've already used up my quota of hope for the day.

Crucially, Nathan hears the siren too, and desperation takes over.

I can't stand by and do nothing.

"Nathan, stop," I plead. "It's over. Put the knife down."

"Drop dead."

"This is crazy. Please, stop."

My plea falls on deaf ears and he switches tactics. Rather than continually jabbing the knife forward — a move Liam counters with ease — he waves it left and right in a slashing motion. It appears to work as Liam has no choice but to back away. The exertion takes its toll, though; Nathan panting and sweating profusely. He never was a fit man, and he's now paying for his sedentary lifestyle.

The siren grows markedly louder, but that only heightens Nathan's desperation. He charges forward, slashing and yelling. His move catches Liam by surprise; forcing him to back-pedal.

With Liam's balance impaired, Nathan — realising this is almost certainly his last chance — barrels forward. He swings the knife again, and in a last-ditch effort to stay out of its way, Liam ducks. The knife cuts through thin air, missing the top of its target by mere inches. Having thrown his entire bodyweight into the swing, Nathan's momentum drags him in the same direction.

Liam regains his balance and shifts his feet with the speed of a flyweight boxer. The siren is now perhaps just a few streets away but still time enough for my ex-husband to flee — that's until a fist slams into his ribcage.

Nathan yelps and staggers to the side; still brandishing the knife but clearly pained. He tries to swing it again, only to discover how much damage Liam's fist inflicted. The swing fails halfway through its arc when he's forced to hold his ribcage. Unable to continue his attack, Nathan's only option is to run. He manages to limp three steps before Liam throws a second, and decisive punch. It connects with Nathan's jaw.

I've never seen Nathan drunk but what follows is a passable impression of an intoxicated man. Glassy-eyed, he staggers a few steps to his left on legs like cheese strings. He attempts a correction but his right leg isn't in any position to offer support. Nathan crumples to the ground; the knife landing a few feet away. There's an effort to reach out an arm, but it proves futile as Liam's Timberland boot steps on the weapon.

A white car with a luminous green and blue livery turns into the lane; lights strobing and siren wailing. It squeals to a halt and two police officers emerge. A second car arrives within seconds and then a third blocks off the entrance to the lane.

What occurs next is like an out-of-body experience. I'm swamped by a wave of delayed shock as a chaotic commotion of people, voices, and lights erupt around me. My own legs come close to giving way as I watch the scene unfold. Again my saviour, Liam arrives just in time and pulls me into his arms.

"It's over," he whispers. "You're safe now."

In times of high stress, people often say they're close to a nervous breakdown — I've heard the term a thousand times in the office over the years. I've never given any serious thought to what an actual nervous breakdown must feel like but, as I sob into Liam's chest, I reckon I'm experiencing a fair taster. I can't stop shaking and my over-burdened mind reacts like a soaked sponge as more emotions rain down; it can't contain, yet can't release.

Liam somehow guides me back to the house.

Next thing I know, I'm sat at the kitchen table. The familiar surroundings and Liam's calming voice are enough to pull me back from the edge.

"A paramedic will be here shortly," he says. "Just to check you over."

I nod.

"In the meantime, I'll fix you a cup of sweet tea. Mum reckons it's the best thing for shock."

"Thank you," I gulp.

He squeezes my hand and smiles.

"I'm afraid the pinny is at home, though."

"Bugger," I splutter in a teary chuckle.

To the best of my knowledge, no one has compiled a Kelly Coburn user-guide but if they have, Liam has definitely read it. I might need tea, but not sympathy. I've suffered more than anyone's fair share of sympathy over the years and it's never worked, never helped. What I really want, what I always wanted, was just someone, anyone, to tell me everything will be okay.

As the kettle rumbles away, I stare into space as Liam prepares the promised tea.

A mug arrives at the table.

"Drink up."

I take the mug and sip the milky, sweet tea. Liam pulls up a chair next to mine and sits down.

"Listen, I'm not going to ask you how you are, I'm not going to ask if there's anything I can do. If you want to talk about it, I'll listen. Okay?"

"I appreciate that."

"Can I just ask one question, though?"

"Sure."

"Did he … did he hurt you in any way?"

Reading between the lines, I think I understand what he's asking. I shake my head.

"Okay, that's all I wanted to know."

I take another sip of tea.

"Can I ask you a question?"

"Shoot."

"Why did you run after Nathan?"

"He said it wasn't over. I don't know what he meant, but I wasn't willing to let the wanker stroll out the house after threatening you."

"I dread to think what his plans might have been, so I'm glad you did what you did. Maybe not at the time, but now, definitely."

"Last time I saw him, they were bundling him into the back of a police car."

"Good to know."

I puff a deep breath and slowly, I'm able to corral a few of the chaotic thoughts stampeding around my head.

"There was something else I wanted to ask."

"Okay."

"Why did you call round?"

"You sure you want to talk about it?"

"If I don't start piecing this together, my brain is likely to explode."

"Well, I was doing some paperwork in the back of the shop when the bell above the door rang. I got up and wandered through to the counter, expecting it to be someone looking for directions. It wasn't — it was Kenneth."

"I … what?"

"I know, the gall of the bloke. He just stood in the doorway calm as you like, and just as I'm about to leap over the counter, he says, Kelly will be dead if you don't get to her house before I do."

"No, that's not possible."

"Trust me: I couldn't believe the police had let him go, either. It took a few seconds to sink in and before I could react, he'd already left. I swear, I was out that door in a heartbeat but he was nowhere to be seen on the street. Anyway, that's when I jumped in the van and got over here as fast as I could. When I finally got inside the house and ran up the stairs, I expected to find Kenneth, not your ex-husband."

"No, no … you misunderstand. It's not possible because Kenneth was in custody … all morning. I left the station just after ten o'clock and Detective Royce assured me they'd hold him for at least another twenty-four hours."

"Eh?" Liam frowns. "Your detective must have changed his mind and let him out."

"Based on what we discussed, there's no way he'd have let Kenneth out."

"Why not? What happened?"

I realise there are only two people who know where we got to with Kenneth, and Liam isn't one of them. As best I can under the circumstances, I relay the highlights of both the interview and my subsequent conversation with Detective Royce.

He listens intently although there's a lot of head shaking and mumbled expletives. By the time I finish, he's just as confused as I am.

"Let me get this straight," he frowns. "Kenneth claimed your psychopathic ex-husband tried to kill you three times because of a bloody will?"

"And an insurance policy, apparently."

"And because he couldn't explain how he knew, the detective presumed Kenneth was trying to frame your ex-husband as he lost money in some investment scam?"

"Yes, although I reached the same conclusion. It made perfect sense; it really did."

"And an hour later, your ex-husband is holding you at knife-point?"

"He pretty-much confessed to wanting me dead. I can't even begin …"

I freeze mid-sentence.

"What's the matter, Kelly?"

"There's … Nathan told me he set up cameras in my bedroom, the lounge … and in here."

"What the hell for?"

"You play chess — he wanted to keep one move ahead of me."

Instinctively, we both gaze around the kitchen in search of a hidden camera. Wherever it is, it's well concealed. Another thought tumbles home.

"He said I could watch …"

God knows how, but my brain finds a reserve of adrenalin and I'm on my feet. Liam catches up when I'm halfway up the stairs.

"What is it?"

Rather than answer, I fly towards the stepladder and clamber into the loft. The light is still on and I scan the floor. There's nothing out of the ordinary; just a few boxes, a suitcase, and a bag of Christmas decorations. I'm about to move towards the central chimney breast when Liam pokes his head through the

362

hatch opening.

"What are you doing?" he asks.

"Looking for something."

A dozen paces forward and I skirt the right-hand side of the chimney breast towards the dark side of the loft. It takes a second for my eyes to adjust but as the shapes and lines come into focus; I find what I'm looking for — on the floor, connected to an extension lead.

"Got you," I whisper.

"A laptop?" Liam asks over my shoulder. "What's that doing up here?"

"Nathan put it up here. He must have used it to gather and store the footage from the cameras."

"Sick bastard."

"Unfortunately for that sick bastard, it's also evidence if it recorded everything he said and did this morning."

"Ahh … probably best to leave it where it is, then."

"I will. I just wanted to see if he was bluffing. This proves everything Kenneth said was true."

"It does."

I turn to Liam.

"It doesn't explain how he knew, though. I think we need to talk to Detective Royce and see if he has any idea where Kenneth is now."

"Are you sure you're up to this? The paramedics still haven't checked you over."

They haven't, and I'm sure they'll tell me what I already know — I'm in no fit state to be dashing around playing detective. However, I've spent too many years being haunted by too many unanswered questions. I'm not willing to lose one single night's sleep to more.

42.

The doorbell rings just as I step onto the landing.

"Want me to get it?" Liam calls down from the loft hatch.

"The door is still on its hinges?"

"Just about. I managed to close it … kind of."

I'm willing to answer the door but I'm not so willing to leave Liam's side. I wait until he's at the bottom of the stepladder.

"It's probably the paramedic," he suggests.

"I might have to tell them a few white lies. Will you back me up?"

He puts his hand on my arm.

"To the hilt."

Looking into his eyes, I can tell he absolutely means it. I have to bite my lip to keep my emotions in check.

"Come on," I sniff.

With Liam one step behind, I make my way down the stairs to the front door; still serving a purpose but in need of some urgent repairs.

I open it, expecting a paramedic, but Detective Royce is on the doorstep. The look on his face probably mirrors mine — pained acceptance we were wrong.

"Thank Christ you're okay," he pants. "I got here as fast as I could when I heard Juniper Lane mentioned on the radio."

"I appreciate that, and I'm … well, I'm still here."

"I've just heard Nathan Thaw is on his way to the station; and he's facing a charge of attempted murder. I don't know what to say, other than I'm sorry."

"For what it's worth, I thought your theory was perfectly sound. Besides, you're not the one who married a psychopath — that's on me."

"I appreciate you being so understanding. Are you up to a chat?"

"Sure. Come in."

I introduce the detective to Liam. They shake hands and the three of us move through to the lounge. Liam sits next to me on the sofa and Detective Royce flops down in the armchair opposite.

"I was hoping for a quiet day, today," he remarks. "Instead, I've got to unpick a ball of string while wearing boxing gloves."

"I'll help as much as I can."

With Liam clutching my hand for moral support, I relay the events after I arrived home from the police station; the detective taking copious notes and posing questions. Several times I have to fight back the tears but I struggle through it.

"Kelly found his laptop up in the loft," Liam adds in conclusion.

"You didn't …"

"It's still up there. We didn't touch it."

"Good, and I take it you haven't found any cameras."

"No."

"Right, well, I'll order a team to come over to retrieve the laptop and remove the cameras. Together with your statement, I think we've got enough to charge Nathan Thaw. And trust me: he won't get bail."

"Apparently, he parked his car around the corner," I confirm. "It's a gunmetal-grey BMW. I don't know if he was telling the truth, but he said the computer is in the boot."

"That would be a great help but I think his phone, and the laptop in the loft will fill in most of the gaps. That said, if he's sensible, his lawyer will probably recommend he makes a full confession."

No doubt there will be months of work for both the police and the prosecution team, not to mention a court case, but as long as Nathan remains locked up throughout that process, I'll get through it. However, before that process begins I need answers to my questions.

"Why did you release Kenneth, Detective?"

He stares back as if I'd questioned his sexuality.

"Sorry, what do you mean?"

"You released Kenneth shortly after I left the station. I just want to understand why?"

"What on earth makes you think we released him?"

"He turned up at my shop," Liam answers. "He said Kelly would die if I didn't get to her house before he did."

"This morning?"

"Mid-morning sometime."

The detective sits forward and places his notepad on the coffee table.

"I think you might be confused, Mr Bradley. Kenneth is in custody, and he's been there since early yesterday evening."

"Maybe you're confused, Detective, because I'm one hundred percent positive he was in my shop this morning."

"With respect, you're one hundred percent wrong."

"Want to place a bet on that?"

The tone of both men is growing testy. I intervene.

"Could you check for me please, Detective, just so we know?"

"If it puts your mind at rest, I'll call the Custody Sergeant."

"I'd appreciate that."

"Give me two minutes."

He gets up and wanders into the hallway.

"It was definitely him," Liam says. "I'd stake my life on it."

"Maybe Kenneth changed his mind and sought legal advice. A solicitor may have secured his release without Detective Royce knowing about it."

"We'll find out in a moment, and I hope he's readying an apology."

"Don't be too hard on him. He's on my side."

"I know," he concedes with a nod. "I'll accept the apology with good grace, I promise."

From the hallway, the detective mumbles a few single syllable replies before ending the call to his colleague. He wanders back into the lounge and retakes his seat in the armchair.

"Right, I've just had a conversation with the Custody Sergeant. As I thought, he confirmed we're still holding Kenneth."

"No way," Liam objects. "He's wrong."

"I asked Sergeant Williams to double-check, and he did …

while looking at Kenneth through the cell door hatch."

Liam's shoulders slump. He turns to me.

"I know what I saw, Kelly, and it was him. There's absolutely no doubt in my mind."

"There is a simple explanation," Detective Royce suggests. "I had a case once where a suspect in a street robbery offered a rock-solid alibi. He claimed to be in a shopping centre six miles away when the offence took place. We checked CCTV and there he was, wandering around the shops. I had no choice but to release him without charge, and he called his brother to ask for a lift home from the station. I happened to be having a smoke when his brother pulled up outside ... his identical twin brother. Our suspect got four years, although both brothers deserved an award for ingenuity and stupidity."

I'm not sure if he genuinely believes Kenneth has a twin, or he's offering a conciliatory suggestion intended to ease Liam's dented male pride. Either way, it only serves to unfurl another long list of questions. There is only one man who can answer those questions, and his name isn't John Royce or Liam Bradley.

"What are you going to do with Kenneth now?" I ask.

"Ideally, I'd like to ask him the same questions I asked this morning, and get some answers. However, I doubt I'll hear anything different; presuming he'd even talk to me."

"Do you have any idea how he knew what Nathan was up to?"

"Honestly? Not a clue."

"Are you going to release him?"

"He's not talking and we've no grounds to hold him. There is still the argument he might have been involved in your ex-husband's plot but any half-decent solicitor will tear that argument to pieces as Kenneth came into the station and volunteered his statement."

"I want to speak to him."

"I don't think that's a good idea. We don't know anything about this man."

"That's my point," I reply. "I can't live without answers."

Detective Royce shoots a glance towards Liam, requesting

backup.

"What do you think, Mr Bradley?"

"It doesn't matter what I think. If Kelly wants to speak to him, it's her decision and hers alone."

Detective Royce turns back to me.

"For the record, I would strongly advise you stay well clear of Kenneth. I think we can both agree he ... let's just say he isn't the full ticket."

"Maybe so, but I'd still like to know why he wandered into my life and how he knew so much about Nathan."

The detective sighs and then glances at his watch.

"I'm heading back to the station now, and I'll be authorising Kenneth's release. Once he walks out the door, there's nothing I can do to stop one free citizen talking to another."

"Thank you."

"Don't thank me," he replies, getting to his feet. "I still think you're making a mistake."

I turn to Liam.

"You'll come with me?"

"Of course."

"There you go, Detective — a compromise. Will you text me when he's about to be released?"

"I guess," he sighs. "And, good luck. I think you'll need it, cracking this particular nut."

Advice given and received, I see him to the door. He says a goodbye and confirms it'll be an hour or two before Kenneth is a free man. I return to the lounge and sit back down next to Liam.

"Thank you," I say, taking his hand.

"For what?"

"I'm great at writing lists, but even I would struggle to list everything you've done for me of late. You've been ... I don't even have the words."

"I've just done what any bloke would do. No thanks required."

"No, bar my dad, you've done more for me than any man has ever done. Christ, you saved my life ... twice ... you've listened, you've supported my decisions, and you've never judged me."

368

"I broke your front door, though. Sorry."

In much the same way Martha uses humour as an escape valve, Liam is in the habit of using it to mask his awkwardness.

"True," I chuckle. "But I'm hoping you'll be around long enough to fix it."

He fidgets a moment and then kisses my hand.

"I'm not great when it comes to saying how I feel, but I hope I'm in your life long enough to fix many, many doors."

"Just doors?"

"Whatever you need fixing, I'll be there. Tomorrow, the day after that, and every day thereafter … until you get bored with me."

My emotions well again. Already well versed in reading my body language, Liam pulls me in to a hug; his hand resting on the back of my head.

By some process I don't understand and can't explain, Liam's embrace sucks all the horrors of the day into the same jar I store all my dark thoughts.

"Do you know why I think you're right to see Kenneth?" he whispers in my ear.

"No."

He slowly releases me from his arms.

"Because you need to thank him."

"Do I?"

"I wouldn't be here if he hadn't wandered into my shop one day and bought a lily."

"A Madonna lily," I sniff, caught in a no-man's-land between smiling and crying. "Not named after the singer, in case you were wondering."

43.

"There we go," Liam declares. "Given I don't have a new lock it's only a makeshift fix, but it is secure."

To demonstrate how secure, he opens and closes the front door several times.

I hand him a mug of coffee.

"You're a hero, Liam Bradley — in every sense of the word."

"I wouldn't object if you got me a cape for Christmas."

Behind his smile, I think he knows the significance of his remark. It's good to know he's thinking about our future, even if that future is just six months from now. Still, if I've learnt anything over recent weeks, it's to live in the here and now. Plans are like sandcastles — outwardly solid but all too easily swept away by forces beyond our control. For now, I'm content to sit on the beach and admire the little sandcastle we've built together.

A text arrives from Detective Royce. Kenneth will be released in fifteen minutes.

We finish our coffee and head out to the van.

"Are you hungry?" Liam asks.

"I haven't eaten today but to be honest, my stomach is still in knots."

"Tell you what: once you've had your chat with Kenneth, why don't we grab some sandwiches and head out to the countryside. I think some fresh air and a bit of peace would do you good … help clear your mind."

"I'd love that."

"That's settled then."

I hop into the passenger's seat and Liam starts the engine.

"Sure you want to do this?" he asks.

"Not sure, but I feel I have to. It could be I'm wasting my time — there's no reason he'd answer my questions now, when he's steadfastly refused to answer them before."

"Only one way to find out."

"Yep."

"Perhaps you can ask a question for me?"

"Sure. What do you want to know?"

"If he has a twin brother."

"You believe Detective Royce's suggestion?"

"I don't know what to believe, but I'm sure it was Kenneth who turned up at the shop earlier."

"There has to be a logical explanation unless he's worked out how to be in two places at once."

"Now, that would be a handy skill to have but, for the sake of my sanity, I'd like to know if he does have a twin brother."

"Okay. I'll add that question to my list."

"You have a list?"

"A long one."

He flashes a reassuring smile and pulls away.

As we trundle the short distance along Juniper Lane to the junction, visions of the earlier bedlam return. All the police vehicles have gone and there's no trace of the chaos anywhere but inside Liam's van, inside my head. It'll be a while before I find the same normality the lane has found so quickly.

It's only a five-minute drive to our destination, and it passes in a heartbeat. I'm still unsure this is a good idea but, before I talk myself out of it, Liam pulls into the car park at the front of the station.

"Are you going in?" Liam asks.

"No, I'd rather talk to him outside."

"Okay."

He reverses into a bay some twenty yards from the station entrance; presumably so we can sit and wait for Kenneth to walk out the door.

The engine falls silent, and it's my turn to fidget. Liam notices.

"If you're not comfortable talking to Kenneth on your own, I can come with you?"

"I appreciate the offer but I think he's more likely to talk if I'm on my own. As long as you're nearby, I'll be fine."

"Whatever works for you."

It only takes a few seconds of silence to push my

apprehension levels in the wrong direction. I turn to my tried-and-trusted method of distraction.

"Can we have the radio on?"

"Sure."

He pushes a button and an overly enthusiastic disc-jockey introduces The Spice Girls, *2 Become 1*.

It prompts a nervous snigger on my side of the van.

"What's so funny?"

"Who's your favourite Spice Girl?"

"Hmm … is this a trick question?"

"No, not at all."

"Okay, Ginger Spice."

My chuckle evolves into laughter.

"I'm obviously missing something here. What are you laughing at?"

"Sorry," I chortle. "Let me explain."

"I'm all ears."

"I'm going away on a girl's weekend in September, and Martha has decided we should dress as the Spice Girls."

"Oh."

"There's a Union Jack dress in her wardrobe … with my name on it."

"Ooh, that's good to know."

"Is it?"

"Have you tried it on yet?"

"I was supposed to, on Wednesday, but I got a little waylaid. Perhaps we should call round tomorrow and collect it."

"Here's an idea. I'll cook Sunday lunch wearing just my pinny if you wear that dress."

"Really?" I reply, turning to him. "And what time do you think we'd finally sit down to eat lunch?"

"Nine, maybe ten in the evening," he grins.

"I'll ask Martha to get it ready."

As I lean in to kiss Liam, his eyes flick to the right. Instinctively, I turn to see what's caught his attention. The flirty atmosphere in the van shatters when my own eyes catch sight of a man in a brown suit, stood outside the police station entrance. I fall back in my seat.

"Still time to change your mind," Liam suggests.

"I know, but I also know how elusive Kenneth is. If I don't ask him now, I might never get the chance again."

I stare out beyond the windscreen. The man himself turns and takes twenty steps to a bench overlooking a small patch of lawn. He looks towards the van — almost as if he expected a greeting party — and sits down.

I grab the handle and push the passenger door open. When I'm stood on the tarmac, I turn to Liam.

"Wish me luck."

"I do, and if luck doesn't work, I'll be ready if you need me."

"Won't be long."

I turn to face the police station and, after adjusting my dress, I stride purposefully across the car park towards the bench. Outwardly, I'm doing my best to appear calm and confident but internally, doubts mount with every passing yard.

I get within a dozen steps and Kenneth gets to his feet.

"Hello, Kelly."

"Kenneth."

"How are you?"

I stop short of the bench.

"I'm tired and hungry. Tired of bullshit and hungry for answers."

"Would you care to take a seat?"

He sits back down and shuffles to the end of the bench. I take a few apprehensive steps forward and sit at the opposite end so there's four feet of space between us.

Now I'm here, the questions I so badly wanted to ask are all swimming away from me. Kenneth, it seems, has no such problem.

"Is Liam well?" he asks.

It's as good a starting place as any.

"You asked me that question earlier and Detective Royce took it as a threat."

"I know."

"He told you?"

"No."

"How do you …"

I stop myself; not wanting to stray too far from my list of pre-prepared questions.

"Liam swears blind you were at his shop earlier, but Detective Royce said you were locked in a cell all morning. Why is Liam convinced the detective is wrong?"

"If I answer that question, it would involve a long and complex explanation."

"Can't you give me the short version?"

"You are now on the right path. Nothing else matters."

"Don't you think I have a right to know? You've interfered in my life over the last few weeks with no explanation and no thought to how your actions have affected me."

"On the contrary. My interference, as you put it, only served your best interests."

I realise my left hand is gripping the wooden armrest a touch too tightly, such is my frustration.

"Am I wasting my time here? Are you willing to answer any of my questions?"

He appears to ponder that question at least.

"You're obsessed with questions, aren't you, Kelly? An inquisitive mind is both a blessing and a curse."

"I'm obsessed with finding out the truth, if that's what you mean."

"And what if the truth only adds to your list of questions?"

"I'd still rather know."

"In which case, knowing the answer to one question would likely answer all the others."

"And what question would that be?"

He turns to me and smiles.

"If you could ask me just one question, what would you ask?"

"I'm really not in the mood for more games."

"This is no game. One question — ask it."

I run the ruler down my mental list and one question stands out from all the others.

"Okay. Who are you, Kenneth?"

His smile broadens.

"I'll try to explain but I ask of you: please keep an open mind."

"Just spit it out."

He delves a hand into the inside pocket of his jacket and extracts a rolled-up newspaper. He then places it on the bench between us.

"Read the front page."

I snatch up the newspaper and unroll it. Not that I've read it in years, but it's a newspaper I recognise from the distinctive blue banner running across the top of the front page.

"What so interesting about the local paper?" I ask.

"The main article. Read it."

My eyes settle on the headline: *One Dead and Four Injured in Bypass Accident.*

I skim the first four paragraphs which relay the basic details of a road traffic accident. A BMW allegedly ran a red light at a busy crossroads and clipped the tail end of a van. Witnesses claim the BMW then flipped over and struck a row of metal bollards on the pavement opposite. Emergency services pronounced the driver dead at the scene.

I turn to Kenneth.

"That's awful, obviously, but I don't see how it answers any of my questions."

"Look at the date at the top of the page."

I glance down. The edition is dated 6th June — a little over two weeks ago.

"I don't see the relevance."

"The accident occurred on Tuesday 4th June. Do you remember that evening?"

"It may have escaped your attention but I've been a little pre-occupied of late, so no."

Frustration mounting, I slap the paper on the bench. Kenneth rolls it up and returns it to his jacket pocket.

"The accident occurred the same evening Nathan Thaw proposed to you."

"So?"

"The driver of the BMW mentioned in the article was Nathan Thaw."

"Don't be ridiculous," I scoff. "Unfortunately, Nathan is very much alive. I know that because he tried to kill me this morning."

"That's correct, but … and this is where I need you to keep an open mind … what if you'd arrived on time that evening?"

"On time? I'm not with you."

"You were five minutes late. The broken heel which proved to be an unfortunate and decisive twist of fate."

"That's the second time you've mentioned my bloody heel. How do you know?"

"Please, can we stick to the relevant facts? You arrived at The Three Horseshoes public house at 8:05pm and left at 8:52pm, correct?"

"Yes," I groan. "Roughly."

"Nathan Thaw left exactly one minute later, at 8:53pm."

My grip on the wooden armrest tightens.

"For crying out loud. If there's a point to this, can you make it, please?"

"If you hadn't broken that heel, you would have arrived five minutes earlier, and therefore left five minutes earlier. Correct?"

"I suppose."

"And it follows that Nathan Thaw would also have left five minutes earlier. In fact, he would have left the public house at 8:48pm rather than 8:53pm. Distracted by thoughts of your conversation, he would have inadvertently passed through a red traffic signal and died as a result of injuries sustained in a road traffic accident; just as the newspaper reports. However, because you were late, he arrived at that junction five minutes later … when the traffic signal was green."

I sense a migraine approaching as I try to unpick the alternate reality theory.

"This is all fascinating fiction, Kenneth, but I did break a heel and Nathan didn't die in an accident, so I'll ask you again: what is your point?"

"You saw the newspaper article, Kelly? That is how events should have occurred that evening."

"Come off it," I snap. "That article proves nothing other than some poor sod in a BMW died."

"Your scepticism is unfortunate," he sighs, a frown creasing his forehead.

It appears my frustration is contagious.

"Perhaps it might be easier if I show you," he adds.

"Show me what?"

He reaches out his left hand and beckons me to take it.

"Why do you want to hold my hand?"

"So I can show you the path you should have taken."

"I'm not leaving this bench, Kenneth."

"I didn't say you had to. Take my hand and your questions will be answered."

"I don't want to."

"Then, you'll never know."

I return a frosty stare. It's met with the same benign expression I've come to expect. I'm presented with a binary choice: take his hand, or walk away without answers I can't live without. It's not a choice, not really.

"Ready?" he asks.

I'm not, but of its own volition, my right arm reaches out and I tentatively take Kenneth's hand.

The moment I make contact, I wish I hadn't. I'm thrust into some kind of hallucinogenic spin; a living nightmare where I'm watching myself tumble through an opaque mist. Confusion, fear … I want to scream, release the panic, but … I've no control over my conscious mind. No … I have no conscious mind, my senses muted and awareness fractured. I can't feel the armrest, can't see the lawn, can't hear birdsong. Where am I? Where is Liam?

Suddenly, I'm no longer watching my body tumble. I'm in that body, staring into the mist as it gradually clears. The confusion and fear give way to an almost ethereal calm as colours and sounds creep back into my consciousness.

I'm looking down on a familiar scene: my lounge. Akin to

watching video footage of an event I cannot recall ever happening, I stare at the woman on the sofa who cannot possibly be me because she's in conversation with a policeman I've never met. Then, in a tone of voice I've heard before, he says he's terribly sorry, but there's been an accident. Kelly Thaw is still listed as next of kin, which is why she's the first to know her ex-husband died last night in a road traffic accident on the bypass.

The lounge scene then fades away and I'm suddenly watching myself walk along a street. I'm in the town centre and dressed in work attire. I recognise the outfit as it's the one I wore the day I first visited Richard at Ramsey Rowe & Associates — the day he told me the true value of Dad's yard. Am I watching that same event unfold? My illusionary self strides straight past the door. I wait for her to turn around as I did, but she continues onwards. Eighty or ninety yards later, she enters a firm of undertakers.

What is this? Why did she visit an undertaker rather than the offices of Ramsey Rowe & Associates?

Then it hits me — she doesn't know.

In this version of events, Nathan died. He never hired a surveyor to value Dad's yard so my tenant never called to complain, and we never discussed selling the yard. I had no reason to visit Richard's office because I had no intention of selling the yard. Equally, I had no clue about its potential value either.

I realise — this is my life unfolding if I hadn't broken a heel. I was on time, rather than five minutes late, and those five minutes were enough to put Nathan in the wrong place at the wrong time. And without Nathan to instigate the chain of events, my life would have continued along the same uneventful path. No million-pound windfall, no plans to visit a clinic, no prospect of motherhood.

My life spiralled into chaos because of a broken heel. A broken heel!

The scene changes again and my illusionary self is in my office at Marston Finance, staring intently at the computer screen. She's browsing what look like funeral wreaths. It appears the task of arranging Nathan's funeral fell at her feet.

No one else would have stepped forward because there isn't anyone else.

I'm back on the street again. This time, the High Street. She crosses the road and approaches a shop. It's a shop I recognise — Avalon Florists. As I watch my illusionary self enter, I'm whisked inside to watch on as she steps towards the counter. Liam appears, and they talk in much the same manner we did when I began my search for Kenneth. I can't be sure but I think it's the exact same day. They chat for a while and then arrange for her to come back and collect a funeral wreath in a few days' time. He takes her number and when she leaves; the broadest smile breaks across his face.

Was my path always meant to lead to this day, to this shop, to this man? Did Kenneth give me the medallion not so I'd find him, but Liam?

I snap back to reality in the same jarring manner I left it.

My left hand is still grasping the armrest, my feet are still resting on the paving slabs, my backside still firmly pressed against the wooden bench struts.

Confusion reigns. I turn to Kenneth.

"What the … what did you just do to me?"

"I showed you the path you were supposed to take."

"No, that's impossible."

"If you say so. Perhaps you simply imagined it."

Whatever happened, traces of serenity remain. It's enough to temper the obvious reaction — full-blown hysteria.

"Any more questions?" he casually asks.

"Liam?" I blurt through confused thoughts.

"What about him?"

"You … you wanted me to walk into his shop?"

"I did. Until that evening when Nathan Thaw's path changed, you and Liam Bradley were always destined to meet. Fate, alas, changed its mind at the last minute when you stepped on that paving slab. I had to redress the balance because you lost sight of what really matters, and it almost cost you your life."

"Why didn't you just tell me about Liam … in fact, why didn't you tell me about Nathan's plan?"

"I told you to give Nathan Thaw the money he requested. If you had, all would have been well after I set you back on the right path. You do now realise the money was never important as far as your ambitions were concerned?"

"What ambitions?"

"To have a family. To find love."

I'm about to ask how he knows that, but I have an inkling the answer won't be one I'm ready to believe.

"The money wasn't important because I met Liam?"

"Correct."

"Are you saying what I think you're saying: I was destined to meet Liam, and we'd ... we'd have a family together?"

"You're getting the hang of this."

A thought occurs. It raises a question I'd rather not ask but need to.

"In the police interview, you said you prevented the attempts on my life. How?"

"I manipulated fate, as far as I could."

"The lift? You stopped it working the evening of my friend's car accident?"

"Possibly."

"And you arranged for Liam to be at my house when that van almost ran me over?"

"I can't deny that one."

"And what about that night when I found the gas turned on?"

"A mutual friend helped me out," he replies with a wry smile.

I sit back and close my eyes in an attempt to find a patch of sanity in all this madness. Everything now makes sense, yet makes no sense at all; the impossible plausible and the plausible improbable. Christ, I can't even make sense of my own thoughts, let alone Kenneth's revelations.

"You see why I never shared my true motive?" he asks. "Why I couldn't tell you?"

"But ... you haven't explained your motive. I don't understand why you ... I don't understand anything ..."

"Do you remember I asked if you believed in fate?"

I manage a nod.

"There is one doctrine greater than fate; a doctrine so influential it has the power to shape one's destiny."

"Which doctrine?"

"Love."

"I … what?"

"Unfortunately, twelve years ago you closed your heart to love and let fate dictate your destiny."

"Twelve years …"

If he'd said eleven years, or thirteen, I might have finished my sentence. He didn't. He said twelve years ago — the year my parents died.

"Do you know why you married Nathan Thaw, Kelly?"

Still reeling, I don't have an answer.

"You married him because you knew, deep down, you didn't love him and you could never love him."

"That … that makes no sense."

"Oh, but it does. After your parents died you were too scared to open your heart again for fear it wouldn't survive another loss. Your marriage allowed you to ignore that fear; a convenient delusion of love you were willing to live with for eleven years."

I'm irked by his observation about my marriage because I fear it might be too close to a truth I'd rather not acknowledge. However, the mention of my parents stings to a significantly greater degree.

"Why bring my parents into this, and … wait … Dad's medallion: how did you know about it?"

"Because I was there the day your parents first met. I was there on their first date, their engagement party, their wedding day. I was there when your father danced with your mother at his fiftieth birthday party."

Ridiculous claims under normal circumstances, but normal left the scene some time ago. However, I'm certain he never attended Dad's fiftieth birthday party because I organised the invites.

"You're talking nonsense," I protest.

He fixes me with his brown eyes; a sombre expression follows.

"I was also there the day of the accident. Whether or not you believe me, your parents never suffered."

I gulp hard. No matter how outlandish his claim, it's one I've waited twelve years to hear. The lack of factual basis is almost irrelevant.

"Haven't you always wanted what they had?" he asks in a low voice. "True, and unconditional love?"

More thoughts gather and cloud my head. I just nod.

"Fate may have taken them away but fate also brought them together and gave them many years of happiness. Not everyone is as fortunate. Not everyone finds true and unconditional love."

A picture forms in my mind; the same picture I see every working day because it lives in a frame on my desk. Two people, one couple, blissfully happy. Consumed by grief — by anger, by a thirst for answers — I never stopped to consider how blessed they were, to have found one another.

"That is why I've tried to help you, Kelly. Love has always been my motive … it is who I am and all I offer. You just lost sight of me, which is why I'm here now."

As the questions continue to swarm, Kenneth checks his watch. He then gets to his feet.

"It's time for me to go."

"You can't just leave," I gulp. "I still don't understand."

"There is a man better placed to answer any remaining questions."

"Is there? Who?"

He nods towards Liam's van.

"There lies your destiny, Kelly. I've gone to great lengths to ensure you two found one another so please, learn to open your heart again."

I look up at him much like a young child might look up at their teacher on the first day of school: scared, bewildered, lost.

"And I'll leave you with one final piece of advice," he adds. "Fate can be unfair, and sometimes seems unfathomably cruel, but love will always provide you with refuge if you're willing to follow the right path."

If it wasn't for my hallucinogenic episode, and Kenneth's

inconceivable knowledge of my past, I might be inclined to pour scorn on his advice. Then again, there was a good reason my parents lied about Father Christmas. There was also a good reason they told me to wear a scarf in winter, and that I should eat my carrots.

Perhaps Kenneth's version of the truth is of greater value than the actual truth.

"Look after yourself, Kelly."

He offers me his hand, but I remain seated, unwilling to reciprocate. Not because I'm scared of revisiting the imaginary world again, but because I just know this will be the last time I see him.

Slowly, I get to my feet.

"Whoever you are," I say, swallowing hard. "Thank you."

I put my arms around him and close my eyes. As I do, the deeply serene calmness descends once more. I can hear birdsong, smell the freshly cut grass, and feel the fibres of Kenneth's now infamous brown suit.

When I open my eyes, only birdsong and the smell of freshly cut grass remain.

ONE YEAR LATER...

44.

Last summer, I queried the true meaning of love.

At that point, my personal experience remained limited to the love I had for my parents, for my best friend, and for my goddaughters. I never loved any boyfriend, not really, and I never loved Nathan Thaw.

Today I know exactly what love feels like.

Perched on the end of the bed, it's just gone nine in the morning and I wouldn't want to be anywhere else. It's the same bedroom in the same house, but everything else is different. I am different. I am someone's mummy.

I lean over the crib, barely daring to breathe in case I should wake him. Even when he's asleep, I can't resist drinking in every detail from the rosy hue of his porcelain-like skin to the faint wisps of blond hair atop his head. This morning, he's dressed in a babygrow patterned with cute bear cubs — a babygrow I purchased as a good luck charm. That luck came good and sixteen days ago, Joshua Douglas Bradley entered my world. My son — my perfect son.

As I sit and watch the gentle rise and fall of his chest, the other man in my life sits up in bed. I turn to him.

"Morning, handsome."

"Morning," he yawns. "Did you sleep well?"

"Not as well as you."

"It's not my fault God gave you the breasts."

"Proof he must be a man," I chuckle. "Coffee?"

"I'll come down with you," Liam replies, throwing off the duvet.

He then creeps around the bed and stands at my side.

"How long has he been asleep?"

"A couple of hours."

He leans over the crib and shakes his head.

"I still can't believe it," he says. "I'm actually a dad."

"Yes, you are."

He wraps his arm around my waist and pulls me tight.

"I must be the luckiest bloke alive."

Maybe one day I'll tell him luck played no part in where we are, and how we got here.

"Let's make the most of your luck and grab some breakfast before his Lordship wakes up."

I take his hand and we tip-toe down to the kitchen — the kitchen which has changed little since the day I cheated death.

A few days after the incident, Martha asked how I felt about living in the same house in which my ex-husband tried to take my life. Actually, that's not strictly true. A few days after the incident, Martha blew a fuse when I brought her up to speed on the preceding events. Despite my protestations, she couldn't believe I'd kept her in the dark, and she insisted I tell her everything. With much reluctance, I confessed the truth about her supposed accident and she cycled through a pattern of shock, horror, and finally, indignant rage. It would be fair to say my best friend's opinion of Nathan Thaw hit a new low that day.

Consequently, as we held hands in the public gallery of a Crown Court eight months later, Martha cheered when the lead juror confirmed Nathan's guilt for all five charges: guilty of money laundering, of market abuse, of conspiracy to murder, and of attempted murder.

The fifth charge related to the death of Beatrice Thaw.

You could almost hear the disdain in the lead juror's voice when he confirmed Nathan's guilt on the charge of murder. His barrister tried the sympathy angle on that particular charge, citing Nathan's desperate financial situation and how he couldn't bear to see his mother's standard of living impinged. The jury, understandably, were unimpressed; who could be so cruel they'd feed their stricken mother a lethal dose of sleeping pills?

With the verdict delivered, an old man in a fusty wig looked across the courtroom at my ex-husband. With as much disdain as the lead juror the judge summarised the crimes in all their shades of selfish wickedness and gave sentence — sixteen years. As Nathan visibly crumpled in the dock, Martha and I hugged. Justice had been served.

"Morning, Frank."

Emerging from his dome-like basket in the corner of the kitchen, my feline friend stretches out the tiredness from his limbs before jumping on to the table.

"Guess I'm now making the coffee?" Liam jokes. "As you're such a dab hand at feeding the small males of the house."

"It looks that way."

Liam switches the kettle on and then reaches up to the cupboard.

"One cat bowl. One tin of tuna."

"Thank you."

Back in the summer last year, Frank decided to take up permanent residency with us; to the point Liam fitted a cat flap, and we bought him his own basket for Christmas. I can only assume he felt it was time to settle down.

His whoring days behind him, Frank now spends his time curled up on the sofa, sleeping in his basket, or generally seeking attention. Oh, and eating tuna, of course.

With the furriest member of the family sorted, I tend to my own needs.

"What do you fancy for breakfast?"

"Don't worry about me," Liam replies. "I'm happy with a bowl of Corn Flakes."

"But, I bought cheese muffins."

"How many cheese muffins?"

"Just the four."

"And do you want to share them?"

"Honestly?"

"Honestly."

"Um, no."

"Thought not," he sniggers. "You go for it."

My lovely midwife, Sandra, warned I might experience a healthier appetite than usual in the weeks after giving birth. She didn't warn me quite how ravenous that appetite would become. I slide all four muffins into the toaster.

"Will you still love me when I'm the size of a sofa?"

"That depends," Liam grins, handing me a mug of coffee. "On?"

"Do they make Union Jack dresses for women the size of sofas?"

"Probably."

"In which case, I'll still love you."

I do still have a Union Jack dress in the wardrobe upstairs but I've not worn it since our girl's weekend at Butlin's last year. The slight flaw in Martha's plan proved to be a lack of originality, and on the second night when every reveller donned their fancy-dress outfit, we might as well have been attending a Spice Girls convention. Any qualms I had about wearing such an unforgiving garment were soon quashed when the dancefloor filled with women of every shape and size, and at least a dozen men, in identical dresses.

Apart from a lack of original fancy-dress, the weekend was amazing, and it proved a watershed moment in many ways. From the moment I booked it until the day we set off for Bognor Regis, I'd experienced the mother of all rollercoaster rides. The weekend came and went in a blur of middle-aged boy bands, cocktails, and carefree laughter, and then I returned to a new life. It was only three days away, but I missed Liam like crazy. So, a little over three months after I first walked into Avalon Florists, I asked the proprietor to move in with me. Without hesitation, he agreed but with one condition; a condition he wouldn't disclose until he was ready.

A few days later, on a bright Saturday in mid-September, Liam picked me up on the pretence of keeping him company on a trip to buy a new van. Fifteen minutes into that journey, he turned off the main road and we travelled along a quiet country lane until we came to a pub. He pulled into the deserted car park and suggested a quick drink as we were running early. Never one to turn down a glass of wine, I tried to open my door but it wouldn't budge. We sat there for five minutes, trying to get the door open but to no avail. In the end, Liam got out and wandered round to my side of the van. The door opened at the first attempt.

Liam laughed it off and took my hand. As I turned to follow him towards the pub, I stopped dead in my tracks at the sight of twenty men in full Army dress uniform; stood shoulder-to-shoulder across the car park. As one, they all saluted. A set of speakers near the door began pumping out music and the twenty soldiers proceeded to do a series of perfectly choreographed dance moves while lip-syncing their way through the Bruno Mars hit, *Marry You*.

I almost fainted.

A minute into the song, Liam's mum and step-dad joined them. Then, my friends Jennie and Rachel — all seamlessly following the routine. Just when I thought I might explode with joy, two more familiar faces joined the ensemble. Stuart danced in from the left, dressed in a morning suit, and Martha sashayed in from the right, wearing a wedding dress and veil. Incredibly, my Uncle Terrence from Edinburgh then appeared; dressed as a vicar. He conducted a five-second service to marry Stuart and Martha as the joyous congregation cast confetti into the air. The whole group then continued their dance routine until they suddenly split apart into two lines; creating an aisle down the centre. I thought I'd seen everything until — both dressed as Cupid — Ella and Millie skipped down the makeshift aisle. They made their way towards us and Ella presented Liam with a small velvet box. He opened the box to reveal a beautiful diamond and emerald cluster ring and then bent down on one knee.

"Kelly Coburn," he said. "Every love story deserves a happy ending. Will you be mine?"

I was so overwhelmed I could barely draw breath. Eventually, I sobbed a 'yes' and the congregation cheered.

There and then, in the pub, we held our engagement party. It remained the most amazing day of my life until two weeks later when I emerged from the bathroom, screaming; a six-inch piece of plastic in my hand. A week on, a particularly young doctor confirmed my pregnancy.

It's hard to imagine how one moment could be so exhilarating yet so terrifying, but as Liam held me in his arms, the fear melted away. Even during the pregnancy, when I kept thinking about Natalie and her heartbreak, my fiancé remained at hand to soothe away my concerns. Mercifully, the worst I suffered was a few weeks of mild morning sickness and, much to

Martha's amusement, piles.

Liam and I decided we wanted to marry before our little one arrived so on Christmas Eve, a small gathering of family and close friends joined us at a gorgeous old hotel in the country. We stayed until the afternoon of Boxing Day, enjoying the sumptuous food, cuddling by the open fire in our suite, and watching the snow fall from our balcony. It should be said, we also spent an inordinate amount of time testing out the four-poster bed.

On the way home, I concluded Richard Curtis hadn't lied, after all.

In late March, as my tummy approached basketball dimensions and the first daffodils arrived, Redwood Homes completed the purchase of Dad's yard. Richard was a little miffed when I threatened the whole deal by insisting a caveat be added to the contract at the last moment. That caveat legally ensures one road on the new development will be named Coburn Close, after my parents, and another, Kellybelle Gardens.

It's a small gesture, but it ensures our family name will live on, as will the name of my parents' beloved old boat.

With the money finally in the bank, I resigned from Marston Finance. Justin, fearing he might have to do some actual work himself, offered me all manner of inducements to change my mind, including extended maternity leave, a significant pay rise, and even a fast-track path to the boardroom. There was nothing he could have offered me to stay. All I wanted was to take it easy for the last eight weeks of my pregnancy. To their credit, my team organised a farewell party in the staffroom, and they even bought me a beautiful, handmade cake — bright pink and shaped like a vibrator. What could I do but see the funny side?

During the impromptu party, a former employee arrived to bid me a goodbye. The moment Natalie walked in, clutching a car seat, half my team swarmed around her to meet Amy — her four-month-old daughter. When the crowd finally dispersed, I took my turn to say hello. The look on Natalie's face when she noticed my baby belly, was priceless. After cooing over Amy for five minutes, I had a long chat with her mother, and explained what I should have explained many months earlier. The wall that existed between us came tumbling down, and she even invited us to Amy's christening.

The toaster pops.

"You sit down," Liam orders. "I'll bring them over."

"You're too perfect, Mr Bradley."

He grins a perfect smile to make my point.

I switch the radio on and do as I'm told. My four buttered cheese muffins arrive and Liam sits opposite with his bowl of Corn Flakes. Frank watches on with big envious eyes before finally accepting no more food will be forthcoming.

We eat breakfast with minimal conversation. Most people would consider it odd but to us, it's now as comfortable as a decade-old pair of slippers. Our quirky mealtime routines aren't the only area where Liam and I perfectly dovetail. Some folks might have questioned why I invited Liam to move in after only three months, and why he proposed to me just days after. To those folks, I'd say this: when you know, you just know. Within those first three months, I fell helplessly in love with Liam Bradley. Not just on a slushy Mills & Boon level, but in a way that made my soul physically ache whenever we were apart; like a part of me was missing. It is a rare and beautiful thing we have, and not a day goes by where I don't stop and look skyward; to thank whatever force brought us together.

Of course, that force has a name — Kenneth.

I only offered Liam the vaguest of details about what happened that day outside the police station; perhaps because I didn't believe it myself. He was in the middle of composing a text message when Kenneth and I hugged, and never saw him leave. I did suggest to Liam maybe Kenneth really did have a twin brother, and it was that brother who walked into his shop to warn I was in danger. A white lie, but how could I explain the truth? How could anyone explain the truth?

With every passing day afterwards, our miraculous meeting felt more like a well-worn anecdote; one which loses credibility on every telling. At some point, you can't swear for sure it happened at all. Maybe I imagined the hallucinogenic visions of the future I lost. Maybe Kenneth himself wasn't real, least not the version who said goodbye that day.

However, one undeniable fact remains: I would never have met Liam if Kenneth hadn't entered my life, and while his motives and his methods remain a mystery, he'll always have my undying gratitude, not least for the fresh perspective he left me with.

My thinking shifted that day. So many questions begged to be answered but as Liam and I sat on a blanket in a woodland glade and ate sandwiches later that afternoon, I realised what I should have realised many years ago — life doesn't provide an answer to every question. I'll never know why my parents died, I'll never know why I turned left instead of right, and I'll never know why I didn't see the paving slab which snapped my heel. Perhaps they really were all twists of fate but not one of them should have determined my ultimate destiny. They so nearly did.

A few months back, while I was waiting for a check-up at the local surgery, I picked up a magazine in the waiting room. I read a heart-breaking article about a mother who lost her teenage son in tragic circumstances almost three decades ago. The lad was at a pop concert when a lighting gantry collapsed onto the crowd. Three people died that night, including the woman's son. She spent three decades chasing the truth, looking for answers, and perhaps, searching for someone to blame. Inquest after inquest, court decision after court decision — all ultimately futile. She died last year, broken emotionally, ruined financially, and with no semblance of closure.

Conversely, the parents of a young woman who also died that night campaigned for better safety at concerts. The father became an influential voice in Government and the mother launched a charity which offered life-changing support to the parents of brain-damaged children.

The same fateful event but two different destinies for the parents involved.

As I sat in that waiting room, I couldn't help but consider which path I'd have taken. Maybe I'd be the mother who wasted a life trying to find answers; none of which would ever bring my son back. Last year, I'm sure I would have chosen that path. Now, I know how quickly the years roll by and how little there is to gain by constantly questioning the fairness of fate.

I prayed that night; begging God never to put me in a position where I had to make such a choice.

I guess it's human instinct to seek the truth but there comes a point where you have to settle on acceptance. Liam put it perfectly when he said you can't drive forward if your eyes are glued to the rear-view mirror — you'll either stay rooted, or crash.

"All done?" my husband enquires.

"Yes, thanks."

He takes my plate and plants a kiss on my forehead.

"Four whole muffins. Are you prepping for the next one?"

"Next one?"

"Baby."

I return a smile. I'm not ready to jump back in quite yet but neither do I want Joshua to be an only child. I've no doubt we'll begin planning the next instalment of the Bradley clan before the leaves turn brown, but for now I just want to savour every minute of motherhood.

My phone rings and Martha's name flashes on the screen.

"Good morning, Mrs Miller."

"Hey, chick. Just checking if you're home at lunchtime?"

"I think so. Why?"

"We were hoping to pop over for an hour. The girls are desperate to meet Joshua."

"Aww, bless them. I'm sure he's just as keen to meet them."

"Hmm … he might change his mind on that. Anyway, how are you doing?"

"I couldn't be perkier."

"How's your fanny?"

"My … what?"

"Mine looked like an angry squid for months after I pushed the twins out. Stuart wouldn't go near it, the coward."

"Yeah, that's way too much info."

"I haven't even started. Shall we discuss the variety of gross ways your body will leak?"

"Eww! Stop it."

"Haha … we'll pick this conversation up later. I'd better go as the twins are playing with the lawnmower."

"My God! They're not."

"Don't panic. The beauty of having twins is you've always got a spare if something goes awry."

"Martha!"

"You know I'm only kidding," she chuckles. "We don't let them anywhere near the lawnmower … not after the hedge trimmer incident."

"You're the worst."

"Thank you, and I really better go."

"Okay. See you later."

"Shortly, shorty. Love you."

I put the phone down and turn to Liam.

"Looks like your fan club are coming over at lunchtime."

"I know," he replies over his shoulder while washing up.

"Eh? How?"

"Stuart texted me. He suggested we watch the cricket while you, Martha, and the girls coo over Joshua."

"Oh, did he now?"

"You don't mind, do you?"

I get to my feet and pull him away from the sink.

"Making plans behind my back, eh," I say playfully. "Is this how it begins?"

He turns and drapes his arms around my shoulders.

"It's a slippery slope, I know, but you wouldn't stand between a man and his cricket?"

"And his beer?"

"That too."

"Fair enough."

"See," he smiles. "You're perfect too."

"Ahh, if I'm perfect, I probably deserve more flowers."

"I'll have a word with Ruth."

"She'll make you pay for them."

"Yep. Nothing gets by that woman."

Ruth took over the running of Avalon Florists in October last year so Liam could re-launch his handyman service. Within a few months the shop was back in profit under Ruth's management so Liam agreed to a fifty-fifty partnership. He's now a near-silent partner and back in his comfort zone of widgets, washers, and wrenches.

We kiss, and my husband returns to his domestic duties. I sit back down at the table to finish my coffee. It doesn't take long for the urge to surface.

"I think I'll just go check on the little man."

"Sure."

I creep quietly along the hallway and up the stairs to our bedroom.

To my surprise, Joshua is awake; his big blue eyes fixed on the colourful shapes of the mobile Daddy made for him.

"Good morning, my beautiful little boy."

Instinctively, I want to gather him up in my arms but he seems so content lying in his crib. I know he'll soon demand a feed, but for now I'm equally content just watching him. Sixteen days is no time but every day since he was born, I've savoured each tiny change in my son — it's like being gifted a surprise present on a daily basis.

I also give thanks on a daily basis. I give thanks for every second of every minute of every hour I'm able to gaze upon this incredible little human Liam and I created.

They talk about the miracle of childbirth but in Joshua's case, his story is more miraculous than most. A few times, when I've been feeding him in those silent twilight hours before the world awakes, I've thought about the journey which preceded his arrival. It scares me to think how many times I might have taken an alternate path to a different future — one without Liam and one without my precious boy. I won't deny I've shed a tear or two in those moments.

However, I've learnt not to let the what ifs control my thinking. I've learnt to appreciate the now.

There is, however, a more profound lesson I've learnt. They say a perfect destiny is where soul mates find one another when they don't even know they're looking — that is true, but sometimes we need a little guidance.

Sometimes, we need a Kenneth.

THE END

Before You Go...

I'd just like to thank you for taking the time to read my latest book. As an avid reader myself, I know a book is more than just the investment of a few quid – it demands many hours of your life, and we know from Kelly's adventure that every hour is precious, and every decision matters. I genuinely hope you feel your decision to buy this book was a good one, and it was worthy of your time.

If you enjoyed reading *Kenneth* and have a few minutes spare, I would be eternally grateful if you could leave a (hopefully positive) review on Amazon. A mention on Facebook or Twitter would be equally appreciated. I know it's a pain, but it's the only way us indie authors can compete with the big publishing houses.

Read More of My Work...

You've just read my eighth novel and if you did enjoy it, there are several more on Amazon's shelves. Hopefully, I'll continue on the right path and many more will follow.

Stay in Touch...

For more information about me, my books, and to receive updates on my new releases, please visit my website: www.keithapearson.co.uk

If you have any questions or general feedback, you can also reach me, or follow me via...

Facebook: www.facebook.com/pearson.author
Twitter: www.twitter.com/keithapearson

Made in the USA
Las Vegas, NV
29 August 2023

76823833R00236